God of Small Affairs

Olga Werby

Printed in the United States of America.

17   16   15   14   13   12   11   10   9
8   7   6   5   4   3   2   1

Werby, Olga

God of Small Affairs : a novel / by Olga Werby

ISBN-10: 978-0-578-56843-0

San Francisco

www.pipsqueak.com

*To Jon, who helped so many find a
path into the future.
1935 - 2019*

Table of Contents

Harvest

Sample Chapters:

God of Small Affairs

Chapter One: Derailed

John Uolan

The sharp sound of ripping leather disturbed Jon's reverie. He looked down with a start; they both did. Ay-Tal's knee-high black leather boots had split along the inside seam. With bated breath, Jon watched as the boot started to swell, letting the gray flesh squeeze out like stringy putty between sheared strips of leather. He of course knew about the metamorphosis—the Change—but it had all been very theoretical up till now. He inhaled subtly though his nose so as not to appear rattled and then looked up and caught Ay-Tal's eyes. This was why he was here with her, right now, on this journey home.

Jon sat across from Ay-Tal in a small but private train cabin. She was almost thirty years his senior, but he thought she was still very beautiful. There was a severity to her features: a strong chin, a slight widow's peak, dark, thick hair cut short with a few stray grays but not too many, full lips and dark gray eyes, long face and slim figure, very light skin. In short, she was everything he wasn't—except for her eye color. Gray eyes were common among his tribe. There didn't seem to be a trace of Inuit in her. And yet Jon knew her tribal roots ran far deeper than his own. His own great-great-grandmother was

English, he was told, one of those who came to Alaska during the Gold Rush all those years ago. Ay-Tal was pure...

"How bad?" she managed to ask. Even under duress, her voice was deep and velvety—a perfect oration organ. It had been beautifully designed by his grandfather.

Jon bent down to examine the boot. In some places, the leather polish was thicker than the remaining leather. Even with extra care and regular repair, thirty years was just too long for city boots. He hoped they would last all the way to the little village hidden on the shores of Alaska's National Coastal Conservation Area, but one didn't always get all that was hoped. Jon's father had made these boots to last the duration, and now it was Jon's job to make them endure these last four thousand miles. Seal fur with a whale hide foundation would have been more durable, but it wouldn't have been appropriate, not for Boston, not for Washington, D.C., and certainly not in front of the Supreme Court.

He lifted Ay-Tal's legs onto his lap for a closer inspection and grabbed his tools. Pressing the sides of the ripped leather together, he started to carefully wrap the specially made leather tape over and over the boot's perimeter to repair the damage. He felt the pressure ease a bit; the gray flesh composed of millions of intertwining threads retreated and resumed the shape of a human leg. The repair wouldn't last long, but perhaps long enough to get home? He pulled the hunting knife to cut the tape and scrape away the frayed edges.

"Tickets!" The compartment door slid open, and the conductor stared at Jon.

Jon looked down at Ay-Tal's legs bound in tape and the long blade in his hand and back up at the horrified face of the conductor. Ay-Tal tried to talk; it came out like strange whalesong moan. She waved to the conductor, but her muscular control was still off, and what should have been a friendly hello turned into spasmodic jerks. She came across as terrifying even to Jon, and he understood what was going on. "It's not what it—" he started to say.

The conductor dropped his pad and whipped a pistol from behind his back. "Stop right there!" he ordered.

Jon dropped his knife and tried to straighten out. Ay-Tal let out a loud howl, more animal than human. It would take some time before she would be able to speak again; too much of the transformation had been triggered by the ripped boot.

"Don't move!" screamed the man.

"It's not what it looks like," Jon tried to explain. But he could guess what it looked like to this uniformed man: a dark-skinned man with a scar above his eye (an old hunting accident) threatening a white woman in a business suit with a big knife after binding her legs together. How could he explain it away? And Ay-Tal wasn't helping. "Officer," Jon tried again. "I was just trying to help Ms. Blue with her—" He reached for Ay-Tal's legal case to pull out some documents.

A shot rang out. Jon felt Ay-Tal twitch and push his body out of the path of the bullet. With horror, he watched a hole in Ay-Tal's chest start to pulse blood. The conductor dropped the gun, terror twisting his face. Jon sprung up and pushed the man out of the cabin, shutting the door with a click of the lock. He picked up the gun and hid it in his own waistband in the back, just like the conductor. The gun was still hot.

Jon looked at Ay-Tal's ashen face. She was losing blood fast. She was his responsibility, his god, his reason for existence. And he owed her his life now too. He felt sick from panic. She blinked and blinked again, but then her eyes rolled back, closed, and didn't open again.

"Aguguq take me!" Jon grabbed the knife and started to cut the boots off Ay-Tal's feet. Cut and pull, cut and pull. It got harder with each incision. Ay-Tal's fibrous flesh started to expand and push out again. But the bleeding ebbed and then stopped. Ay-Tal only bled in human form, Jon was told. *Remove the boots, remove the humanity.* That's how his grandfather shaped her; the whole tribe had worked on finding the right form for those boots. When Jon was done cutting them off, he stood over a gray, twined blob covered in bloody clothing. Well, at least Ay-Tal was alive. It was time to get off this train.

Jon pulled down his backpack, his only piece of luggage, and grabbed Ay-Tal's briefcase full of documents that solidified the tribe's position on legal ownership of its land and mineral resources. Fifty years of work couldn't end just because some white man misunderstood what he saw on the train. Gathering the synthetic blankets that came with their cabin, he wrapped Ay-Tal as securely as he could and stuffed the bloodied clothing under the seat with her suitcase. He wasn't sure why he bothered—the place looked like a murder scene. Blood everywhere...

With the backpack on, Jon put his ear to the door. There were the usual noises of the moving train but no additional screams or suspicious shuffling. He dared to crack open the door and look out. The long corridor, running from one end of the train car to the other between the cabins, was empty. He had already considered jumping out of the window, but he wasn't sure Ay-Tal was strong enough to survive the awkward fall. And he wasn't too sure he was. Too high a risk. That meant carrying Ay-Tal through the train, out to the gangway connection between cars, and jumping from there. Jon deemed that safer. No more than a minute had passed since the gunshot, and Jon expected the authorities to return at any moment, guns blazing. It was now or never.

He felt a slight change in the motion of the train; they

were slowing down.

"Ay-Tal," he said. "I'm sorry, but I see no other choice." With that, he hoisted the gray body wrapped in the Pacific Railroad blankets over his shoulder, grabbed the briefcase, and ran down the corridor.

Jon made it to the back of their train car without incident and slid open the door. Once between cars, only flexible walls separated him from freedom. He carefully lowered Ay-Tal onto the floor. Using his knife, he twisted and jammed the locks to each of the adjoining cars. It wasn't much but it would buy him a little more time. A few quick motions with his knife and he opened a hole in the flexible siding big enough to push through. All those years of practicing on whales, seals, and reindeer...

He picked up Ay-Tal like a baby with one hand, pressing her...it to his chest, and with a briefcase in his other hand, he rushed for the opening and jumped.

He rolled over and over down the steep incline away from the train tracks. The early snow somewhat softened the impact. At least he hoped it was the snow and not Ay-Tal's body protecting him yet again. The briefcase, unfortunately, was slapped from his hand when he hit the ground.

"Are you okay?" Jon asked as soon as he was able; the fall knocked the wind out of him.

The gray, twisting blob that used to be a beautiful woman purred. Jon wasn't sure if that was good or bad. His father and grandfather had told him stories, but even they only saw the Change once. And he didn't think it was this dramatic back then. From what he was told, he imagined it was more like going into a room as one person and coming out as another...after many hours. He didn't know if anyone in his tribe's living memory had seen Ay-Tal for what it was... like this. It wasn't revolting or anything. Jon wasn't repulsed touching the soft, fibrous gray flesh, but he did find it difficult to look at it directly. He needed Ay-Tal to assume a human form again. Fast. Soon. The boots were gone. Ay-Tal would never again have the look of a highly educated lawyer from Harvard, arguing cases in front of the Supreme Court. That person was dead, just like the conductor and the rest would assume...jump to conclusions. Jon knew he would have too if he saw what that man saw. *There will be a murder investigation,* he realized.

"We need to get out of here," he said. He stood up and looked for the briefcase. It wasn't visible. He would have to come back for it once Ay-Tal was safely hidden. Even if the Union Pacific train was far in the distance now, Jon wasn't naive enough to think they were out of trouble. There was going to be a search. He gently gathered Ay-Tal in his arms and carried her—he felt uncomfortable thinking of her as it—farther away into the shelter of the thick low boughs of the evergreens growing on the edge of the forested strip of land surrounding the train tracks. Tucking Ay-Tal out of view, Jon left to look for the briefcase.

All along the railway, there was garbage strewn about among the vegetation, trash snagged on craggy branches and caught among the barren bushes, tall, dead grasses, and exposed rocks of the late fall. Civilization slithered through nature, leaving its slimy discards. Jon felt disgusted and experienced a strong urge to pick the crap up off the forest floor. But that wasn't what he was here for. He scanned the ground for the briefcase; it couldn't have landed too far from where they hit the ground. It was well made so unlikely to have opened and spilled its precious contents all over Wisconsin...or was it Minnesota already? Jon wasn't sure, but he had a map and a satellite phone in his backpack; normal smartphones were not very useful out in the far northern country of his people. Although all the kids had smart tablets and shared educational materials by linking those directly. Technology had changed his people in the last few decades, but far less than Ay-Tal had when she joined their tribe. There might not even have been a tribe without Ay-Tal.

He spotted the brown leather of the briefcase in a ditch off to the side. He rushed over and almost tripped over a kid's Dora the Explorer backpack. It was so covered in mud that Jon almost didn't recognize the friendly face from his childhood. He bent down and picked it up. *Probably fell from the train*, he thought. It felt heavy; he took a quick look inside. Girl's clothing, a coloring book, and...*Yes!* A pair of little pink boots! An idea formed in Jon's head. It was crazy, but it just might work. He grabbed the muddy briefcase in his other hand and rushed back to Ay-Tal.

● ● ●

Jon had never seen the Change ritual; he was only a few months old for the most recent one. He had been told about it, of course, but hoped never to have to personally put into practice the legends of his fathers. There were chanting and singing and some drumming, but Jon believed all that was for his people's benefit and not strictly necessary. He knelt before the gray form that was bundled in the ugly blankets and maneuvered the child-sized pink boots under the soft flesh. It almost felt like the gray tendrils burrowed into the earth beneath the Ay-Tal's body, merging with networks of tubular filaments of mycelia that Jon knew naturally permeated the ground under the tree.

"Ay-Tal?" he said softly. "I know this is not what you would want. And I will help you with...with something else later." He felt uncomfortable even talking about the Change, much less requesting Ay-Tal to become a child for him. But he saw no other way. The authorities would be looking for him and a woman. An injured woman. Perhaps if he posed as a father of a little girl... "Please?"

Slowly, oh so very slowly, thin tendrils snaked their way into the tiny boots. His father told him it took over a week for Ay-Tal to become the woman he met. How long would it take now? Back then, his grandfather spent several years designing the person Ay-Tal would need to become to win the tribe's case in front of the Supreme Court. Ay-Tal knew what was required of her and helped shape that person. *But now? How would it work now?* Jon sat and watched and prayed to Aguguq that the metamorphosis didn't take too long.

• • •

He woke up with a start. It was dark and very cold. The moon was out; he could see its light shining through the branches of their tree. A small hand touched his cheek.

"Jon?" The voice was very high. A small child was staring at him from inside a nest of blankets. "Will this work?"

"Ay-Tal?" It was one thing to know about the Change, but to witness the transformation? Jon was shaken. The child in front of him was no more than five, perhaps even younger. A skinny little arm was attached to a tiny little hand with miniature fingers. The eyes staring at him were deep blue, with just a hint of gray around the edge. A bit of red hair poked out from under the dirty cloth. That and those pink boots.

"Will this work?" the child asked again.

Jon forced himself to focus. "Yes. That's very good, Ay-Tal." It felt strange complimenting a god. "Thank you." He quickly looked at the child's face and then had to look away—too strange. "I have some clothing here." He pulled out the Dora the Explorer bag and gave it to Ay-Tal. "If you could dress, we should try to get out of here as quickly as possible. They will be looking for us."

The child nodded and took the bag. There were some pink tights, a t-shirt with another Dora print on it, and a sweatshirt. The clothing was covered in mud and blooming with spots of mold. *Not enough to keep a child warm*, Jon noted to himself. Ay-Tal wiggled out of the blankets and started to put on the clothing, slipping off only one boot at a time.

The child was male, Jon noticed in shock.

When done, Ay-Tal smiled at him. "Ready?"

"Y-yes," he stammered. "Are you cold or anything?"

"I will be," the boy answered. "But not yet. It takes time to adjust to the Change."

"Yes, of course." Jon had no idea what that meant. "Can you walk?"

"Only for as long as a kid my age can," the boy said with a smile...a very adult smile. "And call me Al. I think it works better for this body, don't you?"

"Al. I can do that." Jon tried to smile back, but it didn't work—his face refused to make it. So he gathered their meager possessions, rearranging his backpack so he could carry all of the legal documents on his back and tied the rest into a bundle made from one of the blankets. Ay-Tal...Al put on the dirty little backpack and tried to bury the briefcase under the many seasons of pine needles and other detritus surrounding the base of their tree hideout.

"Let me help you with that," Jon said and with just a few movements of his wide hands finished the job of concealing the bag. It would be found, of course. But anything to give them additional time to melt into the American landscape was worth it.

The child that was Ay-Tal watched him cover the now empty briefcase and strip a dead branch to make a stick to tie up their bundle for ease of carrying; a hobo stick. They climbed together from under the tree. Jon swung the bundle over his shoulder, resting the stick on the strap of his backpack. Al gave him his hand, like a child would. And they walked into the woods, away from the tracks. Jon hoped to find some shelter before the moon set. In this part of the country, they were really never too far from civilization...for better or worse.

● ● ●

A few hours later, Jon was carrying the sleeping child over his shoulder, wrapped in a blanket like a burrito. He walked on the shoulder of US-12, a highway he had located on his map, pegging their position near the town of Wilkins, Wisconsin. It was still dark and there was no traffic, but Jon was ready to jump into the trees along the side of the road if he spotted any headlights. He was sure there was a manhunt on for him and didn't want to take any chances.

They would need to stop and buy more appropriate clothing for Al. He almost said "Ay-Tal" in his head but stopped himself. That name was dangerous now—too memorable and too easily connected to current events. How many Inuit lawyers named Ay-Tal Blue that just won an argument in the highest court of land were there? She was all over the news last week and would be again now, for totally different reasons. Jon shifted his shoulders, and the child gave a soft sigh. Poor kid tried to walk by himself, and only after Jon pointed out that he was slowing them down did Al allow himself to be carried.

She doesn't just mimic the attributes of the person she changes into—she fully inhabits that person, he remembered his father telling him. For good or bad, Al was a little kid now. Jon wondered if Al remembered all her...his previous lives. *He must. Or it just doesn't work.* He decided to ask later, the next time it was convenient to have such a conversation.

Jon also needed to let his tribe know what happened. He was wary of using phones, but there was an email account set up that he could use to draft a message in code. Messages from that account were never sent, in order to avoid interception in transit. Someone back home checked the account several times a day and read all of the unsent email drafts. Nothing was ever addressed to anyone; nothing ever moved across the network. Ay-Tal had set up the message drop system when the Internet came online, decades ago. Now the whole tribe used this spy-craft stuff. Encryptions, codes, secure passwords, cyber currency, anonymous accounts... It had all been fun and games until now. But Ay-Tal taught them well; clearly, she foresaw it might become necessary someday.

He needed papers for Al. There was no easy way to get over the Canadian border without passports. And the kid didn't look like his son. A shame, that. It would have been so much easier if Al was a dark-haired, dark-eyed, dark-skinned little boy. People would ask questions, the way Al looked. Perhaps they could use hair dye and sunglasses; it would work at a distance, but not at the border inspection or during any other interaction with authorities. Jon felt cold sweat run down his back as he thought of the police arresting him for murder and taking Al away. They would accuse him of child trafficking, too, and put Ay-Tal in foster care. He needed to stay away from people as much as possible and come up with a good cover story. He could change his appearance somewhat; he could shave his head and grow a beard, perhaps. Would that confuse any face-recognition systems? He could use skin-lightening creams. He could dye his hair red to match Al's. But then his passport... He was never into the cloak-and-dagger stuff; he was a traditional Inuit artisan, just like his father and his father's father before him.

A squat building with white walls and a dark-shingled roof surprised Jon out of the early morning mist. "Wilkins Nite Club" said giant letters across the entire facade. On one corner of the building, there were signs of fire damage that were patched up and covered with two giant flags, Wisconsin's and the Stars and Stripes. Jon looked around. There were no other structures close by and no cars parked in the gravel-covered parking lot. He dashed into the lot and behind the nightclub. He needed to rest a bit and change his own clothing. All this mud and blood would attract attention. Back on the train, Jon never got to the point where his and Ay-Tal's tickets were actually checked—the conductor never learned their names. Would the conductor remember what they...he looked like? People were notorious for being lousy eyewitnesses. And he still needed to dispose of Ay-Tal's IDs; it would not be good to be found with those.

He lowered Al, still wrapped in the Pacific Railroad blanket, onto the back porch. The ground was wet and cold, covered in a silvery frost. "These blankets have to go too," Jon mumbled under his breath, which came out as a small silver cloud about his face. "Should have left 'em under that tree for the police to find." But the kid was cold. "Aguguq. So much to do."

Al was sleeping peacefully. He looked like a little cherub from one of those greeting cards. And that was a big problem. Jon actually didn't look like a typical Inuit—those English genes. He was taller than average for his people, just under six feet, and his eyes were an unexpected dark gray, not brown. But who would take the time to check his eye color when looking at Al's wide blue-as-a-clear-March-sky eyes? *Aguguq, help me.*

And looks like a girl too, Jon continued his train of thought. A little white blue-eyed boy...or girl traveling with a guy like him raised eyebrows as well as questions. He needed to get the kid sex-appropriate clothing, something dark and grungy. *But those boots...* He looked at the shocking patch of pink sticking out from under the drab navy-blue blanket. Those *had* to stay. So more raised eyebrows, more questions.

He pulled out Ay-Tal Blue's wallet and passport. *Keep or destroy?* As far as Jon knew, Al would never be able to take on that identity again. If they were discovered with these... Jon stuffed the papers deep into his backpack and lay down next to the child, pressing the little body close. The kid was still cold and made pathetic little snorts in his sleep. *A child who is not a child. How do I keep him safe?* And with that thought, Jon fell fast asleep.

Chapter Two: Wilkins

Jon Uolan

"Hey, Mister!" A voice and not so gentle kick in his back woke Jon up. He glanced at the sky; it was still early. He couldn't have slept more than an hour or so.

Smeared in mud and worse, with a day-old growth, and pine needles sticking out of his disheveled hair and ruffled clothes, Jon knew he looked scary—more homeless drifter than Sunday school teacher. "Cut it out," he barked gruffly, playing up to the scary image he projected. As he sat up, he pushed the bundle of blankets with Al behind him.

"Beat it. It's our porch," a kid no older than sixteen said, taking a step back. He was dressed in torn, ill-fitting black jeans, hiking boots, many layers of sweatshirts, facial piercings, and a biker's leather jacket several sizes too big. Behind him were two more kids, similarly attired, boys or girls, Jon couldn't tell yet. Too dark.

"Well, I'm using it now. Scram!" Jon growled at them threateningly. The boy inched farther back, and Jon felt guilty. These kids just looked tough; they were probably runaways or worse. Why else would a bunch of teenagers bother a sleeping grown stranger this early in the morning? "Look," he said in a softer voice. "I'm just passing through. You can have your porch in a few hours."

"I need it now," the boy said and pulled a knife out of his jacket.

Jon inhaled deeply, stood up, and pulled out his own knife, leaving the conductor's gun in place at the back of his waistband. Seeing how the kid held his weapon, it was obvious he had no clue how to use it. Jon, on the other hand, was an experienced hunter. He knew what to do with a knife... and a gun. He also knew that he would never use them on these kids. Scare them, yes. Hurt them? Never.

The kid took another big step back. He didn't want to fight Jon either. It was all bravado—wear a scary wardrobe and wave a weapon and most people back down without a fight. It was a good strategy for a young kid on his own. *Three young kids.*

"Look, I want no trouble," Jon said. "I just need to rest a bit. Long night. You get that, don't you?" The kid lowered his weapon. Jon put away his. "I'm Jon."

"Arrow," the kid said. "And that's Saga and Hazel." The girls waved hello and smiled. The situation defused somewhat as the knives were put away.

The blankets next to Jon stirred, and a little face poked out and then pink tights and a pink sweatshirt. "And this is Al," Jon said with a sigh. "He is my son." As soon as he said it, he felt relieved—a decision made. "Does this town have a Goodwill?" he asked as Saga and Hazel stepped closer to take a look. Girls always reacted emotionally to cute little kids; it was their weakness. That made Al his secret weapon; people related differently to a man with a small child. Perhaps Al could be an asset, rather than a liability...

"Oooh, hi there, little guy." Hazel crouched next to Al. "What amazing eyes..."

"Yes, so much like *not* yours," Saga commented. And so

it began.

Jon shrugged. "Genetics. What are you going to do? Al's mother is English, and so was my grandmother."

"Cute kid," said Arrow. "Why is he dressed like a girl?"

Yes, why? Jon had no answer.

"I like Dora the Explorer," said Al in his high, bell-like voice. "See?" And he pulled apart the blankets to reveal the cartoon character's face printed on his dirty shirt.

"I see why you might want to visit a Goodwill," said Arrow under his breath.

"Oh, I like her too, honey," Hazel said with a smile. "You want some gum?" She pulled out a pack of strawberry bubblegum from the pocket of her tailored black leather jacket lined with shiny pink silk. Unlike Arrow and Saga, who wore matching black leather jackets with patches and studs, Hazel's look was less sloppy biker and more fashion-forward grunge.

"I want real food," said Al pathetically.

Saga turned to Jon, narrowed her eyes, and asked accusingly, "When was the last time you fed your *son*?" The way she said "son" made it clear she didn't believe Jon was really his father.

Al climbed out of the blankets and, pink boots and all, hugged Jon's legs as if in fear. Jon put his hand protectively on the little red locks. He didn't even have to act; Al inspired empathy, he oozed innocence, roused maternal and paternal instincts. Jon felt it, and he could see how it worked on this band of young ruffians, too.

"There's a kitchen in there," said Hazel, all concern, eager to help. "We can make some eggs. Aunt Ada keeps the fridge well-stocked for us." Seeing Jon's reaction, she explained, "My mom's sister owns this place."

"So this really is your porch," Jon said with a smile. It

explained a few things. Most kids would have left a grown man like him alone. These kids were trying to protect their property. "I'm sorry to have trespassed."

"Oh, it's all right," Hazel said. "Arrow takes his job as a guard way too seriously. Come on in." She pulled out a thick set of keys and stepped around Jon and Al to open the backdoor to the nightclub. "It's warmer inside, and we can make some coffee too. Or tea. Homemade tea. It's Aunt Ada's specialty."

They piled inside a big, bright room with light wooden floors. There were many wooden tables, the same color as the floor, with black leather stools arranged in a circle around each of them. A pine bar stood on one side of the spacious room with dozens of liquor bottles and a large menu above, drawn in multicolored chalk. There were a dozen TVs screwed into the walls, and on the far side there were what looked like a kitchen and perhaps an office. Arrow turned on the lights, and the bar glowed a poison green with purple Christmas lights underneath the counters. All in all, it was a much nicer place than Jon imagined, given the outside of the building, the kind of place that would have done double duty as a community center back in his village...perhaps with a smaller bar.

"Nice," Jon said.

"Thanks!" Hazel strode directly toward the back and motioned for him to follow. Jon took Al's hand and, leaving his hobo bundle on the ground in the corner, followed the girl to the rooms in the back. The documents were still safely stowed away in the backpack on his back.

Hazel made a decent breakfast of eggs, bacon, and some toast. She made Al and Jon scrub up before eating—Ay-Tal's blood, a jump from a train, a night in the mud under a tree, a walk through a forest... They did look like hobos or worse.

They didn't smell so good either.

When they finished cleaning up the kitchen after breakfast, Hazel asked Arrow to draw a Dora the Explorer cartoon for Al to color on a sheet of printer paper. To Jon's surprise, Arrow was able to draw a decent Dora surrounded by some jungle animals in just a simple outline of black ink from his little pen set that he kept in his voluminous jacket pockets. Al set to color Arrow's cartoon with some colored pencils that Hazel found in her aunt's desk. Arrow didn't offer his pen set to the boy. The sight of Ay-Tal coloring felt too wrong, and Jon couldn't help but stare. Al winked at him and continued to allow the girls to fuss over him.

"So what's your story?" asked Arrow when the two of them sat down to some coffee. The girls didn't drink any. Ay-Tal did and liked it, but Jon wasn't sure about Al.

"Not much of one," Jon tried to evade while he thought hard of what to say that would make sense to these kids.

"You were train-hopping," Arrow said, glancing back at where Jon left his stuff. Perhaps the logos on the blankets gave it away. "Not a good idea with a little kid."

"Thanks for the advice, Arrow, but I didn't really have a choice."

Arrow nodded like he understood. He might have; he looked like his life had been rough. Thinking of his own life back with his tribe, Jon felt blessed. He always knew right from wrong, never worried about food or other life's necessities, and there were people who loved him. It wasn't until he had left that life that things became complicated.

"Shouldn't jump from trains with a little kid," Arrow said again.

"Yeah?" Jon wished that he had some access to the news—what was being said on the evening news about him and Ay-Tal? Without basic situational awareness, he was at a severe disadvantage.

"Did you check the boy for injuries?" Arrow looked at Jon over the rim of the huge coffee cup.

"He seems okay," Jon said.

"I broke my collarbone once jumping," Arrow said. "It took weeks to figure out. Hazel's aunt finally took me to the emergency room. Hurt like a bitch."

"Huh. Al seems fine. He hasn't complained of anything. But thanks for the tip." The kid clearly meant well. "His mama is a junkie. Abandoned him about a year ago." Jon felt like he had to share some back-story, something that sounded believable. More empathy...

"He seems like good kid," Arrow said, shifting his eyes to observe Saga and Hazel playing with Al. "The pink shit needs to go. It's not that I have anything against it, mind you. It's just other people...people bully when they don't understand."

"Hmm."

"I'm just saying it would be easier on you and the boy, that's all."

"Thanks," said Jon and meant it. This kid was trying to help him.

"There's no Goodwill around, but the church has a donations center set up in the basement. The girls could go and pick something out for you."

"That would great. Really. And..."

"Yeah?"

"I've got to contact my parents, Al's grandparents. Any place I can use a computer for a few minutes to send an email? A library or a post office?" Jon asked. Arrow nodded. "Need to keep that kid safe until we get home." Arrow nodded again. Jon felt bad for lying, even if he didn't exactly lie, just implied a lot of stuff.

"Are you taking the kid to your parents?"

"Yeah." That wasn't a lie.

"Far?"

"Alaska."

Arrow whistled. "Always wanted to go there someday. Got any money?"

Jon felt his hand twitch toward the inside pocket of his vest. He forced himself to relax, but Arrow noticed and his eye drifted to Jon's chest.

"Some," Jon said. "Not enough for a plane ticket or anything..."

"So, train-hopping," Arrow said. "Tough to do in winter."

"Where did you hop?"

"Down south. It was okay. Won't do it with a kid that young, though."

"Yeah." Jon took another deep sip of coffee. "Any truck stops around here?"

"Good idea," Arrow said after a few beats of hesitation. The boy was a slow talker, Jon noted. He liked that. Not like all those fast-talking dandies back in Washington. "But not too many willing to take hitchhikers nowadays," Arrow continued. "Although with a little kid like that...still, there will be lots of questions. It might be better to ask your parents for money."

"Dad?" Al called from across the little kitchen. "Hazel said that they could get me some clean clothing. Would that be okay? I can go with them..."

Al wasn't asking, Jon didn't think. Al was telling him of some plan. Too bad they hadn't had enough alone time to work out a way of communicating and setting some ground rules. Was Jon supposed to let him go? Would that be too weird?

"Jon? We'll take good care of Al. Saga and I have been babysitting since forever. Years. And the church is just a few blocks away...well, a mile or two," Hazel corrected herself under Arrow's glare. "But not too far." She glanced again at the youth. He obviously had authority with the girls. *Rare, that.* "Anyways, I help with donations sorting, and I know our inventory. There are some good winter jackets in Al's size. He needs warmer clothing," she finished on an accusatory note.

Jon wasn't sure what to say. He really looked the part of a confused young father. Al jumped down and ran toward him. "Daddy, please?"

"Well..."

"Saga and Hazel will take good care of him." Arrow vouched for the girls. "I have to stay here. Job, you know." Jon nodded. "But the girls will show you where the post office is. There's a computer there. Mrs. Nelson would probably let you use it for a few bucks."

"Well, I guess that would be fine," Jon said, looking Al in the eyes. *What are you doing?* he wanted to ask. But his father and grandfather had told him to trust Ay-Tal. He felt his body relax a bit as he made the decision to go with the flow, so to speak. "Sure. Let's go. I'll walk with you guys to this church, and you wait for me there, Al. You hear? Don't go anywhere. Just wait for me there. I will send a note to your granddaddy and then come right back to get you."

Al climbed on his lap and hugged him around the neck, putting his face into his ear. "Mail the papers—it's a federal offense to tamper with mail..." And then, louder, "Yes, Daddy!" Al let go of Jon, smiled, and a little dimple puckered his left cheek. Somehow, it was more adorable than having two dimples. There was something about asymmetry that inspired cuteness. *So memorable...*

"Let's go then," said Jon and set Al back down on the floor.

"Bathroom?" asked Hazel. She clearly had babysitting

experience. She took Al's hand and led him to the back.

• • •

Ay-Tal

"So where's your mommy?" Hazel asked as she soaped Al's hands. She also sniffed his sweatshirt and wrinkled her nose again.

While Al was sure his body smelled fine, the pink clothing they found inside the Dora the Explorer bag did smell terrible. Al was looking forward to wearing something clean... and more sex-appropriate. He didn't know why the Change took on the characteristics of a little boy rather than a girl, given the obvious clues. But perhaps these things really did belong to a boy once...or a girl who wanted to be a boy. Hard to tell, and there was no time to prepare. If there was more appropriate footwear in the church's donations bin, he would get Jon to grab some and then go through another Change in a few days when he got his energy back. There were a lot of advantages to being a cute kid...and a lot of disadvantages. The big one was that Jon wasn't sure how to behave around a small child. And, unfortunately, there was little familial resemblance between them—*why should there be?*

"Al? What's the matter, dear?" Hazel asked. "Are you sad about your mama?"

"No," Al answered honestly. "Just tired." He was very tired. The Change was never easy, even under the best of circumstances.

"You can stay here for a bit," Hazel said. "And get some rest in a real bed. Aunt Ada is a real sweetheart. She doesn't have kids of her own...not since Mason died in fire..." She glanced to check if Al was scared by what she just said. Since

Al didn't react, she continued without skipping a beat. "But that was a long time ago. Don't you worry." Hazel had a way of talking where there were no pauses between the end of one sentence and the beginning of the next. It was as if she was afraid of being interrupted before she could finish what she wanted to say. "Well," she went on, "Aunt Ada lets Arrow and Saga hang out at her house now, but fostering is not the same as having real kids. And they are too old. Anyways, I'm sure she would love to have you for a few days. With your daddy, of course," she added hastily as Al looked at her with his big blue eyes. "You've got beautiful eyes, you know. So not like your daddy's."

"Everyone says I look just like my granny," Al said.

"Of course you do," Hazel said. She moved on to wiping his face with a towel. Al was already as clean as he was going to be; so this was just stalling. "Do you know your granny's name?" she asked sweetly.

"Granny," he answered simply. He wasn't fooled. This was a full interrogation. He'd bet there would be many more questions as soon as he was separated from Jon.

"Of course she is! And how about your mama? Do you know her name?"

"Mom?" Al played the innocent. How many kids his age knew their parents' given names? Not too many in his experience.

"And your dad's? He said he was Jon. Do you know your last name? Your family name?"

Al smiled, pushed the towel away from his face, and wriggled free. "Let's go to the church! Do you think they might have some toys there I can play with?" he asked.

"Oh, they do! They have lots of toys to play with. I bet we can find a nice Dora doll for you," Hazel said and took Al's hand firmly in hers. "Let's go see."

When they rejoined the rest in the kitchen, Al noted that Hazel and Saga exchanged glances. Obviously, Jon's story wasn't believed. But nobody was calling the cops on them just yet...

● ● ●

Jon Uolan

The walk to the church was longer than Jon would have liked. Up the hill from the highway, two-story homes lined the street, looking eerily alike with the same slanted roofs, wide porches facing the street, broad front lawns, and American flags mounted next to the front doors. Aside for a few boarded-up houses, the town of Wilkins looked like a quintessential small-town USA in the lower forty-eight, at least to Jon. Some suburbs of Anchorage tried to emulate this look, but it was difficult to pull off up there; Alaska's climate was much harsher than Wisconsin's. Jon wondered if people knew their neighbors around here or if it was all very anonymous. Back in his village, everyone knew everyone else and everyone else's business. It was a bit claustrophobic in that way, and many young people left for big cities because of that. But Jon liked it; it was home.

He carried Al most of the way to the church—either the little boy's body really didn't have much stamina, or Ay-Tal was exhausted from the Change. Either way, it made Jon seem more paternal to the girls, and that was good. Carrying Al and the hobo stick was a bit awkward, but neither of the girls offered to help—they were repulsed even to come in contact with the dirty-looking bundle. Jon found it amusing... and possibly useful.

The church's basement was set up as a homeless shelter

with a few beds but no customers. Jon figured that this far from a large metropolitan center, there were few homeless about. But there was a large table with books, toys, and old DVDs and many racks of used clothing, all neatly sorted, all clean. These people wanted to help...and there was a lot one could tell from how they went about doing it. *Not a wealthy town, that's for sure,* Jon thought based on the selection of this community's discards. But there was far more of the stuff than he imagined there would be; Wilkins didn't seem to be such a large town.

"I work here most Saturday mornings," Hazel said. "We have washing machines and a big drier in the back. I can even dry-clean some donations."

"Very impressive," Jon said. He meant it. Back home, they did clothing and book exchanges. Everyone had something they no longer needed or wanted. Most of his childhood clothing was second-hand—why spend the money? "Is there something here that would fit Al? Something for winter?"

"Oh, yes," said a middle-aged woman in jeans and a sweater with hearts all over it. *Aunt Ada,* Jon guessed. She looked like every other small-town gossip that Jon had met in his limited experience. He knew it wasn't fair to classify the woman like that, but first impressions didn't often lie, as his grandfather taught him. So he smiled politely and put on his most charming demeanor.

"It's so kind of you to help us out like this," he said and meant it.

"Not at all." The woman came around the table with an old computer and gave him a quick once-over. "I'm Mrs. Wilkins, by the way, but please call me Ada."

"I'm Jon." He extended his hand in greeting. Ada's grip was soft and slippery, not wet, just ungraspable. Jon felt like wiping his hand afterward but restrained himself. A good impression was everything right now. "Is that Wilkins, as in the town's name?"

"Yes, it is." The woman blushed, but her expression showed that she was very proud of the fact. "Wilkinses were the founders of this community." She did wipe her hand on the side of her pants after shaking Jon's. Jon pretended not to notice.

"Very interesting," Jon said. "And your help, it really means a lot to me and Al," he said again.

"Oh it's no trouble at all," Ada said, continuing to unconsciously rub Jon's "germs" off her right hand.

"I told you." Hazel smiled at him. "My Aunt Ada is a jewel." Ada blushed and waved her niece off, but Jon could see that she was very pleased by the praise.

"She's doing God's work," Jon agreed and put on a particularly wide smile.

Al ran around the table to the toys and zeroed in on some book, made a happy noise, and rushed back to hug Ada's legs. The woman was thrilled by the little boy's show of affection, if a bit surprised. Jon just marveled at Al's performance. Over thirty years as a high-powered attorney, and before that a skilled seal hunter, and before that... Jon looked forward to the time when he could safely ask Ay-Tal questions and learn about her past lives and his own tribe's history from her unique point of view. Thousands of years ago, his tribe journeyed over the ice from what was now Russia to Alaska. Ay-Tal was there though it all; she led the original group of families over the Bering Strait during the Ice Age. The Ice Age! *But now?* It was all so awkward now. It was hard to see a little kid as an authority figure, as an elder, as a god. *God?* Jon never really thought of Ay-Tal like that. There was Aguguq, and then there was Ay-Tal. They were...different. But perhaps he should have focused on similarities rather than gods' differences.

"Come on, Al." Hazel took the boy's hand. "Let's go find you something more appropriate to wear."

"But I like pink," Al protested.

"I just meant you need something warmer, okay? And we can wash things here for you while your dad goes to the post office. Wouldn't it be nice to have everything clean?"

Al made a face, and Hazel laughed and took him among the racks of kid clothing. *Ay-Tal is so good at this,* Jon thought again.

"And do you need something, Jon?" Ada asked. "I'm sure we have a few things in your size."

"Oh no, thank you, ma'am. I have plenty." He pointed to the bundle of clothing wrapped in a blanket and immediately realized he had made a mistake. Ada's look turned hostile; he had warm clothing for himself while his kid went without? What kind of monster was he? Jon swallowed and said, "Well, if you don't terribly mind, I could use a warm jacket." Ada's expression relaxed somewhat. She was still suspicious but put on a smile and took him to a different rack with men's stuff. Truthfully, Jon looked like he could use a warm jacket; he was wearing just a puffy vest over a sweatshirt. But he grew up in Alaska—where it might be cold outside for these folks; for him, it felt as warm as a balmy spring afternoon. It was all a matter of what one was used to.

Ada left him to help Hazel and Al. Jon stayed and pretended to look through the selection of jackets and sweatshirts and hunting gear while keeping an eye on Al. That kid had Ada and Hazel eating out of his little hands the way they fussed over him.

"You don't really need a jacket, do you?" Jon was startled by Saga standing way too close to him. Somehow he just plain forgot all about her. The girl barely talked, leaving that to Hazel, and made herself as invisible as possible, even in all that sloppy Goth stuff.

"It couldn't hurt," Jon answered. "But I hate taking charity."

"You could pay," Saga said.

"Good idea. Do you mind showing me the way to the post office?"

"I'll walk with you," Saga said.

"No, really. You don't have to."

"I don't mind," she said and walked toward the door. Jon didn't want the company but he also didn't know how to shake the girl. He wasn't trained for this. He was a good leatherworker, a good hunter, and a lousy bodyguard, apparently. And this? He wished the tribe had sent someone more competent. But his family had been linked with Ay-Tal for at least four hundred generations. Perhaps much longer... there were rumors. Jon shook his head. *Rumors are just that, rumors.*

"Coming?" Saga called to him, and Jon rushed to catch up. He decided to leave the bundle of clothing behind and took only his backpack with the legal papers and Ay-Tal's IDs. The sooner he could get rid of those, the safer he would feel. And the gun, he would need to dispose of it ASAP, too.

The town was quiet. Jon didn't know if it was because it was early in the day or if it was just a really sleepy place.

"Why aren't you at school?" he asked.

"Thanksgiving recess." That explained some of the sleepiness, although back home, school holidays made for the most commotion out on the streets.

They walked along the side of the road. There were no sidewalks here; apparently everyone drove. Back home, everyone walked or skied. Driving was for going distances. No one thought of driving to go across the village. *But here?*

Things here were farther apart, spread out just beyond Jon's comfort zone.

"Over there." Saga pointed. It was the first thing she'd said in fifteen minutes of walking. The squat building she indicated was inside a small shopping center: a dry cleaner, a gas station, a coffee house, and a small grocery store with a post office inside. Everything one could need in one convenient location. Well, that, at least, wasn't much different from where he grew up. He knew some towns up north that were just one building. Restaurants, schools, apartments, medical offices, and even a church and a city hall were all stuffed into one multistory construction. It made sense in that climate—easier to heat, easier to manage. One-stop everything. Instead of cars, there were elevators...

"Thanks," Jon said and cut across the street. He spotted garbage bins and veered off to find a box to package Ay-Tal's papers.

Saga stayed a few steps behind and observed. When she understood what he was looking for, she went around the back and brought out two recycled shipping boxes, one too small and one just about the right size. She handed them over, again without a word.

"Oh, thanks," Jon said and took the larger one. She tossed the small one into the bin.

"She will open at ten," the girl said and went to sit on the curb by the store.

Jon hadn't thought of the time. Of course the store would be closed so early in the morning. Well, he just had to wait. Al could take care of himself. He shouldn't worry. But the kid inspired protectiveness. Jon sat next to Saga in front of the metal cage doors on the cold concrete steps. She pulled out her smartphone and started to text and surf and Aguguq knew what else. They would be here for a while, he realized.

Jon closed his eyes; he hadn't really slept in over twenty-four hours.

"Hmm," he heard her say loudly, clearly intending to get his attention. "Hmm."

"What is it?" Jon asked without opening his eyes.

"They are looking for a guy who might have murdered someone and then jumped off the train."

"Hmm." Jon had been waiting for some news of what happened on the train, and here it was.

"They say he is armed and dangerous," the girl said with forced casualness.

"Who did he kill?" asked Jon.

"It says here that the man grabbed a gun from the conductor and shot another passenger. A woman."

"Do they know who she was?" Jon finally opened his eyes and looked over at Saga. She was being very nonchalant about the whole thing...and so was he. It was hard to do, though. Jon was nervous and felt sweat running down his back. *How long will it take them to figure the identities of Ay-Tal and her companion?*

"Not yet," Saga said. "But the description—dark hair, dark eyes, average height, ethnic-looking—fits you pretty well."

"Does it? Sounds like pretty much anyone."

"That and those Pacific Railroad blankets you stole," she said.

"Got those in a second-hand store," Jon said. "Don't make accusations, kid, about people you hardly know. Some might take offense."

"Are you threatening me?"

"Why should I?"

"Is the kid really yours?" Saga suddenly turned to look him straight in the face. "I mean, he really doesn't look like you." Jon opened his eyes as wide as possible. His features might be "ethnic," but his eye color wasn't. Saga noticed the grays of his eyes, and Jon could practically feel her relax. "I guess genetics does work in mysterious ways," she said, a note of disbelief still in her voice and posture.

"You never know what you going to get." Jon smirked. "So are you and Arrow related?" Both had dark blond hair—Saga's was a bit more mousy than blond—and they shared certain facial mannerisms that only came from family ties or, at least, long time familiarity.

"He's my older brother. But most say we look nothing alike."

"It's not always in the features," Jon said. "Sometimes it's the attitude that's inherited."

"Yeah," she said. "We are both quick to judge."

"He seems like a nice kid."

"He tries," Saga said. "But don't let him hear you call him a kid. He feels all grownup and all."

"Is it just the two of you?"

"For the last three years."

"Sorry."

"Yeah, well, life is not always fair, is it?"

"Nope."

"Hazel's aunt and uncle took us in to foster."

"Ada seems nice enough."

"She is." But the way Saga said it made Jon wary. Something wasn't right there. Why didn't Saga stay with Hazel and Ada back at the church? It couldn't be more fun to trudge to a neighborhood store with a stranger.

"And the uncle?" he asked. He waited, but Saga didn't answer, just turned away into her phone again. *That bad,* he thought. *Well, Al will be fine for a few hours and we will be leaving soon.* And it wasn't really his problem...whatever it was. He glanced at the girl and saw that she had shrunk into her oversized jacket. Hardly anything of her was showing; she was hiding in it like a tortoise in a shell. He felt bad for her, but he was in no position to help. And she had an older brother...

He pulled off his backpack and opened the box Saga brought over. Most everything Ay-Tal had was stored and sorted into waterproof clear plastic envelopes. He slipped those into the box. Ay-Tal's IDs he wrapped in an old t-shirt from the bottom of his pack without taking them out first and then added the bundle into the box. The t-shirt prevented the box from closing.

"Do you have to send that too?" Saga inquired. She'd been watching him pack. He didn't mind too much; it was hard to tell what all this paperwork was.

"I know it's silly," Jon said. "But my mom would like to have something personal."

"Something that smelled like you?" Saga asked.

Jon sniggered. "I guess."

"Well, underwear is smaller and smells more."

"Thanks for the tip."

"You're welcome. And it still won't close. You need a bigger box."

"Is there a bigger box?"

"No."

"Hmm." Jon took out his knife and carefully sawed off unneeded portions of the shirt. "Now it fits," he said triumphantly. Saga just rolled her eyes. "Well, it does. See?" He demonstrably closed the sides of the box, fitting the edges cross-diagonally under each other for a secure closure. "Do they have tape in there?"

"Yeah. Mrs. Nelson will give you some if you ask nicely."

"I will."

"Need a pen?"

Jon considered it. Did he want Saga to see the address of his tribe? No, he did not. "Nah, I'll do it inside."

"Mrs. Nelson likes people who come prepared."

"Does she now? Well, I am. I want to use a permanent marker—don't want the package to go astray due to poor eyesight or something."

Without a word, Saga produced a thick black permanent marker. Jon didn't have a choice now. He took the marker and noted a small smile playing at the corners of Saga's lips—she knew she had won. *Well, two can play.* Jon stood the package on edge and wrote the address on the underside of the box; he was planning on taping up the top anyway. When done, he returned the package to his knees, address down.

"Thanks," he said, handing the marker back.

"Any time." Saga acknowledged that he won this round. He planned to be careful how he carried the box inside.

Another half hour of ignoring each other, and Mrs. Nelson arrived to open the store.

"You are early today." She nodded to Saga and fiddled with the locks. "You look so thin. Grab an apple. I brought a whole basket's worth from my yard yesterday." Jon didn't think it was possible to really tell Saga's weight underneath all of that leather, but Mrs. Nelson seemed to mean well; based on the note of worry Jon heard, it wasn't a jab at Saga's appearance but a genuine concern.

"I figured I owed you a few hours, seeing as I left early the other day," Saga said, standing up and helping Mrs. Nelson manage the door. So the girl worked there. Well, that explained why she walked Jon here instead of just giving directions. It made him feel a bit better. "This is Jon. He needs to mail a package home to...?"

"Home," Jon said. "If you'd be so kind, Mrs. Nelson, I would like to post this right away. I have Hazel, Saga's friend, babysitting my kid at the church. I don't want to take advantage."

Believing she understood the situation, Mrs. Nelson rushed to the back to open up the post office, leaving Saga to deal with the store and starting up the cash register.

"Can I buy a roll of packing tape from you, Mrs. Nelson?" Jon asked, stepping up to the counter.

"Oh, you don't have to buy it, young man. Just take a few strips. It will hold. USPS makes good tape."

"Thank you so much." Jon took the tape and secured the box. "When does the mail get picked up? I would feel so much better knowing this package is on its way."

"Oh, Michael will be by at one or so. He delivers and picks up at the same time. I can usually look up the exact time of arrival; unfortunately, my computer here is busted again. Mason used to..." She stopped and glanced at Saga.

The girl was under the checkout stand in front and couldn't have heard what they were saying, and that clearly made Mrs. Nelson feel better. There was something strange going on here, but Jon had no way of finding out what it was, and he didn't really care. The bad news was that he couldn't use Mrs. Nelson's computer to drop a message for his grandfather and other elders. He needed another plan.

"Anyways, Michael is very punctual. *Very*," Mrs. Nelson emphasized and glanced at Saga again.

"I am sure," Jon said. "So my package will get posted at one o'clock or so?"

"Or no." Mrs. Nelson smiled pleasantly at him. "It gets posted as soon as I take it off your hands. We do everything by the book around here. I work for the federal government, you know."

"Of course. I didn't mean—"

"Of course not." The woman was still smiling. "It's just

some people here believe they could take their mail back." She looked at Saga again. "But the post office doesn't work like that. Once you let go of your package or letter, it's gone. As good as delivered."

"That's what I wanted to hear, Mrs. Nelson. Thank you so very much." And with that Jon paid the express delivery postage on top of certified delivery and walked back into the market section of the store. "Well, thanks a lot, Saga. I'll be getting back to Al now." The girl looked at him strangely but didn't say another word; she just bit into her apple and continued to busy herself at the counter. Jon waved goodbye in the direction of the post office window at the back of the store and left. He practically ran all the way back to the church.

Chapter Three: The Wilkinses

Ada Wilkins

The television blared news. Al was now dressed in ski pants and a clean Dora the Explorer t-shirt with a dark blue sweatshirt on top that completely covered up any pink once zipped closed. He still had his pink boots of course. Ada wanted to get him to wear something more boy-like, but Hazel stopped her when Al started to cry.

"I know you don't believe in this, Auntie, but in this day and age, we all have to be a little more accommodating. If the kid wants to wear pink boots, let him," Hazel told her. "He is traumatized enough."

"I know you are right, dear, but people will make fun," Ada objected but let it go. The little boy just looked so unhappy. "Come here, little one. Tell me where you've been traveling?"

Al sniffed and hiccupped a bit and wiped his nose on his clean sweatshirt sleeve. Ada furrowed her brows; she was not a fan of snot and germs, especially on recently cleaned clothing.

"I'll take him to the washroom," Hazel said, seeing her expression. "Come, Al. We want you to look good for your daddy."

Ada used hand sanitizer to get the "boy cooties" off. *Who*

knows where that child has been? Really, who knows? And then she put the stuff that didn't fit the boy back on the rack.

On TV, an earnest-looking newscaster described a possible murder on the Pacific Railroad train traveling through Wisconsin to Minneapolis. Something about a high-powered attorney for an Alaskan Native American tribe being bound up with tape and then shot, possibly to death, with the conductor's own gun, no less. The conductor, his arm in a sling and a big bandage over one of his eyes, described a desperate struggle for the weapon. It was an ugly story, especially since they hadn't caught the perpetrator or found the body of the woman, Ms. Ay-Tal Blue. The locals were told to keep their eyes open for an ethnic-looking man with a scar over one of his eyes.

Ada went cold—didn't the kid's dad have a scar over his eye? He was sort of ethnic-looking, darkish skin and all, everything but those intense gray eyes. *The TV people would have mentioned the gray eyes, wouldn't they?* His eyes were so distinctive.

She stood up to go find Hazel and that boy and ask the child some serious questions when her eyes fell on a bundle of clothing tied up in the Pacific Railroad blanket with another identical blanket neatly folded up underneath. Ada would have recognized those blankets anywhere. They were so chic. She had one herself, and it cost her a pretty penny, too. And here these homeless hobos had two of them. They had to be stolen. How else would this Jon character get two?

Stolen railroad blankets, a murder mystery, and a kid who decisively didn't look like his papa. Ada didn't understand, and when she didn't understand something, she got nervous and unhappy. She wished her husband Burt was here, but he worked into the wee hours in that bar of his last night... Still, she decided she would feel safer if he was around and used her cell phone to text him to come over right away. This was an emergency. *It would be good if Burt got here before that Jon character.*

Feeling better after calling for reinforcements, Ada walked back to Hazel and the boy. She had an idea.

"Hazel? Hazel!" she called. "Do we think we have time to launder some of Al's dad's things? It seems a shame to let them leave here with all that dirty clothing." What better way was there to snoop through Jon's belongings? And it was all charity work...

"Dad doesn't like it when people go through his things," the boy said innocently in that high singsong voice of his.

"Of course not," said Ada. "And we won't be doing that. We'll just drop it all in a washing machine and have it all ready and nice and fluffy and smelling good when he gets back from the post office. I'm sure he would be thrilled for us to do a bit of cleaning for him. Most men are, you know." She smiled pleasantly, ruffled Al's red golden curls, and walked toward the bundle of clothing. Having made her decision to act, she felt much better. She rubbed the hand that touched Al on the side of her jeans—one never knew. *I'll wash tonight, as soon as I get home.*

Al ran to intercept and sat on top of the bundle. "I'll wait for Dad here," the boy added.

Ada stopped short and then looked back to Hazel for help. "Dear? We don't have much time, even with our new washing machines Reverend Paul bought. Really, child," she turned back to Al, "we told your daddy that we'd get everything cleaned up before he got back. So up you go..." She made shooing motions with her hands to get him off the blankets. "And we have a real suitcase that we can give you for all your new things and for your daddy's. Something with wheels." And then she could keep the blankets for herself.

Why would Jon want them if he has a real traveling case that rolled? And she could even give them Burt's old sleeping bag—*much, much better than these threadbare things.* She eyed the blankets greedily. "Up, up, up, dear." She motioned for Al get up again and looked to Hazel.

"Oh, let it go, Auntie," Hazel said. "It's not worth fighting about. And Jon must be on his way back by now anyway. It's way after Mrs. Nelson opened the post office. There's no time—" She stopped talking at the look Ada gave her. "Well, I guess we can—"

"We can and we must," Ada said. She was going to get those blankets for herself. After all the good she had done for these two, it was only proper. "Take the boy into the kitchen and get him something to eat."

"I'm not hungry," Al protested.

"You have a long trip ahead and should eat," Ada insisted. She was angry now. Where was Burt? Did that man ever show up when she needed him? Honestly, did she have to do everything herself? She leaned down, seized Al by his upper arm, and lifted the boy off the bundle. "I said go to the kitchen with Hazel, young man. Do it now. Hazel?"

"Come on, kid," Hazel said, picking up Al and carrying him away. "I'll give you some ice cream. It's not like real food."

Al stopped protesting and drooped over her shoulder on their way out of the room. Ada exhaled. She hated ugliness. She grabbed the bundle and the second blanket and walked over to the laundry area. Carefully untying the knot, she spilled the contents directly into an industrial-sized washing machine, then neatly folded and put away the blankets into a bag to take home. She could clean them in her own house. With the deed done, she totally forgot to snoop through Jon's belongings.

• • •

Jon Uolan

The moment Jon walked into the church's basement donations sorting room, he saw his stuff was missing. The stick he used to carry the makeshift bundle over his shoulder was left leaning against the wall. He looked around. There was no one in the room; only the television bellowed out the news...and the news was all about him. There was a sketch of the murder suspect now. The good news was that it didn't look much like him, but the bad news was that they got his scar right. He reached up to rub the old injury but stopped himself—no need to attract attention. He needed to get something to cover it up. He walked to a bin with hats, picked out a dark wool cap, and pulled it down over his eyebrows. Simple solutions were always best. Jon turned off the TV set.

"Dad!" He heard Al's voice and saw the kid run toward him. He had to force himself to pick up Ay-Tal and swing him around like a child. It was too awkward. But Al managed to giggle in just the right measure to smooth over whatever paternal shortcomings Jon exhibited.

"Aunt Ada is washing your clothes," Al said.

"Is she?" He put Al down. "You didn't need to do that, ma'am," he said to Ada, who walked into the room with Hazel. Jon noted that the older woman had an expression of guilt spiced with defiance. *Snooping*, Jon thought, but outwardly he smiled and said, "Really, I'm used to doing it all myself. You didn't have to, but I'm awfully grateful."

"It's my pleasure, young man," Ada said. Her face had resumed the normal appearance of slight superiority mixed with righteousness. She truly believed she was doing God's work in this world, and Jon didn't dream of disabusing her of those beliefs.

"It will take a few hours to get through the cycle," Hazel said apologetically.

"I guess that's okay," Jon said. It wasn't; they needed to get out of there as soon as possible—too much discussion on the news. "Do you mind if I pick out a few things for myself and Al? Just a change of clothing. I'd be happy to pay...to make a donation." In fact, he decided that he needed a fresh set of everything; jumping off a train into a muddy ditch didn't improve one's look. He needed to come across as more respectable.

"Of course, of course!" Hazel was happy to see the situation defused and rushed to show him the items that she had already picked out for Al. "See? We have a nice outfit for your boy. And very boy-like. I know, I know—pink is Al's favorite color. But around these parts, not all people are so understanding. It's just easier to wear dark colors on the outside and pink on the inside. Like a chocolate zefir, right, Al?" Jon didn't know what a "zefir" was, assuming it to be some kind of local confection, but noted that Al was holding Hazel's hand already and smiling. He guessed that many millennia of practice gave Al an advantage over mere mortals like him...or Aunt Ada, for that matter.

Jon picked out a pair of old jeans, a thick new lumberjack shirt, and an unopened pack of black wool socks. The shirt was a violent checkered orange-and-green pattern—perhaps the reason why it was still new. Jon was already wearing hiking boots, but they were soaked through. His vest was dirty but fine for warmth, even in a few weeks from now when *real* winter began in these parts. He hoped that the journey north would be short. They just needed to make it to Alaska.

Someone from the tribe would be sure there for them at the border...but not before...

"You should try these on," Hazel said, handing him a bunch of clothing and a pair of old cowboy boots. "You never know about these things. My mom says sizes don't mean much nowadays."

Jon nodded and stepped into a small booth made from some old recycled lumber boards with a shower curtain across the front. There wasn't much room, but there were a mirror and a hook to hang things. He didn't really need to try anything; he just needed to change. He quickly shed his now nearly empty backpack and puffy vest and started to take off the hiking boots when the gun fell to the floor with a loud clank. It didn't go off, but Jon was sure Hazel could see it through the bottom of the shower curtain. *Damn.* He picked up the weapon and stuffed it into his backpack, together with the new socks, his hunting knife, and the satellite phone, whose battery, unfortunately, was completely drained and the charger back on the train. Quickly, he changed his pants and shirt. Then he slipped on the cowboy boots, packed his dirty clothes into his bag, and tied the muddy boots to the backpack straps. Having finished, he opened the curtain. Hazel looked straight at him, her face white as a ghost. Al was over with Ada. Jon assumed he was keeping the woman distracted.

"Fits great," he said with a smile. "Thank you for all your help, Hazel."

"Do you want to wash those?" she asked. She was looking into his eyes, holding his gaze, daring him to say something about the gun.

"I'm good. Let's pack the kid's new things." He walked over to a small pile of items Hazel had set asidepicked out for Al and stuffed those into his bag as well.

"Aunt Ada set aside a suitcase for you," Hazel said.

"That's not really necessary. We like to travel light."

"I bet," she mumbled and went to join her aunt.

It was time to leave. Hazel already knew about his hunting knife and now she learned about the gun. She suspected him. Saga probably did too, along with her brother, Arrow. He pulled out his carefully folded map from his vest pocket and located the town of Wilkins. Wisconsin and Minnesota had plenty of wilderness, just not close enough to where they were now. And hiding in the woods wasn't going to work with Al anyway. Train-hopping was not a good idea for the moment. Perhaps they could catch a ride with a trucker to Minneapolis and rent a car there. There were tribe-friendly establishments in the lower forty-eight. The elders would vouch for him. His father was probably advocating for driving down to pick them up right now—they must have heard the news about Ay-Tal's murder. It was all over TV, at least here in Wisconsin. He really needed to pass on a message, but that had to wait. He glanced over the map at Hazel. She was watching him. He smiled at her. *Damn.*

The doors to the basement swung open, and a big guy walked in with tightly trimmed blond hair and a beard. He was wearing jeans, a red-and-black lumberjack shirt, a puffy vest, and cowboy boots—a strange mirror image of Jon. *I'm probably wearing his rejects,* Jon realized. Too big on Jon, the violently colored lumberjacker was just about right for a hulking fellow like that.

"Hey, sweetheart." The man came over and hugged Hazel. "Ada." He waved in the general direction of his wife. "And you must be Jon." He came over and loomed over Jon, not offering to shake hands.

"Must be," Jon said. "Hazel and Ada have been good to Al and me. Set us up right and proper. We are grateful."

"Of course you are." Having taken Jon's measure, the man decided that Jon wasn't a threat. "I'm Burt Wilkins, Ada's husband. I'm the mayor of this town and run the place down the road where you decided to crash last night."

"Sorry about that," Jon said.

"I guess it couldn't have been helped. Arrow said you were all right. Hazel texted me, and Ada did too. So I guess you make an impression."

"A favorable one, I hope," Jon said. He couldn't really tell why, but he really disliked the guy from the moment he laid eyes on him. Burt looked younger than Ada, too, not that it meant anything in and of itself. *Just strange. A bit out of the ordinary...like this whole homeless donation center.* Jon wondered again how many customers Ada Wilkins served. Were there any homeless around this small town of Wilkins? *Same name and the mayor—coincidence?* Jon didn't think so. It's way past the time we got out of here, he thought again.

"That's your kid?" Burt pointed to Al, who quietly made his way over to Jon and now stood just behind his legs. "Doesn't look like yours," he said. There was a touch of malice in his voice.

"Daddy?" Al said in his little kid voice.

"Let me take a proper look at you, kid," Burt said and reached to grab Al by the shoulder. Al tried to squirm away from him, but Burt managed to grab him anyway. Jon could see that he was hurting the kid...deliberately.

"Let go of my son, sir," he said and stepped forward, right into the man's face. Jon was shorter, but not by very much. He also knew how to stare down predators; he wasn't afraid of facing a bear. Jon wasn't stupid about the confrontation; he knew when and how to appear threatening. And after a moment or two, the man backed off with a smirk. *He's just trying not to lose face,* Jon thought. Burt was a bully, but the man wasn't interested in standing up to someone who could take him down. And Jon knew he could, and he made sure Burt knew it too. It was all in the body language, Jon remembered his father teaching him. *And what works with animals...works with animals.* He felt fear from the guy like an electrical current. He thought back to Saga's reaction to his questions earlier. *Is it this guy?* "Time to go, Al," Jon said and turned toward the door. Al grabbed his hand, and he felt the sweat on the little fingers—Ay-Tal was nervous.

"Oh, don't be silly." Ada came running, blocking the exit. "You can't go until your clothes are dry. And you should eat something. It's almost lunch time." It wasn't—it was not even eleven. "Hazel! Call over to Mrs. Nelson and ask Saga to deliver some sandwiches. Turkey, white meat, hold the mayo for me and Burt. Don't argue, dear. The doctor said you had to watch what you eat. You're not as young as you think, you know. And what would you like, Allie? You don't mind me calling your son Allie, do you, Jon? He just looks more like Allie. Perhaps with time, he will grow into Al, right Allie? How about a nice kid's meal?" Her voice was thick, sweet, and off, like a jelly gone bad. But there was no escaping her, not yet.

Jon hated the nickname "Allie." It was so inappropriate for Ay-Tal. But all he said was, "We'll both take a turkey sandwich just as it comes, if you are ordering." There was no way to leave just now. And it wasn't just Ada. Jon had a feeling Burt would follow them and run them down somewhere where there were no witnesses. Perhaps he wouldn't really hurt them much, but he could surely make the trip north difficult. And Jon liked his bones intact. "Come sit with me at the table." He took Al over to the sorting table, and they both settled down to wait. Jon didn't remove the backpack from his shoulders.

Burt went over to the fridge and pulled out a can of beer—he didn't offer one to Jon or his wife—and sprawled in the corner of the room and turned the TV back on to the news. Ada flittered around, pretending to put things away. Neither Al nor Jon had disturbed much, and what had been moved out of its usual place had already been picked up and put back by Hazel. It was just busy work, all for show. Hazel, unlike her aunt, sat at the table with Jon and Al and stared just above their heads. An uncomfortable twenty minutes passed.

Saga walked in with a big bag of groceries.

"Need money?" Burt barked at her.

Without looking at him, Saga put the bag on the table and started to pull out sandwiches and chips and some sodas. "Mrs. Nelson put it on Aunt Ada's tab," she said.

"That's fine, dear." Ada pulled out some paper plates and some napkins from a cupboard and went around delivering lunch. "There you are, Allie. If you can't eat the whole thing, we'll pack it for you for the road."

"Thank you, Aunt Ada," Al said and gave her a radiant little smile, asymmetrical dimple and all.

Ada shared a look with Burt, but he just shrugged. Jon wondered what she had said to her husband about him and Al. There was all that texting, and telephoning, and probably image sharing... They'd stayed too long. He bit into his food.

"Good sandwich, Saga. Thank you, Ada. Burt." Jon nodded to each in turn. "How much can I contribute for Al and me?"

"Nothing! It's just a little nothing." Ada exchanged another look with her husband. "Of course, of course. We couldn't let you go all hungry and such," she said. "And all your stuff drying..."

"I'll go check," said Hazel, getting up.

"No, you sit and eat," Burt told her. "Saga. Go deal with the laundry."

Without a word, Saga got up and walked toward the back, not looking at or acknowledging Burt in any way. Jon noted that she didn't bring a sandwich for herself, only for her foster family, Hazel, and Al and himself. She might not be hungry or...

"Lazy girl, that. Didn't even bring beer," Burt murmured between bites. "At least her brother works for his keep."

"Saga works," Hazel said quietly but didn't look up or confront her uncle in any other way.

Jon ate his sandwich in two bites. "Thank you. It was great, Ada," he said and got up to join Saga at the laundry room.

●　●　●

It smelled like soap and fabric softener and was much warmer than the room outside. The dryer was still going, and Saga stood with her back to the wall, invisible to all outside of the laundry room.

"Hiding?" Jon asked. Saga didn't answer, just stared at him with those eyes that reminded Jon of black ice cured too rapidly by the cold. "When do you think the dryer will be done?" The girl just shrugged. She didn't seem to care what Jon did, so he went over to the machine and pressed pause.

"I wouldn't do that if I were you," Saga said.

"Why?"

"Aunt Ada is very particular about her machines."

"I thought this was all the church's?"

"Same thing."

"I see." Jon opened the dryer door and pulled out his clothing. It was just an extra pair of jeans, another shirt, and some underwear and socks. They were lost inside the giant maw of the industrial-sized drier. "Well, it's actually dry." He smiled at Saga and quickly stuffed the things into his backpack. It was bulging now with all of the "new" things he got.

"She won't let you take *Allie*," Saga said. She used Ada's tone of voice to pronounce the ridiculous endearment.

"What?"

"Having a kid around makes her feel important," Saga said. "She took me and Arrow because we are direct proof of her good deeds."

"Well, it was nice of her," Jon said. "But Al and I are good. We don't need any more help or good deeds."

"There's a special service tomorrow. She'll want to show the kid off to the congregation. What's in a good deed unless everyone knows about it?"

"I see. Pretty clinical, that."

"Whatever. Do you want to get out of here or not?" she asked. The way she said it, Jon knew there were conditions attached.

"What do you have in mind?"

"The post office truck will be coming by here around one, no later than one thirty. Mike tends to be on time."

"So Mrs. Nelson said." Jon watched Saga's body language. She tried for nonchalant, but the way she wrapped her arms around herself made Jon pity her. He wondered again about Burt. *Is he harming the girl?*

"Well, Mike's a friend," Saga said. "He—"

"What are you two doing in there?" Burt's voice hollered at them from across the church's basement. Jon saw Saga flinch.

"We're just folding, Uncle Burt," she called out. "Be right there."

"If you touch my girl in there—" Burt yelled.

"Ignore him," Saga said.

"I will. So Mike?"

"He rides through town making deliveries. The post office and the church are his last stops."

"Would he take me and Al to the next town over?" Jon asked.

"No." She stared at him, daring him...*to do what?* "But he will take me." *Aah.*

"That's nice. But how is that good for me and Al?"

"If I come, you two can too," she said.

"That's your price?"

"That's my price."

"Why?"

"Why what? Why do I want to help you? Or why do I want to leave this freaking hellhole?"

"Both, I guess."

"Wilkinses." The way she said the name made Jon shudder. "Burt will want his reward for doing all this good work and getting up this early."

"And?"

"I'm not planning on sticking around for it...again," she said. "And I suggest you don't either. He likes little boys too, you know."

Jon felt sick. He glanced out there through the open door. Burt was on his fifth or sixth can of beer. Al was sitting on his lap, watching the news. Ada was helping Hazel clean up after lunch. Jon noticed that Hazel was keeping her eye on Burt. *She knows.*

"Is Hazel okay?" Jon asked.

"She gets to go home," Saga said.

"And your brother? Arrow?"

"He decked Burt once. That's how he got the guard job."

Jon was impressed; he didn't think the kid had it in him. *Good on him.* "Won't your brother worry about you?" he asked. He didn't want to add to an already painful situation, although he felt that he would help the siblings if he could… just not if it would jeopardize his ability to bring Ay-Tal safely home. *Ay-Tal above all else…*

"Arrow can take care of himself now. He's almost eighteen. He'll be able to leave this freaking place soon. I have years…"

"I see." If he could, Jon would have taught Burt the only lesson that man was likely to learn from. *But Al…* And he was already wanted for murder; he couldn't draw more attention onto himself. "Why me? Why now?" he asked.

"You have a gun," she said.

So Hazel must have told her somehow. Jon watched her awhile and thought. The girl wasn't lying. And now that he knew, he couldn't really walk away, could he? "Okay," he said. "You can come with us, but only for a while. I can't take you with me as far as my home. You understand? I just don't have the means to do it. But I will help as far as I can."

"Okay," she said. Jon saw palpable relief in her whole being. She was scared, he realized. Really terrified. *Poor kid.*

"Do you have papers with you?"

"School ID, library card," she said. "I don't have a driver's license yet. Burt won't let me."

"Birth certificate?"

She shook her head.

"Social security number?"

"No. Nothing like that. Aunt Ada has it all locked in her safe. There's money from the state for fostering…"

"Well, we'll solve that problem later," Jon said. "Why don't you grab some change of clothing for yourself and get ready to go? We'll try to catch Mike before he gets here."

"Okay." She slithered out of the laundry room—that was

the only way Jon thought of describing how she hugged the walls and stayed low so as not to attract attention. *She must hide from that monster a lot,* Jon thought. The anger he felt was so intense that he needed time to get himself back under control. He needed his cool to face those people out there.

When ready, Jon walked directly to Burt and lifted Al off the man's lap. He didn't look down; he didn't want to know how bad a monster Burt was. Thank Aguguq, Ay-Tal wasn't really a child, or Jon would have had to kill this man. He pressed the tiny, fragile body to his chest; Al leaned into him. Al knew. And Jon took a deep breath to calm himself again.

"Well, we better be going," he said, stepping away from the table and the monster before he lost control. "Thank you again for all your hospitality," he called out to Hazel and Ada.

"Oh, but Jon!" Ada rushed out to try to stop him from leaving again. "I just made a pot of my homemade tea! You have to try it."

"Aunt Ada!" Hazel tried to intercept her. "Jon has to take Al home to his grandparents. They are waiting for him, aren't they, Jon?" She looked to Jon for support. "The kid needs his Nana and Baba, right? You said yourself, grandparents are so important in children's lives. We have to let them go. We *have* to!" There was no question Hazel knew about Burt. How many in this small town knew and did nothing?

Jon walked past the two women. "Thank you, Ada. And thank you, Hazel. Thank you," he repeated in a small voice just for the girl. From the corner of his eye, he saw Saga rush up the stairs. She had a small backpack on that wasn't there when she walked in with sandwiches, and another bag in hand; she had followed Jon's instructions and packed some things from the donations. *Good.* "Well, goodbye, ladies. Thank you again." And Jon headed for the door, carrying Al, neatly bypassing Ada. Hazel had managed to put herself between Jon and her aunt. He was grateful and hoped that there wouldn't be any dire consequences for the girl. She was real family, after all.

• • •

Outside, he looked around. Saga motioned to him from around the corner of the church. He rushed to her.

"We can't stay here—" they both said at the same time.

"Burt will come after us as soon as Aunt Ada gets him to move. I didn't see. How drunk was he?" Saga asked.

"Drunk enough," Jon said and pressed Al closer to him. If it were his child... "Which way does Mike leave town? We can wait for him en route."

Instead of answering, Saga just rushed down the road back toward US-12. Jon ran alongside her, carrying Al. It took half an hour to walk up to the church from the Wilkins Nightclub that morning, but they made it back in just ten minutes.

Jon veered off to go inside, but Saga stopped him. "If Arrow knows..." She didn't finish, but Jon understood. Arrow wouldn't have a choice...just like Jon wouldn't have had one if Saga were his sister. It was a blessing to leave without a word.

"Which way?" he asked.

"There's a gas station down the road about a few miles or so," Saga said. "Mike usually fills up there before returning to the main postal sorting center in Eau Claire."

"That's quite a ways."

"There used to be one closer, but with the population dropping..." She shrugged and slowed down to a walk. Jon wanted to keep moving fast, but Saga was breathing heavily already, and he couldn't carry both of them. So he let Al walk as well, holding his hand.

"So did Burt—" Al tried to ask Saga about her foster father as soon as he was on the ground.

"Don't," Saga cut him off. "Just don't."

"All right."

Al wiggled free and walked alongside her. "We could report him," he said.

Saga gave him a frightened look. "Did he do it to you, Al?"

"I can take care of myself," Al said. From a little boy, it wasn't very convincing.

"I'm sure," Saga said with a sad grimace. "So can I."

"I'm just saying that you shouldn't have let him get away with it. There are people, services that would have helped you," Al said.

"What do you know about it?" Saga said.

"Al is smart like that," said Jon. But he wished Al would shut up and drop the matter. No legal advice worked coming from a five-year-old. He tried to grab Al's hand again to show his displeasure, but the kid rushed around and took Saga's free hand instead. Surprised at first, she took it. Somehow, Jon knew that if it were him showing the girl sympathy, she would have shut him out. "Let me carry that bag," he said instead and took the tote away from the girl, leaving her with a backpack and Al. The bag was small but heavy. Jon vaguely wondered what was inside.

It took almost a full hour to walk to the gas station. Saga immediately asked for the keys to use the bathroom, leaving Al and Jon alone at the station's mini mart. They picked out a few trail mix packets and a reusable water bottle with a filter and then sat to wait for the girl and the postman by the curb.

"It's heartbreaking that child didn't know how to escape," Al said.

"She's out of there now," Jon said. It was a strange conversation to have with a little boy...but not with Ay-Tal.

"Not yet," Al continued. "Ada and Burt Wilkins have legal custody of the siblings. The law is on their side."

"What do you recommend?"

"If we put some distance between, it will give us breathing room to address the issue in another jurisdiction. The Wilkinses are obviously well known around these parts. It would be their word over Saga's. Once we reach Saint Paul—"

"Saga said that Mike, the postman, can take us only as far as Eau Claire, and that's in the wrong direction—"

"Doesn't matter."

"Suppose not."

"There's a manhunt out for you," Al said. "I saw the news. The hat was a good idea."

"Thanks."

"But not enough."

"I have you. They won't be looking for a guy with a little kid."

"No. But I'm a liability in this form." Jon didn't contradict that. It was very inconvenient to have Ay-Tal as a child. It made them more memorable, too. "I will have to do another change," Al said.

"Can you so soon?" Jon really didn't know how any of this worked. He wished yet again that he had been trained for all contingencies. But this trip was supposed to be easy.

"It will be more difficult the next time," Al said. "More energy-intensive."

Jon had no idea what that meant in practical terms. "You can't while Saga is with us." He immediately felt guilty for saying the obvious. Ay-Tal might look like a little kid, but the mind within was as old as human civilization. Such dichotomy of being was difficult to process, especially under duress. Jon didn't think his father or grandfather would have done any better. "So what's your plan?" he asked, because ultimately, what they did was going to be Ay-Tal's decision.

"As always, we wait and see. Humans are predictable in the long run, but in the short run, you are full of surprises."

There was nothing to say to that. Ay-Tal was speaking from a very different perspective. But Jon still found it hard to be reminded of the vast differences between himself and this creature. *If not god, then what?*

The sound of brakes pulled Jon out of his reverie. A big tractor-trailer pulled into the gas station, taking up most of the space at the outside pump and completely blocking Jon's view of the road. Not wanting to miss the postal truck, Jon stood up and walked around the tractor-trailer. Al stayed with their bags.

The truck driver pulled out the gas hose, but it came short; the eighteen-wheeler had overshot the pump by a few feet, obviously trying to avoid hitting the overhang. Cursing under her breath, the driver climbed back inside and reversed...right into the shrubbery.

The driver was a large woman, about the same height as Jon, with salt-and-pepper hair—mostly salt—big but fit, dressed in loose-fitting pants and a sweater several sizes too big with rolled sleeves, snake-skin boots, and a big silver squash blossom necklace and a matching bracelet with chunky bits of turquoise. Jon guessed her to be in her mid-fifties, maybe a bit younger, it was hard to tell. Half her face—the left half that faced the driver's side window—was severely sun-damaged, wrinkly and brownish with dark spots randomly dotting her chin and forehead. The right half was a lot lighter and smoother. It was like two women were spliced together. By her right side, Jon would have put the woman in her late thirties, attractive with piercing blue eyes that matched the stones in her necklace. But her left... Fifties was splitting the difference.

"The space is really narrow," Jon called out to the woman through the open cab window—the old crow side. "I can help a bit, if you like."

"Drove all night. Tired," the woman said. Her voice was deep, velvety, nice. Jon liked her right away. He acknowledged her with a nod. Women truck drivers got plenty of shit on the road, and he wasn't about to undermine her. But he also didn't want this to turn into a full-blown incident with the police and all. The clerk managing the gas station's little convenience store was already out and videoing the whole thing on his cell phone. Everything was documented nowadays. Jon pulled his hat down a bit lower and, conscious of keeping his back to the camera, used hand signals to guide the woman within the hose-stretching distance of the pump.

"You're good, ma'am," he said. "The bush's okay too. Just a few leaves knocked off, that's all. Will be good as new in the spring." That was an understatement of the damage, but it was sure to grow back—plants did that all the time. So no real harm done in the long run.

"Thanks, kid." The woman climbed back down and walked over to inspect the flattened shrubbery. "Damn. I don't know why they make these places so narrow." Jon noted the lack of space as well. It was fine for regular cars, but for something as large as an eighteen-wheeler? A tight fit indeed. And it would be hard to get out too. Whoever did the landscaping was an idiot.

"I'll help on the way out, if you want," Jon offered. "They didn't leave you much room to maneuver."

"Thanks. We can aim for symmetry, huh?" She winked at him. "Mind watching the pump for me? Got to go use the little ladies room." And with that, the woman walked away, leaving Jon in charge. There wasn't much to do, but Jon knew that it took some time to fill up something of this size, and he was expecting Mike at any time. He looked back at Al and shrugged. Al shrugged back.

Forever later—at least ten minutes—Saga and the woman driver walked back out to the gas pumps. The woman was still as she was, but Saga looked completely different. No more black leather jacket, or black denim jeans, or those heavy hiking boots, or the heavy Goth makeup. Even the facial piercings were gone. The girl who was Saga was now wearing light-colored sneakers, gray tights, and a pink dress underneath a very girly purple puffy winter jacket. She looked much younger now—a total makeover. *Smart*, thought Jon.

"You look good," Al called to her approvingly. Saga shrugged, but Jon could see that she appreciated the compliment.

"They with you?" the driver asked Saga. Apparently they'd met in the lady's room.

"Yeah. This is Al and that's Jon," Saga said. "Thanks for the help in there, Mary."

"Sure thing. Sure thing," Mary said. Jon wondered what help Saga required but decided not to ask. "Thank you for watching my rig, young man."

"No problem." Jon was relieved to be done with that. He walked back to Al and Saga. "So, is Mike late?" he asked. It seemed to be way past the time Saga said to expect the mail truck.

"A bit," Saga agreed. She looked nervous, fidgeting with the straps of her backpack. It looked swollen—the leather jacket, Jon assumed. Her old boots were tied to the straps, just like Jon's.

"Is there a chance that he drove back to his postal station some other way?" Jon asked. But just as he said it, he saw the mail van drive up to the gas station. Burt was sitting in the passenger seat in front next to Mike. A big pickup truck was right behind. *Burt's,* Jon guessed. "We've got to go," he whispered and pulled Saga to her feet, grabbing the bags. "Quickly go around the big rig. Keep it between you and Burt."

There was panic in Saga's eyes, but she rushed to the tractor-trailer, grabbing Al's hand and dragging him along. Seeing that Al understood the situation, Jon ran to catch up to Mary, who was now paying the clerk for some junk food she'd picked up at the mini mart.

"Look," she was saying. "It will grow back. You know it will. So just give me a break. There ain't any—"

"Got to pay for the damage, lady. It's not me. I'm fine with a dead bush. What do I care for greenery? But my boss will make me pay for the new planting. Sorry, lady. It would be two hundred extra."

"Two hundred? For that sickly old thing? I bet they were not even to code!" Mary's hands balled into fists. Her face was contorting in anger and incredulity.

Those shrubs aren't worth two hundred bucks, Jon thought. But they were pretty smashed up, and he could see that this was about to escalate. And Burt was outside already. He might have not seen Saga and Al yet, but he would soon. "Sir, allow me," he said and pulled out two hundred in cash. "This is enough, right?" The clerk nodded, but Mary rounded on him. Jon waited for her to yell and argue, but instead her eyebrows went up and she looked outside to where Al and Saga were seated earlier and then over to the where the mail truck just parked. Burt was staggering out toward them. Something clicked, and her entire demeanor changed right in front of his eyes.

"Need a lift?" she asked.

"Yes." He looked back at Burt walking toward the mini mart and then back at Mary. She followed his gaze and nodded.

"Give this guy another two hundred," she ordered. Jon didn't question it, just counted out the money and placed it on the counter. The clerk watched them both with buggery eyes. "Keep that guy occupied," Mary ordered the clerk and pulled Jon around the counter and toward the back door of the store.

Within seconds, they were slipping out the back. Jon heard Burt bark something at the clerk. The clerk protested. There was a bang, a crash, and glass broke.

"In my rig, fast," Mary ordered.

They crept around to the front. There was glass all over the pavement. From the side, Jon could see Ada standing next to the parked pickup truck, hand clasped to her chest, eyes huge. Mike, the postman, was slowly backing away to his van. It was obvious that he had planned to go into the mini mart but changed his mind and now just wanted to get the hell out of there without being dragged into a confrontation.

"Go," Mary ordered and strode out to the front of the store. "What's going on here?" she barked at Ada. The woman cringed and turned to get back into her pickup truck.

Jon saw his opportunity and ran. He rounded the tractor-trailer and helped Saga and Al into the huge cab. As soon as the kids hid behind the seats with their bags, Jon climbed into a passenger seat, closed the door, and crouched low to watch.

Mary glanced over at him and winked. The woman had nerves of steel. But instead of walking to her truck, she went inside the mini mart.

What is she doing? thought Jon. Next to him, he heard Saga whimper. Al pressed himself into her; Saga hugged him and whispered encouragements. Jon could see that protecting a small child made her feel better, braver. Al obviously knew what to do; unfortunately, Jon didn't. Did Mary need his help?

"Look, mister." They heard Mary's booming voice all the way across the gas station. "The only girl that was here was wearing a pink dress, and she drove away with her father a while ago. So why don't you scram before I call the cops?"

From inside the truck, they couldn't hear Burt's answer. By now, the postman managed to get himself back into his van and was driving out of the gas station. He didn't want to be around for this. Jon didn't blame him. He wished Mary were speeding them away from here, too.

There was more unintelligible screaming from inside. In the side mirror, Jon saw the flash of blue and red lights—the cops. *Damn.* "Al?" he called back.

"Just stay low," Al said. "The local cops won't want any witnesses." Jon considered and agreed—the Wilkinses most likely had pull with the local sheriff. Burt was drunk and had just vandalized the mini mart. There would be a surveillance video to that fact. And Mary. And Mike, the postman. And the clerk inside. That was a lot of witnesses already.

The sheriff pulled up right to the shuttered door and, waving hello to Ada, strode inside. There were more shouts from Burt, but then the man walked out and went around to sit in the passenger seat of his own pickup truck. Jon saw Ada carefully back up and out of the gas station and haltingly drive back the way they came. Al had guessed right—the sheriff wasn't here to arrest Burt but to get him out of trouble.

A few minutes later, Mary walked out of the mini mart holding a giant Slurpee cup. She turned and waved to the sheriff and the clerk, walked to her tractor-trailer, and with a big grin handed the giant drink to Jon.

"Good to go," she said and drove the truck through the other hedge and back out onto the road. "Don't you just love symmetry?" she added with a smile. Jon just stared at the woman. *How crazy is she?*

Chapter Four: They Be Gods

Jon Uolan

They drove fast, faster than Jon thought was safe on this rural road, with all the twists and turns and the possibility of people walking along the shoulder. But one couldn't argue with the results: trouble was back there somewhere, and they were not.

After about an hour, Al broke the silence. "What flavor is it?" he asked, extending his small hand for the Slurpee cup.

"Mango." Mary passed the cup back to the kids.

"Really?" Saga said. "That's my favorite!"

"Don't spill any back there," Mary said gruffly. But Jon picked up the fake note of anger—Mary wanted the kids to have her drink, probably got it for them in the first place. "I sleep there, you know. Don't want anything sticky on my pillows," the woman added.

"Of course not," said Saga. Jon heard worry in the girl's voice.

"So that was the creep you told me about in the bathroom?" Mary asked. Saga didn't answer, just nodded. But Mary looked at her through the rear-view mirror. "He won't get his comeuppance in that town."

"Saga's brother is still back there," Jon said.

"He won't stay long now," Mary said. "With Saga gone, he is a free agent. No system will waste its resources looking for an almost eighteen-year-old." Jon looked back and Al nodded. It made sense. "They will look for you, though," Mary continued.

"I won't go back," Saga said.

"Of course not," Mary said. "I'm just saying they will look."

Jon sighed. Not only was there a manhunt for him, but now there would be one for Saga. And what would the authorities think? Probably that he kidnapped a kid after killing a woman on the train. And he couldn't even begin to think of clearing his name before delivering Al to safety.

"I have to get some sleep," Mary said suddenly. "Know how to drive one of these?" She turned to Jon.

"Yeah, but—"

"Then drive!" She set the speed on auto and started to climb to the back of the cab. Jon jumped into the driver's seat, grabbing the wheel before they spun off the road. *The woman is crazy!*

"Where?" Jon managed as soon as he took full control of the truck.

"Saint Paul," Mary said through a yawn, and soon there were powerful snores coming from the back.

Saga climbed into the passenger seat, leaving Al to sleep in the back with Mary.

● ● ●

Two hours later, they approached Minnesota's capital. It was dark already. Jon drove strictly at speed limit, trying to look as boring as possible to any highway patrol officers in the area. But the truth was that they didn't even pass any that Jon had noticed. Once they got on the interstate, it was a straight road all the way. But now Jon didn't know where to go to next. What was Mary's destination? What were they hauling? He had no idea. Everyone was asleep, even Saga, who had curled up into a little ball in the big bucket passenger seat. He hated to wake them, but it was time.

He pulled into a rest stop. It had a small convenience store, a restaurant, and a gas station. At least two dozen other tractor-trailers were parked at back. Jon maneuvered into the farthest spot, where the streetlight seemed to be broken, and turned off the engine—he was tired too.

"You did well," Mary said from the back.

"Thanks." He didn't realize she was paying attention.

"So what are you going to do now?" she asked. It was a strange question with many possible responses. Jon wasn't sure what Mary was looking for from him, so he waited. "There will be an Amber Alert by now for Saga," she continued. "And then there's that business on the train…"

Jon felt sick. "You know?"

"Of course," she said. "There was some grainy surveillance footage of you boarding the train, but I recognized you right off. It's been all over the news since midday."

"Then why did you take us?"

"Ay-Tal."

The world fell away…

● ● ●

They sat in a corner booth. It was way past dinnertime. The restaurant was full of long-haul truckers with a few "civilian drivers" straggling in for something to eat before heading into Saint Paul proper.

"What do you want to do?" Mary asked Saga.

"I don't know," the girl said. She looked very young. "Find

some work. Find a place to live?"

"How old are you?"

"Sixteen."

"Truthfully?"

"I'll be fifteen…in ten months," Saga answered.

"Not old enough to strike out on your own," Mary commented.

Saga's eyes flitted to Jon. But he was still shell-shocked for having failed to protect Ay-Tal's identity. There was no privacy. No way to ask, no way to really know what to do next.

"She'd be fine if she got a guardian," Al said.

"She has one," Mary said.

"Another one," Al said.

Jon wondered if Al knew that Mary knew that he wasn't what he seemed to be. But if Al knew, he wasn't telling Jon. Jon felt a humming in his ears; his fingers and toes tingled. It was just like the fight-or-flight sensation that happened moments before confronting big game during a hunt. All his blood flowed to his brain, away from his extremities, making him feel slightly buzzed, only to rush back into the legs and arms for action. A seesaw of sensations that some loved but Jon hated.

"That's not the way to set it all right," Mary said, focused completely on Al, daring him to contradict her. "It's not the path into the future that saves the most lives."

"Perhaps not in the long term," Al conceded. "But in the short term—"

Those were not the words typically spoken by a child. Confused, Saga looked back and forth between Mary and Al and asked, "What are you two talking about?"

"Some people have the job of navigating the right course into the future," Mary said. She never took her eyes off Al. "Some people have that responsibility. And it's not something they can just walk away from."

"But Al is only a kid?" Saga said. "What can a kid do to help me?"

Behind the counter, up on the wall, the television was showing photographs of Saga, and the news anchor was describing a possible abduction of a young girl: "Anyone with information—"

Jon glanced at the TV screen. The girl in those photos didn't really look like Saga now, at least not on casual viewing. But if they were stopped...

"—and now the police are linking the murder on a train of a prominent Native American rights attorney with the local girl's disappearance." A still from a surveillance video showed a side view of Jon walking onto the train at the Washington, D.C. station. It wasn't a good image of him, but it still made him cringe. It would only be a matter of time. How was he going to cross the border? "This man is considered a suspect in the murder and in the abduction of the young girl. He is deemed armed and dangerous. He is alleged to be traveling with a small child. It is unclear what relationship there is between the child and the man. The child's description doesn't match any of the abduction cases on file..." The news anchor seemed so earnest, calling for vigilance and information on the as yet unnamed suspect.

"They will figure it out eventually," Mary said, glancing up at the TV. Jon was sure she was right. He didn't try to hide his identity when purchasing the tickets to travel back to Alaska. There was probably more surveillance footage of him walking around the airport when he first arrived in D.C., milling about at the hotel, touring the Smithsonian museums, and then surely of him purchasing the tickets at the train station. What was he to do?

"Did you murder that woman?" Saga asked, and Jon

practically felt her recoil from him.

"Of course not, Saga," Al said. "No one was murdered at all. It is all just a stupid misunderstanding."

Saga looked at him. Jon didn't think she was quite used to having a kid talk like this. Not yet. "How do you know, Al?" she asked.

"I was with him the entire time," the boy said. "He never left me. Never. He took care of me the whole time, even when it was most difficult." Jon saw that Al was speaking as much to Saga as to Mary. The woman just nodded, like that was to be expected. *Of course it is, but how did she know? How does she know anything?*

"I can take Jon and Saga up north," Mary said. "Now that we've finally tracked you down..."

"I'm not going anywhere without Al," Jon said.

"Very admirable, dear Jon. But Ay-Tal has responsibilities, and it is time she took them up again. Twenty thousand years is long enough to rest, don't you think?"

"What are you talking about?" Saga squeaked. She seemed to be folding into herself to avoid the strangeness of this conversation.

"I've done enough," Al said. But he looked tired, beaten.

Mary just picked up her fork and polished off the coconut cream pie she had ordered for dessert. No one else had touched theirs.

When Al stood up to go to the bathroom, Jon stood with him. It was an opportunity...

"You can't slip away again, Ay-Tal," said Mary. "The world has changed. With all the technologies and such... Now that we know who you are, there is really no point in even trying."

Jon interpreted that as a threat. He didn't know who Mary was or whether she worked alone or not, but she clearly meant to take Ay-Tal away from his tribe, from his people.

That can't be.

• • •

They went into the "family bathroom," a non-gender-assigned room to allow families to manage their business easier. It was one of the modern societal changes that Jon approved of; his tribe had been doing it for thousands of years, and the world outside was only now catching up to what was practical. It was a large room with two washbasins, a changing table, and an extra-wide toilet stall with a door for privacy. Al went in alone, and Jon waited by the outside door, which he locked as an extra precaution.

"Well?" he asked as Al came out to wash his hands. He had to help him with the soap; the sinks were set too high. *Nothing's perfect.*

"I had over twenty thousand years with your people, as Mary pointed out."

"What does that mean?" Jon felt way out of his depth. *Is there a way to stop Ay-Tal from leaving if he wants to go?*

"I walked the original tribe over the ice from what is now Russia to Alaska," Al said.

"I know. I've memorized all of the legends." He lifted Al to sit up on the counter to be able to speak to him eye-to-eye.

"I led others through the steppes of Europe and then Siberia," Al continued. Jon just watched the child's face that was not a child. His knowledge of Ay-Tal stopped at the ice bridge that connected the two continents during the glacial maximum of the last Ice Age. "But before that, I led people through what is now the Middle East and up all the way to Britain. And even before, there were groups that left East Africa." He paused and observed Jon.

Jon felt numb. Twenty thousand years was a long time.

Now Ay-Tal was implying that he was around much, much longer than that.

"That's what we do, Jon," Ay-Tal said. "I'm a guide, a dragoumanos, a cicerone, if you will. I find greener pastures for those who can't thrive where they are. I find a path into the future and lead people."

"My tribe is grateful, Ay-Tal."

"Most peoples are...for a while." Jon tried to interrupt but Ay-Tal stopped him. "Your people were the most grateful. So I wanted to stay. Even gods get tired."

Jon felt like he was failing his tribe. Ay-Tal clearly meant to go away, to abandon them. "But why? Why leave now?" he asked. "Aren't you happy? And as you've just said, there are plenty of people in the world now. We don't need guides anymore." And as he said it, Jon felt fear. That had not been the right thing to say; Ay-Tal turned pale gray, almost the color of the ropy flesh that Jon saw oh so briefly just two days ago. "Don't, Ay-Tal. Please don't," he begged.

"My kind won't let me stay, Jon. Now that they've found me, as Mary pointed out, they will not leave me alone. I will be made to do my share again."

"But don't you get a choice?" Jon asked.

"Of a destination, perhaps," Ay-Tal said. "But the duty of all gods is to serve."

"*Are* you a god?" Jon knew that his tribe had always been ambivalent on this point. Ay-Tal was not a force of nature, technically, so she couldn't really be a god. *The* Aguguq. But who said that Aguguq ruled alone? *By all other measures...*

"What is a god, Jon?" Ay-Tal asked, and not expecting an answer continued, "There are all kinds of entities in this world. Some are like me, more or less."

"Guides like you? Or immortals like you?"

"As you well know, I am not immortal." The vision of

bloody clothing and pale face came to Jon. "See? You know," Ay-Tal said.

"But you have ways of living for a very long time," Jon said.

"Yes. That."

"And there are others?"

"From a small band of primates to the dominant species on the whole planet, it's not a bad trick, eh?" Ay-Tal gave a tired smile. It didn't look right on a little boy's face.

Ay-Tal was too cryptic for Jon. Jon was simply not trained for this. "What do you want me to do?" he asked instead.

"Carry me back to Mary's truck. I think I will need to change sooner than I have hoped," Ay-Tal said. The child who was a god but not a god lifted his arms up to Jon's neck in the universal "carry me" gesture. Jon picked up the little boy and took him out to the truck, then left him in the back of the cab and returned back to the diner. He didn't want to witness the transformation, and perhaps he wasn't really permitted to. *But I can still question Mary.*

• • •

When Jon returned, Saga and Mary seemed to be in a staring contest. If he weren't so freaked, he would have found it funny. He was basically an easy-going kind of guy, when he wasn't tasked with bringing home a god, for Aguguq's sake.

"So Mary," he said as he resumed his seat across from the truck driver. "Who are you, and how do you know about Ay-Tal?"

"Is he going back with you or me?" Mary asked.

"I don't know," Jon said honestly. "How does one force one's will on a god?"

"God!" Saga screeched. A few people in the restaurant

turned around to see what was the problem, but seeing nothing out of ordinary, they resumed their meals.

"Don't do that again, Saga," Mary admonished, "or you will be caught and sent back to that family."

Saga just nodded and seemed to sink even further into herself, looking smaller and younger. *If nothing else, it's good camouflage,* Jon thought. He gently patted her shoulder. "It's complicated, Saga," he said. "You must have guessed that Al is really not like other little boys."

"He is not?" Saga said. "I guess. Al's more mature. Quieter. Is there more?"

"More," Mary said.

"So who are you, Mary?" Jon asked, refocusing on the strange woman in front of him.

"I'm like Ay-Tal."

Jon didn't know whether he should run or stay, whether he could even move. One god-not-god was complicated; two were impossible. He looked at the half-wrinkled face and tried to see the gray foundation underneath.

"Like all living things, we learn," Mary said with a smile. "Progress, technology, and all that."

"What does that mean?" Jon asked. Saga was very quiet again, but Jon felt her inch closer to him. She was scared of Mary. He was too.

"Do you know anything about us?" Mary asked. Jon just shook his head. What he knew was clearly inadequate. "Well, for a few millennia, I was a kuhikuhi—"

"What's a kuhi?" Saga asked.

"Kuhikuhi means a guide in Hawaiian," Mary said.

"You don't look Hawaiian," Saga said with a slight hiccup. But Jon was impressed that she was able to form words. He was finding all of this very difficult. And Mary most certainly didn't look Polynesian or like any indigenous people...other than Irish, perhaps. She had strong Northern European features...but what did that matter for her kind? She blended in well in these parts of the country.

"Oh, I did for a while," Mary said with a hint of a smile, glancing at Jon for support.

"If Mary is like Al, she can look like anyone she wants," he confirmed. He wasn't sure it was wise taking Saga into their confidence like this, but it was out of his hands now.

"I liked the ocean and the warm climate," Mary said wistfully. "My people loved me, but I never stayed long." She gave another one of her pointed looks to Jon, as if it was his personal fault that Ay-Tal remained with his people for thousands of years. "Some of us—"

"How many?" Jon heard himself ask.

Mary ignored him. "Some of us like the special status in the societies we serve, but others prefer to be more anonymous, if possible."

"You don't like being a god?" Saga asked. Again, Jon marveled at the girl's composure and acceptance of what was completely unbelievable.

"It's so limiting," Mary said with a dismissive gesture, pulling Jon's plate of apple pie to her side of the table and digging in with relish. "Good," she said, her mouth full. "They do good pie in this joint."

Saga took a bite of hers and nodded. "Not bad."

"Not bad?" Mary said. "Where have you had better?"

"Well, as a god and all," Saga said, "you must have tried a lot of pies."

"My share, certainly. But most places don't care to invest into a quality product any more. Nowadays, it's all fast food, pre- and post-processing. Even the fruit fillings are suspect. I bet my coconut cream pie was mostly artificial." She chewed slowly and swallowed. "Still good, though."

"So can we return to the whole 'there are many of us' thing?" Jon asked. "You might be a guide and all to all those people, but I'm a guide to Ay-Tal. I'm supposed to bring her safely home."

"Her?" Saga asked. Jon just waved the girl off.

"It's hard to raise a species," Mary said.

"So you've said."

"We look for the best paths into the future and then offer our guiding services," Mary said.

"That's all?"

"There's a lot in that, young man," Mary said. "Without Ay-Tal, your people would have perished somewhere in the ice. The Americas would have had a very different history."

"Perhaps we never would have attempted to cross the ice in the first place," Jon said. It felt odd challenging a god, but here he was...

"Perhaps. But knowing Ay-Tal, there was a good reason to go. Not all humans made it to their final destinations, you know. Some perished in their caves."

"I'm not saying we are not grateful. My tribe celebrates Ay-Tal—"

"And relies on her to solve your problems," Mary said. "If you didn't seek legal protections for your land, Ay-Tal would still be safely ensconced among your people."

That was true. It wasn't Jon's decision, of course, but he often wondered why the elders chanced letting Ay-Tal go out into the world like that. They set her free in exchange for doing their bidding. Now their land was safe, for the moment, but their god was gone. Was it worth it? Jon didn't know. He was never asked.

"How is Al...Ay-Tal a god?" asked Saga.

"Well, like Jon here said, Ay-Tal led his people to North America during the last ice age."

"So he is like a living GPS?"

"A *very* long-lived GPS," Mary smirked. "But in a sense... at that time—"

"Sort of like Moses?" Saga asked again.

Mary chuckled. "A *lot* like Moses."

"So Moses was..." Jon started to ask but couldn't. It was all too much to take. One Ay-Tal was a blessing. *Many?*

"Moses and so many others," Mary said.

"Christopher Columbus?" Saga asked.

"Perhaps." Mary's eyes sparkled in a very unnerving way.

"Erik the Red?" Saga asked. "Arrow and I did genetic testing, and it showed we are related to Vikings. So..."

"Erik Thorvaldsson, originally," Mary corrected. "But yes. For a while we thought Greenland would transition to a better climate, but our calculations didn't work out. It's still a pit. Although with all the global warming, it might be a thing again. There's a beautiful canyon that runs down the middle of it, deeper than the Grand Canyon. It will be a sight once the ice shelf is gone," she said wistfully and then finished Jon's apple pie and eyed Saga's. The girl slid her dessert across the table. "Thank you," said Mary and polished off the girl's leftovers in just a few bites. "It's a good thing that fat and cholesterol don't cross the body boundaries," she said, rubbing her belly. "A few of these and I might have to do a change again."

"What would you change into?" Saga asked. Jon couldn't understand why the girl was so easily accepting of this whole thing. *It must the whole postaugmented reality gaming generation thing,* he decided. He had been far more skeptical at her age.

"I haven't made my decision yet," said Mary. "It all depends on Ay-Tal."

"He is changing now," said Jon.

"Of course he is," Mary said. "A child is never a good choice...well, not any more. Everything moves so fast now. There is precious little time to develop."

There were many ways to take what Mary said, and Jon wasn't too confident in his own judgment or swiftness at the moment to gather her true meaning. *Best to try and remember as much as I can for now and tell all to Grandfather and other elders.*

"Do you only do guiding over land and sea?" Saga asked.

"What do you mean?" Jon asked. The girl's thinking seemed more flexible than his.

"Well, there are many different ways to lead," Saga said. "Science, religion, politics, all come to mind. It's not all about going places, like in *places*." She emphasized the last word and used her fingers to walk across the table. "Some things are spiritual and intellectual. There are missionaries..."

"Very good," said Mary. "There are indeed many ways to lead."

"And do you?"

"We try."

Saga nodded. "I want to be guided to safety," she said in a tone one would use to ask for sanctuary in a church or political asylum from the border patrol. "I want to experience what it's like to be a kid again. With real parents...who care." And Jon realized that for the first time in her life, Saga was supplicating to a real god. He wondered if it worked as well as other kinds of prayers.

"Should we go and see Ay-Tal?" Mary asked without answering. There was a strange expression on her face, as if she was daring Jon and Saga to disbelieve her.

"Al said it would take a long time to change," Jon said. He really didn't want Saga to see the crawling, twisting gray flesh seeking to assume its new form. He would never be able to unsee what he had seen, and he figured the girl could do without those visuals.

"Really?" Mary laughed. She was the only one. "Ay-Tal really didn't keep up..."

"I don't know what you mean," said Jon. Saga only stared. He wondered how bewildering all of this was to her; did she really believe any of this or just pretended and went along with the crazy out of self-preservation? If it were him, he would have run at the first opportunity. Jon vowed to keep a closer eye on the girl. He didn't think she would make it on her own, not yet, not this young.

"Well, how long did it take Ay-Tal to become Ms. Blue?"

"Years, as far as I know," said Jon, "if you count all the preparations. A week of actual transition, I believe."

"Ms. Blue," breathed Saga, her eyes wild. "That's the woman who was murdered, wasn't it?" She said it so low that Jon was able to understand her only because of the context. He felt sorry for her.

"She didn't die, Saga," he tried to reassure her. Saga didn't move. Mary just laughed louder.

"Years?" Mary repeated. "Ay-Tal always had a flair for the dramatic. How long did it take her to become a kid?"

"I'm not sure," Jon said. He had slept through most of the transformation...thankfully. And then Ay-Tal had trouble with speech for hours after. It seemed a difficult process, much more so than what Mary was implying.

"Ms. Blue became Al the little boy?" asked Saga. "Where did all the rest of her go? She looked so much bigger in the photos on TV."

"Conservation of mass?" Mary asked. Saga nodded. "Glad you've learned something at school."

"I'm interested, too," said Jon. *I know so little...so little.*

"Everything is conserved, with the exception of the

universe as a whole," Mary said. That wasn't very helpful. "And perhaps even that," she added. "It's a matter of what and how you count."

"I'm not sure I understand?" Saga said. The girl was brave, talking to a god like that. But then Jon believed in Mary, and Saga might not. Not yet.

There was a commotion by the door. Jon stood up to look and felt ill. The Goth girl Jon ran into on the back porch of the rural night club—big dark hiking boots, black jeans, black t-shirt, and that oversized black leather jacket—walked in. Unlike the Saga of old, this young woman wore no makeup or piercings, just the discards of the girl sitting next to him. And right above her, the TV was showing the image of Saga that was a split image of what Ay-Tal had just become.

Ay-Tal walked slowly but deliberately toward their back booth. A hush radiated away from her. All eyes in the restaurant seemed to be on the little rebel in black. *Stupid, stupid, stupid*, thought Jon.

"Hi," Ay-Tal said and sat next to Jon, sandwiching him between the Old and New Sagas. Mary nodded in approval. Saga—the real one—just stared, her face becoming just two huge eyes. Ay-Tal smiled at her. "I hope you don't mind," Ay-Tal said.

"I?" Saga managed.

Jon stared back and forth between the girls. It was close, very close...but yet... The talk resumed among the other customers. Jon was painfully aware of people pointing fingers at them. How long before someone called the cops?

Ay-Tal was eying Saga closely. *Studying her features and expressions,* Jon guessed. Since appearance was more than just physical resemblance, it was all those little tics and micro gestures that gave shape to the physical. If Ay-Tal had a plan to fool people by taking Saga's identity, there was work to do. But as he watched Ay-Tal, he noticed more and more differences, not less. Ay-Tal's eyes were gray, not brown like Saga's. A little thing, but noticeable. The hair color was also off. Saga was a darker blond...mousy. Ay-Tal had light hair, almost golden. But no one would pay attention to hair color—so easy to change. On casual observation, Ay-Tal still really looked like Goth Saga's twin.

"So," Ay-Tal said. "Forgive me for asking, Saga, but I feel like a...a mixture of two people, at least," she said after struggling for the right word. "I don't really understand."

Saga looked scared, more scared than Jon had seen her up to now. Not that he could blame her.

"That was Mason's jacket," Saga said. "Arrow and Mason got matching ones at the church-organized rummage sale." Jon noted that Mary and Ay-Tal were both nodding. "When Mason..." Saga inhaled sharply. "When Mason died, I took it."

"How did Mason die?" asked Mary. Jon saw compassion and concern etched into the woman's face. Somehow, despite all of the sun damage and weathering, the left side of her face was more expressive still...like there was a deep reservoir of empathy pooled in between all of the wrinkles and brown spots. The right side just wasn't that expressive—the emotions didn't imprint there. They just slid off the smooth skin. The result was very disconcerting, and Jon looked away.

"You know..." Saga mumbled.

"No, Saga, we don't," Mary said. "But we would like to. Ay-Tal would like to."

"I want to go back and help the people in that community," Ay-Tal added. "To help your brother. That's why I chose this."

Saga looked at Ay-Tal and nodded. Jon noticed tears in the corners of her eyes, but none slipped down. Saga gathered control over herself and spoke. "They said it was an accident." Mary and Ay-Tal nodded in unison again. "But I know he was killed. They burned his body, you know."

"You mean cremated it?" Jon asked.

"No, she means burned," Ay-Tal said. "That can in your bag are his ashes?"

Saga nodded. "He wanted to travel the world." She said it like that explained it.

Jon remembered thinking how heavy that bag was. *Do ashes weigh this much? Is there so much stuff left over?* He looked at Ay-Tal. She seemed different now. Her face was more angular, the chin more prominent, squarish. The features still bore a passing resemblance to Saga, but no more than that. Saga noticed too, apparently, because she stuffed her fists into her mouth as she watched these changes unfold.

"I meant to go back as Saga. But it seems I might become Mason," Ay-Tal said, and during these two short sentences, his voice dropped a full octave and assumed a male quality. "I might need to borrow your cowboy boots," he said.

"Mine?" Jon asked. "Wouldn't that change you again?"

"The ones you're wearing are from the church, right?"

Jon looked down at his "new" boots and nodded. And then nodded again; these could have been Mason's. He leaned down and started to take them off just as Ay-Tal did the same with Saga's heavy hiking ones on his feet. A minute later, Jon was barefoot, and Ay-Tal had "his" boots.

"Better," the boy said with a smile. Ay-Tal was definitely male now.

"You look like Mason and not Mason," Saga said.

"That's a good description," said Mary.

A waitress came over to ask if they needed any more pie or coffee, but Jon saw that she really came over to stare at Ay-Tal...Mason, now. A look of surprise twisted her features when she saw that the girl who walked into the restaurant just half-hour ago was really an adolescent boy. The surprise relaxed into relief. Jon gathered that she had been sent to double check before calling the police on them. The waitress looked back at a manager who was clearly waiting for her at the reception table and smiled—danger passed. *For now.*

"I would like some more of that awesome coconut cream pie of yours," Mary said with a smile.

The waitress, now completely relaxed, gave her a big smile back. "Coming right up, honey. Any one else for an extra helping?" Her eyes turned dark again. "Where's that cute kid of yours? I bet he wouldn't pass up a dessert."

"All tuckered out," Mary said. "Took him back to my truck cabin to sleep."

The waitress nodded, anxiety cleared up once more—nothing suspicious here. Most truckers spent a few hours sleeping in the back of their long-hauls. Jon bet they kept one of the streetlights broken just for that reason out the back—it was better to let the restless rest when they could. "Be right back," the waitress said and disappeared into the kitchen. They heard her explaining Ay-Tal to her coworkers, and there was some laughter, again sounding like relief to Jon's ears. No one wanted to get into other people's business out here... unless it was about murder and child kidnapping.

"Tell me about Mason," Ay-Tal said in quiet, earnest voice. And underneath all of the changes, Jon could still hear the Ay-Tal that he knew, the one he met in D.C. in what now seemed like a lifetime ago.

"Mason was Arrow's age," Saga said. "They became best buds right away, like in the first hour. Boys do that, you know." Ay-Tal nodded. Jon noted that Saga was avoiding looking directly at Ay-Tal—he was difficult to watch. There was gray blurring around the edges as the changes proceeded to twist his features this way and that. It was very subtle, but still unnerving. "Aunt Ada was still married to Uncle Ben, Burt's brother, back then."

"Wait. Burt wasn't Mason's dad?" Jon asked. And while he was surprised, Ay-Tal seemed not at all. Mary just listened, her expression totally neutral.

"And Aunt Ada wasn't his birth mother," Saga said. "She married Uncle Ben when Mason was just a baby. Burt is...was Ben's younger brother."

"Huh."

"When Mason...passed," Saga continued. "His dad took it poorly. I don't really know what happened. Arrow and I had just started living with the Wilkinses. We got caught train surfing and were placed into the system. Mason was volunteering for the church group Aunt Ada runs. That's how we met. He got his parents to host while they looked for something permanent. No one wants to adopt teenagers, you know. So we stayed with Aunt Ada and Uncle Ben and Mason. But it takes time to take classes and such before a family can foster, so..." This was one of the longest things Saga had said so far, Jon noted. But she was talking to a god...gods.

"And Burt?" asked Mary.

"He was a regular at the house even back then. Mason told us to stay away from his uncle. Told us Burt was bad news. But I didn't know...not back then, anyway." Saga's face was pale, with bright red patches just under her eyes. She looked sick telling the story, and Jon felt sorry for her. "He took Arrow and Mason fishing one day. Mason didn't want to go, but Arrow had agreed already and Aunt Ada forced Mason to go. That's when I first knew. Arrow wouldn't tell me what happened on the lake that day, but from then on he was always there every time Burt showed up at the house. Mason, too. He was protective of both of us. He said it was his job since he got us involved. I wish I knew about Burt. I would have told someone then. I would have!"

"Of course, dear," said Mary.

"But I didn't. I really didn't. And then the accident happened. Arrow couldn't prove anything. He tried to look for clues. He said that he knew Burt did it. Mason wasn't clumsy or a pyro, and he wouldn't have killed himself. He was looking at colleges. He was planning on getting out of there. He and Arrow both. They had plans. And then Mason died. And it was Burt's fault. And we couldn't prove it! And then... and then..." Saga was hyperventilating, tears rolling freely down her face now. Jon could feel her little frame shaking. Frightened and ashamed. Incredibly sad. *Poor kid.*

"What happened to Mason's dad?" asked Ay-Tal. And for the first time, Jon could see a hint of Burt on him—a familial resemblance, a trace of a Wilkins.

"You would have to ask Burt," Saga said, eyes glistening.

"What's the official story?" Mary asked. *She and Ay-Tal make a good interrogating team,* Jon thought.

"Drowned in a lake," Saga said. "Just another accident. The Wilkins brothers went fishing to help each other grieve. Only one came back."

"Do you think Burt's responsible for Ben's death too?" Mary pressed the girl, but Saga just shrugged. "Hmm. So Ben's death was ruled an accident, just like Mason's, but you don't believe it."

"Arrow doesn't either," Saga said.

"How did Burt end up with Ada?" Ay-Tal asked. The face into which he settled had a decent quality to it. Jon liked that kid, Mason, based on what he was seeing now in Ay-Tal's interpretation. So much tragedy in such a tiny town...

"Burt just hung around and wouldn't leave. And, one day, Aunt Ada just said that they might as well get married; it was easier that way. Without Mason and Uncle Ben, she was a Wilkins in name only. Burt made it count more somehow."

Jon found that strange, but who knew what social pressures existed in small towns down here? Even in his tribe, only direct descendants got to keep the status of "Uolan." Wives and stepchildren and such didn't inherit this name. It was the first "family name" in the sense that Europeans use. Before about a hundred years or so, his people had only their given names. Everyone knew which family one came from; there was no need to spell it out. Now, of course, every one had two names.

"When did you and Arrow officially become fostered?" Mary asked.

"The paperwork was all done way before Mason's death, before Uncle Ben's. But Burt insisted on being listed as full guardian, after... The documents had to be amended. So probably like a year ago now, maybe a little less."

They sat in silence after that. The waitress brought more pie and coffee. While they ate—well, Mary mostly—Ay-Tal was slowly "fixing" his features. Jon caught Saga staring at him from the corner of her eye. He got the sense that the girl had been in love with Mason back then. How would it feel to have Mason's ghost come back like this? It was like an answer to a prayer and, like all such answers, was probably not at all what she had hoped for. Again, Jon felt sorry for Saga—the poor kid had it hard up to now.

Chapter Five: Caught

Jon Uolan

The shift in the emotional atmosphere of the restaurant was palpable, and it made Jon's hair stand on end—two cops had walked through the door. They weren't here for pie; they were working. So someone had called anyway. *Well...*

They walked slowly down the length of the restaurant, taking their time. When they reached Jon's booth, each took a position blocking the exits. One ended up next to Mary, the other by Ay-Tal, who was now fully Mason.

"Good evening, Officers," said Mary with a wide smile. Jon and Ay-Tal smiled as well. Even Saga waved; the girl had survived being homeless for a while, traveling with just her underage brother. There was an etiquette to dealing with authorities who took interest in you: smile a lot, stay polite, move slowly, and try to give the appearance of answering questions willingly while really saying little.

"Hello. This is Officer Rogers. And I'm Officer Merry. Please, no jokes," Officer Merry said, returning Mary's smile.

"What a coincidence," she said. "I'm a Mary, too."

"Of course you are," he said. "Can we see some IDs, please?"

"Sure thing," Mary said and pointed at her wide pants.

"Have it in my pocket." Moving slowly—no sudden moves—she pulled out her wallet and handed over her driver's license to Officer Merry. "See? Mary!"

After inspecting her driver's license and photo—Mary's double face was a very distinctive feature—he gave it back with a smile. "Thank you, Ms. Unapedos."

"Mary, please."

"Mary. I see you are enjoying the pies."

"Delicious, simply delicious," Mary confirmed. Saga bobbed her head in agreement.

"Good. Good. And now you, sir?" Officer Merry turned to Jon.

Jon followed Mary's lead, indicating the pocket of his vest and then pulling out his own wallet. "Here you go, Officer."

Officer Merry inspected Jon's Native American Tribal ID while Officer Rogers kept watching over everyone at the table. It felt like his job was to jump on anything suspicious, while his partner socialized and made small talk. They reminded Jon of a hunting pair—one predator distracts the prey while the other zeros in for a kill.

"Your driver's license is Native American-issued, not a settled law around here. Hope you hadn't been driving," Officer Merry said, slowly shaking his head.

"No," Jon assured him quickly.

"You're far from home, Mr. Uolan. So why are you here, if you don't mind me asking?"

Not for the first time, Jon regretted not getting a regular Alaskan state driver's license, but it was so much easier just to go down the street and get one from the tribal authorities, especially since they were all family. And then there was that whole pride thing—a feeling that he should fight for the rights of the native peoples to make their own laws. It felt like foolishness in, retrospect, when confronted with two suspicious cops from the lower forty-eight. Fighting governmental bureaucracy was like wading through half-frozen ice over deep waters—not something to do for the sheer fun of it and dangerous to boot. And given his job of bringing Ay-Tal home safely and quietly, it had been downright stupid. Jon felt sick and hoped his face didn't give away his inner turbulence and anxiety. The name of his tribe and village had been all over the news in the last several days in relation to the abduction and suspected murder of Ms. Ay-Tal Blue, although his own name hadn't yet been linked to the incident, just his physical description, which was wrong, or hopefully, wrong enough. Jon felt his mind spin.

"He's my trainee," Mary said suddenly. Everyone looked at her. *It's not a bad lie,* Jon thought, but he wasn't used to lying on the fly. Planning and careful deliberation were held in higher value than fast thinking among his people. Rushed decisions got one dead faster than salmon in the jaws of a bear. "I do long-distance hauling," Mary tried to explain.

"I wasn't asking about you—"

"Of course not, Officer," she said with a smile. "Jon was looking for something new, and one thing just led to another."

"Mr. Uolan?" Officer Merry turned to stare at him.

These few moments of back-and-forth gave Jon the time to gather himself. "There aren't too many jobs on a reservation, Officer Merry," he said. "When Mary offered to take me on, I jumped at the chance. Literally."

"I see. And how long ago was this?"

"We really just started," Mary said. "A few weeks, I'd say."

Officer Merry didn't take his eyes off Jon. "We met on the East Coast thirteen days ago," Jon volunteered, thinking of the direction from which they just drove. "Ms. Unapedos posted an ad for an assistant driver. I answered. And here we are." He didn't know what made him be so specific, but it felt right. And Ay-Tal had the means of making his statement less of a lie, Jon guessed.

"As long you're aware it's not legal for you to drive without a license," the officer said.

"Jon is still just trying to figure out if this is the life for him. Trucking is not for everyone, you know," Mary said with another brilliant smile. "I wouldn't let someone so green behind my wheel, not without passing some tests. Who knows what the kid could do to my truck?"

"Good." The officer seemed to relax his visual grip on Jon and moved on to Ay-Tal. Jon forced himself to stay as calm and neutral in appearance as he could—he was a hunter, he knew how to wait. "So, young man. What's your story?"

Ay-Tal sucked his head into the collar of his leather jacket. It wasn't as huge on him as it was on Saga, but Jon still got that same sense of a tortoise going into its shell. Ay-Tal's chin all but disappeared. He looked scared—eyes big, eyebrows up, nose twitching with just a slight sniff. The boy came across as young. Ay-Tal glanced at Mary.

"Mary," Officer Merry said without taking his eyes of Ay-Tal, "I'm warning you, let the kid answer for himself."

"I was sleeping in the bushes out back, Officer. Mary and Jon bought me dinner," Ay-Tal stammered out, his voice breaking in the middle. Jon was impressed by the performance.

"A runaway?" the officer asked, but his voice was gentle now, no trace of interrogation, just empathy. Officer Rogers also visibly changed. He stopped the job of constant monitoring, and Jon could see pity in his eyes as well.

Ay-Tal shook his head. It was neither yes nor no, but the cops let it go.

"What's your name, son?" asked Officer Rogers.

"Mason."

"Mason what?"

"Just Mason."

"I see. Nothing else?" Ay-Tal just shook his head. "I thought so. And how old are you, Mason?"

"Eighteen."

"Don't lie."

"Sixteen," Ay-Tal said in a whisper.

"I guess no papers, no ID?"

Ay-Tal just shook his head.

"Been on your own long?"

"About a year now."

"In Minnesota, we have compulsory school attendance until the age of sixteen," Officer Merry said. Ay-Tal shrank even farther into his jacket. "Now, there's no way to tell if you are lying, of course. But we can take you back and check fingerprints and such..."

"But I've done nothing wrong," Ay-Tal protested, his voice peaking into that adolescent high squeak at the end of the sentence.

"We don't know that."

"Precisely. So you can't take me in and arrest me." Al-Tal scooted as far away from the cops as he could get in the booth. Jon couldn't help but pity the kid...and he knew who and what he really was.

The officers exchanged looks but dropped it, with Officer Merry moving his gaze on to Saga. Now, she couldn't lie about her age—she barely looked a teen. But Mary quickly intervened.

"That's Saga," she said, before Saga was able to respond. "We found her hitchhiking on the road back a ways."

"You know of the Amber Alert issued for Saga Turgis?" Officer Merry asked. Officer Rogers already took a step back and pulled out his phone.

"Amber Alert?" Mary said with convincing innocence.

"She said she was going to visit Grandma in Saint Paul. Is that not true?" She turned on Saga. But Saga was too confused to answer and just stared back at her with those huge eyes. Jon also didn't know what he could do or say to support the theatrical performance he was witnessing. It was two gods versus the human authority and law representatives. Who would win? Who had more power? Jon had no idea.

"We have a missing persons report filed by the Wilkins family about three hours ago for a fourteen-year-old Saga Turgis. You?" Officer Merry said while his partner reported Saga's location to the police station. Whatever happened next, Saga would be going home tonight to Burt and Ada.

"But…" Saga tried to protest but couldn't. There was nothing really to say or do. These officers would take her away; she knew it. Jon squeezed Saga's hand under the table. Given Ay-Tal's choice of appearance, Saga wouldn't be abandoned to those people…those murderers. At least he didn't think so. *I hope not.*

"So whereabouts did you find this young lady?" Officer Merry asked. His pad was out; he was prepared to take notes.

"At a gas station a ways back," Mary said. "Not too far from Eau Claire."

"That be Wilkins," the officer said.

"Just like the family?" Mary asked.

"Just like. So the joyride is over, Ms. Turgis. You will have to come with us to the police station, where we will call your parents—"

"Foster parents," Jon broke in.

"Legal guardians," the officer said without even looking at Jon. "You will wait there to be picked up."

"I see," said Saga, tears pooling again inside her huge brown eyes—melting black ice. "And if I don't want to go back with them? What if they are mean people? What if I want to stay with Jon and Mary?"

"Sorry, kid," Officer Merry said. And Jon believed that he truly was. He waved for Mary to get up and let Saga out. Mary did so without a word. Saga didn't say anything either, but tears were streaming down her face. As she climbed out of the booth, Mary placed a hand on the girl's shoulder in support. *God's support.* The thought flittered through Jon's mind.

"And now you, sir." Officer Rogers pointed at Jon.

"What?" Jon had thought the danger was over. He stood up slowly, feeling very conscious of wearing just socks.

"Take off your hat," the officer ordered. Jon compiled; there was nothing else to do. The officer noted the scar above his eye and nodded. "You'll be coming with us, Mr. Uolan."

"But?"

"I've really enjoyed your story," Officer Merry said. "And some of it might even be true. We'll find out. But for now..." He pulled out handcuffs and motioned for Jon to turn around. As he did so, he noticed several other police cars outside. So they were just waiting for backup. He was such a fool. Officer Merry recited Jon's rights as he clicked the cuffs together. "And you, Ms. Mary Unapedos," Officer Merry continued. "Please refrain from picking up hitchhikers in the future. Not everyone walking along our roads are what they seem. And certainly don't lie for them."

Mary smiled back at the officers. *You caught me,* her face seemed to say.

"We will need you and this young man to come to the station as well," Officer Rogers said.

"Are you arresting us?" Ay-Tal asked.

"Just for some questions," the officer reassured, but his face was grim, and Jon didn't really believe him. How long would it be before they started to ask about a little blue-eyed boy who was supposed to be traveling with him? Jon felt sick.

More cops came into the restaurant. Everyone watched as Saga was taken away wailing and pleading for them to let her go. They took Ay-Tal next. Once both "kids" were out of the restaurant, Officers Merry and Rogers escorted Jon out. Outside, he could still hear Saga crying and screaming.

● ● ●

Jon didn't ride in the same police car as Saga or Ay-Tal. After he was taken into the station, he had no idea of what happened to them. He was booked and led for questioning into a bright cold room that smelled odd.

Over the next several hours, he was interrogated repeatedly by a progression of police officers that asked the same questions over and over again. Jon tried not to say much. They already knew where he lived. They knew about his people. They knew of Ay-Tal Blue and her Supreme Court Case win. They knew that his grandfather had led his people for many decades and that someday soon it would be his dad's turn to be the next tribal chief. Theoretically, Jon would lead after his father's death or when his dad decided to take a rest from responsibilities of caring for his people. In a word, they knew a lot about Jon...and nothing.

He had asked for a lawyer and was told that one was on the way, but somehow one never arrived. Finally, he was put into a holding cell. Deathly tired, disoriented, and still barefoot, Jon fell asleep.

● ● ●

He woke up feeling funky. He wasn't hungry or cold, and he was used to sleeping on much more uncomfortable beds than the cot in his cell. His condition was nothing physical, but it felt physical. Anxiety had translated into real symptoms. His stomach was cramping, he had a perpetual headache, and, for the first time in his life, his left eye had a tic. It was an awful sensation. He pressed his fingers against his twitching eye, just under the scar, to try to stop the small eyelid muscle from spasming, but it only caused his fingers to jerk. All of this made it difficult to think. He'd already decided not to lie, although he was hoping not to have to talk much. *Who will believe the truth?* Jon hoped the gods would pity him and find a way of setting him free. But it had been hours, and he had heard nothing. Ay-Tal hadn't come for him...and neither had Mary. *Have the gods abandoned me?*

He was interrogated again.

● ● ●

Jon considered praying. But knowing what he knew, it felt like a silly activity. Ay-Tal only knew what she experienced personally, by actually being present or by reading about events or by some other form of real communication. Ay-Tal wasn't omniscient; she wasn't that kind of god. And Aguguq—the god of the frozen waste and bountiful icy waters—never answered. Life was harsh up north, and Aguguq expected his people to take care of themselves. Ay-Tal was much more approachable and responsive...when she was physically present.

He was placed alone in a cell meant for four. Well, just him and a camera. They were always watching him. He felt uncomfortable, so exposed even in his most intimate moments. In the morning, they gave him food and even coffee. It wasn't as bad as he figured prison food would be, but he couldn't stomach it anyway.

There were five other inmates distributed among the three additional cells that Jon could see. There was a drunk they picked up just this morning. Some kids who had set a car on fire—they claimed it was an accident—had been here before Jon. And there was a drifter full of holes in his face. Jon guessed the holes were from piercings; all jewelry was removed prior to placing the guy in a cell. Jon wondered vaguely if coffee would ooze out of the holes if the man wasn't careful. All in all, based on the inmates, this police station didn't have to contend with a lot of serious crime or hardened criminals. Jon was probably the baddest baddie they had held here in a while...and he was innocent.

● ● ●

No one bothered him for the whole day and night; Jon entertained himself by trying to remember all of the legends of Ay-Tal in as much detail as he could. Jon knew that the last name "Blue" had been chosen for the Harvard Law School application. It sounded less exotic and yet was one of the colors of hard, slow waters—glacial ice. He knew it had taken many months to come to that choice, and he'd bet Ay-Tal hadn't even picked it himself. And funny that—since Ay-Tal changed into a little boy, in Jon's mind he'd started to refer to Ay-Tal as a he...at least when he visualized Al. But for so many years—most of Jon's life, really—he had thought of Ay-Tal as female. And yet, ultimately, it didn't matter. Ay-Tal was not really human and was therefore beyond human gender prejudices.

Jon remembered his grandmother telling him the story of his ancestors, the English ones, the ones responsible for the gray eyes of all the male members of his family since then. He always had his suspicions about that story—it never rang true. That was the generation that adopted the family name of Uolan—"man" in the language of the Yakut, the brothers from across the ocean. Before then, most tribal members only had one name. But as more "progress" advanced into Alaskan territories, people felt a need for last names. Most chose animal-based or nature-based family names, but his ancestors were different. Jon's family asserted their humanity in their very choice of a family name. Given what he knew now, Jon wondered if it was significant. *Do gods have children? Can they?* It was a very prideful thought, and Jon felt ashamed thinking himself related to a god. But, by some teachings, they were all children of gods, right?

●　●　●

On the third day, Jon was the only one left in the lockup. For dinner, they served him a plate of turkey, gravy, stuffing, and canned, jellied cranberries—it was officially Thanksgiving. Of all the holidays, Thanksgiving was the most complicated for his people. Certainly his tribe hadn't suffered the kinds of abuses other Native American tribes experienced, especially those on the Atlantic Coast during early colonial times. Ay-Tal had been good at minimizing damage from racial tensions. In school, Jon's teachers treated the holiday in a more nuanced manner than schools in large population centers like Anchorage. And while this federal holiday was a late addition to his tribe's yearly celebrations, it was still embraced; but no one was made to wear pilgrim hats or feathers and other such nonsense. His grandfather took the opportunity before Thanksgiving to visit all the classrooms and talk about their people's heritage. But tribal pride was always mixed with a message of thankfulness and sharing. Jon thought it was a good approach—it made his people feel American and yet didn't whitewash the nasty details. And turkey was good food. Back home, kids collected wild cranberries for the communal feasts...much better than the canned stuff.

Jon ate in silence, keeping the food tray on his lap. He felt bad for the officers who had to work this evening. He saw that the cops who got stuck with the holiday duty ate the same turkey plates as their only prisoner. They had missed the holiday dinner with their families to keep an eye on Jon. It was sad and so unnecessary.

● ● ●

Passing the time was the hardest thing to do in jail. Unlike the others, Jon wasn't allowed to go to the common room to watch TV. His only change of perspective was to move about the cell and lie on each of the four beds in turn. It wasn't much. With nothing to do, he took lots of naps and used the opportunity to practice guided dreaming. He had never been any good at that.

He was awakened by Officer Rogers informing him that he had a visitor. Jon didn't really know anyone from around here other than Ay-Tal and Mary, so he felt a nervous hope. His gods might not be able to free him, but at least they remembered him and knew he was innocent. He was taken back to the small interrogation room and left alone to sit and wait.

There were just two chairs and a metal table. Jon took the far chair that he sat in during the previous questionings. After about twenty minutes, a woman dressed in a business suit came in and took the seat closest to the door where the policemen had sat before. The officer who let her in closed the door to the room with a click, leaving just the two of them.

But Jon was sure he was being observed through a two-way mirror or via a camera feed. He'd watched enough TV to know that prisoners were never left alone with anyone.

"Mr. Uolan? Jon?" said the woman. She was pleasant-looking. Jon noted that she was of an average height, had shoulder-length dark brown hair with a touch of gray, a very fair complexion, and lots of smile lines radiating from the corners of her eyes. Her eyes were gray; left one with a large orange-brown starburst at the center. The asymmetry made the woman more striking, rather than detracting from her looks. Jon also noticed small earrings with orange stones and a matching gold necklace, nothing ostentatious yet matching the strange marking in her eye. She was about Jon's age and wore sensible shoes, and she practically exuded trustworthiness. He was immediately suspicious.

"Yes?" he said. *Who is she?*

"I'm Roberta Hand. I am a detective assigned to your case."

Jon didn't say anything. He had been interviewed by so many people already. What was another one?

"So let's get right to business," she said with a warm smile. Jon felt his eye tic rev up to a new, higher rhythm. "There was a push to charge you with the murders of Ay-Tal Blue and Al Uolan."

"Really?" Jon didn't realize that they already tried to declare the little boy dead. *Seems fast...with no bodies or other evidence.*

"But unfortunately, without any concrete evidence," the woman echoed his thoughts, "we simply can't hold you any longer. We are now past the customary seventy-two-hour rule."

"A what?"

"The maximum time the police can hold a suspect

without charging him is seventy-two hours," Ms. Hand said. "Now, that's not a strict rule, of course."

"Of course. And it's been longer," Jon pointed out and immediately felt like kicking himself. *If they want to let me out, let them. Don't argue...*

"Yes. With the holidays and all, the police can sometimes get away with keeping a suspect incarcerated longer. But I've argued that it is way past the time you can be held without actually filing charges with a judge."

"And without evidence...huh?" Jon wondered why she was telling him all this. She wasn't his attorney; she was more like the opposite. "Does it mean I'm free to go?" he asked.

"You will leave when the paperwork gets sorted out," Ms. Hand said. "Now, given that it's a day after Thanksgiving—"

"I get to stay here longer," Jon finished for her.

"Yes."

"I see," Jon said. "I asked for a lawyer..."

"It's the holidays, and we are a small town, Mr. Uolan," the detective said.

She was being disingenuous. They were right outside of Saint Paul, and there had to be plenty of public defenders around even on Thanksgiving. But Jon didn't challenge the assertion—they were setting him free, so it would be stupid to put up a fight now.

"You will be free in a few hours, days at the outmost, so..."

"Days?" Jon cried out, but the woman just shrugged. "I see," he said, controlling himself. "Do you by chance know what happened to that kid we found in the rest stop parking lot? Mason?"

"Not really," she said, staring at him, taking his measure, judging him.

Jon refused to be intimidated. He did nothing wrong... well, he had stolen a gun and lied to the police. "Was the boy let go?" he asked.

"I assume so." She looked at him, willing him to ask more questions, to share information.

"I see. And Mary? What happened to Mary?"

"Mary?"

"The truck driver? I thought you wanted to interview her too," Jon said.

"*I* didn't." She emphasized the word "I" and smiled again. Ms. Hand made Jon nervous. "I assume you will be traveling back to Wilkins?" she asked.

"Why?" Jon had no idea what would happen next or what he should do. He *needed* to find Ay-Tal. He *wanted* to go home. He *had* to help Saga and her brother. The woman detective just watched him as he struggled to figure out what he would do, but he wasn't about to volunteer any information.

"I can arrange for you to travel back home," Ms. Hand suggested. Jon shook his head; he didn't want her help. "Well…" She stood up, and so did Jon. "It was a pleasure to talk with you, Mr. Uolan. I'm sure it won't be the last time." And, with that, Jon knew that this woman wasn't giving up on him. She was still on his case. "Oh, and Saga told me everything," she added. With a smile, Ms. Hand knocked on the door and was let out by Officer Rogers.

Jon exhaled and practically fell back into his chair. A few minutes later, he was escorted back to his cell. It wasn't fair. They'd kept him way too long, according to this Detective Hand, but he wasn't about to argue the point. He had no idea where to go, not even shoes to go in.

Chapter Six: Going Back to Move Forward

Jon Uolan

It's always faster coming than going. Jon noticed that even as a child, going on hikes with his father and grandfather. But it still felt like no time passed between finishing breakfast in jail and walking into the Wilkins's nightclub parking lot some hours later. He assumed Ay-Tal...Mason was already back in town. He wasn't sure how to find him, but it was a small town, and Mason would know that Jon was released from jail. He was a god, after all. And he still needed Jon's help.

It was nine in the morning on the Sunday after Thanksgiving. The ground was covered with a layer of frost and a blanket of low-lying cold fog. It was no longer dark, but it felt like it would still be hours before it was properly daylight. This time of year, the dark lingered.

Jon scanned the area for any signs of cops or Detective Hand—did they follow him? He was sure they did. Why wouldn't they? But he hadn't seen anything all morning. When he left the police station, everyone had been polite and seemed uninterested in his plans. It was unnerving. But as he walked to a bus terminal from the police station, he was sure he was followed, only to be the only passenger on the local bus to Eau Claire, Wisconsin. He asked the driver to stop a few miles down the road from the Wilkins's nightclub. Most of the way, the highway was completely deserted, not even a passing car all the way to Wilkins.

Jon bet that Arrow wouldn't be at the club—with all that happened, he would be too worried about his sister to leave her alone for the night with those people. Jon would have been. *What was Saga's punishment from Burt for running away? Did she really tell the cops everything?* Jon made another bet: the girl didn't tell. Burt was a pervert—Jon already knew that, observed it first hand with Ay-Tal as Al—but was he a murderer too? Jon was here to find out.

Jon went around to the back porch and sat and waited with his back against the rear door. If in a couple of hours, Mason didn't show, he would go into town. The church, probably. Ada and Hazel would be there; it was Sunday morning, after all. Saga too, probably. That would be the first time he had really spoken with anyone since the arrest; interrogations by the police and a detective didn't count.

He had nothing but the clothing on his back and his old hiking boots; he had assumed Mary dropped them off for him at the county jail. He also had a rubber-banded wad of a hundred twenties. It was most of the money the tribe gave him to deliver Ay-Tal home, minus the train fare, minus the postage, minus the four hundred dollars he had to give to that gas station clerk for the smashed shrubbery. A god had asked him to pay. It wasn't his tribe's god, but could Jon really have said no? It was money to smooth out Ay-Tal's journey back to the tribal lands. The cops didn't ask him about the almost two thousand in cash, and he didn't bring it up. But it was all there; he counted. That and his tribal ID. His backpack with the gun, his hunting knife, a change of clothing, including stuff for "his son Al," and the satellite phone, was somewhere back with Mary. Jon hoped that the gods managed to get rid of the incriminating evidence, but he wasn't too sure. These gods seemed somewhat inattentive to such details. Although as Ms. Blue the attorney, Ay-Tal had been very focused on her objective of securing the mining rights for their tribe. Did the Change, one human form into another, affect behavior? Personality? Or was there a central core of traits that survived morphing from one person to the next? Having experienced Ay-Tal as Ms. Blue, and then as Al, and briefly as Mason, Jon thought there might be such a core. And he actually missed her...his company. But thinking about Mary, he couldn't imagine her as anything but the dual-faced, always-smiling, gregarious truck driver.

"Move and I'll shoot."

A muzzle of a shotgun was pointed into Jon's right ear. Burt Wilkins had his finger on the trigger. And Jon had no doubt whatsoever that Burt wouldn't hesitate to kill him. For the second time, Jon had managed to be caught unawares on this stupid back porch.

"Hi, Burt," he said. "Glad I ran into you here." He used a calm, low voice, just as he would with an overly excited hunting dog.

"Glad?"

"Why else would I come here?"

"To kidnap my girl again," Burt said, and Jon could almost hear a growl in his voice.

"I'm sure Saga told you that I did no such thing."

"That little bitch lies all the time," Burt said and spat on the ground. The aggressive, emotional display was making Burt feel better; he lowered the shotgun to point at Jon's lap.

"I came here hoping to find a job," Jon lied. "The nightclub seemed like a good place to start."

Burt gave him an appraising look. "Where did you stash the kid?"

"Al? With his grandparents, like I've told you," Jon said.

"So you didn't make that shit up?"

"About his grandparents?"

"Yeah."

"Of course not. He's a kid; he needs stability. I've used all my money to send him up north. Was hoping to make some cash and follow him home in a few months."

Burt nodded thoughtfully, leaned on his shotgun, and scratched. Jon still didn't move. He didn't know this man well enough to be able to predict his next move. But he hoped Ay-Tal...Mason had the sense to stay away from here, at least until the weapon was removed from the scene. *Gods bleed, gods can die, if not careful.*

"I'm freezing cold," Jon said after a few moments. It wasn't that bad, but the weather seemed a safe topic of conversation.

"Wanna drink?" Burt asked. There was excitement in his voice again.

Jon didn't think Burt needed his permission to have a drink on a Sunday morning at his own bar, but perhaps an excuse? If so, Jon was happy to give him one. "Sure," he said and allowed himself to get up slowly. No sudden moves.

Burt swung his shotgun over his shoulder and pulled out a giant mass of keys. "Well, get out of my way, Jonny boy. I won't be jumping over you." Jon moved aside, and Burt unlocked the door to his nightclub.

It was just as Jon remembered—clean, mostly wooden surfaces, purple and green accent lights around the bar, and half a dozen TVs, all dark, along the walls. "Nice place," he said.

"Yeah," Burt agreed. "Brings in a pretty penny too. Not

too many places to go and relax around these parts. And our preacher is a regular."

"You don't say."

"Sure. Paul knew my parents. Was tight with my brother for all those do-good activities. And now the same with Ada. The guy likes to support people who support him. And the Wilkinses provide a lot of support."

Jon just nodded to indicate he was paying attention. Burt went behind the bar and, without putting down his shotgun, pulled out a couple of beers from a fridge under the counter. He popped the cap of one, passed it to Jon, and did the same for himself.

"Thanks," Jon said and took a small sip. He had never been much of a drinker—alcohol and cold weather didn't mix, despite all the myths—and now he preferred to keep his head clear.

Without taking a breath, Burt downed the whole bottle and pulled out another one, popped it open, and took a big swig. "That's better," he said.

A few more minutes, and Burt was done with his second beer. Jon sat a few tables away from the bar and watched.

"My brother built this place," Burt said after a while. "With his own hands."

"He did a nice job," Jon said, looking around appreciatively.

"Yeah. Nice."

"Does he still work around here?" Jon asked.

Burt visibly winced and took out another beer. "Nah. He's gone now," he said. "It's just me and Ada."

"She seems a very capable woman," Jon said, pretending to sip from his bottle. "Really had that church organized. Al and I are truly grateful for all the things she gave us."

"Yeah. That woman has a soft heart." Burt leaned the shotgun against the wall, and Jon felt better. It was still within easy reach, but so was the exit. "She wanted me to see if your kid needed fostering. Picks up every sad stray she sees on the street. Seven cats..." He sort of petered out at the end, as if he lost his voice...or his train of thought.

"And Hazel?" asked Jon.

"Her sister's kid. Hangs out at the church a lot," Burt said. "I think she just likes riffling through all that crap. Ada and her go to the donations warehouse up in Saint Paul and buy by the pound."

"Really? I didn't know it was a thing." It explained how a small town like Wilkins had managed to get so much "donated" clothing.

"She tells Reverend Paul that his money goes further this way."

"And he lets her?"

"There's no Wilkins without the Wilkinses." There was a twisted grin on Burt's face that made Jon very uncomfortable, but it was good to have the man talk like this, volunteering information. Jon wasn't only getting the facts, as such—he was also getting Burt's take on them. *Useful.*

"So your family founded this town?" Jon asked.

"Several generations back," Burt said. "The Wilkins family did everything. Raised the money for the church. Gave to the school. My grandpa even donated to have a library built." He made a sound between a huff and snort.

"You don't approve of book sharing?"

"Can't buy respect no more."

Jon thought on how differently his own small village operated. His family had produced chiefs for as long as anyone remembered, probably as far back as the crossing. *There would be no tribe without the Uolans.* The snarky thought echoed Burt's claim. And yet it seemed very different. Back home, everyone worked together. The tribe came first. Uolans just had more responsibilities than most. Jon might be a chief one day, yet it had fallen on him to deliver their god back to her people. And he was failing mightily at that.

"Mind if I smoke?" Burt asked and pulled out a cigarette before Jon answered. But he did ask—more than Jon expected from this guy. "Ada hates it when I smoke. Ben never smoked," he added.

"Ben?" Jon asked quietly. He wanted Burt's side of the story.

"My brother. Dead now. Never smoked, but he's dead. What's the use in that?"

"How did he die?"

Burt grabbed the shotgun and turned on Jon so fast that there was no time to run for the exit. *So much for goading the bear,* Jon thought. *This would be a mighty stupid way to die.* He forced himself to stay relaxed and appear unconcerned.

"What do you know about it?" Burt asked.

"Nothing, man. Nothing," Jon said and took a deliberate gulp of beer—a reminder that they were engaged in friendly drinking. "Just the way you said it made me think it was lung cancer or something," he lied. He was never any good at lying, but Burt was on his third...or was it fourth beer?

"Nah," Burt said and sat down again but kept the shotgun on his lap. "A stupid accident."

"Most accidents are."

"He fell out of a fishing boat," Burt said, scratching his head with his beer bottle. "The next thing, he's dead. Drowned."

"Darn shame," Jon said sympathetically, but he could see that Burt was lying. Maybe he was lying about how Ben "fell out" of the boat, or maybe about how his brother hadn't managed to get back in. Either way, Jon was now sure Burt was responsible for Ben's early demise.

"Yeah. Darn shame. One day the guy's the mayor of town, getting respect from everyone, the next he's just worm fodder rotting in dirt."

Jon nodded slowly—*no sudden moves.* "I thought you were the mayor?" he asked.

"I am now," Burt said, threw his empty bottle into the recycling bin, and took another one out of the fridge. Jon wondered how many were in there. Had they gone through a whole six-pack yet? "And you know what? Still no respect. Ben this and Ben that. Always about Ben. Well, I rule differently." His mouth opened up in a wide yawn.

"You're a different man than your brother, of course you do things different."

"You bet!" Burt slammed his beer onto the bar so hard that Jon thought the bottle would shatter. It didn't. Burt finished it in one go. "Everyone wants something, but Wilkinses built this town. We built it! And it's mine now." Having exhausted himself with all of this complaining, Burt put his head on the bar, and soon Jon heard heavy snores. He had survived his second encounter with Burt. *Didn't get a job at the bar, though.*

• • •

It was time to leave. Ay-Tal...Mason would find him when he thought the time was right. God-chasing never worked. Jon forced himself to use the name "Mason" so as not to accidentally slip up. Just saying "Ay-Tal" seemed fraught with danger now.

Outside, it was wet and drizzly. The kind of drizzle that was more frozen than not. Within a few minutes, he was totally wet.

As he was walking up the hill, scanning continuously

for anything suspicious, Jon saw a dark figure running across the street.

"Ay-Tal!" he cried out and immediately berated himself. "Mason!" he tried again.

"Jon?" It wasn't Mason after all, it was Arrow. He didn't react to hearing Mason's name. The boy either didn't catch it or was in the loop, Jon decided. "What are you doing back here?" Arrow asked when he got close, holding up his hood to keep the rain out of his eyes. "Saga said you'd be back, but no one believed her."

"Really? Did Mary send you?"

"Who's Mary?" Arrow asked but didn't wait for an answer. "Can we go inside?" He pointed down the hill toward the nightclub. It was obvious that he wasn't here on Jon's account. "I'm soaked," the boy added.

"Burt's in there, and he has a gun. Drunk too."

"Huh. Then let's go back to town. The Sunday service is still going, but we can wait for Saga in the basement." And with that, Arrow turned and dashed back across the street. The big leather jacket, the dark pants, the black hood—he looked a lot like Ay-Tal's version of Mason. Jon raced to follow.

In the few days of Jon's absence, the little town of Wilkins had transformed. American flags were still everywhere, but now there was an ostentatious display of Christmas kitsch all over the houses and lawns of its residents. Snowmen and Santas competed with Baby Jesuses for space on the front lawns. And if all those lights were still the old incandescent kind instead of LEDs, Jon was sure there would have been a surge powerful enough to blow out this whole part of the state. Even the shuttered-up houses had a few decorations— an old Santa or some tinsel on the trees, and even Christmas lights powered by wires stretched from the neighboring houses. People here cared...at least about appearances.

Jon and Arrow ran all the way to the church, and Jon thanked Aguguq that there were powerful dryers down in that basement. They were soaked through.

Like the rest of this little town, the church was heavily decorated. There was a life-size nativity scene, complete with a homemade but expertly built barn, figures carved out of wood, including several camels and a donkey, and even fake snow draped over the roof. It was the most elaborate display Jon had ever seen; the entire front lawn of the church was used. Over to the side, next to a small, gated playground, someone had put up Christmas lights and decorations on a living pine tree, obviously grown there for this purpose. Jon could see a wire strung from the top church window to the tip of the ten-foot tree. Oversized and plainly fake Christmas present boxes were laid out underneath, wrapped in colorful outdoor paper and tied with golden ribbons with bows.

Jon must have looked impressed, because Arrow turned to him and said, "Aunt Ada and Hazel's mom, Beth Olson, chair the WINGS decorating committee on alternate years. This thing has been getting bigger and bigger every year. Beth and Ada are sisters, and you know how it is with siblings."

"Huh," said Jon. "What's WINGS?"

"Wilkins Initiatives to Nourish God's Service. It's a lame acronym, but the ladies like it." Arrow smirked. Like so much in this town, the name of the charity was saccharin-sweet, but that was no longer a surprise. "The town decorating committee is just a little piece of it. Shall we get inside?"

Last time Jon was here, he went through the front door and down the stairs just off the church's gift store. But given that most of the town inhabitants were inside there at this moment—the parking lot was full—Jon preferred another way.

Seeing Jon's discomfort, Arrow pointed to the back of

the church. "By the side door."

Once inside, Jon and Arrow went down the stairs, through the cavernous basement area filled with stackable chairs, and into the laundry room. They stripped down to dry their pants, socks, and shirts, which they stuffed into a dryer. Arrow's hair was totally soaked, his lips were blue, and he was visibly shivering. Jon was just as wet, but not as uncomfortable. The laundry room was very warm; one of the machines had clearly been in use earlier, and the smell of detergent and fabric softener clung to the air. On second thought, Jon shoved his puffy vest into the dryer—might as well. Arrow's jacket couldn't go in, obviously—it was leather. It smelled of mildew, and Jon judged it would take days to dry. Fancy leather was not an ideal material for this weather.

They stood awkwardly, barefoot, in just their underwear and damp t-shirts inside a small room, actively avoiding looking directly at each other.

"If someone discovers us like this..." Arrow smirked. "Actually, they probably won't be surprised. There's crazy shit that goes on in this place."

"Nice jacket." Jon changed the subject. Arrow was too uncomfortable.

"Thanks. Hazel picked it out."

"Really? She did good by you," Jon said.

"Yeah, well it's a perk of working in this second-hand mercy factory."

"Al and I are grateful," Jon said.

"Sure. But Wilkins is a one-town industry, and once they get you..." Arrow spoke to a corner, away from Jon. That gave Jon a chance to surreptitiously check the boy out. He noticed a big scar on the Arrow's upper thigh and bruising that was pretty much evenly distributed along the visible skin. "You're back for a while, aren't you?" the boy asked. He sounded hopeful, and that made Jon angry. Was there no one in this whole town that these kids could turn to for help?

"Tell me about Mason," Jon said. And Arrow immediately shrank back, eyes huge, hands curled into fists. "Saga mentioned him," Jon added. He didn't know what Arrow knew, and he needed to find out in a hurry.

"Ada's stepson. The only child of Ben Wilkins. Ada's only kid," Arrow said in almost a whisper. The room was small, but the dryer was so loud, Jon had to lean in to hear him. "Saga stole his ashes, you know." Jon nodded that he knew. "But now they've gone missing. We've been looking for a paint can just like the one he was stored in. Figured we would put some dirt and such and just pretend that it was never missing." Arrow speech was frenetic, driven. "Saga stole his real ashes from the funeral home in the first place. They buried sand from the lake in his grave. Ada knows. Burt too. But no one else. Well, perhaps the reverend too. Ada caught Saga doing it. I guess it made her feel good that someone cared that much about her son...Ben's son. Burt was pissed. Ada was stupid to tell him."

"Is Ada looking for them?" Meaning the ashes.

"Nah. She's scared to even touch them. But Burt would notice. He notices everything...eventually."

"Are you scared of him?"

"Of Burt? Sure. Aren't you?"

"Yeah." And he was. Burt was physically dangerous and surprisingly politically powerful in this small, sleepy community.

"Did Saga tell you that he killed Mason?"

"She said you suspected it," Jon said carefully.

"Not suspect. Know. Mason and I were best buds. Even if he got us, Saga and me, into this town. It was good for a time. The best Saga and I had in forever. Mason and I had plans to go away to school together. I figured Saga would be safe here on her own. Ada and Ben seemed like decent people. Ben liked us. Saga is a good girl. And other than Mason, Ada and Ben didn't have kids of their own. But then Burt screwed it all up."

"Burt wasn't around at first?"

"He was in prison when we first got here. But I didn't know anything about him. Mason said he was bad news. Told us to stay away. We tried, but Burt is family, and so..." Arrow shook his head. He was as far away from Jon as the space would allow, all the way against the wall. Jon felt pity for the kid. This boy should be worrying about college exams and such, not murder.

"How is it now?" Jon asked.

"Now?" Arrow laughed, and it sounded like a sick bark. "Ada knows, you know. But she pretends that it is all fine. Spends all her time here, in church, organizing, arranging, harassing people for donations. I think if she stopped for just a second, she would really go crazy. The whole f-ing town is pretending. The sheriff too. You know they say that life is like an ocean? We all swim, but some catch a wave and some end up swimming against the tide. It's been against the tide for me and Saga for as long as I can remember. Burt, though..."

"Huh."

"Burt's been a bad seed from way back. He always got into trouble, even as a kid, I was told. But it was only the last time that he couldn't just get out of it. Everyone always covers up for the Wilkinses. I think it's been going on for so long that the people forgot how not to pretend."

"What'd he go to jail for?" Jon asked.

"Assault? But I don't really know. It's not like I can just ask him for details."

"No." It wasn't surprising that Burt did time for something

violent, but it would help if Jon knew the whole story.

"Mason and I were going to get out of here," Arrow continued. "And Saga would follow us in a few years. We even talked of a way of getting custody of her."

"You?"

"Yeah. You can do it when you turn eighteen, you know. And she's my kin."

"Would they let you?" Jon asked.

"It wouldn't have been easy, but I figured once we got out, we could seek real help." Jon noticed that Arrow was talking about adopting his sister in the past tense. "But now I don't know." Arrow stopped the dryer and pulled out the slightly damp clothing, throwing Jon's over to his side of the laundry room. They got dressed quickly, without looking at each other. "I can't leave her here by herself," Arrow said. "Not the way she left me." There was a lot of resentment in his voice.

"I think Saga felt that by leaving, she was freeing you to do what you needed to do," Jon said.

"She is too young to be on her own."

"I agree. We talked about her going to live with my people," Jon said. It wasn't exactly true, but they would have gotten to that eventually, if the cops hadn't shown up.

Arrow whirled on him and got real close. Jon could smell his breath; it smelled like bubble gum. "And what's in it for you?" the boy growled. "Are you one of those—"

"Easy now, Arrow. I'm here to help. I didn't have to come back. But I wanted to." And it was true. "You and Saga and Hazel—"

"Hazel is just fine."

"This town is sick, and I want to find a way to help."

"But why?"

"Because it's the right thing to do? Because I think I can help...a little. Because you need help."

"Lot's of adults talk like you." Arrow dismissed him. "And look where it's got us now. It's Saga and me against the world. You want to stay and help? Fine. But I will make the decisions on what's right for me and my sister. You help her run away again without me, and I'm coming after you. You're going to have to deal with me." Arrow grabbed his wet jacket and rushed out of the room.

That didn't go the way Jon hoped. Nothing did.

Chapter Seven: WINGS of Mercy

Jon Uolan

He heard the sound of many feet descending the stairs; the sermon must have ended. Jon stepped out of the laundry room to meet the congregation.

It was the first time he got to see almost the entire town's population in one go...well, half the town. It was mostly women and girls making their way down into the basement, young kids in tow. It was a far more diverse population than Jon originally supposed. Historically, the first wave of immigrants to the area was of German descent. Even now, the majority of people were obviously from some Northern European country or another. But Jon noticed some Asian and Hispanic faces—this part of the world was changing faster than his. Hardly anyone in his hometown was anything other than native-born, his immediate family notwithstanding.

"People. People!" He heard Ada's voice above the hum of multiple conversations. "We have work to do. Remember?" The room settled down. "Thank you," Ada said. "This is the first day of our official WINGS committee gathering this Christmas season. As you know, this year I will chair..." There was a rise in volume as the women of Wilkins expressed their opinions on the matter. If Arrow was correct on the lock on this position by Ada and Beth, Jon could see that they weren't as popular as these sisters hoped. But then Ada clapped her hands loudly, and the room settled down once more. "We really do have a lot to do, ladies. The first priority is to pick a cause for this season, and we can organize around that." She looked about the room. Some hands went up in the air, and Jon heard proposals for adopting an orphanage in East Ukraine, supporting a drive for some remote village in the Congo, creating a sister-church partnership in Venezuela, and a dozen other similar ideas, all involving putting together a large collection of Christmas presents and shipping them far away.

A woman spoke up. "How about something closer to home this year?"

"What do you have in mind, Dorothy?" Ada asked.

"How about helping the victims of that earthquake in Alaska?"

Jon was startled. He hadn't heard anything about an earthquake, but of course he had been out of it for a few days.

"You mean that native village that was swamped by a tsunami?" Ada asked. And all at once, everyone was talking animatedly about it. Apparently it was a big deal.

Jon felt his heart pump at a higher rate—*where? Where is this?* He wished he had his satellite phone on him, but it was still in his backpack somewhere in the back of Mary's truck. And it was dead. He searched the room for Arrow, Saga, or Hazel, but not seeing any of them, he spotted a woman standing off to the side, quietly observing the scene. He walked over to her and tapped her shoulder.

"Excuse me, miss—" he started, but as the woman turned around, he staggered back. It was Detective Roberta Hand, dressed in a nice wool dress and rubber boots, blending perfectly into the crowd of Wilkins townswomen.

"I thought you would be here," she said pleasantly. Jon felt sick. "Looks like Wilkins Initiatives to Nourish God's Service committee will be adopting your tribe this year, Mr. Uolan. Isn't that nice?"

Stumbling, Jon ran up the stairs and out the back door of the church. It was pouring rain, and he stopped—there was nowhere to run.

"Ay-Tal?" he prayed. "What am I supposed to do? What do you want of me? How am I to help?" He shook his head and sat on the wet wooden steps. "Tell me what to do...please."

• • •

He didn't know how long he sat there. He felt complete torpor swallow him whole, leaving him unable even to stand. Aguguq had always been a distant god, the god of the universe, the god of everything and thus nothing in particular. It was comforting to know that Aguguq was there, but such a god was incidental to one's life. Aguguq focused on the large picture; one person's life was just not very significant in the grand scheme of the universe. But Ay-Tal was always very present, tangible, real, approachable. She was there, *really there*, for all of Jon's life. And she had been with his people as far back as their tribal memories went. And given what he had heard from Mary, she had been with the ancestors of his people even before that, perhaps even before they were one people, in the time before the tribe. Ay-Tal was in the now, but she was also deep time. She was the continuity of identity, a direct connection from the past to the present and into the future. She was a god who was somehow more and less than Aguguq. And Jon needed her to answer him...to find him and to help him figure out what he was supposed to do. Ay-Tal needed to answer his prayers.

"Jon?" He heard Saga's voice piercing the veil of the torrential ice-threaded rain. "Are you all right?"

Jon forced himself to focus on the girl's voice, then on her face, and then on answering her. "I don't know what to do," he said honestly. And he knew it was an unfair burden to place on the girl—Saga was just a child. It was his job to keep her safe. It was wrong to put the weight of his indecision on her young shoulders.

"You will," she told him. "Come on. It's wet out here. It won't help if you get sick."

She pulled, and he stood up, allowing her to lead him back into the church basement. Was she the answer to his prayers?

● ● ●

"Oh, look who is back," Ada announced in a loud voice when Saga walked in with Jon. If she had said, "Look what's the cat's dragged in," she would have used the same tone. "Everyone, this is Mr. Jon...what's his last name again?" she asked Saga in a loud stage whisper.

"Mr. Uolan," Saga answered clearly enough for the whole basement room to hear. "He is a member of the Omuktal tribe—the First Nation people who suffered the devastation from the Alaskan earthquake and the following tsunami."

"Ada! How did you managed to get a tribe member to work with us so fast?" someone exclaimed in surprise. There was a loud murmur of excitement as the women of the WINGS committee pushed forward and surrounded Jon and Saga.

Ada shoved people aside and stepped into a tight circle

with Jon and Saga as its center. "Ladies, ladies. As you can see, Mr.—" She looked over at Saga again.

"Mr. Jon Uolan," Saga repeated.

"Mr. Jon." Ada simply gave up on Jon's last name. "Jon came here to help us organize relief efforts for his village. He will be making a presentation soon. But in the meantime, I think we should give him something dry to wear." She brushed away the water that dripped on her neatly pressed jacket, making a face.

More excitement and conversation. As Jon looked around and tried to contain his initial shock, someone swept in with a sewing tape and quickly measured his height, shoulder width, and inseam. The last made Jon jump, and the women around him laughed. His size was determined, and a stack of fresh-washed clothing appeared as by magic in front of him.

"You can change in the laundry room," Ada informed him. "I believe you know where it is?"

"I'll take him, Aunt Ada," Saga said and pulled Jon out of the tight gaggle of churchwomen.

● ● ●

"What was that?" Jon asked when he was back inside the warm, detergent-scented room.

"Aunt Ada at work," Saga said sarcastically. "Change and come out. She's not done with you yet." It sounded like a threat.

Jon changed into a dry lumberjack shirt—gray-green this time—and a pair of jeans, which fit surprisingly well. He put aside things he didn't think he needed and stuffed his puffy black vest back into the dryer, together with his other wet clothing. He wanted a few moments to think. What he really needed was a phone. Were his people okay? His family?

He needed to know ASAP.

There was a knock on the laundry room door, and Jon answered "come in" out of habit. He regretted it as soon as the woman detective walked in and closed the door behind her, trapping Jon in a small room with her.

"I bet you want this?" She waved her cell phone in front of him.

Jon considered it and nodded—there was nothing he was going to tell his grandfather that this woman didn't already know. She handed him her phone, and he frantically dialed his home number. Cellphones were ubiquitous in his town, but landlines were more reliable. During an ice storm, antennas often collapsed, cutting all cellular communications. But a buried landline? It survived. That and the radio—his tribe still used that old technology as well.

When the landline didn't work, Jon tried his grandfather's cell, then his father's, and then his uncle's.

"Damn," he cursed under his breath.

"In a church? Really?" Roberta remarked sarcastically.

"How big was the quake?" he asked.

"Seven point five."

"Damn." Jon's heart sank, and he felt rather ill.

She tsk-tsked him again.

"When?"

"Two days ago. It was all over the news."

"I didn't know..."

"Now you do. What are you going to do about it?"

Jon dialed again and again got nothing. "The lines and the tower must be down," he said. "Do you know how bad it was? Did anyone...did anyone die?" He heard himself saying the words as Roberta took back her phone.

"One dead. But there might be more casualties, they just don't know yet. Too soon," Roberta said. Her voice was kind, dropping all sarcasm. "Some people were hurt—broken bones and such—and were airlifted to Providence Alaska Medical Center." It was the largest trauma center in Alaska.

"Buildings collapsed?" Jon asked.

"A few." She wasn't volunteering information.

"I need to see what's going on," he said, regretting giving her phone back. It sounded like begging. "And the tsunami?"

"Just a foot. It was unpleasant, but no loss of life," Roberta assured him. "Your village did suffer catastrophic devastation. Most of the structures are red-tagged, and people were evacuated. Authorities think they got everyone, but as you know, tribal information is not well integrated with the US government databases, so..."

"That's horrible." *Who died?* Jon was scared to find out. And he couldn't even imagine how it would be without a place to call home, without the stable community of his tribe. He felt adrift. Lost. It was the start of winter. There wouldn't even be an attempt to rebuild anytime before spring... summer. No one would be able to assess at the full extent of the damage before then. And in the summer? There would be people who wouldn't come back. There was always some attrition of the youngest members of the tribe—no work, the conservative lifestyle; those were just not the life choices that his generation was comfortable with. A lot of his childhood friends had left already. Left for good. And now their families would probably join them in Anchorage or some other large population center. Who would want to live in a shelter when there was family to go to? And after a few months of dislocation, people would find jobs, start relationships; many would choose to stay and rebuild a new life in a city rather than rebuilding the village. All that work of protecting their land would be wiped out in just a few short months. *In just one stroke by a natural disaster, all is gone.* He needed to get back there to help his dad and grandfather organize his people. Help them believe.

It was as if Roberta could read his mind. "You can leave today and be there in just a few days." Jon just nodded. "What would keep you here?" she asked.

Yes, what? Ay-Tal, came the answer. Ay-Tal wanted him to stay here and help these people instead. Jon felt his heart tear in two.

● ● ●

When Jon rejoined the church ladies, Ada already had them organized into teams assigned to various projects on a disaster relief effort for his tribe. One group was assembling packing boxes. Another was sorting things on long tables: children's toys and clothing, adult toiletries and clothing arranged by sex and size, school supplies and old books, homemade preserves and crafts, and a dozen other items Jon couldn't even name. It was obvious these ladies had done this before and were good at it. For all the petty power struggles and local church politics, these people really did do good, and Jon was very impressed and humbled.

"There you are." Ada called him over. Jon made his way to her table, and Roberta followed. "Given the news reports, it sounds like your people will need everything."

Jon just nodded mutely. He didn't really know, but he assumed the worse. *Who was the person who died? Is it known? Do I want to know?*

"There was a crisis center number provided by the woman on TV," Ada continued. "We generally want a bit more information than that, if you know what I mean." Ada stopped everything she was doing and drilled into Jon with her eyes. "Saga said your little boy was already with your family? Is that true?"

"Al left five days ago, so he would have been there by then," Saga helpfully suggested. She too was looking at Jon, willing him to listen to her. "The quake happened Thanksgiving night, so it's obvious that Al would have been with his grandparents by then. Right, Jon?"

Jon looked at Saga. He felt like he was moving through molasses. Nothing was making sense. In his mind, his town still existed just as he had left it. *Nothing changed. Nothing.*

"Jon? Jon? Are you all right?"

"Of course he is not all right, Aunt Ada," Saga said. "For all he knows, his son might be dead."

"Saga! Don't say things like that." Ada whirled on the girl. "I'm sure that charming little boy is just fine."

"Do tell us, Mr. Uolan, what happened to your son?" asked Roberta Hand.

"Jon? Why don't we go over to Hazel?" Saga tried to help. "She's doing research on Aunt Ada's computer over there. You can see the news for yourself." Saga pulled on Jon's arm, and he followed her like a zombie.

"That girl has turned so bossy all of a sudden," Ada said from behind them. "You'd think one night in prison and she gets all tough and such..." Jon didn't hear the rest.

Hazel was looking through the various news sites and donation portals on the computer on Ada's desk. There were aerial drone images of the devastation: buildings toppled and then flooded; clothing, toys, books, and kitchenware floating randomly, some already frozen into strange ice sculptures; cars, trucks, and fishing boats upside down and sideways, strewn randomly on buckled roadways. How did anyone survive this? Hazel stopped what she was doing and let Jon sit in her chair to browse the reports himself.

"Did you learn who died?" Saga asked Hazel in a low tone.

Jon didn't hear the answer; he dove into the news. It was far worse than he imagined...and far better. In addition to one known fatality, only three people had ended up in the hospital, and with relatively minor injuries, according to the reports. Given the widespread destruction, it was a miracle more people weren't badly hurt or dead. Page after page, image after image, video after video...

Jon stopped when he heard the newscaster in Anchorage announcing the death of his grandfather. It wasn't how she put it; she talked of the years of service and dedication of the tribe's chief and elder, but in his head, Jon heard his grandfather's name over and over again. He also learned that his uncle and grandmother were two of the three people in the hospital—lacerations and severe bruising, broken ribs. Both were expected to make a full recovery; but Jon had a feeling that his grandmother wouldn't make it out of the hospital alive. After sixty-five years of marriage, she would see it as her duty to die with her life partner. It was crazy, but Jon knew her, and she would insist on dying. Just like that—she would make the decision and go through with it.

"Aguguq take me..."

"Were those your relatives?" Roberta asked. Her voice was sympathetic. How could it not be? It would take a permafrost heart not to show some emotion at such a catastrophe.

"My grandfather died." Jon heard himself say. "My uncle and grandmother are in the hospital. Sounds like my uncle tried to help pull my grandfather to safety. Another neighbor is hurt."

"And your boy?" Ada asked. Saga shook her head to stop her questioning. "Would you like a cup of tea, Jon?" Ada asked instead and without waiting for an answer went to make some, giving Jon some room to grieve.

"I can make some phone calls to the local authorities,

Mr. Uolan," offered Beth, Hazel's mom. "They might know something."

"The news people didn't mention a hurt child," Saga pointed out. "They would have."

Jon didn't know what to say. He was too numb. Fortunately, everyone, even Roberta, decided to give him some space. There was a low murmur across the church basement room as the information about Jon's family was passed on from person to person. People looked in his direction but quickly lowered their gazes. It was obscene to observe a man in so much pain. Only Saga stayed by his side.

"What are you going to do, Jon?" she whispered for only him to hear.

"I don't know," he said just as quietly.

"Was it okay to make them think Al wasn't dead?"

Jon just shook his head. He didn't know.

"Perhaps if we said he was dead it would explain...well, you know."

"Do you know where Ay-Tal is?" he asked.

"The new Mason?"

"Yeah. Do you know where he is? Did he come back here with you?"

"No. I haven't seen him since I've returned," Saga said. "I thought you would know."

"And Mary?"

"I saw her briefly dropping off your boots at the county jail that night. But that's all. Burt and Ada came and got me after that. I was grounded in my room with no Internet access of any kind until after Thanksgiving. I didn't know about your people until Arrow said something at the dinner table. And I haven't had much private time with him either."

She was apologizing to Jon for not knowing enough, and he felt bad about that. When they first met only days ago,

Saga hardly strung two words together. Now she sounded more confident, more in charge. She had changed.

"It's okay, Saga. We'll figure it out." It was his job to help her. It was his job to know things.

"So you won't be leaving?" Jon could hear fear beneath the facade of bravado.

"No."

"Even to help your own people?"

"I will help them from here." He could practically feel the tension lift from Saga's body. He couldn't leave her. He wouldn't.

Chapter Eight: Bed & Breakfast

Jon Uolan

Unlike Roberta Hand, Jon didn't have a car and couldn't stay in a motel outside of town. And there were no accommodations for travelers in Wilkins. There used to be a bed and breakfast run by Mrs. Nelson, but after her husband died, she decided not to continue. Business had been bad anyway. She simply closed off that part of her house and turned off the heat. But now she generously offered to rent a room to Jon for a very low cost…really just the cost of heating, electricity, water, cleaning, and perhaps a bit of wear and tear.

"You'll be able to walk to church in just thirty minutes, easy," she was telling him. "And I will even throw in a breakfast now and then." She smiled pleasantly, pleased by her own generosity.

Jon really didn't have too many choices. He could probably ask to sleep on one of the cots set up as a homeless shelter down in the church's basement, but he decided it was too fraught.

"Thank you for your kind offer, Mrs. Nelson," he said, accepting the invitation. Hopefully he had enough money to stay for as long as was necessary to help these people...and his own.

"Good, good. Please call me Nora. Now, Jon—you don't mind me calling you Jon? Good, good. Now, we need to get some clean bedding for you. I'm sure we will find something here." She was all business now. "I'm afraid that after so many years of disuse, mine might be all mildewy." She hastened away to a corner of the basement that presumably contained the supplies she needed. A small group of women accompanied her like a pack of squawking chickens rushing after a meal. Jon felt that he might live to regret his decision to stay with Mrs. Nelson.

For the moment, he was left alone to read on Ada's computer and gather as much information as he could about what had happened to his people.

* * *

Nora returned after about an hour. Behind her, a dozen women and girls were dragging huge boxes full of pillows, sheets, blankets, towels, and some basic household cleaning items. It seemed like she not only managed to gather endless supplies for her bed and breakfast, Nora also put together a brigade of helpers to get her stale premises in order for Jon to move in.

"Oh, if this goes well, perhaps I will need to start up again," she said with a note of trepidation. "There is a need for hospitality in this town. Roberta? Roberta!" she called into the crowd behind her.

Jon looked and saw the woman detective smiling at him from across the room.

"Did you know that Ms. Hand also needed a place to stay?" Nora asked Jon. "When things happen, they always happen all at once."

Jon just stared at her and then back at Roberta. So he was going to live with the detective who was assigned to shadow him. *How convenient.* He wondered, not for the first time, where Ay-Tal was staying. It wasn't possible that a god was living out there in the rough. Or was it? When Ay-Tal was a child, he had the energy level of a child. Now, as an adolescent boy, he would presumably have the physical stamina of that body. The Mason kid looked strong, but not in a way that would let him sleep in the woods in the icy rain. *So where is he?*

"Shall we go and set up, Jon?" Nora tugged on his shoulder. "I'm sure one of these ladies would be happy to give you a ride. Dorothy volunteered to drive people in her minivan. There should be plenty of room for everything and everybody. Do you have anything? Any other clothing? A bag?" She seemed very anxious for Jon to have luggage. He didn't have anything other than the stuff spinning in a dryer.

"Give me a second," Jon said, smiling. He went to find Saga or Arrow before leaving.

Saga was hanging out by the laundry door. She smiled at him when he caught her gaze.

"I folded your clothing," she said and nodded over to a small stack on top of the white plastic folding table in the laundry room, clearly placed there for just that purpose. "You should grab a few more things, if you are really staying."

"I'm really staying," Jon said.

"Good," she exhaled.

"Thank you for all your help, Saga. If you need anything before I see you again, I'll be—"

"At Nora's B&B," Saga said with a crooked smile. "Good luck with that."

Jon just shrugged; he didn't really have a choice. Not

really.

"And I'm really sorry about your family," the girl said, her whole demeanor changing to sympathy and compassion. She shook her head and then stepped up and hugged him, quickly disengaging and lowering her eyes. Jon couldn't help liking the girl. After all that happened to her, she was still able to be funny and caring. Others would have just turned off. Jon had seen people beaten by life give up all hope. Saga hadn't done that...*yet*.

"Thank you, Saga. I'll see you soon, okay?"

"Okay."

Jon grabbed his stuff, such as it was, and left to join the church ladies on the cleaning mission to Nora's.

● ● ●

He rode in Nora's station wagon with at least seven other people. It was more people than the number of allotted seatbelts, but he was told that since Nora's place was just around the corner, it was perfectly safe. There were two other cars caravanning with them, including Roberta's. The detective was coming to look over the place before getting her stuff from the motel in Eau Claire and moving in. It seemed a sensible precaution.

One thing about so many people in a car jammed in together like sardines was that conversation was all but impossible. It saved Jon from answering the unending questions about his tribe, and his people, and their way of life, and on and on. Given the tragedy, he really didn't feel like discussing any of that, but it was all these ladies wanted to talk about. It felt like their price for giving aid and support, and Jon didn't feel like he could deny them. Even so, any respite, even one as short as riding in the car for a few blocks, was welcome.

"Here we are," announced Nora with flair, pulling into a circular driveway.

Jon spilled out of the car in front of what he could only describe as a house that had another house attached to it. The original one—where Jon assumed Nora lived—was a typical two-story dwelling with two big windows on either side of a white porch and two white-trimmed windows above. The siding had been painted robin's-egg blue some time ago, and Jon could see some of the paint peeling away, revealing Wilkins's standard off-white color underneath. It was a modest, unassuming home. The second house, built into the side of the first, was painted the same fancy color and was clearly a newer construction. It was also about one and half times bigger—three windows above, three below. The house-plus-a-house had two chimneys and one long, aged-looking black-shingled roof. The front yard featured a giant American flag, waving in a breeze, just like every other house in Wilkins, and a collection of holiday lawn tchotchkes. It all looked old and tired.

All three cars in the caravan parked in the driveway, and the ladies flowed out carrying cleaning supplies and extra linens appropriated by Nora for her "do-good" project. Jon grabbed a big plastic bin with unknown contents and carried it up onto the porch.

Inside, the house was decorated in a style popular several decades ago. Jon doubted that anything had been added or replaced since its original placement. But Nora was beaming; she obviously was very proud to have so many of the church's WINGS ladies in her home. She quickly waved everyone in and shut the door to keep the warmth in. She then ushered the group through a large kitchen and into a spacious sitting room—part of the newer construction—that clearly used to serve as a breakfast area for her B&B guests. Small, wheeled, square tables were discreetly tucked in the four corners of the room, and chairs, sofas, and a few armchairs were strategically placed in little groupings. This portion of the house was obviously furnished more recently, but was designed to look like it hadn't changed from some previous century. There were more doilies on tables, armrests, shelves, and pillows than Jon had ever seen in his entire life. It was also as cold as an icebox in there. But there was a nice fireplace, currently unlit, set into the wall separating the two houses.

"Beautiful place, Nora," said one of the women; Dorothy, if Jon remembered right. "I had no idea it was so luscious." It was a strange word to describe a room so full of clashing flower and tartan patterns, in Jon's opinion. But who asked him?

"Can we start the fireplace, Mrs. Nelson?" one of the teenage girls asked. She refused to take off her jacket and hugged herself for warmth.

"Oh no, honey," Nora said. "That thing hasn't been lit in years. We wouldn't want to accidentally set the house on fire."

"Can we at least turn the heat on?" the girl whined.

Nora huffed, said something under her breath, and then declared that with so many people, the house would heat up in no time. And then she demonstrably went to close the weatherproof door separating her warm kitchen from the bed and breakfast addition.

"It will be fun," Roberta ribbed Jon. He was startled—it seemed way too familiar a gesture for a detective hunting her prey.

"It's only for a little while," he managed to say.

"You don't say? And here I thought you were staying..." Roberta smiled at him and followed Nora upstairs to inspect the condition of the guest bedrooms.

Jon was handed a vacuum cleaner and went to work sucking in years of dust. On the bright side, with the noise the machine made, no one tried to talk to him.

● ● ●

When everyone finally left, Nora took Roberta and Jon into her kitchen for some tea. While the kettle heated, she turned on music and from the speakers built into the ceiling poured an obviously amateur recording of old French jazz.

"That's lovely," said Roberta. Jon noticed that the detective was mouthing the words to the song. She knew French? "How did you get this music?" she asked.

"Oh, that." Nora waved her off but was obviously very pleased to be asked. "It's something my grandpa recorded at the end of World War Two. He was stationed overseas as a reporter and... Well, he had the equipment and traveled the whole country recording cafe music."

"Wow, that's interesting," said Roberta. Jon didn't know if she was in fact interested or if it was just her way of keeping people talking—a professional snooping strategy, if you will.

"Oh, Mom and I had these recordings for years and years. Well, I was too young to really appreciate them, but Mom grew up with them." Nora flitted around her kitchen gathering milk, sugar, and little homemade silk tea bags. She already placed the cups and the rest on the counter for Jon, Roberta, and herself. It looked very professional. Jon could see that she did in fact have some experience running a place that served food to guests.

"And so one day..." she continued, telling a story to a fresh audience that she had clearly told many times. "My late husband was watching a podcast, and they were discussing lost music treasures. And so he just responded to them. He was brave like that," she said confidentially, and Jon and Roberta nodded. "And they asked him to play some, right over our computer microphone. And the people on the show got so excited. And so the next week, we had these people show up, asking if they could buy the rights to our music."

"Really?" Roberta asked.

"Well, I was all hesitant, but my Norm just said yes. Just like that." She snapped her fingers to demonstrate her husband's decisiveness and poured hot tea into everyone's cup. "And that's how we got the money to build the addition and to start our bed and breakfast business."

"They paid that much?" asked Jon. He had no idea that music could be translated into buildings or other tangibles.

"Oh, they gave us plenty," Nora said, waving sugar and milk in front of his face. He politely declined both. Roberta, on the other hand, helped herself to plenty of each. "For years, we didn't even need to have any guests, and we could still make ends meet. But then Norm passed on, and... Well, here we are." She forced a smile and settled down to her own sweet, heavily creamed tea. "Cookies?"

"No, thank you, Nora. But it is so lovely of you to offer," Roberta said.

"But of course, of course. I used to bake my own, but this being all sudden and all." She shrugged at the package of supermarket cookies.

"These are very good," Jon said, even as he hadn't touched any.

"When tragedy strikes..." Nora started but didn't finish, just looked at Jon with a face tuned to compassion and understanding. "Unfortunately, Jon, I should inform you in my capacity as a federal official of the United States Postal Service that your package probably didn't make it to its destination in time." Jon sat up. "I'm sorry about that. But while 'neither rain nor snow' and such are true, earthquakes and tsunamis do make postal deliveries difficult."

"What will happen to my package?" Jon asked. He saw how intently Roberta was paying attention.

"I assume it will be stored at some central postal location, in Anchorage, I suppose. And if someone doesn't claim it, it would be returned back to the sender. That would be you, Jon. And isn't it convenient that you just happen to be staying with Wilkins's postmaster?"

"Very," said Roberta.

● ● ●

Jon's bed was comfortable enough, but it smelled badly of mildew. *It would be good to get a dehumidifier,* he thought. He had lots of practical thoughts like that as he lay awake through the night in Nora's B&B. By daybreak, he'd have been back in town for a full day, and there was still no sign of Ay-Tal...Mason. Or Mary. *Where are they? Are they together?* He needed a safe computer to communicate back home. He was sure that the drop email was still functional. People didn't just give up on their gods like that. With his package stranded in the U.S. postal system, his tribe would be waiting for a word, worrying over his silence and the news coverage of murder on the train. And Jon was desperate for some information from home. He felt so alone.

Finally, giving up on sleep, Jon got dressed and walked out of his room. Upstairs, there were four guest rooms and two large bathrooms. He and Roberta occupied the two street-facing bedrooms, the only ones that were cleaned so far, although Jon planned on making the other bedrooms of Nora's B&B fit for occupation. It was the least he could do...

and he had the time. He walked quietly down the corridor, trying not to creak the disused floorboards and accidentally wake Roberta, and descended to the first floor.

Downstairs, there were four doors leading out of the sitting room: one to Nora's residence, through the kitchen; one to the small washroom; one to the hallway leading out to the backyard and a small guest parking lot; and one more. Jon tried Nora's kitchen door first. It was locked from the other side. He immediately tried the door to the backyard. It had a standard bolt that could be opened from the inside, so he could go out, if he wanted. He felt better learning that he wasn't a prisoner here, although he could easily have climbed out of his bedroom window if need be. He went to the last door he hadn't explored. It wasn't locked and led to a small office that had been converted into a sewing room. Several sewing machines lined the walls. It seemed to Jon that no one had used this room for a very long time.

He rooted around the desk that had been pushed over to the side and in one of the drawers found an old laptop and Norm Nelson's business cards naming Norm the manager of Nora's B&B. *Bingo!* Jon had the impression that Norm had died at least a decade ago, so his computer equipment would be at least that old. He plugged it in and waited for the charge to reach usable levels. It took a long time...or at least it felt like it did. Jon stood and watched the denuded trees in the overgrown backyard through the window. The gray, predawn scenery matched his mood.

Before the boot-up sequence was completed, Jon pressed several command keys at the same time to interrupt the loading of the regular operating system. He wasn't a hacker or anything, but this he was taught by Ay-Tal herself, just as he was instructed on the proper use of the secret email drop. Moments later, he was in an admin mode and managed to connect to Nora's Internet connection. A few minutes more and he was writing a brief report to the tribal elders of what happened to him and Ay-Tal, asking for instructions on what he should do next.

When done, Jon turned everything off, returned Norm's computer to the desk's drawer, and tiptoed out of the office.

• • •

"Coffee?" Roberta's voice woke Jon. Despite—or perhaps because of his inability to fall asleep all night—Jon had passed out in one of the chairs of Nora's B&B sitting room.

"Yes?" he said and stretched out his limbs; the crackles and pops were easily heard in the hush of an early morning. "What time is it?" he asked.

"Six. Not too early for you, is it?" she asked.

"No. Not usually. Nora?"

"She is up and making us coffee. Sees it as her duty as a B&B hostess—it's a bed *and* breakfast, you see," she said with a smile.

"I see. We should tell her that she doesn't need to do that—"

"Speak for yourself. If you don't want coffee, fine. But I'm good with getting up to a ready pot," Roberta interrupted. "I live alone, and, if I don't make coffee, it doesn't magically get made by a coffee fairy."

"Oh." Jon didn't really know how to talk to this woman. She was nice and friendly...and she was looking for evidence to lock him away for murder. It was a fiendish combination.

"I bet your mom made you coffee every morning," she said and sat in a chair across from him. "You still live with your folks, right?"

"My people don't tend to go off on their own until they

are ready to start their own families. Otherwise, it's a waste of resources." Jon felt particularly defensive for some reason.

"Of course. Your people do things differently." She smirked.

There was something about how she said it, but Jon couldn't catch it. "It's not like that," he said.

"How is it?"

"Well, we take taking care of each other as a great responsibility. And... Never mind." He realized that Roberta was just trying to get him talking. And he didn't really want to do that, especially with her. "And it was my grandfather," he added, despite himself.

"What?"

"The coffee. My grandfather made it for everybody."

"Hmm." Roberta stood up and gave him a searching look before going into the kitchen. Jon could hear Nora in there humming some old tune that he didn't recognize. He decided that he liked it.

● ● ●

After taking a quick cold shower, Jon joined the women in the kitchen. Nora seemed particularly happy to have guests.

"This is the part I've missed the most," she was saying to Roberta. "When you have guests, it's like getting to live another's life for just a little bit. It's almost voyeuristic."

"Strangers sharing breakfast," Roberta said. "I can see that."

"Exactly. Coffee?" Nora turned to Jon, and, before he even had a chance to answer, he had a large, steaming mug in his hands.

"Thank you," he said and joined them at the counter of the large kitchen island.

"You know, Norm and I got those rolling tables to serve our guests breakfast over in the sitting room there, but everyone always ended up here, around our kitchen island." She pushed cream and sugar Jon's way.

"Life is like that," Roberta agreed. "You plan one way, and things work out differently." Jon couldn't agree more. "So, can we have the keys to the front door?" Roberta asked.

"Oh, that." Nora seemed uncomfortable.

"Well, we need to come and go, even when you are not around," Roberta said.

"You will," Nora agreed and still hesitated. "I will need to go and open the post office in a few moments. It is really just up the street, walking distance." Roberta didn't say anything. "You could just—"

"Nora, I'm a cop. If you can't trust me..."

"Oh, of course, of course," the woman said. She opened a drawer and pulled out a thick ring of keys, carefully separating the keys into two sets but giving both sets to Roberta. "Here you go. This one is for the side door that opens into the garden. And these are for each of your rooms. I will have to lock the door dividing the private and guest residences, you know. It's just what Norm and I did. Always."

"That's fine," Roberta said and pocketed all the keys.

Jon waited, but when Roberta didn't hand over a set of keys to him, he said, "I will need a set too, please." There were a few moments as Nora's face reflected a host of mixed emotions, but then she nodded to Roberta who gave a set of keys to Jon.

"I guess that makes sense," she said. "It's just back when we ran the B&B, one of us just always used to be around. Most guests never needed keys because Norm and I were here."

"But now you are the postmaster for the whole town," Jon reminded her.

"Yeah. Things change." Nora visibly forced herself to smile at her guests. "Just make sure to lock the outside door. I know we are a small town, but one never knows in this day and age."

"We'll make sure to," Jon promised.

"Well, I guess it's all good," Nora said, her lips remained stretched into a very uncertain smile. She glanced at the clock. "I really do have to leave now..."

Jon continued to sit and drink his coffee. Nora stared at him pleadingly.

"Come on, Jon," Roberta said and pulled on his sleeve.

They left the kitchen, and Nora locked the door separating her "private residence" from the sitting room with a loud click. Roberta and Jon kept their cups.

"So I guess no refills?" Roberta smiled. She downed her coffee and placed the empty mug on one of the rolling tables. "So what are your plans for the day, Mr. Uolan?" She looked at Jon. Her gaze was steady and a bit sarcastic.

"I guess I will go back to the church and help with the relief effort," he said. He wanted to check if there was an answer from the tribe waiting for him at the email drop, but he couldn't do that with Roberta snooping around.

"Good idea," she said. "I'll go and grab my jacket. Need a lift?"

"Why?" Jon stuttered out. "I mean why do you want to help? It's not your people, not your problem."

"These people are Americans? Humans? They need help?" Jon nodded.

"The local church and the people of this small town are willing to do what they can. I guess so can I."

"But don't you need to work or something?"

She smiled widely. "Who says that I won't be working?" And with that, she ran lightly upstairs. Before he even knew how to handle or even process what she said, Jon found himself in the passenger seat of Roberta's car on the way to the church.

●　●　●

"Breakfast first," said Roberta and pulled into the same small shopping center where Nora worked. "I saw a coffee shop here earlier."

Jon considered just walking to the church from there, but he too was hungry, and making important decisions on empty stomach was not advisable. He followed Roberta into a tiny, two-table coffee house. They served baked goods and hot dogs with a side of coffee or soda. It wasn't much, but then it wasn't one of those fast-food chains either. From the selection of baked goods, Jon guessed it was all homemade. And even the hotdogs were knockwursts—a thicker, spicier, and fancier version of regular sausages.

"What's your specialty?" Roberta asked the young woman manning the counter.

"Good morning!" the woman said brightly, and Roberta and Jon replied in unison. "Well, all of our jams are our middle school home-ec winning entries from our local county fair. So they are all the best. We have been rated number one jam-makers for twenty-three years in a row."

"You don't say," Roberta said, and the young woman beamed with pride. She looked really young. Jon guessed about eighteen, fresh out of high school, if that.

"We teach our girls and boys skills to last a lifetime," she said. It was a well-practiced phrase...like so many others Jon heard while in Wilkins.

"And your favorite?" Roberta asked.

"I like chokecherry preserves; it's a more complex taste."

"I've never heard of chokecherries," said Jon.

"Wild cherries?" the girl asked. "Really? We are taught to collect them. You have to be careful. Some look like cherries but in fact are not. If it's bitter, spit it out—bitter berries are poisonous. That's what our Reverend Paul always tells us."

"Thank you for tip," Jon said.

"Native Americans collected wild cherries to make trail mixes," she added. Jon wasn't sure if she was being demonstrative of her knowledge of the local flora or if it was a commentary on his appearance. "So I've heard about you," she said, looking at Jon. "You are from that tribe that got wiped out." So it was the latter.

"Not wiped out," Roberta corrected her.

"The tsunami—"

"Thank you, dear," Roberta interrupted her again. "We will take that jam with some wheat toast. And two coffees, please."

"Coming right up," the girl sang out and rushed to make their breakfast.

Roberta pulled out a chair at the table as far away from the counter as possible and sat down, watching Jon all the way.

"Thank you," he said.

"The girl just doesn't know. She didn't mean anything..."

"I know."

"I'm sorry about your grandfather. And the rest of your people. Sometimes life just takes a hard turn when we least expect it."

It was a nice thing to say, Jon knew. He just didn't really want to talk about it, especially with Roberta.

"So what are you going to do?" Roberta pressed. "Are you going to return home?"

"I must," he said. "It's my job to return...eventually."

"Sometimes there's not much to return to," Roberta said quietly. "Yet we still do." She stared out of the window. A light rain started to fall again. It was gray and sad, as only a fall morning could get sometimes.

"What do you want from me?" Jon asked. "What do you *really* want? I didn't kill anyone. I might not be able to prove it, but I didn't. There won't be any evidence to the fact. There are no buried bodies..."

Just then, the door slammed open and close, and Nora rushed in with Jon's package.

"I knew I recognized your car," she said excitedly to Roberta. "Here you go." She handed the package to Jon. "Mike arrived extra early today. And as I predicted, they couldn't deliver it." Jon took the package with all of Ay-Tal's legal papers and IDs. "You insisted on sending it certified mail, and there just wasn't anyone to sign for it," Nora finished breathlessly.

Roberta looked at the package and then at Jon. Something about her demeanor made Nora make excuses to run back to the post office next door right away.

"You were saying?" said Roberta to Jon.

● ● ●

After eating the toast and jam in almost complete silence, Jon insisted on walking the package back to his room at Nora's B&B. Roberta drove slowly alongside him as he walked. It was stupid, but he didn't want to sit next to her, even as the rain soaked him through again.

Back in his room, he looked around for somewhere to hide the package. The room had a queen-size bed, a small side table with a drawer and a bible placed carefully inside, a virtually empty chest of drawers, and an easy chair with a white doily over the top. Concealing the package under the bed or mattress seemed stupid. There weren't any hiding places in the room that weren't obvious to a seasoned detective. After a few minutes of looking around, Jon simply placed the package unopened on the side table and locked the room. Roberta would have to break into his room and then rip the package open to see what was inside. According to the TV shows he had watched, she would need a warrant to do that. And then what would she find? Ay-Tal's papers and IDs. But she already knew that he had been traveling with Ms. Blue. How much more incriminating was it to have these papers? Once again, he wished that Ay-Tal...Mason would make his presence known. If nothing else, he could advise Jon on the law.

When he finally came outside, he saw Roberta waiting. She opened the car door for him. He rushed and climbed inside. There was a large towel thrown over the front passenger seat.

"Thanks," he said.

They drove to the church in silence. What was there to say?

Chapter Nine: Those That Haunt Us

Jon Uolan

Inside was the hustle and bustle of a well-oiled mercy sweatshop: pumpkin spice potpourri mixed with chemical cleaners and that sweet odor of many bodies that had stepped from the wet and cold into a hot room. The ladies were set up on rows of tables with sewing machines, furiously making something. There were stacks of packed boxes each labeled with different colored packing tape. On the wall, Jon saw a large board with an explanation of the color key codes. Next to that was a huge scheduler with tasks and outlined dates, again in different colors. And finally, there was an assignments board, where people could sign up for various jobs and list their available times for volunteering. It was all very official and efficacious.

Roberta whistled. "Very impressive," she said and walked over to Ada at the head table. Jon, the oldest male in the room, was left to drip on the stairs. It was his own fault for insisting on walking in the rain.

There was a careful click of an opened and closed door, and a fresh smell of rain and ice seeped into the church. "Do you want to use the dryer?" asked Saga behind his back. Jon turned and saw that the girl came here directly from school, her wet umbrella neatly folded and stowed into a plastic bag to avoid making a mess. She was still wearing her "disguise" outfit from a week ago...or at least the purple, puffy jacket and runners. Saga had also never reinserted any of her facial piercings and was now using some foundation to cover up the holes in her face. Jon hoped that for her sake those were only temporary and would close over with time without too much scarring.

"Hi, Saga," he said with a smile. "I guess I'd better." He was too wet to interact with people and "products." They walked through the WINGS "factory floor" and into the laundry room. All machines were running full blast.

"Don't worry," Saga said and took his wet vest and shirt and stuffed them into a spinning dryer load, leaving him in a damp t-shirt and wet jeans. "At this rate, you'll wear out all of the weatherproof coating of that vest thing of yours," she said. She put her backpack on the floor and slid down next to it, settling down to wait out the clothing.

Jon sat on the floor as well; he wanted to be at eye level with the girl. It all felt very familiar now. "How have you been?"

"Coping. That's what I do."

"And Burt?"

"With the big effort to send relief packages to your people, he got a few local papers and even a TV station to interview him as the mayor of Wilkins. He's happily entertained for now."

"That's good. And Arrow?"

"I tried telling him what happened...about Mason and Al and all," Saga said. "But he won't believe me. He is very sore that I left him like that."

"So he'd said."

"But you agreed with me—it was the right thing to do. In just a few months, Arrow could leave Wilkins for good. And I want him to. I want him to be free of here."

"That's what I told him," Jon said. "He didn't believe me either."

"He needs to see Mason," Saga said, and her eyes bored into Jon's. He couldn't hold her gaze for long. "So you don't know where Ay-Tal is either," she finally said. "I thought it was your job to protect him, to get him home safely and all that. You're failing your god."

"I know." The weight of failure was almost too much to bear.

"I tried praying to Ay-Tal—"

"It might be better to call him Mason now."

"Okay." Saga shrugged. "I prayed to Mason. But I'm not sure I'm doing it correctly. I've never prayed to a living god before."

"Well, it's easier when you can just talk to him directly, face to face," Jon said.

Saga smiled. "It is easier. I wish I could do that all the time. I like seeing the expressions on God's face. It gives me clues if I'm asking for too much."

Jon felt his heart break. "You've never asked for too much, Saga. All children deserve a childhood. You shouldn't even have to pray for that. It should be a given." He made himself calm down. Large displays of emotion were rarely the answer.

"I agree. But here we are." Saga was remarkably stoic given her situation. Jon admired her for that.

"I will take you with me to my people," he tried to reassure the girl nonetheless. But he was clearly failing her too.

"How? And where? And to whom exactly?" Jon recoiled; Saga's questions felt like slaps. "The people on TV are saying there is no one left in your village," the girl went on. "No one is likely to come back. There isn't a village to come back to. And it just doesn't make any sense to rebuild. Some scientist said that, with the global warming, it would have been a lost cause even if there were no earthquake and tsunami. The sea would have claimed it all. It was just a matter of time before your people left that place." She was right, yet Jon felt sick to his stomach when confronted with the truth so bluntly. Still, he tried at least to appear strong for this little girl; she needed him to be strong. "I think it's because your god was no longer there," Saga continued. "If Ay-Tal was there, this never would have happened."

Jon didn't know about that, but he didn't want to argue. "I need to find a computer that I can use privately," he said, moving away from discussing Ay-Tal's godly powers. *What do I know?*

After considering his request for a few moments, Saga said, "Mason had a computer."

"And?"

"It's still in his room. Aunt Ada never put his things away or anything. She just sealed her stepson's room, and that was that."

"Really? The police didn't go in and search his room? Didn't he die in a fire?"

"Yes. And as I can only assume you've heard a bunch of times now, this is a Wilkins's town. If a Wilkins doesn't want her house searched, her house doesn't get searched."

"But that's crazy. Didn't anyone do an investigation of Mason's death? He was a Wilkins too."

"Aunt Ada ruled his death an accident."

"And people let her?"

"And people let her."

"I see." Jon didn't understand how the law could let a young kid's death slide just because his mother didn't want to know what really happened. "So he had a computer in his room?" he asked as a change of subject. There were few topics that seemed safe to discuss right now.

"Has. It's still there."

"Are you sure?"

"Arrow and I used to spend a lot of time in Mason's room. We all used to climb the tree outside of his window to get in and out of the house without his parents' knowledge. It was fun."

"Huh."

"After Mason died, Arrow snuck into his room to try to figure out what really happened."

"Did he find anything?"

"He got scared and left after just a few minutes. But he said that it was left just like Mason left it. Even his dirty socks were still on the floor by the bed three months later. The door to his room was locked from the outside. I know because I tried to go in once, pretending that I left my textbook in there, and Aunt Ada yelled at me never to do that again. In the end, the school gave me a new textbook and I had to burn my old one in the woods." Saga spoke with passion but without fear, simply telling Jon what she knew. She seemed very different to Jon from the girl he first met just days ago. "Everyone in this town is scared of the Wilkinses," she continued. "The school, the teachers, the neighbors, the town hall, the sheriff. Everyone. That's how Burt can get away with everything. It's easy because no one ever questions anything he does. Ever!"

"I see."

"So do you want to go in?" she asked. "Half the town is at work or at school, the other is here making old shit into new—'upcycling,' as they say."

"Is that what all these church ladies are doing out there?" Jon asked, really just as a way of giving himself time to think over Saga's proposition.

"Most people don't like to get other people's used stuff. By crafting unique objects and improving the presentation, Aunt Ada and her mercy gang change the emotional value of their donations." It was another well-practiced line. This town was good at indoctrinating its citizens. "I read the research," Saga added. "People don't consider stuff used if it's been upcycled."

"I see. What do they make?"

"Mrs. Nelson is really good at making advent calendars from men's shirt pockets or jeans back pockets. She sews a quilt-like thing with twenty-five pockets and then adds little things like candy or Christmas toys or little toy animals she makes out of orphaned socks or even just office supplies in each one. It's very cute, actually."

"Did she make one for you?"

"Yes, and one for Arrow for our first Christmas in Wilkins. Mine is out of flannel shirts, his is made from denim. His is nicer, but I'm not complaining or anything."

"Of course not. I understand." He smiled at the girl.

"Mrs. Nelson filled mine with all kinds of hair clips and such."

"Sounds like she is a nice woman." Personally, Jon still reserved judgment. Staying with Nora Nelson had been a bit strange.

"Nice, but crazy, right?" Saga said. "Well, that describes a lot of people in this town, doesn't it?"

"Not all."

"Nice? Not all. So do you want to go break into Mason's room?"

Jon really needed to check the email drop. What was actually happening with his people? What could he do to help? He realized that this was really the first time he was cut off like this, making decisions that were wholly his own. It was strangely unwelcome.

Saga didn't interrupt his cogitating. After a few moments, Jon looked up and saw her waiting patiently for him to make a decision. She just let him have the time to reason out what he wanted to do. But as much as he needed to use that computer, he couldn't risk getting her into trouble, not more than she was in already.

"Show me where it is," he finally said. "I'll go in alone. You can keep an eye on people around here for me." He knew that, without an assignment, Saga would just follow and break into Mason's room with him, regardless of how much he protested. He could see it plainly on her face.

"You won't be able to get in without me," she said.

"Why not?"

"You have to wiggle the window frame just right."

"I can figure it out, Saga. It would be more helpful if you were my lookout back here."

"You will get into trouble," she argued. "It's my home...or at least I live there. You? You would be a burglar. Add that to the murder of Al and Ms. Blue—they will haul you away so fast!"

The door to the laundry room opened, and Roberta walked in. "I agree with Saga. Breaking and entering in addition to murder? Tell me more, Mr. Uolan."

Saga bit her hands, eyes huge. Jon felt like he was falling helplessly into a hole in the young fragile ice, and there was no bottom, just cold water all the way down...and he was drowning. *Aguguq help me...*

Roberta closed the door behind her. With the three of them and all of the laundry machines, it was claustrophobic— hot and humid, not enough air and not enough space.

"So please tell me why you are conspiring to break into

Mason Wilkins's room?" Roberta asked again. There was a touch of triumph in her voice, in the way she just stood there as Saga and Jon died inside.

"It's not what you think, I promise," Jon said. Saga was mute. The girl looked petrified; what little color she had in her face all drained away until she looked snow white. And he didn't even know how long Roberta had been listening at the door. *How much did this woman overhear?* "Saga was telling me about her friend who died," he said. Saga let out a small moan. *Poor kid.* Roberta just stared at him, giving him space to snag himself on the barbs of lies. *There are so many lies...* "Mason died," Jon started over; Roberta remained silent, expression inscrutable. "He was Ben Wilkins's only son. Ada's stepson." He watched Roberta's eyes, trying to guess how much she already knew. "He died in...in an accident."

"It was no accident!" Saga cried out. "Burt killed him!"

Roberta turned to consider Saga. She stared, unblinking, as if Saga was some alien species washed up on spring ice. It made Jon sick. He reached out and placed his hand on Saga's knee. It wasn't much, but it was a bit of comfort he could offer.

"Why do you think Burt Wilkins killed his only nephew?" Roberta asked.

"Because Mason was my friend, and I knew him well. He wasn't into starting fires, and he didn't want to kill himself. Mason was careful, thoughtful. He was good with computers, as good as Arrow is with his hands. Mason and Arrow were going to go Chippewa Valley Technical College together. Arrow would have gone for mechanical engineering or architecture or something and Mason for computer science."

"The community college in Eau Claire?" Roberta asked. She had pulled out a notebook and started taking notes.

"Saga, she's a cop," Jon said. "You don't have to talk to her." He squeezed the girl's knee hard. He wanted Saga to stop talking.

"She can talk if she wants to," Roberta said. "Saga, tell me why you think Burt killed Mason?"

"Saga, please," begged Jon. But he could see that the girl was going to tell Roberta everything. After holding it all in for so long, she couldn't help herself. *Telling Saga that Roberta is a cop is probably an incentive to talk and not a deterrent,* he realized.

"It was way before Jon and Al came here," Saga started. "We've only met them a week ago." The girl caught her breath, making a sound somewhere between a sob and a hiccup. Roberta just nodded for Saga to go on, positioning her body so that the girl couldn't really see Jon's face and vice versa, leaving his hand on her knee as the only bridge between them. Saga didn't even notice Roberta blocking her off like that; Jon did, but there was not enough room in this small laundry room to outmaneuver the detective.

"Do you know what happened to Al?" Roberta asked.

"Yes."

"Do you believe the little boy is all right?"

"Yes." There was no hesitation in Saga's voice. "Ay-Tal is just fine."

"Ay-Tal Blue? Do you know her too?"

"No... Well, yes. It really doesn't matter. They...she...he is just fine. I promise," Saga said. "But Mason...the old Mason is not."

"There's more than one?" Roberta was relentless.

Jon was losing his mind. There was no way to explain any of this. It was all so twisted and staggeringly unimaginable. Who would believe in god-who-walks-among-us without meeting him first? They would put him away for the murder of Ay-Tal Blue, and Al, and maybe even Mason...

"Mason Wilkins died twenty-five months and four days

ago," Saga said. "It was just two days after his sixteenth birthday." Her eyes were closed, and Jon was sure she could see Mason's face as clearly as if he was right here with them. *Aguguq, where is Ay-Tal?*

"I'm sorry, Saga. This boy clearly meant a lot to you," Roberta said. There was something in the woman's eyes that was familiar—recognition of the pain at a loss of a loved one? "Tell me what happened to him. I promise to help," she said. *Aguguq, she sounds so convincing.*

And Saga told. About three years ago, Ada and Ben Wilkins added a full kitchen to their nightclub down by the highway. There hadn't been a restaurant in Wilkins for decades. It was a good thing. Everyone was into it. Everyone but Burt, Ben's younger brother. Why? He was just released on parole that year and was living in the back room of the nightclub. A new kitchen meant no more free room. He argued and had temper tantrums. Saga was even present for one—he broke every TV in the place, just shattered them with his bare fists. Ben made his brother move out anyway. He said it was good for him. A few days later, Ben and his son went into the building to rewire everything and install new TVs. Mason was really good at all the tech stuff. Some time that evening, Ben went home, leaving Mason alone at the club. He was just gone for an hour. Saga and Arrow were doing homework back at the house. Ada said it was a good father-son bonding time and forbade Arrow to help with the installation at the club.

They smelled the smoke through the open window. They rushed out onto the street and saw the fire above the treetops. By the time they got to the club, the whole side of the building, the one with the new kitchen...where Mason was working... it was gone. Burt was standing outside the club, watching it burn. He told them that he could hear Mason's screams, but there was no way to get to him. Too much smoke. Too hot. When the fire was finally put out, they saw that the back door was barricaded by two unopened dishwasher boxes, delivered earlier in the day, apparently. Mason tried to get out that way and couldn't. He was trapped in the fire. Later, Burt moved into his brother's house.

Saga stopped. It was clear that she couldn't go on. Inside her head, she was reliving the tragedy. Her shoulders shook and tears streamed down her cheeks as she cried without making a sound.

"Sometimes, when I lie in bed at night, I think I can hear Mason's screams for help," she whispered.

Jon found that he could hardly breathe. "It was all about a place to sleep?" he asked.

"Burt punished his brother in the only way that would truly hurt him," Roberta said.

"You know about the case?" Jon asked.

"It was all over the papers, community posts." She shrugged. "It was big news around these parts."

"Why didn't you investigate back then?" Jon was so outraged by the authorities' indifference. *A kid died, for Aguguq's sake. How could they just let it go? How could they let Burt get away with murder?*

"I don't make the calls on what we investigate and what we don't," Roberta said.

"Not even after Ben died? Wasn't that suspicious?"

 Roberta just shrugged again.

"Well, are you going to do something now?" Jon asked.

"Well, it's my vacation," she said.

"It is?" Jon thought she had been following him in an official capacity, but perhaps not. Did it change anything?

"I'm free to do what I want with my free time," she continued. "So are we going to break into Mason's room?"

That was unexpected.

*   *   *

They drove to Ada's house in Roberta's car. It had stopped pouring, but the temperature had dropped; everything was covered in a layer of verglas. All of the Santas, elves, and wise men standing guard outside the houses had grown icicle beards. It was almost pretty.

They stopped right in front of Ada's house. It was just like every other house in Wilkins, perhaps a bit bigger and a bit older. It was as if it was the original and the rest of the community had just built clones of the Wilkins's home—off-white wood siding, a black-shingled roof, a wide porch, and holiday lights wrapped around everything. Just to the right side of the house, there was a large oak tree, easily a century old by the size of its limbs and the width of its bole. Some ruby-red leaves, now encased in ice, were still hanging from its tips. One of the broad branches extended just about to the top right window—Mason's bedroom, Jon guessed. It would be an easy climb up to that window, but without the cover of the leaves, anyone doing so would be completely exposed to all passersby and neighbors. It was stupid to do during daylight. It would be stupid to do while the family was home.

Saga started to get out of the car. She was ready. Determined.

"Wait, Saga." Roberta stopped her. Saga looked at her defiantly. "I'm not reneging on my offer to go into Mason's room," Roberta said. "But perhaps we can just go through his bedroom door?"

"It's locked," Saga said in a flat voice.

"That won't be a problem." Roberta smiled at her, and, surprisingly, Saga smiled back.

They got out of the car and walked to the front door. Saga opened it with a key and let them into the house. It was way too warm inside and smelled of alcohol and cigarettes, potpourri and cats.

"I thought Ada doesn't like Burt smoking at home," Jon said.

"She doesn't," Saga said and led the way upstairs.

Despite the smell, the house clearly belonged to Ada. There were little trinkets and doilies all over the place. Jon wondered idly if the whole town had simply adopted Ada's taste. The furniture was feminine, and there was a lot of it. Dried flowers clung to random bits of shelving, and lamps were topped with giant lace shades. Cloying was the only way to describe Ada's decorating style. Jon found it hard to breathe, just like in that church laundry room.

There were family photos on the walls, but Jon didn't see any of Ada and Ben. It was all Burt, in every shot, except perhaps in the very old photos. There was one featuring Ben and Burt as little boys standing at their mother's knee in a formal family portrait. None of the photos were of Mason... but there were obvious faded spaces on the walls where those photos probably used to hang. *Did Burt make Ada pull them all off? She let him?*

"It's just down the hall." Saga pointed to a white door at the end with a poster of Yoda from *Star Wars* that proclaimed, "This room is protected by the Force, but not cleaned by it." It was the only door that was decorated.

Roberta stepped out in front and walked purposely to the door. She tried the handle; it was indeed locked. Roberta swung her handbag off the shoulder and rummaged for something, pulling out a small drawstring bag. With a smirk, she took out a long, thin metal instrument with a waved hook at the end and confidently inserted it into the keyhole.

A twist, a turn, a click, and the door opened. Roberta flashed a self-satisfied smile at Jon and walked into Mason's room. Saga and Jon rushed to follow.

The room was small, with a slanted ceiling. The walls were painted deep blue and dotted with glow-in-the-dark plastic stars. The curtains were a similar blue with galaxies and starbursts printed on them. The messy bedding matched the curtains and was littered with dirty clothing and books. A huge poster of the periodic table took up most of one wall, and a homemade orrery hung from the hook where a chandelier used to be.

"Arrow made that," Saga said when she noticed Jon looking at the model of the solar system. "He said it was as accurate as he could make it."

"Very nice," Roberta said. And Jon nodded. It was good work. The boy had some artistic talent.

"Arrow also worked on some of those models," Saga added, clearly proud of her brother.

Models of NASA's Mars rovers and *Star Wars* spaceships were placed carefully on top of a chest of drawers. Some of the drawers were opened, with contents spilling out onto the floor. A pair of black socks lay in the middle of the room. Perpendicular to the window, there was a small table with a computer and a spinning office chair.

Jon looked around, took in the room, and really liked Mason. A lot. Whatever happened, the world was a poorer place for this kid's absence. He walked around Roberta and Saga and stood in front of Mason's computer. It would be password-protected, but he could just boot it up in admin mode. He didn't need to look at Mason's information, just his own email. But there was no way of doing that with Roberta in the room. *Why did I agree to come here? What's the point of being here if I can't even use Mason's computer?*

"Do you want me to log you in?" Saga asked. "I know Mason's password."

"Huh." Jon didn't know what to do again. He glanced surreptitiously at Roberta, but she caught him. "Sure," he said. "There may be clues there," he added, proud of himself for thinking fast.

Saga sat at the desk and turned the computer on. It made sad, whining noises for a while, but then a happy message announced a welcome to Mason's digital life. Jon would bet that kid spent a lot of his life on that computer. Would there be anything in there to implicate Burt in his death?

"There you are," Saga announced and stood up. There were notices of hundreds of unread messages from various online groups, and it showed thirty-five new emails. Only thirty-five.

"Why don't I take a look?" Roberta said and sat down in Mason's chair. Quickly and expertly, she scanned the unread messages and emails and forwarded them to some digital storage box. Was she preserving evidence? Was that how it was done? Jon had no idea. And from where he stood, he couldn't easily read over Roberta's head.

There was a loud bang of the front door, and Burt bellowed, "Saga! Get down here! You had chores at the club. I looked for you at church. No one saw you..." They heard heavy footsteps as Burt made his way up the stairs.

Roberta stood up and softly, like a cat, without a sound, shut Mason's bedroom door, and locked it from the inside. She turned to Jon and Saga, pressed her finger to her lips, and then pointed to the window. Jon turned and tried to pull up the window. It wouldn't budge. Saga came over to help. She pressed on a lower corner while pulling the windowpane up. Again and again. The window was stuck. The girl looked panicked. Jon tried to emulate what she did but gave it a bit more force. Nothing. It had probably been more than two years since it was opened. It could have easily warped or the wood expanded in that time, fusing it permanently shut.

Roberta tiptoed over to them and tried fighting the window open as well. It was all done in complete silence, just as Burt screamed for Saga to come out of hiding. He knew she was home—her school bag was left in the hall down by the front door.

Jon looked at Roberta—now what? She shook her head and pointed to the closet door. No sooner had she done that than they heard a key in the door's lock. Quickly, Jon and Saga made their way into the closet. It smelled musky and mildewy. Saga did say that no one had been in there since Arrow prowled the room just a few months after the fire. The closet had a severely slanted ceiling. There was barely enough room in there for one person and definitely not all three of them. Jon pressed against the back wall and stooped with his arms around Saga, her elbow digging into his side. The girl was breathing hard, and he could feel how fast her heart was beating. Roberta closed the closet door, indicating the space under the bed. And they heard a quick shuffle as she presumably hid under there.

A heartbeat later, Burt walked into the room and locked the door behind him. They could hear him standing in the middle, breathing. Just breathing. *What is he doing in here?*

It sounded like Burt walked over to the bed and lay down on top of all of Mason's clothing and blankets and sheets. On top of Roberta. He was muttering something. Jon couldn't really understand through the closed door and the muffling of Mason's clothing.

"I know you're dead." They heard an exclamation and a bang. Jon imagined Burt hitting something with his fist. "Don't you come looking for me, you little bastard," Burt yelled.

"I know you're dead. I know..." There was muttering again, and Jon again couldn't catch what Burt was saying. That went on for some minutes. There was more banging. Then they heard Burt get up off the bed and rip something. *The periodic table?* "That. That. And that!" Some furniture got moved or shoved. Something hit the door of the closet, and Jon felt Saga jump. *Poor kid.* He hoped Roberta was safe.

There was a scream. It was Burt. Jon tried the closet door—if Roberta was in trouble, he had to help her. The closet door was locked. *What?* Saga whimpered. He pressed her to him—it was going to be all be okay, he tried to promise. He was making so many useless promises.

"You're dead! You're dead! I watched you die, you little devil. You can't fool me. Not again. I had you. I had you!" Burt raged and screamed. Saga was silently crying. Jon could feel her body shake and the wetness of her tears. *Did Burt discover that the computer is on?* They hadn't turned it off. There wasn't enough time. *Aguguq, what is that man going to do?* There was strange, hysterical laughter and another bang of something hitting the floor. *Computer? If Burt can destroy the evidence, of course he will! Did Roberta have enough time to transfer Mason's data? Is Roberta all right?* Jon tried the door again, but it was still a no-go. Roberta must have locked it; Burt didn't come close. He only threw things.

The laughing stopped. There was a crash of a broken glass, a barrage of swearing. And then they heard Burt storm out of the room, screaming for it all to stop; he'd had enough of "f-ing tricks and foolery." *What triggered that man? Does he go into Mason's room often?*

They heard the slam of the front door and then the screech of tires. Many more minutes later, Jon knocked on the closet door. "Roberta? Roberta? Let us out!" With no response, Jon decided to break down the closet door. What was more damage with the amount of destruction clearly inflicted on Mason's room by his uncle? He braced his back against the sloping wall of the closet, lifted his right leg against the door, and pushed. It would have been easier without Saga, but he was a strong man, and the door didn't stand a chance...in the long run.

Saga tried to emulate him. She pressed herself against his chest and pushed with both of her legs. They heard a creak. The doorframe complained. *One. Two. Three.* With a bang, the door flew open. And Roberta flew with it. She landed hard on the floor and made a sound like all the breath had been knocked out of her.

"Are you all right?" Saga rushed to the woman and tried to lift the door off her. Jon helped.

"That was the worst time I could have picked to unlock that door," Roberta said with a crooked smile. Saga actually laughed in relief.

Jon helped Roberta up. She was a mess. Her clothing was ripped in places, and she had a big black eye developing where the door had thunked her face.

"Is anything broken?" Jon asked. "Did that jerk do anything to you? And why did you lock the door? I couldn't help you—"

"I didn't want you rushing out to rescue me with Saga in tow," Roberta said. "I'm a cop. I can take care of myself, even with guys like Burt."

"Huh."

"And he never found me under the bed."

"So why didn't you open the door when we called for you?"

"I wanted to be sure he was gone." Roberta rolled her eyes, and Saga let out a nervous little laugh. "I didn't want him to discover Saga, of course."

Jon stood up and looked around the room. As messy

as it was before, it now looked like there was a fight or a tornado went through the room. The window was broken. The computer was no longer on the table. The chair was smashed and was lying sideways, wheels spinning, next to the closet. The poster of the elements was indeed shredded, and pieces of models were scattered around the room. Jon stepped to the window. There was broken glass down below, but no computer.

"I got the emails downloaded," Roberta said. "We should get out of here," she added.

Saga ran out of the room.

"I don't think we can let Saga and her brother stay here tonight," Roberta said.

Jon agreed with her. "What do you propose?"

"Nora has two more rooms," she said. With that, she brushed herself off and followed Saga out. She looked like shit. Jon was impressed by her bravery and composure.

●　●　●

Jon was taping together packing boxes in the far corner of the church—the only job he had been judged qualified to do. The girls, Saga and Hazel, were assigned to keep an eye on him; Roberta stuck around too. Her black eye was thickly covered up with concealer; the makeup almost worked as long as she stayed in the shadows.

There were more than two dozen boxes of various sizes already filled with goods. They were putting together dozens more.

"Do you know where all this stuff will be sent?" Roberta asked.

"Aunt Ada and Mom usually figure that stuff out," Hazel said. "With the reverend's approval, of course."

"Of course," Roberta said. "But this is a lot. How will it all get delivered?"

"Depends," the girl said. "Sometimes we use mail. Sometimes we hire a truck and someone drives all of the donations to the destination."

"Makes sense," Roberta said, expertly working the tape to reinforce the box she was putting together. She was surprisingly efficient. In all this time, Jon had only managed to make three boxes. The girls, working together, had a stack of ready-to-go packages two layers deep and way above their heads. It was as if they were building a cardboard barrier between themselves and the rest of the WINGS community.

"It might be good to drive all of this stuff to Alaska," Roberta continued. Jon looked up at her, but she didn't acknowledge him paying attention. "With the tribe so dispersed by the disaster, it might be easier to actually go there and set up a help center. Perhaps a few of the WINGS members can go and help. I'm sure Jon would be happy to help, too."

Jon was about to reply, but then he saw the look on Saga's face and held off, pretending he hadn't heard what Roberta said.

"Hazel? Why don't we go and check out the plans for the delivery?" Roberta said and walked around the wall of boxes to where Ada and Beth Olson, Hazel's mom, had set up the center of WINGS operations. Hazel followed her, obviously happy to be asked to do something more interesting than taping boxes together.

Jon was left alone with Saga. They worked silently for a while, but then Saga started to talk.

"Roberta is very nice, don't you think?" Not waiting for Jon to answer, she continued. "And I think she likes you." Jon stopped what he was doing and stared at Saga. "Well, she did move into the same place as you, right? And she's been following you around. And you've mentioned that she was very brave. So you like her too."

"I—" Jon tried to respond, but Saga just talked over him.

"And she is pretty. Did you notice?"

Jon did notice, in fact. Roberta wasn't pretty as in magazine cover girl pretty, but she was undeniably attractive in an understated sort of way. She wasn't in-your-face pretty; she was quietly, dignifiedly beautiful. Yes, he did notice, but didn't say so to Saga. He wasn't sure what the girl wanted.

"And Roberta is super nice," Saga said again, as if running out of positive things to say about Roberta.

"You do know that Roberta is a detective, right?" Jon asked.

"Yes. It's a good job. Very responsible. She protects people."

"Huh."

"She said she is looking into Mason's murder...death. She said she would help. She didn't have to, and yet she did."

"True. But she has also been assigned to investigate me, Saga. She is looking to prove that I murdered Ay-Tal. You get that, right?"

"Is she, though? She is here on her own time; she said she was on vacation. I heard her myself. And she is volunteering here to help your people. She didn't have to do that."

That was true. But Jon decided that Roberta was working with WINGS just to be around him, to keep an eye on him. He didn't think she had a genuine interest in the plight of his people. She might care—a person would need to have a lump of ice for a heart not to care, given all of what they saw on the news—but she wouldn't had been here if not for Ay-Tal's murder investigation. Jon was sure of that. As nice as she was, Roberta was on the other side. Or at least not on his side. *But how to explain all that to this child?*

"So what I'm saying," Saga said, "is that you might want to spend more time with her. Like a friend or more."

"What?"

"Well, she is nice. You are nice. You can go out. You can ask her out."

Jon stopped what he was doing and watched Saga in total disbelief, but she wasn't looking at him. She focused her attention on taping a box together, as if she was too afraid to find out his reaction.

"If you two got together," she added, her head still down, "you might really find out that you like each other. A lot. You might want to be together. And...and...and then you might decide to start a family." She took a deep breath. "You might adopt me. Become my guardians. And...and it would all work out again. Right?" She finally looked up at Jon with eyes full of tears.

"Oh, Saga," he said and reached for her hand. But she moved and smashed her face into his shoulder, sobbing softly. He put his arms around the girl and held her awkwardly. "It will be okay. I promise. It will be okay," he kept saying over and over.

● ● ●

Roberta returned some time later.

"You and Arrow can stay at Nora's tonight," she said. "I worked it all out with Ada. You and your brother can spend a few nights at Nora's B&B to give Ada a much needed rest. I didn't mention the broken window yet, but it will come out eventually. I just thought it best if it came from some other source." She smiled weakly. "I told Ada that she's been working very hard organizing this disaster relief. In fact, I suggested that she go stay with her sister for a few nights, and everyone thought it was a great idea. The two of them can make plans and work out the details of deliveries and so on. Reverend Paul is going over there too to have dinner tonight. So the house will be empty..." She looked at Saga and Jon and back. "Did something happen?"

Saga was working on putting together boxes again, her face to the wall. Jon was just staring at Roberta. He was at a loss. Roberta did go out there and smooth things out for the kids. She didn't have to, but she did it anyway. It would be harder to run her investigation of him with Saga and Arrow underfoot. *Why did she do it?*

"What did you do?" Arrow charged at them, knocking over some of the boxes from their neatly stacked wall, startling Saga.

She looked up at her brother. "What's up?" she said as matter-of-factly as she could and let go of the packing tape roller. It immediately twisted in on itself and stuck to the wrong side of the box.

Jon swore and started ripping off the bad tape. The custom boxes were all branded with the Wilkins name and had little religious decorations and prayers printed on all sides. The tape ripped off some of the words from the Isaiah 35:4, leaving "...be afraid! God is coming." *Aguguq help me.*

"Hi, Arrow," Jon said over the box, considering if it could still be used, blasphemy and all. "Want to give us a hand?"

"No, I don't want to give you a hand." Arrow was in a bad mood and practically swinging punches. More drama, more emotional damage on display—all things that Jon was poorly equipped to deal with. "I want to know what you did," the boy yelled at Jon. "Burt made me drive his truck all the way to Eau Claire to get plywood and a bunch of two by fours."

"Huh." Roberta stopped making her box, sat back, and

observed Arrow.

"And when I got back, he was burning something in club's parking lot. From the street, I thought there was another fire. I thought..." He lost his breath; the boy was obviously freaked. "What did you do?" he screamed, shaking his fist at Jon. "Nothing is good since you came here. What is he burning out there?" It almost sounded like "whom."

Roberta stood up and took out her notebook. "When did Mr. Wilkins ask you to go get the building materials?" she asked, looking very official.

"What? Who are you?" Arrow turned to face Roberta. Jon realized that they haven't met yet; somehow he'd thought they had already.

"Detective Roberta Hand," Roberta said and extended her hand to Arrow. He shook it out of habit. He seemed shocked to be speaking with a cop and immediately clamped up. All those years on the run must have taught the boy to avoid any authority, since such interactions would have surely been fraught—Arrow wasn't old enough to keep custody of his little sister. Arrow's freaked-out eyes sought out Jon's. "What am I supposed to do?" they seemed to ask, going from rage to supplication. Jon shrugged; he had no idea.

"We burned the leaf litter just last Saturday, two days ago," Arrow added meekly, all bluster sucked out of him. "There wasn't enough to start another burn."

"Did you stop to look at what Mr. Wilkins was burning?" Roberta asked. Her voice was gentle, soothing, full of authority. Jon recognized that voice. He used it to talk to dogs when they were scared or uncertain of what to do. It was a voice aimed to arrest skittishness.

"I...I didn't," Arrow managed to stutter out.

"So Mr. Wilkins is still in the process of doing a controlled burn at his nightclub?"

"Yes. Probably? He was just minutes ago."

"Why don't we go outside and take a look?" Roberta took Arrow by the elbow and escorted him out of the church basement. Saga and Jon rushed to follow.

Outside, they could clearly smell smoke. It was acrid and didn't smell like leaf litter.

"Plastic?" Roberta turned to ask Jon.

Jon looked at Saga, and they both nodded. It smelled like Mason's computer melting. Burt was getting rid of the evidence.

"Why did he wait so long to do it?" Jon asked.

"Do what?" Arrow looked from face to face. "What is Burt burning? You know, don't you? You all know!"

"He threw Mason's computer out of the window," Saga said. "And when we looked afterward, it was gone. Just glass everywhere, but no computer."

"This happened today?"

"Just a few hours ago," Jon said. "Saga took me to see Mason's room." It wasn't exactly true, but it was not wrong either. "When we got in—"

"You snuck into Mason's room?"

Saga shrugged. "Jon needed to use a computer."

"You're crazy. You're *both* crazy!"

"Well, Roberta was there too."

Arrow was so taken aback, he almost tripped over his feet. Behind him, parked just in front of the church, Jon saw Burt's truck with lumber stacked neatly in the back.

"He must have asked for the lumber to fix the window," Roberta said. "Can't leave a hole in a house like that. Not during this time of year."

"Did Burt know you knew what he did?" Arrow asked.

"Jon and I hid in Mason's closet. Roberta was under the bed. Burt didn't see us, but he was really crazy...more crazy.

Something set him off. What did he do this morning in the club?"

"How should I know?" Arrow was so shocked by Saga's confession, he lost his anger all over again. His emotions were roller-coastering. "I was at school, just like you," he said, looking at his sister.

"We had a short day." Saga shrugged. "My class is working on a plan to help the kids of Jon's village not to lose any instructional time. I was sent to the church to coordinate."

"Is that what you were supposed to be doing?" Roberta asked. Saga just shrugged again. "All right. You two stay here." She motioned at Saga and Arrow. "Jon and I will drive down to the club and see what's up."

"But—"

"No, Arrow. I want you to make sure your little sister is okay. That's your job. Ours is to figure out what's going on with Mr. Wilkins. Come on, Jon. Move it." With that, Roberta turned and walked to her car. Jon followed.

● ● ●

They drove to the club in silence. The dark cloud of smoke was rising above the treetops. Jon wondered why no one called the fire department. *Is this how it happened with Mason? No one called because it was a Wilkins's property?*

They parked right off the highway and walked around to the back of the club. Even from the street they could hear Burt yelling and screaming. It was primal, completely unintelligible, except for Mason's name. *What had set him off?*

Roberta put a hand on Jon's shoulder, restraining him. Jon stopped. From where they were, they only had a partial view of the parking lot. Burt had dragged an old oil drum into the middle of the lot and was hopping and waving his arms in some sort of dance around the acrid fire.

"What—" Jon tried to ask.

Roberta shushed him. She pulled out a Taser from her purse and walked toward Burt. Jon tried to follow, but she pushed him back. *Stay.*

She walked so that her approach wouldn't be a surprise, but it still took a few moments before Burt managed to notice Roberta in front of him. She didn't raise the Taser. *She isn't trying to contain him,* Jon realized. *She is trying to talk to him, to get information.*

Having spotted the woman, Burt's manic jumping and screaming intensified. He got up into her face, so close and threatening that Jon almost ran to help Roberta, but she stopped him with a look. Burt was yelling so hard that there was foam around his mouth. He had even wet himself. It was terrifying. Jon was watching a man totally lose control. Roberta spoke to Burt. Jon couldn't hear what she said, not over the screaming and the roaring fire. But he could tell that she spoke in an even tone, completely unperturbed by the emotional storm raging around her. She never even flinched. Jon couldn't help but be impressed by her nerve. Saga was right—despite his better judgment, he liked her. He couldn't help it.

After what felt like forever, Burt simply collapsed into a sitting heap on the gravelly ground. Exhaustion had gotten the better of him, Jon guessed. Roberta motioned for him to stay where he was and went into the club through the back door. She returned with two pitchers of water. There was no way that was going to be enough, but she poured them into the metal drum anyway. The black smoke became mixed with white steam. It was so thick that Jon couldn't even see Roberta standing behind the drum. He couldn't stay back any longer and rushed forward into the smoke.

The air felt poisonous. He started coughing, his eyes stung, and he found it difficult to breathe.

"Get back!" Roberta yelled at him, and he felt her grab him by the arm and pull him away from the noxious air. "I told you to stay back!"

"I...I..." Jon couldn't catch enough air to talk. His chest hurt.

"Burning electronics is very stupid. They are full of toxic chemicals," Roberta said partly to him and partly to Burt, who was completely unresponsive. Her eyes were red; her nose was running. Jon noticed that she was working hard to suppress coughing. "Let's get inside and wash up," she said and guided Jon into the nightclub.

It was just as he remembered: clean, smelling vaguely of disinfectants and air fresheners, with a touch of stale beer. They walked into the men's room together, and Roberta made him wash his face with cold water. She washed hers too, including washing out her nose. Jon did the same. It was a strangely intimate activity, but Jon felt better for doing it with this strange woman.

"Shouldn't we pull Burt out of there?" he asked, finally feeling a bit better.

"He has been burning and inhaling that poison for a lot longer," Roberta said. Her eyes were blood-red, and that was on top of the large black and purple bruise spreading from just below her orbital ridge. She looked awful. Not that he looked any better. His eyes were almost swollen shut, and his skin was a quilt of red, white, and blue patches. "Burt's on the ground now and below the worst of the noxious cloud," Roberta added. "But he won't be okay whatever we do now."

"Shouldn't we call an ambulance?" Jon asked. "I'll pull him out." He turned to the bathroom door, but Roberta moved fast and blocked him, locking them both inside. "Why?" he asked.

"He killed Mason. He killed his own brother. I wouldn't be surprised if he has killed others," she said.

"But we don't know for sure..." Jon was confused. He hated Burt; he was truly disgusted by the man. He couldn't understand him...but he also couldn't understand leaving someone to simply die. It was wrong. "The authorities would—"

"Would let him go again," Roberta finished for him.

"But—"

"Just wait, Jon. We can call the sheriff, if you like."

"I would. I would very much like to do that."

Roberta smiled and pulled out an old-fashioned cell phone. It wasn't a smartphone, or an Internet phone, just a small plastic brick with number buttons. Jon watched as she dialed 911 and explained the emergency. When she was done, she slipped it into her purse.

Suddenly, there was a large boom, and the whole building shook. Jon grabbed the sink for support and looked up at Roberta. She smiled.

"Let's get out of here," she said. She unlocked the bathroom door and led him outside. Jon didn't return to pull Burt out of the toxic smoke to safety. He simply got into the car with Roberta, and they drove away. Behind them, they saw flashing lights of the police and then the sirens of the fire trucks. Someone must have finally called about the fire.

"Huh. So what now?" he asked.

"We go back to the church. Make sure the kids are okay. Make instant chocolate for the congregation while we wait for the news on Burt. Do the small things that make life better for others," she said simply.

Chapter Ten: Wilkins's Wounded

Jon Uolan

They stopped at Nora's minimart to grab some groceries. Roberta bought all ten gallons of whole milk that had been delivered to the store that morning and grabbed several boxes of instant chocolate mix.

In back, strangely out of place, there were several large packages of sweet curry powder.

"You have quite a lot of those," Roberta said to Nora.

"It was an ordering error," the woman explained. "Unfortunately, not the type of merchandise that sells around here. I tried telling Saga..."

"Huh. Well, print a simple chicken curry recipe, post it above the shelf, and make a big sign 'only two per customer' and see if it moves," Roberta suggested. "People always want what they can't have. It's human nature. Oh, and Nora? Do you by chance have any fresh parsley?"

"Oh, not here, dear. This is strictly an in-and-out, just dry goods kind of place," Nora said just as Jon was paying for the fresh milk next to a basket of lopsided apples labeled "free." "But I still have some plants alive in my garden. Plenty of apples, too. Just help yourselves."

"Thank you, Nora. We'll do that," Roberta said. She helped Jon get all of the groceries into the trunk of her car.

Just as they were about to drive away, Nora asked, "You know both of you look kind of bad? I don't really feel right telling you, but perhaps you are allergic to something?"

Knowing the way they both looked, Jon was surprised Nora didn't mention something right off. She did stare, though, when she thought they weren't looking.

"I think it's all the smoke." Roberta pointed to the dark cloud down the road that was still visible. "Not sure what Burt is burning over there..." Jon saw Roberta watch carefully for Nora's reaction.

"Men around here burn all sorts of crap." The woman just smiled and nodded. "I'm glad the fire department got around to shutting him down. You two do look dreadful..." There was an unspoken question there at the end: *What happened?* But since Roberta didn't volunteer an answer, Nora let it go. "Just go to my garden, dears. I'm sure you will find some parsley in there somewhere."

"Thank you, Nora. We'll do that. And as soon as you can close up the store, come join us for some hot chocolate at the church."

Jon nodded his goodbye as the women smiled and exchanged a few more polite words. Women were always better at keeping up community ties, Jon noticed. Even as his male relatives ran the tribe, it was the women of his family that kept the tribe together. He now wished he had learned some of those "soft" skills from his grandmother and mother, although he felt that it might make him feel foolish to act like Roberta and Nora. But better foolish than tribe-less...

"Come on," Roberta said. "We need to get that parsley ASAP."

"Why?" Jon sat in the passenger's seat of Roberta's car as she drove to Nora's bed and breakfast.

"We can neutralize some of the chemical exposure with parsley."

"If it's that bad, why don't we just go to the emergency room?"

"For one thing, it's too far," Roberta said as they pulled into the circular driveway. "And I would rather not have to explain," she finished.

"Is Burt going to be okay?"

"That man was never okay," Roberta barked out and rushed into the backyard.

Jon looked at all the milk in the trunk and decided that it was plenty cold enough to leave it there. He ran after Roberta; the mild exertion burned his lungs.

Roberta was a strange woman, not at all like he had first judged her to be. Well, she was still relentless, but now it wasn't all directed against him. She seemed practical and compassionate. Jon believed that she genuinely cared about Arrow and Saga. And more importantly, Roberta believed the kids about Burt. She believed that Mason was wronged, and Jon was sure she would follow the leads wherever they led. Roberta didn't seem to be cowed by the Wilkins name like everyone else around these parts. If she stayed here, Jon felt he could go home and leave the kids in her care. *Roberta's protection should be enough for Saga, right?* It was strange to realize how much he trusted this stranger.

"Here we are," Roberta called from the far corner of what looked like an abandoned vegetable and herb garden. At one time, Nora must have grown a lot of produce there, but it was an all-volunteer affair now. Nothing was pruned, watered, weeded, or even picked—spoiled brown apples littered the ground. Whatever was left growing on this plot of land was a self-fertilizing and hardy survivor, no sheltered hothouse plants in sight. Wild potatoes, radishes, and rosemary had practically taken over the backyard. But there was a patch of something that resembled parsley. Not the kind of parsley that Jon was used to—the dried kind in a glass jar—but stalky, willowy, with giant, umbrella-like heads of small yellow flowers and with a few wilting leaves left. But as this was way past growing season, he was surprised they found anything at all. Jon watched Roberta carefully collect the remaining leaves into the front of her shirt that she folded up into a sling. He caught a glimpse of the bare skin and turned away, embarrassed.

"It might be enough," she muttered.

"Do you want a hand?" Jon asked.

"Nope, all's good. Open the door, and let's get these washed and steeped."

"You want to make parsley tea?"

"I want us to drink it. I want us to wash our hands and faces with this stuff. I want us to inhale the vapors."

Jon had never heard of parsley as a detoxicant for chemical exposure, but his lungs ached and his face and eyes burned. He needed to do something.

Roberta managed to get into Nora's kitchen; apparently she had been trusted with the keys for the door between Nora's private space and the guesthouse. Jon watched as she deposited bunches of leaves in the sink and put on the kettle. She carefully washed and then mashed the parsley leaves in a large glass bowl with a smaller one. When she was satisfied with the consistency of the paste, she poured boiling water over it. Immediately, the whole kitchen smelled of the herb.

"Grab some bath towels and come over," Roberta ordered.

Jon rushed back up into his room and got the one towel that Nora gave him. He had no way to get Roberta's—her room was locked. One towel would have to do. He hurried back down, and even this small bit of activity made his lungs feel sick. He struggled not to cough.

"Here," Roberta said. "Pull the towel over both of our heads and lean over the bowl."

Jon did as he was told, and the fragrant steam seeped into his pores and lungs and mucous membranes. His face got quickly wet, as did his hair. Next to him—close enough to touch—Roberta was taking big breaths of heavy air through her mouth and exhaling through her nose. Jon emulated. It hurt to inhale and burned as the moist air made its way into his damaged lungs, but he did it anyway—as long as Roberta did it, he did it. She had been exposed to a lot more of the poison. Jon wondered again how bad Burt's lungs were— would that man have permanent damage? Would Roberta? Would he?

"Parsley is old medicine," Roberta said between deep breaths of parsley-laden steam. "It's high in vitamins B1, B2, C, and K. It's a potent antioxidant and has anticarcinogenic and anti-inflammatory properties. It's even a good laxative," she added with a smirk.

"I see."

"And it's cheap and widely available."

"I just hope it works on a swollen face and painful lungs," Jon said. He wasn't feeling the effects just yet, but nothing in life was instantaneous. Even Ay-Tal needed time to change form. He wondered yet again what could have happened to the god he was charged with protecting. It'd been days since he saw the New Mason. But perhaps Burt's freakout had something to do with Ay-Tal—nothing like meeting a boy who should be dead face-to-face...

"What are you thinking about?" Roberta asked. And Jon noticed that she was actually staring at him. He was so busy inhaling that he didn't notice.

"Nothing really. Just about Burt and Mason. And Saga and Arrow. That's three kids that we know Burt abused. How many others are out there? We might never know. Mason never talked—"

"Not until he was worried about Saga and Arrow."

"Right. And Saga only spoke up when she thought Ay-Tal...Al, my son, was in jeopardy." Jon felt the heat flash to his face as he spoke the name Ay-Tal out loud. That was what happened when thoughts got interrupted by conversation. He had to be more guarded, more careful. Trust was not his friend at the moment. "Well, hopefully it's no longer an issue," he added to create some distance from his mistake.

"Al." Roberta mused over the name but didn't comment further, adding to Jon's discomfort.

"How much longer should we inhale parsley?" he asked. He wanted to move away from this woman...*from this cop*, he reminded himself. It was so easy to forget what Roberta was—she was so easy to be around, so easy to talk to. Jon guessed that was her secret super power—people just trusted her. It came effortlessly for her.

"We can do some more this evening," she said and pulled down the towel. "Let me look." She leaned in to examine his face and eyes. "I think the swelling is a bit better. How's mine?" She thrust her chin at Jon. He instinctively backed away but then leaned in to inspect her skin and the whites of her eyes. Even bloodshot, the starburst in her left eye stood out.

"Better?" he asked. "I mean I think it's better." The contusion above eye was still ugly. The makeup oozed off, revealing the full color spectrum of her bruise. *It must be painful*, he thought. Yet Roberta hadn't once complained.

"Well, let's just say it's better, shall we?" Roberta smiled at him and got busy cleaning up Nora's kitchen. There wasn't much to do, but she carefully collected the rest of the unused parsley, stuffed it into a small plastic bag, and stored it in Nora's supersized refrigerator. "For later," she said and waved Jon out of the kitchen.

● ● ●

The atmosphere in the church basement was strange, confused. Now that Burt had been taken away in an ambulance, there was worry and sympathy...mostly for Ada. People crowded around her, touching her gently, brushing her with soft words and caring smiles. It reminded Jon of a queen bee in the center of the hive, surrounded by her dancing workers. He could see how much Ada enjoyed the attention. It was obvious that she had cried earlier and still had an occasional tear roll down her face, to the oohs and aahs of the women around her. But she was here and not at the hospital with Burt, he noted. If she really felt scared for her husband, wouldn't she be there? Jon would have been at the hospital if anyone in his family were there...except that he wasn't. His mood grew dark, and he withdrew to the far corner and lapsed into the role of an observer again.

After some time, Saga joined him. "You look bad," she said.

"Thanks."

"Roberta looks worse."

"She was closer."

"Closer to what?"

"Closer to the wrong side of the closet door," Jon said. "And to Burt's stupid fire."

"They say there's permanent damage," Saga said casually. "Burt might end up in a wheelchair or on an oxygen machine. Or both."

"You'll outrun him for sure then."

Saga's face broke into a huge grin, but then she covered her face into her hands, and Jon could see her cheeks turn deep red underneath her fingers. "I know it's wrong to wish him dead, but I do," she whispered so quietly that Jon could barely hear her over the din and hum of dozens of conversations going on simultaneously in the vast basement room.

"Wishing doesn't make it so, Saga. You had nothing to do with Burt's exposure to a toxic fire. It was all his own doing," Jon said to reassure the girl. Her guilt was touching; his own guilt was something else. In any case, Jon didn't think Burt deserved any sympathy, surely not from Saga. And if he could judge the mood of this congregation, the town of Wilkins wasn't giving Burt any either. All the emotions were tightly focused on Ada. Jon wondered how much these people suspected. Surely they didn't know about Burt and his nephew and brother. If they did, they would have turned on him a long time ago. Still, Burt clearly wasn't popular around here. The town's high regard was for the Wilkins family name, not for Burt in particular. *If Burt wasn't a Wilkins...*

"Do you think now that he's gone, it would be okay for me to stay?" Saga refocused Jon's attention back on her.

"You want to stay here? In Wilkins?" he asked.

"Well, it's not like there is something to go to with you. Your people are no longer a community...I didn't really mean it like that, Jon." Saga's eyes got huge; her concern was very real. Strangely, Jon believed that it wasn't just for herself, but for him and his tribe, too.

"It's okay," he said. "You're probably right. In the near future, there's not going to be much of a community back home. Not in the sense of a real place to go to."

"That's what I meant." Saga breathed in relief. "Like your parents won't really have a spare room for me to move into or anything. Right?"

"For the moment, that's true. So do you want to stay here?" Jon asked again. "With Ada?"

"I'm not sure about Aunt Ada," Saga said carefully. She didn't bring up her idea of Roberta and him taking up guardianship of her and her brother again. "She would be busy with Burt, no? Perhaps someone like Mrs. Nelson can take me in. She has room, and she has always been very nice to me. Do you think she would want to?" The girl's whole face pleaded for a yes. But he had no idea about Nora. Would she want to raise a teenage kid? "I'd be good," Saga added. "I'd do all my homework, and make dinner, and clean, and work with her at the store. She wouldn't even need to pay me or anything. I can be a lot of help." She was pleading with Jon for a home, but it wasn't something that he could give her. Not any more. Not here.

"If I was in Nora's shoes, I would want you," Roberta said. Jon turned to see her standing right behind him. *How long was she here? Did Saga know? Of course she did.* That woman had an uncanny ability to be at just the right place, where you least wanted her.

"Thank you!" Saga said. She rubbed her face with the sleeve of her sweatshirt, and Jon was sure the girl was wiping away a tear.

Roberta pushed past Jon and embraced the kid...*or perhaps just where and when she needed to be.* They were both almost the same height, but Saga crushed into the woman's shoulder and looked small, like a little child. Jon was sure he heard a wet sniff coming from underneath all those layers of clothing. Roberta just held the girl and patted her hair and stroked her back. It was what Saga wanted from Jon, but he couldn't do that, not in front of all these people. He was never taught how to give such fulsome comfort.

"For now, we can go get your stuff from Ada's house and move you into the spare rooms at Nora's," Roberta said. "Arrow too." Jon was astonished by the look of hope mixed with gratitude on Saga's face. She was anxious to be free of Burt's evil influence.

"We'll...I'll make sure that you and your brother are safe before I go back to my people," Jon said. "I won't just leave you."

Saga pulled away from Roberta and hugged Jon just as fiercely.

Roberta caught his eyes. "You better make good on all these promises," she said.

● ● ●

Roberta pulled her car all the way up to the front door of Ada's house. They saw Arrow up on a ladder, nailing a large sheet of plywood into the broken window frame. A few other young men were assisting. One was picking broken glass up off the lawn. Others were holding things up, including the ladder Arrow was perched on to do the hammering. It was a nice community effort. Jon approved. He also noted that the other boys listened to Arrow and looked up to him, figuratively and not just literally. Arrow was liked and respected by his peers, and Jon approved of that too. He was proud, even, although he didn't have any right to be.

"Let's go get your stuff," Roberta said.

"All of it?" Saga asked.

"Well, as much as we can take right now," Roberta said. "We need to get Arrow's stuff too, and I don't know how much will fit into my car."

"All of it," Saga said with conviction.

"I can walk to Nora's from here," Jon offered, "if we need

space in the back seat. Saga can drive back with you. I'll walk with Arrow."

"Sounds like a plan." Roberta and Saga went to pack the siblings' belongings, while Jon went to see if he could help with cleanup and weatherproofing.

He went up the stairs to Mason's room. A bit of plastic and tape could help keep the water and wind out of the house until the window got fixed. Jon wanted to see what could be done from the inside and perhaps it would give him a chance to look around Mason's bedroom for some clues to the boy's last days. There wasn't any time for snooping the last time he was there, just hours ago.

The room was just as they left it that morning—a complete mess. Jon wasn't sure if Ada knew how bad things were in there. He wasn't even sure if she knew how much damage Burt had done to her house. When Burt threw Mason's computer out the window, he didn't just break glass; he shattered part of the window frame. The whole thing would need to be replaced.

There was no large sheet of plastic—neither inside nor outside. Arrow hadn't bought any Visqueen. Improvising on the spot, Jon took the galaxy-covered bedspread from Mason's bed and used nails, easily found in one of the kitchen's drawers, to hammer the blanket to the window frame. Jon didn't feel bad about putting holes in the wooden frame; it would have to go anyway.

He considered Ada and Burt. Frankly, he didn't understand what kept those two together. It would take willful unknowing to turn a blind eye to Burt's crimes. *Why would Ada do that? Why did she marry him and why would she stay?* Jon couldn't understand, and thinking about it didn't help.

Jon tried to speak to Arrow through the window, but

the boy chose to ignore him. Jon actually understood him—Arrow had almost no control over any part of his life. One way to cope was to shut down, try not to care, and yell when all else failed. At the moment, Arrow was doing good carpentry work outside, Jon noted with approval. The sound of his electric drill overlapped with Jon's hammering to make strange work music. It was soothingly mind-numbing.

All these thoughts twirled in Jon's head like large snowflakes in the wind. He felt that nothing he was doing was actually important, and yet he was working hard to keep things neat and tidy, while the world around him was in chaos.

Chapter Eleven: Looking for Shelter

Jon Uolan

The siren of the police car shattered the peace.

"Jon?" Roberta looked into Mason's room. "It's time for you to go."

"What?" Jon felt sick to his stomach. For just a few hours, he had forgotten he was a wanted man.

"The cops will want to question everyone who was with Burt as he burned Mason's computer," she said. "And of course what happened earlier... I really don't think it's a good idea for you to be questioned about yet another incident right now." She was looking him in the eyes, calm, patient, willing Jon to figure it out.

"Why are you telling me this?" Jon asked. "Aren't you a cop?"

"Yes. But I'm now trying to solve the murders of Mason and Ben Wilkins. I know you are not responsible for those."

"But the other—"

"And," she interrupted him, "I now also have to consider what's best for Saga and Arrow. It's complicated. So I want you out of here. Right now. To remove the unnecessary complications." She punctuated her speech with slaps on the doorframe. "Now!"

The sound of her direct order to move finally got Jon mobilized. He put down the hammer and rushed from Mason's room. From the hall, he could hear the cops talking by the front door. Arrow was answering their questions. Saga squeezed past Jon, holding on to Roberta's hand.

"There's a back door through the kitchen. The house in back is unoccupied. Go," Roberta said quietly. "We'll keep them occupied."

Saga and Roberta walked down the stairs together. Jon held back to wait for the right moment to get out unobserved.

"Hello, Officers," he heard Roberta say. "I'm Detective Roberta Hand with the Eau Claire police department. This is Saga Turgis, that young man's little sister. They live here with Ada and Burt Wilkins as their legal guardians."

That was the last thing Jon heard as he sneaked downstairs, out the kitchen door, and into the backyard. He vaulted over the fence into the backyard of the adjacent property. Like Ada's and Nora's, this yard had an overgrown quality. It was wet and smelled of decaying leaves. The ground felt very soft, almost spongy—it must have been years since anyone had raked the dead foliage from the ground. In the early dusk of late fall, the place had a haunted quality. Hunching low, Jon ran around the empty house behind the Wilkins's and out onto the parallel street. The front yard mirrored all the other front yards in Wilkins: old holiday decorations mixed with a Nativity scene and a giant American flag drooping low on its pole, saturated by the recent rainfall. There were Christmas lights woven about the trunks of the trees in the front, but they were all off for the moment. The whole street looked dark and unfriendly. Jon didn't see a single lit window in either direction.

He couldn't stay there. The cops would be looking for him, and this time he didn't think he would be lucky enough to leave prison so easily. Unfortunately, he didn't really have anywhere to go. He couldn't go back to the church—if the police were not there now, they would be soon. He couldn't go back to the nightclub—it was the scene of the accident. He couldn't return to Nora's—if the police were after him, they would surely go there, too.

Jon's mind flashed to the package on his dresser—Ay-Tal's papers. He needed to get those. Keeping his profile low, he ran down the street. He was about a mile from Nora's B&B, and he could get there in under ten minutes, even if he was careful and didn't run full-out—it wouldn't help to look suspicious. People in Wilkins didn't run, not for fun, not for exercise. He hoped he got there soon enough.

● ● ●

He saw the flashing red and blue lights from a long way off—the cops had beaten him to Nora's house. What would they think when they found the package? Regardless, he couldn't retrieve it now. Jon slowed down, ducked into the overgrown shrubbery, and watched.

The police stayed at Nora's B&B for over an hour. He only had a change of clothing and the package in his room. Jon couldn't think of why it would take them so long to go through the place. He was pretty sure it was clearly established by now that it was him staying with Nora Nelson. The police wouldn't have to prove that, not that his fingerprints weren't all over that place; they were in every room, aside from Nora's personal area. And there were plenty of people in this town who were witnesses to the fact—Jon wasn't keeping his stay at Nora's a secret.

He considered the old computer in the drawer of the office/sewing room. Perhaps the police would notice that it had been used recently and would match his fingerprints to those on the keys. But there wouldn't be any additional information they could learn beyond the fact that he used that computer—Ay-Tal taught her tribe well. There wasn't anything to discover, even if they turned the computer on. And there was a very low chance that a key-tracer had been installed on that thing. It was old, and why would Nora's husband want such a thing? No, Jon was pretty sure his communication to the tribe was secure. His detailed account of what happened to him and Ay-Tal was safely tucked away on an anonymous server and hopefully had been read and deleted by now.

So what now? The question spun around and around in Jon's head.

● ● ●

Three hours later, Jon was still hiding in the bushes and watching Roberta drive up with Saga and Arrow. Now that he knew they were okay, it was time to go. He stealthily left his hiding place. He needed a secure space to spend the night, preferably away from all the places the cops would be searching for him. At least the kids would be staying some place safe. Roberta could take care of them. Jon exhaled, feeling relief, for he was truly anxious for them. They were good children and deserved so much better.

He wandered randomly along the deserted streets. A surprisingly large percentage of the town was left abandoned. Yet house after house that Jon passed was decorated. It was like the citizens of Wilkins had made a decision to fight the rural flight with flags and holiday displays. It was sad and uplifting at the same time.

After several turns and about three miles, Jon wound up in front of a municipal park on the beach of a small lake. There were a few picnic tables, a porta-potty, and a small boathouse. With a start, Jon realized that this must be the lake where Ben Wilkins drowned.

He walked over to the structure. It was right on the shore, with a long ramp going into the water. There was a big padlock on the front door. But as Jon walked around to the side of the boathouse facing the lake, he noticed a crack in between the barn doors that were used to let boats down into the lake. He jumped over the narrow gap of water onto the ramp. The whole wooden structure groaned under his weight. Stepping carefully toward the double doors, he tried to see inside. He wished he had a flashlight or a cell phone—it was darker in than out. But it was shelter. Another downpour threatened to unleash, and Jon didn't want to spend another night out in the open. He slid through the opening and felt his way inside.

Almost instantly, he smashed his knee on something hard. There was in fact a boat inside the boathouse. He walked around it, stepping warily and holding on to the boat's perimeter. It was just an old wooden rowboat. By the condition of the paint that he could feel with his fingers, Jon guessed that not only had it been many seasons since the boat had left this storage, but it was probably not fit for water any more, more likely to sink than to float. Boats, especially wooden ones, required lots of maintenance. His memory flashed on going out in a sealskin canoe with his grandfather as a kid. It was light and maneuverable, practically skiing over the surface of the water and sea ice mush. Sitting low, head almost even with the water, Jon had felt one with the arctic environment back then. *Will the next generation of kids in my tribe get to have such childhood experiences?* Jon felt the loss of their traditional way of life keenly, all his emotions close to the surface.

Carefully, testing first if the boat and its supporting structure could hold his weight, Jon climbed over the side and clambered into the boat. At the bottom of the boat, there were old rags, stiff with age, a few empty beer cans, what felt like old newspapers, and a coarse woolen blanket that smelled like the church's laundry room—a very familiar scent now. Maneuvering only by touch, Jon moved some things aside to make room for his body. The space was dry and as secure and out of the way as he could find this night. Curling into a ball and pulling the blanket over himself, he got his body as comfortable as possible to spend the night. His mind was another problem. Thoughts and memories swirled, making sleep unlikely.

● ● ●

He must have slept, for the sound of a barking dog made his eyes pop open. A steady gray light was streaming into the boathouse from a small crack between the two doors facing the lake. Someone was just outside the walls of the structure, walking a dog.

"Don't you go in the water," the man yelled, presumably at his pet. "I don't want to have to hose you. But I won't let you into the house like this, hear me, Angie?"

Jon caught his breath. His body was spasming from having spent hours in a cramped position. Slowly and silently, he tried to work the kinks out of his stiff muscles.

There was a thud, and Angie poked her nose through the double doors. It was a medium-sized dog with long golden fur and insanely blue eyes. If not for the eyes, Jon would have guessed it was a Golden Retriever. But the eyes pegged Angie for an interesting mutt—a retriever with a touch of Husky. Jon was good with dogs and with Huskies in particular. His tribe had a large pack...*had. Where are they now? Did the animals survive the tsunami?* The news people didn't mention any animals in their coverage of the earthquake and subsequent devastation. Not that Jon heard.

Good dog. Good Angie. Nothing to see here. Go back to your human, Jon thought, willing the dog to go away. But the dog had obviously found him and had no intention of leaving.

"Angie!" the man called, his voice a mixture of fake anger and indulgence. He clearly loved his dog, even as she was being naughty. "Get back here! And don't you go getting wet. Bath time! I'm telling you again—bath time. I know you know what that means." The dog poked its head back out and made a whimpering sound. She knew. And yet moments later, she was pushing her way through the doors of the boathouse and toward Jon.

"Easy, girl," Jon whispered. "Go home. Go home, Angie, or you'll get a bath." The dog stopped but didn't go away. She just stood there, wagging her tail.

"Angie, don't you make me come get you," the man called. His voice was vaguely familiar, but Jon couldn't really place it. Most of his interactions in Wilkins were with the women of the WINGS club. Aside for Burt, he hadn't really met any grown men.

Angie barked. And then barked again, obviously calling for her master to come and check Jon out. There was another big thump, and Jon heard the pounding of the footsteps on the ramp. The man was going after his dog.

"Bad dog, Angie," Jon said and sat up. There was no point in hiding; he was about to get discovered. It was better not to surprise the guy. Jon didn't want the man to accidentally trip and fall in his haste to get away from an unknown man hiding in a boat.

"Bad dog," the man said and walked into the boathouse, opening the doors wide and letting the early morning light pour inside. "Well, hello," he said and stopped, staring at Jon from just inside the doorway.

"Hello, Reverend," Jon said, trying to smile. As soon as he saw the man, he recognized the preacher from Wilkins's church. Even without his customary religious uniform, the reverend was memorable. His dark hair was cut short and had a heavy sprinkling of gray. His eyes were intensely blue, with a dark gray ring. He was tall and lean, wearing rubber boots, an orange windbreaker that would have been appropriate for hunting season, and jeans—not very churchy.

"Well, hello there. It seems like my Angie found the man the police have been searching for all night." The reverend stepped inside.

Jon climbed out of the boat, his legs unsteady. The reverend rushed up, ready to catch Jon if he lost his footing, but didn't touch him. Jon stomped his legs on the floor, and Angie rushed behind her owner for protection.

"Yeah, she is a real attack dog." The reverend laughed. Jon smiled too. "It's not a bad place to spend the night," the man observed.

"It kept the rain out," Jon said. "Forgive me, I just realized that I don't really know your name, Reverend."

"Paul Wolf," he said, smiling again. His teeth were perfectly straight and very white. He extended his hand, and Jon shook it. "Pleasure to finally meet you, Mr. Jon Uolan."

"So the police are looking for me?" Jon asked.

"You've got our whole town all confused, young man." The reverend couldn't have been more than a decade older than Jon. "My WINGS crew has been working overtime to help your people—"

"I know. And I'm very grateful. Truly."

"I know you are. I also don't believe you've hurt anybody. Not the way you've taken to those kids."

"You don't believe that I've killed Ay-Tal Blue?"

"Of course not. Why would you? She was part of your tribe."

"True. But all of the news—"

"News people have a way of getting things wrong. And then the authorities get involved, and for a while there's all this confusion."

"Huh." The reverend sounded like he spoke from experience.

"Did you kill Ms. Ay-Tal Blue?"

"No! Of course not!" Shock and anger welled up in Jon's chest, despite his efforts to control his emotions.

"See? Confusion!" The reverend smiled at him and patted his dog. "Angie and I are almost done with our morning constitutional. Why don't you come home with us and get some coffee and pumpkin bread? Or herbal tea, if you prefer less caffeine. Ada Wilkins mixes a mean blend of spices for me. Her brews cure everything from a headache to a cold. Awesome stuff." He flashed another smile—all teeth, wolf-like...like his name. "And Mrs. Nelson baked the pumpkin bread herself," he continued. "That woman can bake, I tell you. If not for running with Angie every day, I would have gained five sizes easy since I moved to this town."

"Was that recently?"

"Depends on how you measure time," he said with another easy smile. "Two decades just about."

Paul must have moved here as soon as he was done with his religious studies, Jon realized. He would have been a very young man back then. *Too young to lead a congregation? Well, not any more.* And the Wilkins townsfolk seemed to like him.

"Come on. What do you have to lose?" the reverend asked.

"Freedom?"

"You will lose that one way or another, if you can't clear your name." And with that the reverend stepped back onto the ramp and jumped back to shore. Angie wagged her tail at Jon and then followed.

It was true—Jon couldn't run forever. He kept hoping Ay-Tal would make her presence known and make everything okay again. But time was passing, and Ay-Tal was not around.

Jon walked to the doors and looked out over the lake. A white mist was drifting over the cold gray waters. It was very different from home, and yet it reminded Jon of his. As he turned to close the boathouse doors, he saw an old carving on the inside wall. It was a heart with the letters A and B cut into it.

"Jon?" the reverend called for him, and Jon quickly closed the doors and jumped onto the sand. His body had almost recovered from the long night. That was the advantage of youth, as his grandfather had been fond of saying.

"Coming, Reverend Paul." Jon ran up to the road and joined Angie and her man as they walked back to his house.

Jon glanced to check if the reverend had a wedding ring—Lutheran pastors were allowed to marry—but Paul seemed to be a bachelor. The man noticed Jon looking and raised his left hand to show his empty finger. "Never found the right woman," he said.

"Are you looking?"

"Given up," Reverend Paul said and continued walking. His stride was wide and steady. They made good progress past all of the abandoned homes.

"What happened?" Jon asked, pointing to yet another obviously empty house.

"Kids grow up, move away. There's not much to do in Wilkins," Reverend Paul said. "But it's not like we are special. Many small towns around here are half empty...or half full, depending on your perspective. But we try and keep up appearances. Everyone chips in to do basic maintenance on the unused homes—mow the lawns occasionally, do the tree trimmings, fix roofs, and keep the animals and elements from getting a foothold inside."

"And decorate," Jon added.

"That too. Everyone wants to live in a pretty town. Ours is better than almost any other around these areas. We don't let progress strip away appearances."

"I see."

"I'm sure your town was no different. Didn't everyone chip in to help a neighbor fix his roof?"

"Of course, but—"

"There's no but. We hope that these homes are only temporarily empty. God will find us new neighbors," he said with conviction.

"I guess it's a good thing." Jon found Reverend Paul strange but charming.

"Sure. And here we are." Reverend Paul pointed to a small white house right behind the church. He led the way inside and into a tiny kitchen. With all of the empty houses, it seemed that this man could have had a large mansion, if he wanted. He was a popular and well-loved spiritual leader of this community; all he had to do was ask, probably. And yet he chose this tiny home. As if reading Jon's mind, the reverend said, "I spend all my time at the church. I don't require a lot of personal space. And frankly, I'm lousy at housekeeping." He beamed yet another dazzling grin at Jon. One couldn't help but like this guy. "Coffee or tea?"

"Coffee, please," Jon said and settled down at a small

kitchen counter.

"The bathroom is over there," Paul said, pointing with his shoulder. "If you would like to wash your hands."

Jon turned red at the reminder and went to wash his hands. The bathroom was right off a short hallway. Through an open door, Jon could see a small bedroom with a single bed and bookshelves on all the walls, even above and below the window. Just like in Ada's house, there were many photos on the walls. People were smiling at church weddings, communions, church picnics, and standing around packing large boxes decorated with snippets of scripture. Next to the bathroom door, there was one picture frame with two photos in it. One was of a young girl, around ten or so, with pixie tails and a brightly striped bathing suit standing inside the boathouse—which was in much better condition than at present—together with a young boy about the same age. They were smiling and holding hands right underneath the carved heart with A & B. The boy was showing off his pocketknife, clearly indicating that he had just carved the symbol of young love into the wall of the boathouse. Jon leaned in. He was sure the girl in the old photo was Ada—A for Ada. He wasn't sure about the boy. The second photograph was also of Ada but much older. Again, she was standing next to carved heart with A & B, but the man next to her wasn't Burt. *Ben,* guessed Jon.

"I see you found my external memories," Paul said and stood uncomfortably close to Jon. "That's Ada Wilkins."

"I've guessed," Jon said. "Is that Ben as a young boy?"

"No. Burt."

"Really?" It just didn't make sense. *Didn't Ada marry Ben and only settled for Burt after her husband's death...murder?*

"Burt and Ada were an item as long as people could remember."

"Then why did she marry Ben?"

"Ada wanted to be a Wilkins. As you can imagine, being a Wilkins in this town means a lot. Everything..."

"So she could have married Burt. He was a Wilkins too, right?" Jon didn't understand.

"Burt got into trouble with the law. Well, he did that a lot, but then one time, he wasn't able to walk away. He served over a decade in jail for the assault of his brother...and a few other things."

"What?"

"Burt was over at his brother's house," the reverend went on, "Ada's house now. There was a fight. Burt punched his brother, and Ben fell down the stairs. He ended up in the hospital with a fractured skull."

"Oh, Aguguq." At Jon's reaction, Angie made a small howling sound, walked over to her master, and rubbed her head against the reverend's legs. The man patted her head, and reassured, she trotted back to her bed by the door and went to sleep.

"Ben's wife was very pregnant at the time and suffered from preeclampsia—very high blood pressure induced by pregnancy. While Ben was in the hospital, she collapsed alone in the house. Ada found her the next day. Elsa Wilkins died giving birth to Mason, Ben's only child."

"I had no idea..."

"It's not something people around here talk much about. It was a tragedy. A private tragedy. Ada stepped in and took care of the baby while Ben healed and Burt sat in jail. One thing led to another, Ben married Ada about a year later."

"I imagine Burt wasn't happy about that."

"No, Burt never forgave his brother. And Ben never forgave Burt."

"But Saga said that Burt came and stayed with Ben and

Ada when he came back to town. Why would Ben let him?"

"It wasn't Ben. Ada insisted. She said that it wasn't right for brothers to fight forever. Burt never meant to hurt Ben's wife or Ben, for that matter. It was a tragic accident...accidents. Ada wanted them to get along. After all, they were family."

"Reverend, I don't know how much you know about Burt Wilkins, but—"

"Burt is not a good man. I know, Jon." The reverend's sad eyes bored into Jon's. Jon tried to hold the man's gaze but after a few heartbeats dropped his eyes. There was something about that man.

"I think you might not know the whole of it, Reverend," he said. "Arrow believes that Burt killed Ben and Mason. And I believe the kid. I saw what Burt did to Saga and my own son. Burt is a very evil man. It's one of the reasons I came back to Wilkins. I felt it was my duty to protect Arrow and Saga from him." Jon felt lightheaded, having told this stranger the heavy truth, shifting the burden like that. He wasn't sure if it was right to share the siblings' dark secret. *But if not this man, then who?* Who could he tell this to? Ay-Tal knew...

"I heard suspicions about Ben's death," the reverend said, leading Jon back into the kitchen and pouring each of them a cup of black coffee. "His was a strange death. Ben was a good swimmer. But the family doctor thought his old head injury might have led Ben to become disoriented under the water. The lake water is dark, cold, and murky. It would be easy to get turned around under there, especially if he bumped his head against the boat, as Burt said."

"Did a coroner examine Ben's body? Did Ben have a bump on his head?" Jon asked.

"Ada insisted it was an accident and refused to permit further investigations. She said the family had enough tragedy as it was. This was just weeks after Mason's death."

"About that, Reverend. Mason died in a fire at the nightclub. But I've heard that he was trapped—a box was left blocking the exit door. Doesn't that sound suspicious to you?"

"Yes. But not everything that sounds suspicious is sinister, right, Jon? Accidents do happen." And he looked at Jon again.

Jon felt trapped. What happened to him and Ay-Tal on the train was not really an accident, but a misunderstanding. Suspicious but not sinister. *Still.* "Accidents happen to the Wilkins family way too often," he said softly.

"It's all a matter of perspective, isn't it? When we are close to a sequence of events, it feels like clustering, even if statistically it's not really all that unusual."

"I still feel like it's pretty unlikely to have so much accidental death in one family," Jon pushed. He believed Arrow. "Three Wilkinses died in less than two decades, right?"

"Five, if you count Ben and Burt's parents."

"How did they die?" asked Jon. He took another sip and noticed that he had already managed to finish his entire cup of coffee. His stomach felt sour. Paul got up and poured him another one.

"Pumpkin bread?" he offered.

"No, thank you, Reverend. I don't think I can stomach food just now." Jon took another large sip of hot coffee, trying to restore his emotional equilibrium. "How did Ben and Burt's parents die?"

"A car accident," the reverend said. "The boys were both still teenagers. Nineteen and seventeen. It was the year I arrived in Wilkins. I married Ben to Elsa, his childhood sweetheart, and the two of them agreed to become guardians to Burt until he reached eighteen." Jon judged Burt to be about forty-five or so, so Paul Wolf was yet another ten years older than his previous guestimate.

"What about those photos on the wall?" Jon asked.

"The ones of Ada and Burt?"

Jon nodded.

"Well, that's at the heart of it, isn't it?"

●　●　●

The reverend left for the church, leaving Jon at his house with Angie. It was very generous of him—both in his belief that Jon was innocent and in allowing him a hiding place from the authorities until all of this shook out. The reverend also told Jon that there would be a congregation-wide vote today on what the next steps in the disaster relief project should be. It was Jon's tribe, and he couldn't even be there while strangers were deciding on how to help his own people. It was frustrating and left Jon feeling very powerless, trapped by events and fate. *For Aguguq's sake, where is Ay-Tal?* Unlike Aguguq, Ay-Tal was about the minutiae of life's decisions—a gentle push, a kind word, an inspirational example that led people to change their minds or act in ways Ay-Tal wanted them to. Ay-Tal was never a pushy, "do this or else" kind of god. Life was hidden in the details of daily choices to do one thing over another. Ay-Tal was good at helping people make the right decision for each particular moment in time. Just as Jon was not.

Jon looked around the house. Reverend Paul didn't seem to have a television set or a computer or even a phone, not out in the open. *Although who has landlines nowadays in the lower forty-eight?* After fretting and feeling guilty for a few hours, Jon decided to search the reverend's house for a computing device. *In this day and age, everyone is connected, right?* People even hooked up their refrigerators to the Internet— the Internet of Things and all that. Well, Jon's people didn't do that. What use was a freezer that ordered meat that couldn't be delivered for several months? People adjusted to their environments in ways that was most practical for how they lived. City folk had self-stocking pantries; Arctic folk flew planes—each to their own.

Starting with the kitchen and the adjoining small sitting room, Jon systematically searched every drawer and cubbyhole. There was a shelf with homemade preserves marked with hand-written labels by their makers; some names sounded familiar. Apple jam, apple butter, wild strawberry spread, blueberry jelly, cranberry conserves—there were a lot of jars. There was also a shelf of little cans that looked like homemade spices or teas. *Ada's headache remedies?* Jon found two jars of curry powder from Nora's store. *Did Roberta's marketing scheme work on Paul?* There was a surprising variety of cleaning supplies under the kitchen sink. The drawers were well-organized by function—spoons small and big in one, forks in another, knives in a third, one large butcher's knife and one small paring knife in the last. The utility knives looked like there were hardly ever used; the manufacturer's stickers on the handles were still attached. Other kitchen utensils hung on little hooks organized by size. Not one had a burn mark or even a slight discoloration from use. Jon checked inside the oven—*might as well*—it looked like it was never used. Same for the stovetop. One of the knobs still had the protective plastic cover on it! The only used items appeared to be the coffee maker and the electric kettle. Similarly, in all of the kitchen cabinets, all the dishes and pots and pans appeared practically brand new. Only mugs, clearly not part of the ordered set of dishes, showed wear. Jon would bet that all of the kitchen stuff came new with the house when the reverend moved in several decades ago and remained in their original condition.

The small sitting room had two reading chairs, a small table, and more bookshelves. The reverend didn't seem to entertain much at his house, but he did read. The books were mainly folklore, ancient history, and philosophy. Granted, Jon hadn't met too many adults from Wilkins, but based on his personal reading interests, Reverend Paul seemed to be poorly matched to the community he served. One thing Jon's own tribe had was a sense of intellectual and spiritual cohesion. Everyone in his hometown shared the same history, the same legends, the same family ties to each other and the land. It was easier to be the spiritual guide to the people who shared the past, the present, and the future. Wilkins was very different from Jon's town in this respect. The strongest social drives that he noticed here were the need to hold things together, to keep up appearances, and to help others. But the last one was huge—what better tie than empathy for strangers to keep the townsfolk together? Jon wondered whose idea was it to start WINGS? *Did Reverend Paul arrive to lead an existing do-good enterprise? Or did he start it?*

Exhausting the search in the public-facing part of Reverend Paul's home, Jon turned back to the small hallway and the bedroom. He scanned all of the bookshelves, looking for a fake book-hiding place. Nothing. It was a crazy idea anyway—why would the reverend need to hide anything? It was obvious that not too many people visited him at home, and Jon didn't think anyone in Wilkins, not counting Jon himself, would want to snoop on their parson. He looked under the bed—plenty of dust and spiders, but no boxes or bundles or anything worth investigating. Under Jon's bed, there was his entire childhood-worth of junk—toys, collectables, old sports equipment, trophies that weren't worth the display space, ancient school projects, rocks he collected along the sea shore, even an old computer and videogame console or two. Reverend Paul didn't seem to be very sentimental, at least not in the way Jon was with his childhood things.

Similarly, in Paul's closet there were only a few simple sets of warm- and cool-weather gear, a few black clergy shirts, and an old black cassock. It all felt very impersonal to Jon. In fact, in the whole house, only the books and photos on the walls showed any individuality. Having given up of finding a means of communicating with his tribal elders, Jon went to examine those photos more closely.

There were several collages of kids' photographs, obviously family snapshots turned into Christmas cards. The kids were carefully cut out and arranged against a large shot of the Wilkins's church all decorated for the winter holidays. The year of each collage was drawn in a thick gold magic marker. Based on the dates, the reverend did one of these every three years. There were seven altogether, with a space for a new one already marked out on the wall as a large blank area. Jon looked for Mason, Saga, Arrow, and Hazel, the only kids he knew in this town. Hazel appeared in three collages—there was one where she was maybe only two years old, if that, but still recognizably Hazel. Jon identified Mason in a few. There were no collages with Saga and Arrow. At first Jon was taken aback by the omission, but then he realized that the siblings were probably not in Wilkins yet for the last collage. Saga said Mason died a little over two years ago. She and her brother arrived not too long before that. Going by dates, Reverend Paul would be making another one of these photo collections this year. Saga and Arrow would be in that one...if they stayed in Wilkins.

Jon looked at the earliest one, and sure enough, Ada and Burt were there. Ada was dressed in a flower-covered summer dress. Burt's photo, though, was the mug shot from his juvenile arrest. Behind a few heads of other Wilkins town children, Jon could see the arrest numbers on Burt's chest. It was a strange photo to use, but perhaps it was the only one

Reverend Paul had from that year? Jon tried to find an image of young Ben, but he didn't really know enough of what the man looked like, having seen only the one wedding photo and a picture of him and Burt with their mother back at Ada's house. Mason was represented in four images. Just four, and then he was dead.

There wasn't some great truth that Jon could glean from these photos. The only thing that jumped out at him was that the number of children diminished with each collage. The oldest one showed at least fifty children, the last one only twenty-three. Now, it could be that the reverend just didn't get the photos from all the parents, but given that he even included a jail mug shot, Reverend Paul was clearly proactive about getting the images of the town's kids for his walls. It could also mean that the town of Wilkins was dying out; fewer and fewer kids lived here with each passing year. Based on the number of shuttered homes, Jon guessed the latter. Did Paul know that he was adopting a dying town when he moved out here all those years ago?

The thought led Jon to consider his own tribe. They too had fewer and fewer children in their hometown with each passing generation. It wasn't exactly that the tribe's numbers shrank; in fact, it was probably the opposite. It was that the members of his tribe chose not to live together anymore. People moved and took their children. If someone made collages of his tribe's kids every five years, wouldn't there be the same trend of diminishing numbers? And now that everyone was uprooted, granted not by choice, would Ay-Tal stay with his tribe? Mary said that gods like them led people to new worlds or to new lives. If there were no people to lead, there was no need for a guide. After nearly a thousand generations, his tribe would lose its god of direction, its god of decisions large and small. Their personal god of small affairs. Their beloved god. Would that be enough to cause his people to disband and go their separate ways? Would his grandfather be the last tribal elder? *In some ways, it would be a relief,* Jon realized. That insight made him sick. He went to the bathroom and threw up.

Chapter Twelve: Ghosts

Paul Wolf

"Ladies, ladies, please." The reverend raised his voice again. He had to. The police had shown up with a search warrant for their church this morning! It was an unheard of move in Wilkins. Blasphemy, some people were saying. They also insisted on searching Ada's home and Nora's house. Such an invasion of privacy was simply not done, not here in Wilkins's town. Not to a Wilkins! "Officers Merry and Rogers are just doing their jobs. I'm sure they didn't want to intrude on Mrs. Wilkins at such a difficult time. It's just routine police business," Reverend Paul said over the loud grumble of discontent. "And since they didn't find anything—"

"They even assaulted their own detective!" someone shouted out.

That was not true. Roberta Hand came to talk to the officers willingly and even allowed her own room at Nora's B&B to be searched. Again, the cops found nothing. The woman's black eye was from an earlier accident, he was told. There was really nothing to find—Jon was safely ensconced in his house, Paul hoped. *Unless that man isn't smart enough to stay put.* But Roberta had vouched for him. She convinced Paul that Jon was innocent of the charges against him. She also told him her suspicions about Burt, which matched rather closely with what Jon told him. If what she and Jon said got out, it would drive the community apart. Tear it beyond repair. *With Burt safely away in a hospital, wouldn't it be better just to let it go?* There were the kids to consider, of course. Saga and Arrow deserved better. On that, Paul agreed with Roberta. But as a spiritual leader of his community, Paul always had to consider the needs of the many over the needs of the few. Still, whatever happened, Burt couldn't be allowed to hurt any other child ever again. Things like that tended to get out eventually.

Ada, dressed all in black, sat off to the side, surrounded by a protective circle of women. She looked like a widow, even as Burt wasn't dead yet. And everyone was treating her as such. If he did die, Ada would be widowed twice over, and she would be the last surviving Wilkins...by marriage only. No blood kin left. It was surprising just how much superstition was wrapped up in the belief that without a living Wilkins among them, the town would die. Paul had already heard that people were making plans to move to Saint Paul or Eau Claire if Burt died. And if more people left, there really wouldn't be a town worth saving. Who would be left? Ada? Her sister and family? Beth Olson would move too. Her husband Ron was a long-distance trucker; Beth could live anywhere, waiting for her husband to visit several days a month. As it was, those jobs were disappearing. The Olsens hoped the change to self-driving trucks wouldn't come until after Ron retired. The whole town held its breath to retirement. There was no future in it. None that its people saw. *Only I can save them*, he realized again. There really wasn't anyone else.

WINGS served to glue these people together. But the glue was failing. The town of Wilkins needed something else. Yearly Christmas disaster relief efforts were not enough anymore. It needed a new reason to come together. It needed a cause to rally behind. In an event that Burt would be identified behind the spilling of blood... The reverend couldn't even conceive what the discovery of a murderer in their midst would do to their town. *Disaster! Total disaster...*

"Ladies, ladies!" he cried out. *Get the women to stop talking and to pay attention, and the men followed.* He made his voice carry; he was good at that. Slowly, too slowly, he got his congregation's attention again. "Thank you," he said in a more moderate tone. He wanted them all to hush up and focus on his words. "We've been through a lot as a town." Heads nodded, and "amens" rippled through the gathering. "More than some, but certainly far less than others." More agreements were voiced; this was a town full of empathetic people. Paul was proud of nurturing their empathy. "We've dedicated ourselves this Christmas to helping Mr. Uolan's people. Those Americans are just like us. They have families. They try to make ends meet in a new world that is not very supportive of traditional ways. Mr. Uolan lived in a small town like ours, with all the same problems of a small town."

He let the similarities sink in, but avoided mentioning the name Wilkins; it was not a thing to bring up at the moment. "Just like us in so many ways. And then one disaster scattered Jon's people to the wind." He looked over his group. Most were late middle-aged, with teenage or grown children. Not a toddler in the crowd. They were set in their ways. They didn't want to change, not at the pace the world was changing around them. The few young people that were still in the audience were working hard to do well on exams to score placements at faraway schools and universities. Youngsters itched to get out of here. And when they finished with their educations, they wouldn't be coming back home. Not to these homes. They would be making homes elsewhere. It was the truth everyone knew and no one discussed openly. They all worked hard to save the empty houses, to keep them weatherproof and tidy, all in the hopes of having some of these kids return to start their families here, to keep their community from dying out. But it was unlikely before and much more so now. They were on the razor's edge.

"Our town is broken." There, he said it, and the hush caused by those words felt heavy on his shoulders. "And Jon's town is torn apart." Paul paused, letting them absorb his words, forcing them to find a solution to the dilemma.

"I saw Mason." A small voice broke through the tension in the room. That was unexpected. The room shifted to face Hazel—Beth and Ron's girl, Ada's niece. "I saw Mason," the girl repeated a little more forcefully now. "I know you might think it is crazy, but I think it's a miracle." She looked directly at Paul, challenging him to contradict her. People started to push Hazel to the front of the church. And in no time, she was standing next to the reverend.

"You saw Mason Wilkins?" he asked, defeated. He had hoped that the town would spontaneously think up of a solution for a new blood, so to speak. But now this. "Recently?" He made his voice neutral.

"I saw Mason Wilkins," Hazel repeated loudly. "Ben Wilkins's son."

The reverend noted that she didn't mention Ada or Burt. People around here remembered, even those who weren't born at the time. People always knew more than the authorities or politicians suspected. It was one of the reasons Paul loved this town, specifically requested coming here when their need arose...especially when no one else answered the call.

People called on Hazel to speak—everyone liked a good old-fashioned miracle.

"I was walking home last night from church, and you

know how we all like to take the road by the lake, when we can?"

There were murmurs of assent. The road around the lake was the prettiest path in Wilkins. It was one of the reasons Paul loved to walk his dog there—the lake never looked the same in the decades he called Wilkins his home. Even after its waters took Ben's life, it still held on to its severe beauty and became a memorial of sorts.

"Mason was sitting at one of the picnic tables at the lake," the girl continued. "I was skeptical at first. He could have been just some guy sitting there, you know? But he was wearing the jacket I picked out. *I* picked it out," she emphasized. "I knew it was the one. I recognized it right away."

Paul knew of Hazel's hobby—passion, really—of finding vintage clothing and matching it to people she knew. She had found special pieces for everyone in town. Even Paul had one—a silk tie from the sixties with a large print of a shaggy orange-brown dog on it. He got Angie partly because of that tie; it was just too much of a coincidence when, as a stray, Angie walked into his life, looking like the dog on his special tie. He wore that tie on all notable occasions and on the days the disaster relief donations left Wilkins, every December seventeenth. So everyone knew of the jacket Hazel was talking about—one of the matching pair she got for Mason and Arrow. It was a way to celebrate the boys' friendship and upcoming brotherhood. Saga took Mason's jacket after his death. People knew how Arrow's little sister felt about Mason. Even Ada didn't object when Saga started wearing that jacket continuously, in summer and winter. *Although not recently,* Paul noted.

"I was scared." Hazel went on with her story. "But we never saw the body...not with the fire and all. And if it was Mason, I had to know." The emotions in the room were rolling like waves; the crescendos of pain followed by the troughs of despair and up again. Paul felt like he could drown in the stormy sea of anxiety in this room. "I walked to the boy," Hazel continued, voice a bit shaky. "I wasn't afraid. He was sitting, facing the lake. And it was getting dark. For a moment I thought it was Saga, but she and Arrow went with Ms. Hand to Aunt Nora's house a while back. It couldn't have been her. I called to the boy. I called him by his name. 'Mason,' I said. 'Mason Wilkins, is that you?' and the boy turned and looked at me. And it was him. Except it wasn't..." The room caught its collective breath. "The boy was my age. Well, more like Saga's. Fourteen, maybe? This Mason was the age he was when he died. That's when I knew I was talking to a ghost. Mason's ghost."

Ada cried out and collapsed into the arms of the women around her. Dozens of people started talking all at once. It was one thing to see Mason—perhaps the boy really didn't die. It wasn't like there was a true investigation at the time. Ada forbade it. But Mason's ghost? It was too much even for the folks of Wilkins.

"I saw him too." A high voice cut through all the conversations in the room. "I saw Mason Wilkins and talked with him too," said Saga. She pushed her way to the front to stand next to Hazel and the reverend. "It was just as Hazel said. Mason was the same age as he was when he died. I saw him," she repeated firmly.

"I did too!" Dorothy called out from the back of the room. People moved away from her, forming a little empty space all around—a stage. "I saw Mason Wilkins walk down the road. I wasn't sure, at first. I was driving. But then I turned around and drove back to find him. And there he was just walking toward the nightclub. The boy must have wanted to visit the place where he died," she concluded.

"Did you see what he did next?" "Did you talk to him?" "Did he go in?" "Are you sure it was Mason?" "Did he look young to you too?" The questions avalanched on the poor woman. The reverend couldn't catch Dorothy's replies for the roar in the room. Everyone was talking at once.

"You know how Arrow said that Burt was all agitated and all?" Hazel turned to Paul and spoke just for him to hear. "Perhaps the ghost of Mason Wilkins came for him, too. Mason never liked his uncle. They said Burt burned Mason's computer to hide something, and the smoke poisoned him. It feels like Mason came back to punish Burt. Don't you think?"

Paul looked as Saga reached out, took Hazel's hand, and squeezed it in support. The two girls were friends, even though Hazel was a year older than Saga. Did one of them lie to support the other? The reverend would have guessed that, except that he had seen Mason too, at the boat house. At the time, he blamed the early morning mists and his imagination. But the weather and overactive minds couldn't be responsible for all the other sightings, for Saga's and Hazel's and others— Paul was overhearing as other members of his congregation shared stories of spotting Mason. It seemed like the boy had been haunting the town of Wilkins since his death, walking the path by the lake, visiting the nightclub, even wandering the street in front of the church. It was crazy talk. If people truly noticed something unusual, he would have heard about it right away. Mason died over two years ago. This was all revisionist history. People wanted to believe, and they wanted to personally be part of the miracle. *Soon the whole town will claim to have seen the boy,* Paul thought with exasperation.

"Reverend Paul?" Saga pulled on his sleeve. He guessed that the girl had been trying to get his attention for a while.

"What is it, Saga?" he asked.

"Officers Merry and Rogers are waiting just outside to

question me and Arrow," Saga said.

"They said they wanted to question me too," Hazel chirped. "But they can't do that, not without our parents, right?"

"And Arrow and I don't have parents—"

"You have legal guardians," Paul heard himself say, but he knew that wouldn't work. He glanced toward Ada Wilkins. She was still going through the theatrical display of various emotions. *Some might even be true...* "No, Saga," he agreed. "The police shouldn't question you without an adult present. Someone who has responsibility over you. Ada—"

"I don't think Ada would like what Arrow and I have to say," Saga said. He supposed not.

"Why don't we go back to my house, and you can tell me what you want to say to the police?" Paul asked and looked around the pews for Arrow. He wanted both siblings to get out of there without encountering the police first. The boy was in back with Ms. Hand. Paul still wasn't sure where Roberta stood in all of this. She worked for the police, and yet her spirited defense of Jon put her on the other side of the law, or so it seemed to him. "Hazel? Why don't you go get Arrow and Ms. Hand and bring them up here to me? And then stay with your parents. Tell them to wait on speaking to the police. Tell them I told you so. God knows we have enough going on right now."

Hazel ran and Paul watched her progress. People stopped to ask her questions about her experience with Mason's ghost. She was more than happy to retell what she saw over and over again. Paul was sure that with each telling, there was more detail to share. Memory was funny like that, especially when one was the center of attention...and young.

The doors to the church opened, and Paul saw the officers walk in. Roberta and Arrow were just to the side of the entrance, separated from the two men by a few townsfolk. A turn of the head, and they would be spotted. Paul willed for Roberta or Arrow to catch his eye. They didn't, but, to his relief, they did edge away from the door and carefully descended the stairs to the side of the front entrance into the basement.

The officers made their way toward the pulpit where the reverend stood. Without looking directly at them, Paul took Saga's hand and walked to the side hall and to the back of the church, where he had his office.

"Come quietly," he said. "Don't look around." Instantly, the girl's head snapped back and then forward again. She saw the cops. *Did they see her look?* "I saw Arrow and Ms. Hand go into the basement," he said. "We can join them through the back door."

"Reverend Wolf! Reverend Wolf!" one of the officers shouted over the crowd, and like sheep they parted before him.

"Run down and tell Ms. Hand what's going on. She'll know what to do," Paul said and gave Saga a slight push on the back as he turned around, blocking the policemen's view of the disappearing girl. *God, please let them figure it out,* he thought. He'd told Roberta that Jon could stay with him if he ever found the man. Now, he hoped Roberta took the brother and sister over to his house too. The police wouldn't dare to search there. *And why would they? How would they even get a warrant?*

"Gentlemen." He turned to greet the uniformed officers just as he heard the back door to basement softly click closed. "How may I help you?"

"Reverend Wolf," Officer Merry said and extended his hand.

The reverend shook it. It wasn't that he disliked these men.

Their timing was poor, that's all. Too much was happening at Wilkins all at once, and he needed to figure out what to do before the law took away all his options.

"I'm Officer Merry, and this is Officer Rogers. We were assigned to investigate the murder of Ms. Ay-Tal Blue, the attorney for the Alaskan native tribe that your community is working so hard to help. We have a few questions."

"I thought only detectives investigated murder," said Paul and carefully ushered the men away from the main floor of the church. "Would my office work for you?" he asked. It would be better to deal with whatever these men wanted of him away from all the volatility in the pews. Having these officers barge in was bad enough. If Wilkins people started to approach them with ghost stories, it wouldn't help the situation any. *Not at all.*

They walked into his office. Paul showed them to the three empty wooden chairs in front of his desk and walked around to sit at his leather-covered office chair.

"So how can I help you, Officer Merry? Officer Rogers?"

• • •

Saga Turgis

Saga crept into the church basement. On one side, it was stacked almost to the ceiling with WINGS boxes. More packages were in the process of being assembled on the many rows of tables set up for that purpose. There was a giant container full of letters to the children of the Omuktal tribe written by the Wilkins school children. More letters were collected from members of the congregation; people here believed in starting conversations with the disaster victims they were aiding. Reverend Paul said material support alone wasn't enough. They needed to give spiritual comfort as well. Aid was always personal around here. Some people continued corresponding with individuals and families they helped for many years after, becoming decades-long pen-pals and even visiting each other over the holidays.

Saga had written a card to a girl named Onida from Jon Uolan's tribe that she made herself in art class. The girl's name meant "the one searched for." The teacher gave the students a list of the names and ages of some of the kids from the tribe. Saga wrote to this girl because of her name. She knew nothing else about her, including her current address. But they were told not to worry about that—all the letters and packages would be delivered together to Native American Center in Anchorage to be sorted out there.

There were so many WINGS packages and letters that Wilkins's little post office couldn't hold it all. So, every year after Thanksgiving, Mrs. Nora Nelson designated part of the church basement as an official post office, keeping only the regular mail processing at the back of her store. There were no cages or walls that separated the temporary post office from the rest of the space. But everyone here respected Mrs. Nelson's rules over the mail—once a letter or a package was accepted, it was as good as sent, even if the whole batch wouldn't be going out until the middle of December. *Some rules make life easier,* Saga thought, *and some just the opposite.* Laws that tied good kids to bad people were wrong, and they were meant to be broken. And Saga meant to break them.

There was no one working down in the mercy factory now; everyone was upstairs in the nave for the vote on the next steps of this year's WINGS project. Except that didn't happen. Hazel stopped it somehow. At least Hazel's story explained to Saga what happened to Ay-Tal. Saga had been worried that the God of Small Affairs had left for good, left them to deal with all this disaster alone. *God* God—the one that Jon referred to as Aguguq and people around here called Jesus—he felt too far above it all to care about Saga's problems. *Wouldn't he have intervened if he knew Burt was about to murder Mason?* Saga wanted a god that was more approachable, someone you could ask for help and who would answer...using real words and such. Saga was never good at reading signs from above. *What do crows have to do with sorrow?* Aunt Ada always went on and on about crows being bad omens. *But would Jesus send crows to communicate for him?* Saga didn't think so. Ay-Tal was so much easier to relate to. And now Ay-Tal was hanging around as Mason—so many people had said that they ran into him in Wilkins. So Ay-Tal hadn't abandoned them. *He is here to help, although not very helpful yet,* Saga noted.

"Arrow? Ms. Hand?" Saga called out into the darkened space. "Arrow?"

A hand slapped across Saga's mouth, and she jumped.

"Stop that," Arrow said. "Do you want the cops to know we are hiding down here?"

"The reverend told me to come find you," Saga said. The prickles of adrenaline still stubbed into her armpits. "Why did you have to scare me like that?" She pushed her brother away from her.

"Sorry."

"Saga? What did the reverend tell you we should do?" Roberta asked, coming up to them.

"He said that the cops shouldn't just talk to Arrow and me without an adult," Saga said. "And since we don't really have an adult..."

"Is Ada okay?" Roberta asked. "I saw her in distress."

"She's probably just acting." Arrow dismissed Roberta's concern. "Whatever's going on, it is always about her. You might break your legs, but somehow it is Aunt Ada who is suffering the most. Just ignore her."

"I see," Roberta said. "And yet her husband is very sick in the hospital." Arrow tried to interrupt her again, but she stopped him with a look, and he just rolled his eyes. "And people are saying that the ghost of her son is wandering the streets of Wilkins. She might be genuinely under duress, Arrow."

"Mason was only her *stepson*," Saga said. "It's not like she really grieved when he died."

"She is still the woman who raised him from his very first day, as your reverend told me. She must truly care for him."

Saga just shrugged.

"Why didn't she want his death investigated then?" Arrow said. "As a detective, don't you think that's suspicious? A little?"

"I grant you it's strange," Roberta said. "But everyone has their own idiosyncratic reactions to death and grieving. Don't be too fast to judge, Arrow."

"Look, I don't know why Burt freaked. But if he saw Mason's ghost, it just might explain his wacked—"

"Hazel said the same thing!" Saga jumped in. "She said that's why Burt burned Mason's computer."

"Hah," Arrow said. "That was to get rid of any evidence. He must have used Mason's computer to watch porn. Why else would they keep that room locked all the time?"

"Enough," Roberta said. "I have some of that computer's files archived. Granted, that's not everything, and we didn't have a search warrant—"

"But why would we need one?" Arrow asked. "It was in our house. We live there. Shouldn't Saga be allowed to use her sibling's computer?"

"You know that's not how it was," Saga said. "I spent the

entire time hiding in the closet with Jon."

"So we lie," Arrow said.

"I would prefer that neither of you did any lying, especially to the police," Roberta said. "Your situation is complicated enough as it is."

That stopped Arrow from talking. He just looked sullen and angry. But all Saga felt was fear. She had almost full four years before she could gain her freedom. *Arrow will move away, go to college, get his degree. But I'm stuck in Wilkins... with Aunt Ada and Burt. Alone.* It was bad enough when Mason and then Uncle Ben died, but without Arrow to protect her, Saga was worried she wouldn't make it that long. Mason didn't, and he was a Wilkins. What chance did she have? She wrapped her arms around herself; she needed a hug. And suddenly she felt Roberta pull her in, holding her, rubbing her back, saying soothing nothings into her hair. Arrow patted her shoulder in support too. Saga stifled a sob.

"We will find a solution, Saga," Roberta said. "You and your brother will be fine. I promise. Now, the police managed to get permission to search this place. We can't stay here."

"Where can we go?" Arrow asked. "Back to Mrs. Nelson's?"

"No. The cops were there too. We need to go someplace where the police haven't been yet and are unlikely to go," Roberta said.

"Reverend Paul's house," Saga said.

"Do you know where it is?" Roberta asked. Arrow nodded. "Good. Let's move. Double time," Roberta said.

* * *

Paul Wolf

"I'm telling you," the reverend said again. "I've spoken to Jon's tribal elders. They said that Ms. Ay-Tal is fine. They know where she is. No one from their tribe was murdered."

Officer Merry exchanged a look with his partner. "Reverend Wolf—"

"No one calls me that. Please call me Reverend Paul." He stretched his face into a wide grin. He felt how uncomfortable these men were with having to search the church and interview its pastor about a murder. "You don't honestly think that I would hide a murderer?"

"Well, Reverend Paul," Officer Merry started again, "we had Mr. Jon Uolan in custody. He was to be transferred to a more secure facility, right after Thanksgiving."

Paul just looked at the man through his steepled fingers—it always made people uncomfortable when he did that.

"But strangely, an order came to release Mr. Uolan while we were off for the holiday," Officer Rogers said. "We spoke to Detective Hand, and she said that she received the order to let him go, but she was already on vacation by the time he was released."

"And the strange thing," Officer Merry picked up the story again, "is that Detective Hand is not someone who works with us regularly. In fact, neither of us had ever heard of this woman before."

"Well, did you check out her credentials?" Paul asked.

"We did."

"And?"

"They checked out. Roberta Hand is a detective in Eau Claire."

"There you go." Paul smiled and leaned back. "Personally, I find Roberta an excellent woman. She has spent her whole vacation so far helping Wilkins Initiatives to Nourish God's Service—we call it WINGS. Roberta saw the news of the devastation in Alaska and came here when she found out our town was planning a huge aid initiative. She's been working nonstop. Everyone in Wilkins has."

"That's very commendable—"

"You are both welcome to come and contribute in your spare time," the reverend said.

"We are working, Reverend Wolf."

"Reverend Paul," Paul corrected him with a smile. "Of course you are. I'm just saying that your colleague Roberta Hand took her vacation time to help out." He could see that this conversation was exasperating the officers. He didn't particularly want to thwart them; it was just the way they barged into his town, accusing people, waving search warrants. Such behavior was not to be condoned. Especially since he and Roberta had, in fact, talked with the tribal elders, and they had assured them that there was no murder, just some misunderstanding. Jon was an innocent man.

"But you see, Reverend Paul," Officer Merry tried again. "We did find evidence not too far from Wilkins."

"What kind of evidence?"

Officer Merry looked at his partner, and the man shrugged. "Well, typically we don't share details of the investigation with the public. But you are not the public." The reverend just smiled at them. "Okay then. We found a woman's bloody clothing."

"Ms. Blue's?"

"Well, we don't have a way to genetically tying the bloody clothing with Ms. Blue. Surprisingly, we never found any medical records."

"Did you try to contact the tribe?" Paul asked.

"Yes."

"And?"

"The first time we talked with someone from the tribe, we got a very different account of Ms. Ay-Tal Blue. The man from the tribe wouldn't give us his name other than to say he was one of the elders. But he was just as interested as we were in what happened to Ms. Blue. He was obviously worried about her."

"Well, things tend to be a bit confused in the beginning," Paul said. "Was that before or after the earthquake?"

"Before," Officer Merry said. "But we've spoken with the elder again yesterday, and the story changed completely. Basically, we got the same answer you did—there was no crime committed against Ms. Ay-Tal Blue. She is just fine."

"I see. If there is no crime, why are you chasing Mr. Uolan?"

"He still stole the gun from the conductor," Officer Rogers said. "That is a crime."

"And there's the bloody clothing," Officer Merry added.

"Are you sure about the gun?"

"We've interviewed the conductor. We have his statement."

"Did you interview Jon?"

"Yes. He told a very different story. And there's a matter of Mr. Uolan's son. The boy seems to be missing too."

"Not according to the tribe," Paul said. "I asked about him too and spoke to the boy's grandfather directly, in fact. So aside from someone's bloody clothing and a missing gun, you have nothing. Is that right?"

"Reverend Paul," Officer Rogers said. "This is not our first interview."

"No, it is not." Paul remembered the interrogations over the death of Mason and then Ben Wilkins. These people couldn't take no for an answer. "But you see, we here in the town of Wilkins like to do things our way. Accidents happen.

Even to the same family over and over again. You've looked into it, our sheriff looked into it, and no one ever found anything suspicious. So why bring it up again?"

"That's not exactly accurate, Reverend Paul."

"That's how I remember it."

"Both deaths—Mason Wilkins's and his dad's, Ben Wilkins—were deemed suspicious. But you blocked all access. The bodies were cremated before the police even got a chance to look into anything."

"That's not exactly accurate either, Officers. There were no remains, really, in Mason's death. Interrogating his parents right after such a horrific accident was not the right thing to do. You know that too. Why bring it up again?"

"Because we went to the hospital and spoke with Burt Wilkins."

Paul sat up. With all that was going on and with how sick Burt was, he didn't think that the police would go there. *Why would the doctors let them?* There was an explicit order for family-only access. "Mr. Wilkins is very ill and heavily drugged," he said. "His wife is beside herself. I wish you'd leave well enough alone." He instantly regretted adding the last thing. What he wished for was his own private business.

"We thought you'd feel that way, Reverend *Paul.*" Officer Merry put a lot of emphasis on the name. "But this is yet another case of a Wilkins here who is on the verge of an accidental death. That would be the sixth Wilkins, would it not? In fact, it's every single Wilkins in town."

"There's still Ada Wilkins," Paul said. "And Burt is not dead."

"Not yet. But we've asked the doctors. His prognosis is very grave. Burt will never fully recover."

"I'm sorry to hear that. But it's still early, Officers. And I would rather you didn't harp death on any member of my congregation. Mrs. Wilkins is very upset as it is. Is there anything else I can help you with?"

"We have a search warrant for your church."

"So I was told."

"We plan on going through your donation center below."

"You're welcome to it," Paul said. "Of course, the items that have already been packed up are off limits—even the police are not allowed to search mail and open packages inside a post office without a specific warrant for each item, I believe." The officers exchanged a glance again. Paul felt like he had scored a small victory.

"Your church basement is an official post office?"

"Every year, from Thanksgiving to the end of the day, December seventeenth."

"I see. Do you mind if we take a look right now?"

"Not at all." Paul stood up and motioned for the officers to follow him. He hoped that there had been enough time for Arrow, Saga, and Roberta to leave. Roberta had told him that these men wanted to question the kids about Jon and Burt. It was all just to stir up trouble, and he didn't want any more trouble. He hoped that Hazel and her parents had left the church by now as well. The town of Wilkins didn't need another investigation. Some accidents should remain accidents for the good of the people of his town.

Chapter Thirteen: Running

Saga Turgis

Saga watched as Roberta grabbed a large duffle bag and pulled out a package. Saga instantly recognized the box—Jon's package, the one he wanted to send back to his parents. Roberta then carefully pushed Jon's box into a pile of ready-to-go boxes, stacked for shipping. *It's a smart way to hide the package,* Saga thought. Now it was as good as mailed. Roberta then led them back up to the nave by the front steps.

The church was still full. There was a lot of chatter about police activity in Wilkins. Their sheriff was freely giving out his opinions on the matter, and people, mostly men, formed in a large circle around him. The other big gathering was around Ada. Apparently, she was still unwell enough that it warranted a supportive mob about her. Saga harrumphed and felt herself pushed toward the church front doors.

"Go, go, go," Roberta whispered into her ear. "We don't want to get stuck in here."

"Reverend Paul's house is back there," Arrow said, pointing to the back of the church. "But if we go that way, we will be seen from his office window."

"Got it," Roberta said and pulled them along. "My car is parked back at Nora's. I would rather it didn't identify where

I was at the moment. So we will just have to walk around to Reverend Paul's house."

There were several police cars in front of the church—the local sheriff's car, and three more from the state of Minnesota. That was a lot for a sleepy little town like Wilkins. Saga had only seen two cops; who were all of those others? It made her nervous. Arrow seemed on edge too. So was Roberta, which was weird, since Roberta was a policewoman. Saga didn't understand why she would try to avoid her colleagues. But who was she to know what was really going on? Roberta did break into Mason's room with her and Jon. That wasn't something cops did either.

"We can cut through the playground," Arrow said and turned away from the police cars. They ran past the elaborate Nativity display. All the statues were full size—tall as grown men, big as real camels. They were heavy, too. Not only had Saga helped to set them up, she also helped touch up the paint with her school's art class. The high school did this maintenance every year, in September, as part of its arts curriculum. The shop class also helped with repairs. There was always something—an ear that fell off or a finger that snapped. Saga had a lot of personal experience maneuvering those wooden giants.

They crouched low and tried to keep the decorations between themselves and the church. The leaves were mostly gone now, and the denuded braches weren't much cover. If anyone saw them, they would look mighty suspicious running like that. Saga tried not to think that way—it didn't really help, did it?

There was a white picket fence all the way around the church's property. At the back was a parking space for the reverend, but only Aunt Ada and Burt ever used it. Everyone else in town either parked on the street on in the main church parking lot. Reverend Paul liked to walk everywhere, even though the town had provided him with a small car when he first arrived here. Saga had seen the car a few times. It was now over a quarter of a century old—much older than Saga—and still looked relatively new. The reverend was a strange man. Saga tried telling him about Burt several times, even before Mason died, but he never really took her seriously. He kept saying that sometimes we see things that are not really there. Burt wasn't a great guy, he agreed. Burt was ill-tempered, fast to take offense, slow to forgive, always suspicious of everyone. Reverend Paul said those weren't good traits, but we had to keep our feelings in check when accusing people of serious crimes. Saga never knew if the reverend believed her or not, but either way, he said it would break the town if Saga's accusations about Burt came out. True or not, Saga didn't want to break the town. There were too many things broken in her life already.

Arrow jumped the waist-high fence like it wasn't even a barrier. Roberta and Saga had to climb over it. They were shorter than Arrow. He did help. He even insisted on carrying Roberta's bag. After his initial coolness, Arrow was "all in" with Roberta. And it was his attitude toward this strange woman that made Saga trust Roberta even more. They had only known her for a few days, and yet she felt closer to Roberta than she did to Aunt Ada. Roberta didn't know Arrow and Saga as well as Aunt Ada probably did, but she seemed to care for them more. *Roberta might not know us as well,* Saga decided, *but she knows us better.* It wasn't the details like "I hate spinach" that counted in the knowing. It was those parts that made you truly you—your dreams and aspirations, your fears and anxieties, your needs and desires, your courage and heart. Aunt Ada didn't know any of those about Saga or Arrow. She probably wasn't even interested in knowing. Saga sniffed. Her feelings got to close to the surface sometimes.

"Are you okay?" Roberta asked. She always noticed. "We are almost there. We can talk when we get into Reverend Paul's house, okay?"

Saga nodded and hurried. There was a little creek that ran between the church and the houses on the next street over. They jumped, but the fallen leaves hid the far bank, and Saga felt her feet slide into the freezing water. It was as if the earth itself was tripping her up, grabbing her ankles, pushing her down. She yelped loudly and instantly felt guilty. She was just so clumsy...

A strong hand pulled her back to her feet—Arrow. "Are you good?"

"Yes." Saga nodded and tried not to cry. Her feet were soaked through, her clothes covered in mud, and her left knee really hurt. She must have hit a stone or a root hidden underneath all the dead foliage. She limped after Arrow and Roberta. They were almost there, just up the little hill and over another fence. Roberta took her hand and gave it a little squeeze. Tears practically exploded from Saga's eyes.

"It will be fine," Roberta said, looking back over her shoulder. "No one heard anything. Let's get to the reverend's house, and we can dry you off. I have some extra clothing in my bag. Okay?"

Saga was able to nod, even as Arrow gave her a look of something between concern, fear, and reproach. Sometimes, he simply didn't get it. Saga sniffed and tried to limp faster.

There was a small gate in the reverend's back fence. If one looked closer, it was easy to see there was a narrow path that went down to the creek below from there. Saga turned back, and sure enough, there were several large, flat, artificial paving stones placed in the creek just a few yards from where they crossed; Reverend Paul must have used this shortcut all the time. They should have looked around before jumping, but it was too late now. Arrow reached over the fence and pulled a string that lifted a latch. The gate swung open, and they rushed inside.

"We're good," Arrow exhaled.

"Let's get into the house," Roberta said. "We can rest there."

Saga glanced back. The church was still visible through the trees, so they would be visible too. They walked around the small house and were greeted by barking—Angie, the reverend's dog. Saga loved Angie. She always had a treat for the dog in her pocket, usually a Slim Jim, sometimes a piece of jerky that she bought at Nora's minimart. Arrow told her that it was probably bad for the dog, but Angie loved the treats and loved Saga for giving them to her. What could be bad in that? Saga felt her pocket for a treat but found nothing. It must have fallen out when she fell. She felt bad about that too. Still, she tried to wipe her face before anyone really noticed she had been crying. Well, Arrow and Roberta would know anyway.

"Do you have keys?" Arrow asked.

"No," Roberta said and pulled out a little set of lock-picking tools. Saga recognized them instantly. But before Roberta had her tools ready, the door opened. It was Jon.

"Roberta? Arrow? Saga?" he said uncertainly.

"We—" Roberta said, looking over her shoulder.

"Come in," Jon said, noting her concern and opening the door wide for them. Angie rushed in to lick everyone's hands, treat or no treat.

"Good girl. Good girl," Saga said over and over again as Angie licked the tears right off her face.

"The reverend sent us here," Saga heard Roberta explain.

"The police from Saint Paul are here. You know them—Officers Merry and Rogers." Jon took a step back, scanning the street over Roberta's shoulder and then quickly closing the front door with everyone inside. "They have a search warrant for the church."

"They can't search the packages," Saga said. "It's officially a post office down there now. And Roberta hid your package among the outgoing mail."

"You noticed," said Roberta.

Saga just shrugged. It didn't seem like Roberta was trying to hide what she was doing.

"Well, she is right, Jon. Your package to the tribe, the one that was marked 'returned to sender,' is now back in postal custody. I hope that's okay."

"Thank you," Jon said. "That was very kind of you."

"I figured you would rather not have the police open it," Roberta said with a twinkle in her eye. Saga loved her for that.

"Yes," Jon said. He seemed confused by Roberta. "Can I get you something while you wait for Reverend Paul?"

"Maybe some tea," Roberta said. "And Saga needs a bit of medical attention. I think she scraped her knee."

Jon looked at Saga and immediately motioned for her sit in one of the reading chairs.

"Let me see, Saga," he said. "I have first-aid training. Let's see what we can do, all right?" Very gently, he pulled up Saga's tights, exposing a bloody knee. Arrow whistled. It did look ugly. Saga actually felt better—here was a good justification for her tears. She smiled.

"It doesn't hurt that much," she said and winced as Jon tried to straighten her leg again. He stopped, looked, and then proceeded to take off Saga's sneaker and sock. They were soaked through. As he did, he exposed a dozen little scars all over Saga's ankle, below the sock line.

"What's that?" Roberta asked.

Saga tried to cover up. Arrow leaned in to look, his face grim.

"Burns?" Jon, crouching on the floor at Saga's feet, looked up at her.

"Many burns," Roberta said. Arrow exhaled deeply, and it sounded like a growl. "Saga, are those cigarette burns?"

Saga felt her face flash with heat. The burns had been her little secret. She had forgotten about them with all of the attention she was getting. "It's nothing," she managed but she knew that wasn't going to work.

"Who did that?" Roberta asked, her voice as soft as honey.

Saga looked from her face to Jon's—his was full of concern and empathy—to Arrow's. Her brother's face was a mask of sheer anger. His fists were clenched. Saga quickly looked away.

"Saga? Who did this?" they asked again.

"I don't know," she heard herself say. Tears were back in her eyes and running freely down her cheeks. "I don't really remember."

"I'll kill him," Arrow said and went for the door.

Jon was instantly on his feet, gripping Arrow's arm. "No, Arrow. No. That's not the way we are going to handle this." Arrow tried to shrug Jon's hand off, but Roberta also reached out to him.

"He won't get away with this any more, Arrow. I promise," she said.

Saga cried. It wasn't how this was supposed to be. She'd spent months applying creams to help these heal, but then Aunt Ada would just burn more. She said that there were more nerve endings near the bottom of the ankle—the punishment needed to be administered where Saga would feel it. She was careful to burn on top of the same places over and over again so that only a few would really show. And as much as Saga tried, some burns weren't healing any more. They just stayed scabbed until the next time Aunt Ada needed to punish her.

"I'm going to kill him," Arrow said again but no longer pulled for the door.

"It wasn't Burt," Saga said in almost a whisper. They all leaned in, trying to hear her. "It wasn't Burt," she said louder. "He didn't do it."

"Did Ada do this?" Roberta asked. Jon and Arrow were shocked into silence. "Did she burn you? You can tell me, Saga. I'll keep you safe. She will never do this to you again."

"She only did it when Burt was mad. She said that his punishments were worse. When she was done, she always took a photo to show Burt later. As proof that I had been adequately disciplined."

"Oh, Saga." Roberta leaned in to hug her. It felt nice. Saga looked up and saw her brother crying. She turned away, burying her face in Roberta's shoulder. They stayed like that for a long time, it seemed. And then Roberta patted Saga's back and said, "Why don't we remove all of that wet stuff? I can throw them over the chair next to the oven to dry. And Jon will clean your knee and put some ointment on it."

"We can also put ointment on the other wounds," Jon said and went to get the reverend's first aid kit from the bathroom.

Saga pushed Roberta away and took off her other shoe and sock and then pulled down the tights, leaving only her underwear and sweater dress on. There were more scars on her right leg. Roberta saw them but didn't comment. She picked up the wet stuff and went into the small kitchen to try to find a way of getting things dry while Jon washed the blood and dirt from Saga's knee, sprayed the disinfectant, and applied bandages. He did the same for each open sore on her legs.

● ● ●

Jon Uolan

Reverend Paul didn't come home for dinner. Jon and Roberta found some canned beef stew in his pantry that wasn't too out of date and warmed it up in one of the never-before-used pots. Arrow said that the reverend never had to look too hard for a dinner invitation in this town. His pantry was proof that he rarely ate alone.

Angie was allowed to go outside in the backyard and then was fed just as the rest of them sat down to the little dinner. Saga's socks and tights dried over the stool, but her shoes ended up going into a low-heat oven. The whole house smelled of rubber and glue and a bit of a sour old sock smell. Arrow managed to joke about it, but Jon sensed just how stricken the boy was. He hadn't been able to protect his little sister from a monster. But who knew? Monsters often came in shapes no one suspected.

After dinner, Jon offered to read something to the kids. He had found a book on Greek mythology on one of the reverend's shelves earlier. Reading was a good way to pass the time. They were all waiting for Reverend Paul to return, but it was after ten and he was still out. Through the bathroom window, which faced the backyard, they could see the windows of the church all lit up. But there was nothing they could learn from just staring at the church. And Roberta insisted that it was better not to show any lights in the house, so they stopped turning on the lights when going to the bathroom. They even decided that turning on the lights in the living room, which faced away from the church, was a bad idea. So Jon read from the light of a streetlamp up the road. It wasn't much, and when he finally gave up, Roberta resolved it was time to put the kids to bed. Saga got the reverend's bed. Her brother insisted on sleeping on the floor in the bedroom, right next to the bed, guarding his sister. Roberta and Jon took the two reading chairs in the living room; they didn't plan to sleep anyway.

● ● ●

"It's dark enough to go in the backyard without being seen," Roberta said just moments after sitting down. "I will take Angie in back there to do her business and try to figure out what's going on." She stood up, and Jon stood up with her.

"We'll go together," he said. Roberta shrugged, and they both crept outside.

The wind was cold, but the day's intermittent rain showers had finally stopped. It was a relatively clear night, with a few big black clouds flying across the star-lit sky, obscuring for the moment an almost-full moon. They walked carefully around the house, Angie trotting along with them. Standing right next to the back fence, they could see the bright, abstract patterns of colorful glass illuminated from the inside—the church's windows. The Christmas lights hanging on the surrounding trees were turned on. It was a beautiful display. *More beautiful from outside than in,* Jon thought.

"They must still be voting," Roberta said.

"Voting?"

"They had a big, town-wide meeting today. Reverend Paul was making his people decide on what to do about your people," Roberta said.

"I don't understand. What is there to decide? They will

send the aid packages and that will be the end of it. Not that I'm not grateful," he quickly added. "But I didn't think there was anything left to decide."

"Your tribe is dying," Roberta said. Jon tried to interrupt, but she reached out and stopped him with a light squeeze of the hand. "Don't deny it, Jon. That was even true before the tsunami. There won't be any rebuilding, not with climate change. It doesn't make sense to rebuild the town on land that is going to be under the sea in just a few decades."

Jon thought of all those years of getting Ay-Tal to protect their land, the legal battles that went all the way in front of the Supreme Court. *Was that all for nothing?* "We can't just—" he started.

"You can't make people come back against their will, Jon," Roberta said. "And if you've noticed, the town of Wilkins has similar problems."

"They are not going to be under water any time soon."

"Not under actual water, no," Roberta said. "But this town is dying just the same. Young people are leaving. This might be Wilkins's last generation."

"How does this relate to my people?"

"Different causes, similar outcomes."

"But—"

"Sometimes solutions to problems lie in unexpected places. Reverend Paul figured it out days ago. He is now helping the rest of his congregation to catch up." She waited for him to catch up too, but Jon refused to see the solution. His people were tied to their land. They were one and the same. "Not true, Jon," Roberta said as if reading his mind. "Your people didn't always live where they do now, right? Your tribe traveled the world to find its place in it."

"But we did find it," Jon said stubbornly.

"Time and space, they are one, right? Sometimes as time

moves, so does the location."

"You mean for my people to move here? To Wilkins?" Jon thought it was a preposterous idea. "We have nothing in common with these people."

"Hmm." Roberta turned and faced Jon. And then, suddenly, she reached up and pulled his head down and kissed him right on the lips. There was a feeling like their skin merged, like some part of this woman entered Jon and explored a bit before letting go. He staggered backward when she pulled away, it was so unexpected...so different. Roberta's features rearranged themselves ever so slightly. But in the dark of the night, it could have been just his imagination playing sick tricks. "I've always wanted to know what Ay-Tal saw in you all those years," she said quietly.

"Ay-Tal?" Jon's head spun. He didn't understand.

"All those millennia, she stayed. We all moved on, but she stayed."

"Are you one of..."

"I'm surprised you didn't recognize me right off, Jon," Roberta said, one eyebrow raised slightly above the other, the starburst in her left eye more prominent somehow, making her face a bit unsymmetrical. "And there I thought I made an impression on you."

"Mary?" Nothing and everything made sense.

"I think it's time for me to visit the reverend to make sure his vote goes as planned," she said, the crooked smile clearly visible in the moonlight. Jon recognized that smile—somehow there was a shadow of the two-faced woman he met just a week ago in Roberta's expression. "Take care of the kids for while, will you? I'll be back," she said and whistled for Angie. And together they walked out of the back gate and across the creek. Jon watched them go. God and dog.

• • •

Ay-Tal

Ay-Tal walked casually into the Eau Claire General Hospital. She was Mason Wilkins again. She'd had two other bodies since she parted ways with Jon, but this was the one that was resolving the clearest path into the future. She kept the set of clothing—the leather jacket, jeans, cowboy boots, and a black t-shirt—in the small boathouse by the lake. With all of the abandoned homes around Wilkins, it was easy to stay mostly undiscovered. So far, only Burt had come into direct contact with Mason, and that triggered his massive panic. Ay-Tal was horrified that Saga almost got hurt in one of the man's more berserker moments. It still worked out okay, though. Burt was now damaged enough never to be able to abuse another human...*well, not physically.*

Smiling at the nurses and waving hello, Ay-Tal carried a large bouquet of flowers—*just a young boy on his way to see his sick uncle.*

"Excuse me! Excuse me!" a woman at the nurses' station called to him. Ay-Tal stopped and gave her another wide smile. "Where are you going? Who are you here to see, young man?"

"Burt Wilkins? I'm his nephew, Mason Wilkins," Ay-Tal said and walked over to the woman, an attending nurse in the intensive care unit. "I was told he was taken here after an accident? My parents are talking with the doctors. But I just wanted to come up and see Uncle Burt right away. They said he is very sick, is that true?" He added just the right amount of hesitation and a mixture of concern and youthful ignorance. The woman smiled at him and checked her books, but Ay-Tal could see Burt's name written on the wall above the station. Based on the room number, Burt was just around the corner from here, close to the stairs. The door to his room was not directly visible from the vantage point of the nurses' station—*perfect.*

"It says here only family is allowed to visit," the woman said and looked up at Ay-Tal. He smiled back, nodding—he knew that he looked like family. There was a strong familial resemblance among Wilkins men. She nodded back. "But I'm sorry to say you can't take those flowers into your uncle's room." She pointed and looked genuinely sorry. "Mr. Wilkins is suffering severe bronchial distress and lung inflammation. We just can't have flowers in his room. Sorry," she said again.

"Well, will you take them?" Ay-Tal said and pushed the giant clump of flowers across the desk and into the woman's face. She giggled and took it from him.

"I will place them here on this table, okay? This way, whenever Mr. Wilkins is being wheeled in and out of his room, he will be able to see them."

"That's perfect. Mom said that these are his favorites." Ay-Tal smiled again as the woman took the flowers and laid them on top of her desk. "Can I just have a little peek into my uncle's room? I promise not to disturb him. I'm just so worried for Uncle Burt. We all are."

"Of course you are," the attending nurse said. She looked him up and down and then made up her mind. "Just for a few minutes, mind you." She walked around the desk and walked Ay-Tal to Burt's door. "Here we go. Just sit quietly in that chair. I'll be back when I get your flowers in some water. Just need to find something to hold them." She smiled at him and rushed away. Ay-Tal walked into the darkened room.

There was a lot of large medical equipment around Burt.

He had tubes sticking out and machines breathing for him. He looked to be in bad shape. Ay-Tal smiled. *Good.*

"Hello, Uncle Burt," he said and pulled the chair close to the bed, where Burt could see him. "Remember me?"

Burt had his eyes closed when Ay-Tal walked in, but now the eyelids fluttered and his eyes opened. They were completely bloodshot. They remained unfocused for a while, but then they found Ay-Tal...Mason. With a start, Burt's whole face transformed into a mask of terror. The heartbeat indicator went crazy. Ay-Tal leaned out and saw that the nurse wasn't back yet. He carefully turned off the heart monitor.

"No need for all that noise, right, Uncle?"

"How? How?" Burt managed, his voice raspy, no tonality left in it, just sand rushing past rocks. "You're dead."

"I *am* dead, Uncle," Ay-Tal smiled widely. "And it was *you* who killed me."

"I...I..." There was hardly any sound coming from Burt's lips, just the motions outlining the letter forms. "I didn't," he finally managed.

"First your parents, then Mason, then your own brother." Burt's eyes widened. "Yes, I know about your parents, too. They knew about you and the little kids. Even back then, you were into it already. They caught you, didn't they? And told you they would send you away."

"How?"

"Reverend Paul. He knew why the previous reverends left. A string of them who didn't stay more than a few weeks. Your parents managed to smooth things out, though. They managed to keep things hushed. All who knew were carefully removed, put in doubt. But they knew. And you knew that they knew. And you couldn't stand that, right?"

"It was just an accident," Burt breathed out.

"The car burst into flames. They never managed to

get out." Ay-Tal watched Burt squirm in his hospital bed. "Those were just the first murders. Oh, I know there is no way to prove it now. I just want you know that I know." Burt whimpered, trying to reach for the emergency call button. Ay-Tal snatched it out of his hand. "None of that now, Uncle Burt." Burt fell back onto his pillows. "Somehow Reverend Paul knew, though. When you hit your brother and sent him to the hospital, the good reverend managed to send you away to prison, didn't he? They thought it couldn't be done. Not to a Wilkins. Not in the town of Wilkins. But Paul Wolf managed it. And yet he is still with us. You know that man keeps impeccable records, don't you?" Burt's eyes widened beyond what seemed to be possible. "He thinks of it as an insurance policy. He is a strange man, that Reverend Paul of yours."

Ay-Tal leaned outside again. The nurse wasn't back yet. *Good.*

"And then when you were finally released from prison, you found out that your girl went ahead and married your brother. Ada didn't wait for you. I think it was another one of Reverend Paul's schemes. He didn't want a good girl like Ada to be stuck with you for the rest of her life. And that baby needed a mother. It was perfect—"

Burt's chest started to heave. He had a grimace on his face. His whole body was racked...with laughter. Ay-Tal was taken aback as he stared at this sick man. It was not the reaction he was expecting. He came here as a Ghost of Christmas Past, so to speak. He was here to scare Burt, to death if necessary. Laughing to death was not part of the plan. And this was what it looked like—Burt was laughing hysterically, turning blue for the lack of oxygen in his lungs.

"What's going on here?" the nurse walked into the room. "Oh my..." She quickly pushed Ay-Tal out of the room and called emergency.

Ay-Tal stood just outside the door, watching Burt watching him. Burt was evil. He knew that evil first-hand as a little boy.

Doctors and nurses swarmed the room in mere moments. Soon, Burt was obscured from view. Ay-Tal turned and rushed down the stairs. Something was wrong.

● ● ●

Arrow Turgis

Arrow heard Jon and Roberta leave by the front door. He was lying on the floor, unable to sleep. How could he have missed Ada's sadism? He knew about the verbal abuse...and the emotional stuff. But words were nothing to them now, right? He didn't care what Ada or Burt said about them as long as he and Saga could stay together for just a few more years at the most. As soon as Saga turned eighteen, they could leave. It would be easier than trying to spirit his sister away from this place. And as bad as it was, there was a clean place to sleep, enough food, and schooling. What could he offer his little sister? A space on the dirty floor of a dank train car? And then what? What could they accomplish without education? What could he do to earn enough money for rent somewhere? It would have to be somewhere safe for Saga to be alone a lot. The more he thought about it, the more hopeless it seemed. But if he knew about the physical abuse... He felt his fists clench—he would have killed her, if he had known. He would have burned that woman ten times as many holes for each one she dared to inflict on Saga. This town was just so evil. The worst.

"Arrow? Are you asleep?" Saga whispered from the bed.

"No."

"I'm sorry about...you know."

Arrow felt tears prick his eyes. He coughed to cover up the emotions in his voice. "There's nothing to be sorry about. You did nothing wrong."

"Well—"

"Nothing. You hear me? Nothing." He dug his fingernails into his hands to distract his mind from the horror he felt. "You should get some sleep, Saga. You still have school tomorrow."

"So do you. Right?"

"Sure."

"We *are* going to school tomorrow, aren't we, Arrow?"

"I said yes."

There were a few minutes of silence as he heard Saga breathe. She wasn't sleeping. "Arrow?"

"Yes?"

"My clothes are all dirty."

"So?"

"I can't go to school like that. People will ask questions."

"Oh." Arrow didn't know what to do about that. All their stuff was at Mrs. Nelson's B&B.

"Roberta said that she had something I can change into in her bag. Can you see what's there? I just want a sweatshirt or something. Mine is all muddy."

Arrow got up and trotted out into the living room. It was still empty, but Roberta's duffle bag was right there. He bent down and unzipped the bag. There was a Christmas sweater folded on top. He recognized it as one of the donations from years past. No one could wear those more than one season in a row. Sometimes, Arrow thought that there was a nation-wide, decades-long Christmas sweater exchange via Goodwills and other thrift stores around the country. *Ugly sweaters drifting from place to place, person to unwilling person.* One of the WINGS ladies must have insisted Roberta take it. He smiled. There was no way Saga would ever wear that; she would die of hypothermia first. He pushed it aside. A patch of shocking pink was sticking out from the bottom of the bag. He pulled just as he felt cold sweat break out on his hands and head. It was Jon's little boy's boot. There was no mistaking it—old, plastic, pink, with Dora the Explorer face printed on the side. With shaking hands he pulled it out and then pulled out the little pink sweatshirt with a matching print and the other boot, little tighty-whities with red trims and Superman flying across the butt, little girl's pink tights that Al insisted on wearing. *What the?* Jon said his boy was home with his grandparents. Al wouldn't have given up his Dora the Explorer crap unless... Arrow literally felt like he was going to puke. His head spun, and his vision tunneled on just the inside of the bag. He pushed his hand deeper, past some folded up clothing, and felt the cold grip of a gun. He spun away as if he was burned. They had to get out of here. Fast. Before Jon and Roberta returned.

He rushed back into the reverend's bedroom and pulled Saga out of bed, placing his hand over his sister's mouth.

"We've got to go," he managed and pushed the pile of muddy but now dry clothing into Saga's chest. "We've got to get out of here. Get dressed, Saga. Fast."

Saga did as she was told. In all the years the siblings were on their own and hopping trains across America, she had learned to follow Arrow's instructions first and ask questions later. He watched her dress, listening for the front door. "Hurry," he mouthed. Her eyes were as big as saucers. She made minimal noise and followed his gaze to the wall, as if trying to see through to the backyard.

As soon as Saga was done, Arrow grabbed her hand

and tiptoed out to the living room. Jon and Roberta hadn't returned. Trying not to make a sound, Arrow opened the front door and looked out. There was no one up or down the street. In the stillness of late evening, he heard a slight murmur of voices from behind the house—Roberta and Jon were talking in hushed voices. He motioned for Saga to wait for him. On a whim, he turned back, opened Roberta's bag again, and pulled out the pink boots. A large Native American bracelet with turquoise stones fell out of one of the boots. Arrow dropped it back into the bag. Quickly, he stuffed the little boots into the front of his jacket and carefully zipped the bag back up. He now had evidence. He walked back to Saga and signaled for her to follow him. Together they ran silently across the street and into the bushes in front of the abandoned house. Arrow kept pulling Saga deeper into the shadows, away from the reverend's house, away from whatever crimes had been committed by Jon and that detective woman.

"Why?" Saga asked when they were more than a block away and there was no chance they would be overheard. "What happened?"

"Not now," Arrow said. "We should get our stuff and get out of this town." He kept running, pulling Saga along. "We should have left this s-hole years ago. As soon as Mason died."

"What are you talking about? What happened back there? Did Roberta say to run?"

"We are not listening to anyone from now on," Arrow said. "It's just you and me, kid. We can make it. I can take care of you. I promise."

"But..." Saga tried to speak, but it was too hard to run and talk at the same time. And her knee still hurt a lot.

Chapter Fourteen: The Long View

Roberta Hand

Roberta walked into the church through the back door, Angie at her heels. The dog knew exactly where to go, obviously very familiar with the route from the house to the reverend's office inside the church. The office was empty now, but there was a lot of noise from both the stairs leading down into the basement and the hallway into the nave of the church. Roberta considered her options and went into the main church. Reverend Paul was standing at his podium at the crossing.

"Our town has always been extremely diverse. Immigrants from all corners of the world made Wilkins their home. We've always welcomed strangers, hoping to make friends," he was saying. "How many of you traveled to Japan? To Ethiopia? All the way to New Zealand to meet face to face with the people our WINGS had helped? How many of those friends have been welcomed into our community over the years?"

"A visit is very different from a permanent residence," someone shouted out from the congregation. But Roberta felt that most of the people here were agreeing with Paul.

Wilkins was on the verge of welcoming Jon's people into its midst. The reverend was convincing them. She moved back to stand by one of the walls, observing the turning of the tide.

The room was still divided into more or less two large clumps of people: the women clustering around Ada Wilkins and the men around Wilkins's sheriff. Each group would need their own reasons to make up its mind. Roberta saw that the men were nodding in approval, while the women still seemed to be unsure. There had been no new jobs created in Wilkins for many years, but none of the men felt that the influx of strangers would take anything away from them personally. On the contrary, all those abandoned houses would need construction done to get them ready for habitation. Those people would need services. The state and federal government would grant assistance with resettlement, and that would mean money for the whole town, for schools, for roads, for healthcare. And then there were some possible perks that came with Jon's people having First Nation status. Some of those rights had just been reestablished by the Supreme Court in the case won by Ay-Tal Blue. Reverend Paul reiterated each reason why Jon's people would be good for Wilkins several times, stating it a little differently with each telling, highlighting some aspect or another that fired up the imaginations of different townsfolk.

The reverend then went on to talk about WINGS, which was mostly run by the women of Wilkins. And it was one thing to organize help for the faraway outsiders and another to have all those refugees move here. Women felt it would disrupt WINGS too much. Ada in particular pressed hard against all those strangers invading their lives this way. Roberta could see the worry of losing her status as Wilkins's Queen Bee in Ada's whole demeanor. Her sister, Beth Olson, seemed to be arguing both sides. Her husband was on the side of inviting Jon's tribe to stay in Wilkins, so she seemed torn.

Someone brought up the differences in religions, but Reverend Paul said if it didn't bother him, why should it be a problem for anyone else in Wilkins? Americans had the freedom of religion as a right. Most of the people who came to settle in this part of the country did so due to religious persecution back in their ancestral homelands. Religious tolerance was their thing, right? The reverend kept reminding them, and people kept agreeing...at least vocally. And Roberta knew if one asserted a thing multiple times, eventually saying something was true made it true. It was human nature. It was still fun to watch, though.

"Our town has suffered so much tragedy," Ada spoke up, and the whole congregation hushed. It was universally agreed that she had suffered more than most. And she was a Wilkins. When a Wilkins talked, the town of Wilkins listened. "And Mr. Jon's people have suffered," Ada continued, still unable or unwilling to pronounce Jon's family name, Uolan. "How can we heal with so much trouble all piled up one on top of the other? We need time," she finished. And surprisingly, many of the women agreed. Even the men seemed to agree—there was no rush. *We can always invite the tribe in the spring,* the sentiment was emerging.

"But those people need a place to live now," Reverend Paul spoke up in his powerful voice. "As unsettled as we are by tragedy, Jon's people are even more so. A wound, any wound, shouldn't be left to fester. We have enough to share. In giving, we heal ourselves." He looked over his congregation and the many small conversations within and spoke in a larger-than-life tone. "Jon's people are pressed for time. But so are we. We, the people of Wilkins, are running out of time." He looked around, trying to catch the eyes of many in his audience, insisting that they hear him. "There was no kindergarten this year. There was no first grade. Wilkins no longer needs an elementary school or even a middle school. All our kids are of a high school age. And when these young people graduate, when they are gone, what then? Wilkins is a dying town. We can hang on for a few more years. Watch as our neighbors and friends move away to live with their kids and grandkids in some distant communities, our homes devalued to nothing. We can dwindle away to become yet another ghost town, those left behind to live out their old age alone and isolated, no one left to take care of them." He paused dramatically and then finished. "Or we can transform."

Roberta admired the presentation and the argument. *Hit them emotionally and financially. Show them a grim future and then give them hope.*

"We need to grow our community to survive. We need new people to call Wilkins their home. I move for a vote," the reverend called. "All those in favor inviting Jon's First Nation tribe to move into our town raise your hands."

Almost all hands went up into the air. Roberta observed Nora looking surreptitiously at Ada but then defiantly raising her hand. Mrs. Nelson wanted to run her B&B again, Roberta knew. An influx of new people would mean she would again get to do what she loved. It took time, but by the end, only Ada and a few women right next to her didn't raise their hands. Reverend Paul didn't ask for the show of hands of all those who opposed the proposal of merging the people of Wilkins with those of Jon Uolan's tribe. There was no point of setting up sides, allowing opposition to rot the town from the inside. It was clear that he had won the day; Jon's tribe would be invited to move to Wilkins.

What Roberta found strange was that no one even considered the possibility that the tribe might say no. Not that it would happen—Ay-Tal still led her people...for now. If asked by their god to pick up and move again, Ay-Tal's tribe would come. That's what gods like them did—they found a way forward for the people they served. Gods found ways of creating new "we's" from isolated "me's."

Roberta looked around. The police officers from Saint Paul weren't in the audience. She shook her head and silently moved to check on what was happening in the basement.

• • •

Downstairs was an orderly pandemonium. There were about half a dozen police officers sorting and cataloging the mountains of donated clothing and home supplies. But given that part of the basement was designated an official post office, there was a tight division between the items already packed and "mailed" and those that WINGS was just getting ready to send. Many women of Wilkins had volunteered their time to upcycle the old items into handmade creations. There were tables set up for quilting, others for stuffed toy making, and yet more for assembling "welcome home" baskets. Based on what Roberta observed, the women who were doing the craft work would be furious when they saw what the cops did to their setup. All of the careful work of organizing the materials by color, shape, texture, and other physical properties had been disrupted. Roberta let out a low whistle—it would take days for some of the women to get their workspaces right again. *It will be ugly.*

"Detective Hand," Officer Merry called to her as soon as he spotted Roberta on the steps leading down into the basement. "Over here, please." He motioned for her to join him from her observational spot.

Roberta walked over to him and Officer Rogers. The two

men seemed to be in charge of the search. "Good evening," she said. Officer Rogers harrumphed. He looked frazzled. "Have you found anything interesting?" she asked.

"Interesting? No," Officer Merry said. "But we did find things."

"Do tell." Roberta perched on the corner of one of the folding tables and smiled.

"Well, we did find three railroad blankets at Mrs. Wilkins's house. As you know, two blankets were missing after the Ms. Blue incident."

"But you found three?"

"The Wilkinses seemed to be collecting railroad memorabilia. There were other items—an antique train whistle, some cups and cutlery clearly taken from the train kitchens—"

"Are you planning to arrest Ada Wilkins for stealing railroad crap?"

"No, of course not."

"Then why are you bothering with all that stuff?"

"Did you know about the broken window at her house?" Officer Merry asked.

"Yes. It was the talk of the town," Roberta said. "Sounds like Burt Wilkins threw his nephew's old computer out of the window. He also did a number on the room. It looked like a tornado went through it—I was there to help late that afternoon. And from what I understand, that was the computer that Burt burned inside the metal drum in the back parking lot of his nightclub. Is there something else?"

"You seem to be very well informed, Detective," Officer Rogers said.

"Thank you. But this is a very small town. Burt's strange behavior was the biggest thing that happened here in a long time—"

"No, not really," Officer Merry interrupted her. "Jon's arrival and then Saga's departure were the biggest things to hit this community."

"Yes, you're right," Roberta said and stared at the man.

"Jon and his son's arrival," he repeated. "Saga's departure and later retrieval. Jon's return—"

"Without his son," Officer Rogers added.

"Without his son," Officer Merry continued. "And then the choice of Jon's tribe as this year's beneficiary of WINGS's charity, making the faraway earthquake and tsunami big news in this small town. And finally there was the strange behavior of Burt Wilkins and his subsequent injury landing him in a hospital with an uncertain future. That's a lot for a sleepy place like Wilkins."

"Yes," Roberta agreed. "A lot has happened in a short time."

"You are not seeing connections?"

"With what? If you are talking about Mr. Uolan and the choice WINGS made for their charity, then certainly. But I think of it more like serendipity. Mr. Uolan's presence in this community shone a spotlight on the fate of his people. All Americans, I might add. The people of Wilkins got an inspiration for their charity goals, and the people of a First Nation tribe will get some desperately needed help. It seems like a win-win situation. Don't you think?"

"Very convenient," Officer Rogers murmured.

"Yes, very. So what's really the problem here?" Roberta pressed. She spun around, pointing to the heaps of stuff being processed by the police. "Do you have any idea of how much trouble you are going to be with the women who run this joint?"

"What do you mean?" Officer Rogers jerked his head up and took a look around. His eyes bulged and he took a deep breath. "I see."

"Yes," Roberta continued. "It will be ugly as soon as anyone above figures out what's going on down here. Did Reverend Paul know what you gentlemen are up to?"

"He told us to go for it," Officer Merry said. He too looked grim now. "We can clean up before we go," he added uncertainly. Roberta just shook her head. No amount of "clean up" would return this basement into WINGS's charity factory. Not by these men.

"What were you hoping to find?" she asked.

"Evidence."

"Yes. But sometimes it is easier to just ask," Roberta said, shaking her head. "I assume you've spoken to the new tribal elder? Mr. Uolan senior? Jon's dad?"

"Yes, we have. Have you?"

"Of course. I spoke with Ms. Blue directly too," Roberta said. She wasn't really lying either—she had spoken directly to Ay-Tal...just not as Ms. Blue. The expressions on the officers' faces were priceless. "She seemed perfectly fine. Not a hair out of place. She rushed back home when she heard about the disaster." That was a lie, but Ay-Tal would have rushed home if not for the problems in Wilkins.

"But Jon..."

"You put Jon in prison. You told him to stay around, right? Did you tell him he wasn't allowed to travel?"

"I...I'm not sure about that, Detective. You were one of the last ones to talk with him—"

"Don't be silly, Officer Merry. I spoke to Mr. Uolan almost two days before he was released. I'm sure there were people at your station who spoke more with that man than I ever did. You can check your records. At the time, my sum total of exchange with your prisoner was under ten minutes. Way under." That was also true...well, it was true for Roberta, just not for Mary.

"But you let him go—"

"I did no such thing," Roberta said, making sure outrage seeped into her carefully moderated tone. She loved theater and had introduced the concept of well-structured plays to the Greeks way back...well, it wasn't that far back—only a few thousand years ago, a nothing in the grand scheme of things. "I was assigned to interview Jon by my superior officer in Eau Claire, since the supposed crime was committed in Wisconsin and not Minnesota, our jurisdiction. And when I got to your station, I saw that, by law, you had to let Mr. Uolan go. Holding a man without charging him beyond the legal time—"

"It was a holiday," Officer Merry tried to argue.

"—beyond the legal time limit could have jeopardized the case against him. I followed procedures. I was taking the long view. I don't know what you guys were doing." She gave them a chastising look. Technically, detectives outranked field officers, but she wasn't interested in bringing that up... not yet, not unless it became necessary. "I took time out of my vacation to do my job. I even interviewed the tribal elders on my own time. I wanted to make sure that I wasn't socializing with a dangerous criminal. Did you know that Mr. Uolan is a highly respected member of his community? That he is in line to become the next elder of his tribe? That there are no violations in his record, not even a parking ticket?"

"We did run a background check."

"Good. Then what are we doing here?"

"There's still the matter of a missing gun and a missing kid."

"I've read the statements of the conductor. His story changed several times. At one point, he told one of my colleagues back in Eau Claire that he dropped the gun and it went off accidentally."

"I've read that too. He also said that he didn't exactly remember how he lost the gun, but he saw the woman shot."

"Are you sure that he didn't accidentally fire the gun? And then got scared and invented the whole story of a struggle?" Roberta asked. "Because whatever happened—and I agree with you about the importance of finding that gun—Ms. Blue is not a victim. If she was shot, I'm sure she would have gone to a hospital. Given the conductor's story about the amount of blood he saw—"

"What about the blood we found in the cabin? And the ripped boots? Your story doesn't make sense, Detective." He practically spat the word "detective" at Roberta.

"Perhaps my story is not complete, Officers," Roberta said. "I don't really understand what happened. But we have no victims. At least not from the incident on the train."

"The blood stains in the train passenger compartment were very degraded," Officer Rogers said thoughtfully. "It was too soon for so much deterioration. We couldn't get a DNA sample. Strange," he repeated.

"Strange," Roberta agreed. "But not a reason for turning this community upside down."

"Detective?"

"Yes?"

"Did you happen to speak with the kid too?"

"Al? Mr. Uolan's son?"

"Did you?"

"No. I haven't." Roberta wasn't sure why she lied. But she was worried that she might have reached the threshold of what these men would accept from her. "The people of Wilkins just voted to invite Jon's entire tribe to come live here," she said. The men's faces registered shock. Yes, that was unexpected. "Perhaps you will be able to find your missing kid then," she said. In the bottom of her duffle bag, back at the reverend's house, there were pink boots and pink tights and Dora the Explorer sweatshirt...together with Jon's knife, the conductor's gun, and the tribe's satellite phone. With those boots, Ay-Tal could make an encore appearance as Al before leaving these people for good.

"We better get this place in order," Officer Merry said, looking around again at the mess they'd made.

"Good idea. You might also want to interview Ada Wilkins herself—she might know something more about Burt's strange behavior." That was a real clue. Roberta wondered if these men would follow it. Ada needed to pay for her crimes.

Leaving them to it, Roberta ascended the front stairs and went back to check on the kids. There were a lot of loose ends in this town. She hoped that she could tidy it all up before Ay-Tal's people arrived. Ay-Tal would never leave if she didn't feel like her chosen people had a good course into the future.

● ● ●

Ay-Tal

Ay-Tal made it into the hospital's parking lot without being stopped. She was shaken. That was not how it was supposed to go. Perhaps all those millennia sitting among the ice with people that made her feel so comfortable was a bit too long. She was losing her touch. How could she have misjudged this so badly? She knew Ada wasn't a good person, but she hadn't noticed the true evil right before her face. That just never happened to her before. All those years of leading tribes of humans around this planet, and she had never miscalculated the trajectory of events in such a grand fashion. Mary was right, it was time to move on...as soon as she set these people to right. Gods weren't free to leave just because they got tired or made a mistake. Not that Ay-Tal had conceded yet that staying with the Omuktal was a mistake. She always stayed longer with her chosen people than others of her kind. It was many tens of thousands of years before she could finally admit that the peoples now known as Neanderthals were a dead end. All the rest moved on, but she stayed. She tried. She interbred the humans to make something even better. Modern humans were partly the result of her work. She scoured the planet for remnants of different species of humans, and with all she tried to save some genetic information in the hybrid populations she'd created. She wove the tapestry of unique DNA lines; it was such hard work. It required a very long view of humanity. Each mating, each child or individual who survived to maturity, changed humanity as a whole. She ruthlessly pruned and tended to her stock with a long view yet a micro focus on each human being.

After millions of years, one got tired.

It was very late, and there were few visitors now. The parking lot was mostly hosting hospital staff's vehicles. Ay-Tal ran to the farthest, darkest corner of the lot. The dark blue minivan was hers. For the past two days she had used it as her home, as well as transportation. The boathouse was nice, but it took too long to get from place to place without a car. There was a time when several days here or there didn't mean much. But the world had sped up. The high tempo of events, paradoxically, meant that taking a long view was more difficult; it was too easy to get distracted by minutia. Saga got it right— Ay-Tal was the God of Small Affairs. But there were just so many more affairs to focus on now, who had the time?

Inside the nondescript minivan—there were thousands

on American roads just like this one—there were several changes of clothing. Each set made a different human. Mason was her favorite. He was a good kid. Several years out from his death, and Ay-Tal could still feel the impact his life might have had on the people around him...if he lived. When there were fewer humans, it was easier to spot the Masons of the world. Ay-Tal used to protect kids like him, ensure that they got more than their share of luck. It was good for the community when she intervened to grant them additional success. Everyone benefited. Some tribal elders even used to point out those they deemed worthy of their god's extra protection. Those were the days when people were more aware of gods like her. Those days were mostly over. Well, her tribe still knew who their god was. But how many other communities knew? How many even cared? Mary didn't even look like she belonged to a permanent community. What tribe did American truck drivers belong to? They were not one people, but many.

Slipping into the back of the minivan, Ay-Tal considered what to do next. Each human community had a nexus, a pivot point around which individuals and events turned. There was no question that Burt Wilkins was a nexus, but perhaps he was not the main one. Mason was one. The kids, Saga and Arrow, were having a larger impact on their community than other kids their age. And Ada. Ay-Tal berated herself for not seeing that woman for what she was. Ada was a true psychopath. *How many did she kill?* Ay-Tal needed to find out. Slowly, she pulled off her cowboy boots and oozed out of Mason's form.

● ● ●

Roberta Hand

Roberta watched Paul pat his dog with a satisfied grin. Job well done, she had to admit. The man had managed to bend the will of his people to his will. For a man who was just a man, it was commendable, praiseworthy. She went over to express her admiration...and to inform the reverend of the disaster in the basement. That would take a lot of sweet-talking to smooth out all of the WINGS members' ruffled feathers.

Just as Roberta beelined for the reverend, Ada marched in his direction as well. If Roberta had noticed that woman sooner, she would've slowed down or moved off purposely to talk with someone else. She was not ready to deal with *her* just yet. But unfortunately, both of them ended up in front of Paul at just about the same moment.

"Reverend," Ada said, her voice insistent and harboring deep resentment. "Ms. Hand? How lovely to have you join us," she added just as Roberta came up. In Roberta's mind she added "not"—Ada was anything but happy to see her here.

"Ladies," Paul said and stood up. "What a wonderful outcome of the vote. Our small community is about to double, triple even—"

"About that," said Ada.

"I think you did a great job guiding your community to the right decision, Reverend," Roberta said. "I am truly impressed."

"You heard?" The reverend seemed pleased.

"Well, that." Ada moved her body to block Roberta off from the reverend. Roberta almost laughed—as if. But Ada was not deterred. "How are we going to deal with all these strangers, Reverend? We don't even share the same faith? Or values, or culture."

The reverend waited until Ada finished. "Remember the time you, your sister Beth, Hazel, and I all went to county fair?" he asked. Roberta saw from Ada's look that the woman remembered but didn't say so. The reverend went on regardless. "There was a mirror maze as one of the attractions. You hated the way some mirrors made you look fat and others distorted your face into an almost unrecognizable grimace." Ada made a face; it was clear she hadn't enjoyed the experience. "It was Hazel, if I remember correctly," the reverend continued, "that said that all the mirrors reflected real people, even if strangely. No matter how twisted the reflection, it was us in those mirrors."

"What's your point?" Ada asked. Roberta was also intrigued.

"Jon's people are truly spiritual people, just like we are here in Wilkins. I know, I've spoken with the elders of his tribe. Tukkuttok Uolan, Jon's dad, now leads his people's congregation—"

"They are not even Christians!" Ada's voice was loud enough to attract attention.

"As you know, Ada, I come from a family of preachers and chaplains."

"How many generations?" Roberta asked. She had a feeling about this man. Gods like her occasionally had children, and those offspring were always focal points for change in their communities. Having kids was one of the ways she and her kind shaped the human race. There was a time when it was done openly—Greece, Old Russian animists, even Christianity, all had myths of human-god offspring. Could Paul Wolf be one of theirs? The problem with so few gods and so many humans now was that they stopped keeping track of all their children and their children and their children... All moderns had some god in them now. *Some more than others, though.*

"Oh, many." Paul smiled at Roberta.

"What are you saying, Paul?" Ada asked, dropping the honorific. She did look peeved.

"My grandfather served overseas during World War Two," the reverend said, his voice patient, kind. "He helped all kinds of people. I believed he knew Nora's grandfather." And suddenly, Nora's sale of the French street jazz music collection made more sense to Roberta—focal points had a lasting impact.

"Paul—" Ada tried to interrupt him.

"I'm saying, Ada, that differences in spirituality are like those differences in the funhouse mirrors. The reflections all look different, but they show the same source."

It was an interesting analogy, and Roberta was sure she'd heard it before. She had some investigating to do when she got out of Wilkins.

"Well, I see it differently," Ada said. "Some reflections are true, and some show evil."

Roberta saw frustration on the reverend's face. She did give him credit—the man was trying very hard. And he had succeeded in making his people see things his way on the vote...but not Ada Wilkins.

"Our community is in flux," Ada pushed, "in case you haven't noticed, Paul. My husband might be dying right now—"

"Sometimes the greatest good comes from the times of greatest change, don't you think, Reverend?" Roberta said with a sympathetic smile. Burt was vile, but Ada? Roberta flashed on the image of Saga's burns. Could Burt make a good person do that to a child? Ada was twisted in some fundamental way, even if it was her husband who had forced her to hurt the girl.

"My life has been all about change for as long as I can remember," Ada said, turning on Roberta, her nostrils flaring with exasperation. "And it has rarely been for the good. Tell her, Paul. Tell her how many changes I've had to live through."

"Ada—" the reverend tried, but she spoke over him, airing her grievances.

"First Burt's parents, then Ben's wife. That tea you made me make. And the stupid home brew for Burt..." Words were coming fast and furious from the woman's mouth, tripping over themselves, filled with the unfairness of her life as she perceived it. There was so much emotion that Roberta noticed herself stepping back from the woman. "All my life you've made me do things!" Ada practically screamed that at the reverend's face. Those still left in the church backed away, pretending not to notice.

Roberta too took another step back, her ears pounding, her heart beating too fast. She didn't really know the details of the car accident that killed Burt and Ben's parents, but Ben's wife died in childbirth, from a preeclampsia-induced seizure. So what did Ada have to do with that? She kept backing up, away from Ada and the reverend. There was a dark look of concern on that man's face. He took Ada by the elbow and started to move her to the back of the church, giving Roberta a sympathetic smile. Roberta felt so confused that she smiled back automatically. *What is going on? What's wrong?*

"Why don't we go into my office, ladies?" The reverend smiled at them. Roberta felt a strong grip on her elbow as the man drew her and Ada through a small crowd continuing to discuss the vote. "Right this way, please," he said. "Ada, you clearly have a lot to tell me. And I would love Ms. Hand's opinion on all of it."

His voice smelled oily, and Roberta felt herself chilled. God or no god, she was only as strong as the body she was using at that moment. The reverend was stronger. She felt pulled, and there was nothing she could do other than attract attention. Roberta looked around wildly. Where were the cops? But they were not there, and no one was paying attention to them now. People actively tried not to notice. Ada saw Roberta's fear, and a sick smirk twisted her lips.

"I don't think you need to include me in this conversation, Paul," Roberta managed. But the reverend just dragged her even faster. Ada was following on her own, eyes blazing. *Oh gods,* Roberta thought.

"Here we are." The reverend pushed both of them into his office and closed the door. Roberta felt herself shoved into one of the chairs in front of the reverend's desk. Ada took another. She heard the click of the lock and caught Paul slipping a large brass key into his jacket. "Forgive me for the lack of amenities tonight," he said. "Usually Nora supplies me with cookies and cakes, but tonight?" He spread his hands, indicating a lack of pastries. Roberta felt her head spin. *What is going on?* "But I can make tea," the reverend said and stepped over to an antique sideboard with an electric kettle and a tray with a few cups and saucers. "I know how you like yours, Ada. But what about you, Ms. Hand? Black or something floral? Sugar? Splenda? Unfortunately, I don't have any fresh milk tonight. Nora sold out. So we will just have to make do, won't we?"

Roberta found herself holding an old-fashioned teacup on a matching saucer full of aromatic amber liquid. It didn't smell right.

"And one for you, Ada." The reverend placed an almost identical cup and saucer into Ada's hands. "I know you like peppermint." He walked around and sat at his desk, hands steepled, fingers forming the roof of a church.

Here is the church, and here is the steeple. Open the doors, and there are all the people. The nursery rhyme played through Roberta's head as if on a loop. "I don't think I need to be here," she said and tried to get up, but somehow it didn't work. The steam from her tea was making her dizzy.

"Drink some tea, Ms. Hand. It will make you feel better," Ada said with a smile and took a slurpy sip of hers. "Go on. That's it, go on," she said somehow with almost hypnotic compulsion. "As you drink, I'll tell you what really bugs me about all these new people coming into my town." Despite herself, Roberta took a big gulp of tea. It was good, very good, and she felt herself relax. She was feeling much better now.

"You see," Ada continued as the reverend nodded for her to go on. "You see, I'm about to be the last Wilkins in this town. The last Wilkins standing, so to say." She giggled a little.

"You're not a Wilkins by blood," Roberta heard herself say. She found herself floating by the ceiling, observing the strange tea party. Why was she drinking that stuff? She couldn't say.

"Blood is not everything," Ada said, her voice sounding poisonous. "Blood did nothing to keep Ben or his little wife alive, did it? Or his parents? What did blood do for Mason? He is as dead as his mother, as his father, as his grandparents, as his whole rotten kin...almost."

"Burt?" Roberta managed.

"Blood won't keep him alive either. He is too stupid to live. For almost seventeen years I had to put up with the Wilkinses. Who wants their blood? How good is it? Just enough to keep this town together. Well, I don't need it anymore. I am the last Wilkins standing," she repeated. "This town is mine. And my kids'," she added defiantly.

"Kids? What kids? Arrow? Saga?"

"God, no!" Ada laughed. "Ben wanted to make them full Wilkinses, did you know that? He was going to adopt them! As if we needed more of that kind."

"I don't understand," Roberta said. She felt a pounding headache. It was rare for gods to experience pain. If she ever got so sick that it was uncomfortable, Roberta just switched bodies. Gods suffered emotionally; they didn't need to add to that with physical discomfort. Perhaps it was time to change...

"I will be the last Wilkins standing," Ada announced. "After all those years of suffering, I deserve it. Tell her, Paul."

"You see, Roberta," the reverend said, and his voice felt all wrong somehow. "The Wilkins clan is sick. It was a strong stock when they settled this town. But over the years, they've changed."

"What?"

"Sometimes even the strongest breeds get corrupted," the reverend said, his fingers wiggling. *Why?* "I've asked Ada to help."

"And I've spent half my life helping," Ada said, screamed almost. "How much more of my life should I give to you and your schemes? No one can ask for all of me. Half is enough."

"I know about Burt," Roberta said. All those stories that Arrow told her—that man was sick! "But Mason? He was a good kid. Why didn't you protect him, Paul?"

"Sometimes we have to make sacrifices," the reverend said. "This town needs to move on. Don't you agree?"

"Yes? I thought you helped your people make the right decision tonight." Roberta noticed that her arms and legs felt numb. The teacup tilted, and the hot liquid spilled into her lap. It burned. She felt wrong. She needed to change. *Now. Right now!* She didn't have a foot fetish like Ay-Tal. She built her bodies from little tokens. Sometimes it was just a shirt that coalesced into a unique human. But it was difficult to wear the same shirt day after day, year after year. Most often, it took several items—a piece of jewelry, a watch, a type of undergarment. Sometimes even shoes. But never just one thing. It was always a collage of things. Now, she needed to remove those. She tried to raise her arms to pull out the little earrings Roberta Hand wore all the time. And the necklace with a small orange stone that matched the ones in her earrings. And the small gold chain bracelet—sensible, yet feminine. There was a matching anklet around her left leg, just underneath the wool sock, completely invisible from outside. Her hands wouldn't move. And strangely, she no longer seemed to care. She looked down at her lap, sure that the hot tea burned her, yet it felt distant somehow. She hated pain.

"With them dead, I'll be the mayor of Wilkins," Ada said. "But you had to go and invite all those others, didn't you, Paul? What if they don't want me? Don't need me like our Wilkins people do? What if they don't understand how it works?"

"Oh, I think you are overthinking this, Ada," the reverend was saying. It felt like he was all the way across town. Small, far away, fuzzy. "New people will come, and we will make them into Wilkins people, just like we did with all those others who came and joined out town, escaping disaster in their homelands. I'm sure you are strong enough to handle a few newcomers, Ada. You've been so strong already. We need those people. Without people there is no town. So what would you be a mayor of? Right, Ada? You can handle them."

Roberta couldn't turn her head, but she saw from the corner of her eye that Ada was sprawled down into her chair, hands loose by her sides. Her tea spilled on the floor. *What is going on? What? What? Paul?*

Thoughts became more and more difficult to hold to, the God of Small Affairs—*wasn't that what Saga called them?*—felt a twinge of panic. But then she let go. All was as it was.

• • •

Ay-Tal

Ay-Tal felt the death of Roberta...Mary...Kuhikuhi... All the gods were linked. While they might hide from each other in life, in death there was no anonymity. Ay-Tal's tendrils moved and twined and pushed into the earth, trying to reach the dying god, twinning with the mycelia under the ground, reaching out to feel the pulse of the planet, sensing for others of her kind through the vast network of filaments filling most of the top soil almost everywhere on Earth.

There was a time when moving information through the world was faster through the gods' mycelia network than by any other method. All trees talked to each other that way, too. The earth gave, and the emotions poured from one end of the continent to another. Ice and water were barriers, but there was no need to speed data across vast distances. The pace of life was measured, leisurely, even.

Kuhikuhi moved her people across an ocean and stayed with them until it took. Ay-Tal moved over an ice bridge and hid in the permafrost for thousands of years, protecting her chosen people from disaster and sickness. It was easy to pick out where the gods hid—just look for villages where the flu didn't kill, where people survived earthquakes, where wars passed by. Modern humans learned to map such anomalies. Soon, the gods would have nowhere to hide. Information moved too fast. Emotions couldn't catch up to the speed of the modern data flow. There was a disconnect.

Tendril by gray tendril, Ay-Tal dissolved herself into the short patch of grass on the perimeter of the hospital's parking lot. She flowed deep and out, seeking for memories of Roberta, hoping to catch some of her before she dispersed back into the void from which she came. Others came as well. Ay-Tal felt them all. There were fewer than she remembered.

It took hours. By morning light, Ay-Tal was in the ground of the church in the small town of Wilkins. It was too late for Roberta. The world was vast now, and humans occupied most of it, making touching fellow gods difficult. Gods used the Internet now instead of mycelia. Language was better at transmitting informational details than raw emotions. Back in past millennia, all humans lived close enough that the gods could feel each other almost continuously. Ay-Tal remembered the bonds, recalled spilling herself into the ground to merge as one. But she disagreed about culling the humans that were different. She believed in maintaining the diversity of minds, while other gods sought the one true perfect human form. When her group of Denisova hominins was purged, she got angry and left for another continent. She was the first to lead a group of people into the New World. And while others followed to colonize those continents, she stayed in the north, bitter over her loss. Her band of humans survived where so many others didn't. She was not the only one who was bitter. Some other gods resisted the purge and took their people to faraway lands as well. Aboriginal Australians left with their god and hid from the world for almost fifty thousand years, as she slowly added a bit of her own essence into her people's DNA.

The sky grayed around the nativity scene.

$\bullet\ \bullet\ \bullet$

Paul Wolf

The reverend waited until Roberta passed away. It would look like a heart attack. No one would even question it. The detective had been under so much pressure lately. Ada was sleeping in the other chair. The woman was agitated; she needed to be taken back in hand. Another half hour or so, she would be as good as new. He had taught her to make these teas himself. Ada loved tinkering with chemistry...brain chemistry. The world was filled with interesting compounds.

Paul looked at his watch. It was hours past midnight. Most of his congregation went home by now. It was a school night, after all. He smiled. He liked it when everything worked smoothly and predictably.

"Ada? Can you hear me, my little sweet?" He bent over, lifted one of Ada's eyelids with his finger—dilated—and checked her pulse at the neck with another. Slow, steady. A nice, regular heartbeat. She was perfect. Ada's tea contained a bit of stinking nightshade. It was a common enough weed. It didn't take much to have the desired effects—memory loss, sleepiness, extreme susceptibility to suggestion, hallucinations. The chemical derivatives of this plant had wide uses in medicine, but it was also used for darker purposes, as a truth serum to aide with interrogations or to facilitate sexual assault, robbery, killing even. But Paul used only enough to make Ada remember what he needed her to remember and to go along with his plans for Wilkins's population spurt. Stinking nightshade was his favorite, and he had years of practice getting his dosages just right for his favorite parishioner. He was very confident that he knew what Ada needed to make her more pliable. Sometimes, that woman was too stubborn and selfish for her own good.

Roberta got something else, of course. She had ground leaves of foxglove in her tea, another common purple flower used as a pretty decoration in many gardens around town. Foxglove was often confused by lay people with Symphytum. Both plants had flowers of similar height, arrangement, and color. But while foxglove was poisonous, Symphytum's leaves were commonly used to make herbal tea.

"It was an innocent mistake, Officer," Paul mumbled as he set himself in a chair in front of Ada. "Mrs. Wilkins grows herbs and makes her own teas. We've sent out hundreds... thousands of homemade gifts from her garden over the years. Never once... Yes, so tragic. She did say she was having trouble with her eyesight of late... Yes, I should have been more careful. But once the leaves are ground into a tea bag, who can tell? It was a shock. Shock." He shook his head, tears running down his face. "What a tragedy." He felt so much compassion for the detective. And for Ada. *Poor woman, always here to help others... Tragedy on top of tragedy.* Of course it might never come to that—*just a heart attack...*

"Ada? Can you hear me?" he called in a soothing voice. The woman made a grumping noise, and the reverend smiled. "Good, very good. Ms. Hand and I tried to comfort you, with Burt being in the hospital and all. You've truly suffered the most, Ada." Ada sniffed a sob. *Good, good.* "But if everyone leaves, who will take care of you? Who will take care of our little town? How would you lead our WINGS if all of the feathers were gone? You see, we need more busy, busy bees for our little operation, don't we?" He made it sound like the buzzing of the bees, and Ada smiled and nodded. "You are so good at this, my little sweet. We need you."

"You need me," Ada mouthed.

"Ms. Hand—"

"The detective lady."

"That's right, the detective lady, Roberta Hand. She came with us to my office so we could discuss the expansion of our operation."

"We need more people."

"Yes, yes, we do," Paul agreed. "How can you be a leader if there is no one to lead?"

"I will be Wilkins's mayor now," Ada said. Her eyes were

still closed, and a beatific smile fluttered across her face. *Good, good.*

"Of course you will," Paul confirmed. "You are our last Wilkins."

"The last."

"The only," Paul said and rubbed Ada's bony fingers. "And your reservations during our vote were voiced only because you have that responsibility on your shoulders. You wanted to give our people a safe place to air their concerns. By saying you were worried, you gave some of our ladies the permission to say what worried them. You laid it all out in the open. Sliced open a festering wound to prevent rot."

"I support my ladies, my WINGS."

"You do, Ada, you do. Roberta was new, and she needed to understand how things worked in our little town."

"That woman knows nothing." Ada's lips curled in a cruel grimace.

"So we went to my office for some quiet discussion and some of your home-made tea."

"I make great tea."

"Yes, you do, Ada, yes, you do."

"It always relaxes me and makes me see feel so much better," Ada added.

"Me too, Ada, me too."

"Sometimes I get headaches and stomach aches, though." She pulled her hands out of the reverend's hold and hugged her middle. Paul knew she would have an upset stomach all night and day tomorrow. But it couldn't be helped. There was a time when he watched her on a stretcher with what everyone assumed was food poisoning. She got better, and he got better at portioning. Sterility was an unfortunate side effect. Well, maybe not that unfortunate; Ada was a lousy mom. And she didn't know about that...not yet.

"Elsa almost lost the baby, though," Ada said.

Paul's face turned into a cold mask. It took years for Ada to stop talking about that. *Stupid girl.*

"She—"

"Ada? You know we never bring up the past. Remember?"

She clutched her middle and rocked, tears streaking down her face.

"We don't need a reminder, do we?"

"No, no," Ada rushed to say, fear almost crushing her ability to speak.

The reverend pulled her hands back into his own and held them like a vise. "That's a good girl, Ada. Good girl."

"Good girl," Ada echoed.

"Unfortunately, when we spoke with Roberta, she started to feel ill. You made her one of your special teas. I have a nice gift basket of yours right here in my office. Tea is always a nice thing to make people feel better." Ada's eyes fluttered, almost opening. Paul leaned in to be as close to her face as he was willing to get. "You grow plants in your garden, Mrs. Wilkins. You make tea. Beautiful purple flowers—great in flower arrangements as well as in tea pots."

"Symphytum."

"That's the one."

"You taught me about that flower—"

"No, I didn't, Ada. It was *you* who taught me, remember? Remember?" He squeezed her hands until the woman cried out, eyes opening, full of terror. "Remember, Ada? You are the one with that beautiful garden. I'm just a bachelor reverend."

"You love my tea," she said.

"I do, Ada, I do." He smiled gently at her and kissed her fingertips. Ada exhaled and relaxed. "Good, good." He let go of her hands and stood up. "I need to go get some of those officers from down below. I think our good friend Roberta is not feeling so well."

Ada's eyes were as huge as saucers. She stared at Roberta's lifeless form, rigid with fear.

"Stay here. Don't move. Wait for me." Paul leaned into her face again. "You can do that for me, right, my little sweet?"

Ada wasn't able to answer. He gave her another smile and left his office, closing the door with a loud click.

• • •

The God Network

The cold autumn dirt in the churchyard moved ever so slightly, heaving with millions of tiny tendrils, oscillating, flowing between the roots and the dirt and the rocks. The gray tendrils reached out of the earth and pulled themselves onto the walls of the structure, sliding up and up. Around the low-set windows, sliding past the cornices, slithering almost two stories up to the window in the back. Plants can split stone, given enough time. The animate always wins over the inanimate.

Testing for weakness, pushing into the weathered wood of the window frame, the gray tentacles wormed their way into the office of the reverend. There was a plant by the window, an orchid. Orchids were the oldest flowers on the planet. There were more varieties of orchids than any other flowering plant. Orchids lived everywhere—high on mountain slopes, in the canopies of tropical forests, among the brush on jungle floors, in between the rocks of temperate woodlands, out in the open, in the deep shade, in the cold, in the heat, in the most remote ranges, and in most human buildings. Orchids were pervasive; they were survivors, happy to please and tease and seduce their owners into taking care of them. Their roots were a tangle of tentacles reaching for moisture. They loved the feel of mycelium tendrils, feeding off the nourishment they provided, giving back the water and sugar produced by photosynthesizing leaves.

Into the roots, out again. Down to cold floor. Splicing, twining, searching, covering the floor with the mycelium lace. Rubber, leather, cloth. Heat, heartbeat, sweat. Disappointment. More searching. Feeling. Rubber, leather, cloth... This time, relief.

As the micro tendril reached Roberta's flesh, she started to dissolve, to become one with the searchers. There was no longer a memory of who she was, that died. But the body of a god doesn't die just because its mind has.

Ada sat and watched as the body of Roberta deflated, the clothing collapsing onto the floor, making a mess of dirty laundry right there on the reverend's floor. There was a sick movement. Something gray and slithering like angel hair pasta moved in and out and around the pile of cloth, in and out of the dead woman's eyes. The movement spread to cover the floor and the wall with the window.

The potted orchid fell, and Ada screamed.

● ● ●

Ay-Tal

Ay-Tal felt the others move with her, envelop her, support her as she supported them. It was never easy to lose one of your own. For them, the loss of one was more akin to losing a part of one's self. It had happened occasionally over the many millennia gods walked the earth. Each loss was a tragedy beyond measure.

Ay-Tal remembered each loss with immediacy as if no

time had passed.

Chapter Fifteen: Confusing Gods

Jon Uolan

Jon walked back into the reverend's tiny house and sat back down on one of the chairs in the living room. There was a lot to think about. Theoretically, he knew about other gods. He had met Mary...now Roberta, for Aguguq's sake. And his grandfather once talked to him about gods when they were way out on the ice. Jon asked him about the difference between Aguguq and Ay-Tal. Back then, he didn't get a satisfactory answer other than it was good for his people to have a god they could talk to directly, a god who personally saw to things and took care of them, a god of smaller things. And it was true, Ay-Tal was always there, always available.

Jon's grandfather also told of the 1918 flu epidemic. Many Alaskan tribes were decimated by that flu. There were villages where no adult survived, and only the very old and very young were left. But in their home village, not a single person died in that flu epidemic. And it was like that as far back as the elders could remember. Things just always worked out for the Omuktal people. Always. It was good to have a god living among them, just as it was good to have Aguguq tend to the world at large. Both gods were good, both were necessary, but only Ay-Tal took tea with you and talked local politics.

"We should never have sent Ay-Tal back into the big world," Jon said just under his breath. It was a mistake. And now they were paying the price. His people played the game of American politics and won. But now gods played politics in the affairs of men. *Who wins when gods play?* However closely Ay-Tal was aligned with his people, Jon always thought that she had her own motives and agendas. The tribal elders worked hard to keep their god's goals aligned with those of their people—that was their job. But they made a mistake. They used their god as a pawn for a short-term benefit, and it cost them the game.

Gods wanted his people to relocate to Wilkins. Roberta was clearly working on that. Jon wasn't sure about Ay-Tal, but even one god's intentions were difficult to circumnavigate. He wished he knew what Ay-Tal was doing. He tried to think back on the people he met in Wilkins—was one of those Ay-Tal? Did someone feel out of place? New? He just didn't know enough. He needed to talk with his grandfather...no, his father. His grandfather was dead now. Jon found that difficult to remember. He needed to talk to Ay-Tal. If God wanted his tribe to move to a small town in Middle America, did they even have a choice? *There is certainly plenty of available housing...*

He would miss the ice...the many shades of blue.

Jon's gaze fell on Roberta's duffle bag. It was partly open. He didn't remember it being left so. It was wrong to want to look through God's things, but Jon needed more information. What if something in that bag could lead him to Ay-Tal? He got up slowly, trying not to make a sound and wake the kids. He glanced at the bedroom door; it was closed, lights out. The siblings must have been exhausted. Emotional tiredness was harder to push back than physical one.

He leaned over the bag and pulled the zipper all the way open. Inside was a mess, a jumble of clothing stuffed haphazardly into the bag. Somehow, Jon always saw Roberta as a neat freak. Ay-Tal certainly wanted things just so, and he just figured all gods did. But different gods might have different ways. He pushed his hand inside and rummaged. He felt the cold metal of the gun almost immediately. It took an effort not to cry out. He stilled himself and then curled his fingers around the handle and pulled the gun out of the bag. It was his gun...the conductor's gun.

"Damn it, Roberta. Why did you have to bring it here?" he cursed. It was dangerous to have this gun here, even in the reverend's house. He glanced at the front door. He was sure he would hear Paul and Roberta return. He carefully placed the gun on the floor next to the bag with a soft clank. He waited, listening for the kids, but there was no sound. He exhaled and started to pull one item of clothing out of the bag at a time. *What else did Roberta bring with her?*

There were a man's jeans and a lumberjack shirt—Jon was sure they came from the church's donation collection. They were too big for him and would be enormous on Arrow. *Why would...* He dropped the shirt as the realization hit him—Roberta was carrying the seeds of her body changes in her bag. He remembered the feel of gray, writhing flesh against his skin. Goosebumps erupted all over his body. A few moments of breathing deeply, and Jon continued his search. Mary's chunky silver jewelry was there. A flash of pink was enough to tell him that it was the outfit Ay-Tal wore the last time he saw her as a little boy. *Why? Why would Roberta do this to me?*

Pink tights, a pink sweatshirt with a Dora the Explorer print, the little underwear. But Ay-Tal would need the little pink boots if she were to assume this body again. It would be convenient if he could prove that he didn't kill "his little boy." He felt around for the rubber boots. They were not in there, but he stumbled on his phone—the satellite phone. These were all the items he left behind in Mary's truck. Mary must have taken it all with her when she became Roberta. But when the cops came to search their rooms at Nora's…it had been smart not to leave any of these things behind there. Roberta took the package too—Saga said so—and then hid it among the outgoing mail in the church basement. Jon wished that Roberta did the same with the rest of this stuff. But maybe the phone would be useful.

The phone batteries were dead, and Jon looked around for something to use to charge them. The reverend's wasn't a high-tech home. Jon slid the phone into his jacket pocket, wrapped the gun in Ay-Tal's things, stuffed it with the rest of the clothing back into the duffle bag, and zipped it closed. The reverend wouldn't go snooping into Roberta's bag. *He is a man of the cloth, he wouldn't do that,* Jon reassured himself. Patting the bag with his hands, he made sure that the gun couldn't be felt from outside the bag. He casually placed the closed bag behind one of the chairs. Hiding it would only attract attention.

The weight of the phone made him feel anxious. If the kids weren't sleeping in the room next door, he would have made a run for it. But Arrow might have a way of charging the phone; it was a standard plug connection. He really needed to get hold of his tribal elders. Making the decision, Jon stood up and walked to the bedroom door. He would only wake up Arrow, if possible.

Soundlessly, he twisted the door handle and looked

inside. The room was empty. Jon staggered back.

• • •

Arrow Turgis

Arrow stood behind a trunk of a big tree. Saga was at his back. They were watching Mrs. Nelson's house. The woman had just arrived home and was getting out of her car in the crescent driveway. From Saga, Arrow knew that Mrs. Nelson was an early morning person. Saga complained endlessly about her boss's incessant chattering early Saturday mornings when they opened the little store together. It was way past midnight now; with luck, Mrs. Nelson would go straight to be bed, and he and his sister would be able to get into the adjacent B&B and grab their stuff unnoticed. Arrow fingered the set of keys Mrs. Nelson had given them earlier for the back door and the room he and Saga shared. *In and out. Fast.* He could do that. They were both already packed... well, they never unpacked to begin with. They didn't need more than what they could easily carry anyway.

They watched the kitchen light and the flickering shadows from Mrs. Nelson moving around her home. Ten minutes. Fifteen. Half an hour.

"What is she doing?" Arrow asked in frustration. He was tired and cold; he could feel his sister trembling next to him. He put his arm around her and pulled her close. "Cold?"

"Yeah," Saga said, her teeth chattering. "It looks like she is making tea."

"What? At this hour?"

"Well, you saw her. That was the kettle. The big copper one she uses when she has company."

"You think she is expecting Roberta and Jon back here

tonight?" Arrow asked. That would be bad. Saga just shrugged. "Perhaps I should just go in and get our stuff. I'll be quick. You can wait here and text me if you notice anything, okay?"

"Okay."

"I'll be quick."

"Okay."

But Arrow hesitated. He didn't really want to go in there. It would be so much better to just leave. But their stuff was in there, including the checkbook for the account Ben Wilkins had set up for them. Both he and Saga had been putting most of the money they earned into that account. They needed that checkbook. Arrow inhaled deeply and let go of Saga and the tree. "I'll be quick," he said again and dashed to the house, keeping to shadows and bending low. Saga hid behind the tree.

● ● ●

Saga Turgis

Saga watched as her brother crept up to the back door of the B&B. Mrs. Nelson was still moving around the kitchen. She hadn't seen or heard a thing. Arrow waved from the back door and slipped in. *So far, so good.* Saga felt her heart pounding as if it were her sneaking through the house to retrieve their stuff.

The street was empty and mostly dark, other than a streetlight at the far intersection and the lights from Mrs. Nelson's home. Most other homes on this street were abandoned. *It is such a shame,* Saga thought, *so much wasted space. Some people would love to live here.* Well, she wouldn't, but others who needed a place...like Jon's people. She wondered why Arrow was making them leave. She never liked the reverend—the man never listened—but she liked Roberta and even Jon. She was willing to go live with his people up north, with his family even. She wished Arrow explained what was going on, but when he was like this, there was no arguing, and he usually did have a good reason. Saga trusted Arrow, trusted him to keep her safe...just as she knew not to tell him certain things so he wouldn't feel like he had to defend her all the time. She wished he never saw any of those stupid burns. They didn't really hurt, not really. *Not much.*

A flash of light jerked Saga's attention away from Mrs. Nelson's windows. A car rounded the corner and turned onto their street. The car was driving slowly, as if searching for an address. It was a white minivan, like the kind everyone around here drove—white was good for reflecting sunlight in the summer to keep the interior cool, good for hiding the salt stains during winter. Arrow had explained to Saga why car colors were important for reasons other than simply liking a color. The car stopped in front of Mrs. Nelson's and then pulled into the circular driveway, parking just behind her car.

Saga pulled out her cell phone and tried texting Arrow. She nearly dropped the phone; her fingers were clumsy with fear and cold.

"Come on, come on, come on," she whispered to herself. "Work!"

Several people got out of the car—two men and one woman. One of the men must have been old or frail, because his companions helped him out of the car and then supported him as they all walked to the front door.

People are coming into the house, Saga typed furiously. *That's why Mrs. Nelson didn't go to bed. She was waiting for people!* She watched as the front door opened and Mrs. Nelson welcomed her visitors inside with smiles and handshakes. The strangers introduced themselves. Mrs. Nelson didn't know them, but she was expecting them. *Arrow! Get out! Now now now!*

Saga watched the visitors go into the kitchen and Mrs. Nelson serve them tea. If Saga knew her boss, she was also serving them pumpkin bread or something. Mrs. Nelson was a good baker. Saga searched the windows on the B&B side for any sign of her brother. Arrow should have gathered their stuff by now. He'd been in there for hours, it seemed. All the windows on the B&B side were dark, and Saga couldn't see in. Arrow wasn't responding. Didn't he get her texts?

She swallowed and pushed herself away from the tree. She felt weak, as if that trunk was supporting her body more than her legs. Cautiously, she ran to the back door. She tried the handle—it was locked! She felt panic spread through her body like poison. Her knees felt wobbly. Pulling out her phone again, she typed, *Get out now! Strangers inside.* Putting her ear to the door, she tried to listen for her brother, but all was quiet inside. *What is he doing in there?* Saga walked around the house and tried to peek through the backyard windows into the B&B's sitting room on the first floor. It was dark. She couldn't see anything...and then the outside spotlight turned on. The lights were motion activated, Mrs. Nelson had told her earlier. The ones by the back door must have been out, but these shone brightly, revealing Saga standing shocked in the backyard.

Mrs. Nelson's fearful face poked out of the kitchen window. She saw Saga, and fear turned to smiles and concern. She waved to Saga, and Saga waved back. She had been caught.

Moments later, the back door leading directly into the happy, warm, well-lit kitchen opened, and Mrs. Nelson called out. "Saga, honey. What are you doing standing out there in the cold? Did you lose the keys? Well, don't just stand there, honey, come on in. Come on. Get in. I don't want to let all the warmth out of the house. I'm not paying to heat the backyard." She waved frantically for Saga to come in, so Saga walked into the kitchen. There was nothing else to do. She clutched the phone, hoping Arrow was paying attention somehow.

"This is Saga Turgis." Mrs. Nelson introduced her to the strangers sitting around the kitchen island drinking tea and eating cake. "She and her brother Arrow are staying with me for a few days. But don't you worry. I have an empty room at the B&B, and you can use my spare bedroom upstairs. You won't need more than two beds, will you?" she asked almost in panic. The woman stranger smiled and shook her head. "Oh, good. Good." Mrs. Nelson visibly relaxed. "Then it is all settled. You stay here for as long as you need to get your people settled in Wilkins. Isn't it exciting, Saga? Jon's whole tribe is moving here. To Wilkins!"

"What?" Saga managed.

"We are the elders of the Omuktal Tribe," the woman said. "Mrs. Nelson told us all about you. My son did too. Jon even said something about you staying with us? I didn't understand; Jon can be so opaque sometimes. But don't you worry; whatever Jon promised is fine with us. Saga, right?" The woman extended her hand to Saga, and she shook it. "I'm Jon's mother. Mrs. Uolan. But please call me Amka."

"A pleasure to meet you, Mrs. Uolan," Saga said. These were Ay-Tal's people.

"These are Tukkuttok Uolan, Jon's father, and Lenno Uolan, his uncle."

"Nice you meet you," Saga said. She felt like she was having an out-of-body experience, like she was looking at everyone from somewhere far away, from some place safe. She hoped Arrow got out safely. And then she hoped that he would come here and be with her. She didn't really know what she wanted. "I like Jon," she finally said. Ay-Tal liked Jon. Jon was his god's chosen one. "He told me that Arrow, my brother, and I can come live with you. But that was before... before the earthquake and all." She swallowed hard. Here she was begging to live with these strangers, even as they had people dead, injured, homeless. "I'm sorry," she added and wasn't really sure for what in particular. *Everything, really.*

The woman got up, walked around the kitchen island, and took Saga into her arms. The hug was warm, and the woman smelled sweet but unfamiliar. It made Saga want to cry into this stranger's shoulder. She sniffed, and, instead of pulling away, the woman pulled her even closer.

"It will all be okay," she said. "I promise." And Saga cried. She couldn't help it. Was this the answer to her prayers?

* * *

Arrow Turgis

Arrow heard what was going on in the kitchen through the door that separated the B&B sitting room from Mrs. Nelson's home. Saga left her hiding place and came into the house! What was he supposed to do? How was he supposed to keep his sister safe? If Jon killed his little boy, what kind of people were his parents? Did they even know about Al?

"Sometimes life is too much to be handled alone." Roberta had said that. Arrow had judged her a decent woman until he discovered little Al's things stuffed into her bag. And the gun. He patted his jacket. The tiny pink boots made awkward lumps under the leather. Sometimes it was better to get help than to run from trouble. He listened at the door. Saga was crying. He could always tell by that telltale sound of little hiccups when she wasn't breathing right due to sobbing. He made his decision, softly dropped the backpacks by the side of the door, turned, and ran out of Mrs. Nelson's back door. The cops would still be sorting through all the junk in the church basement, he was sure of that. However this turned out, he needed help. This was all much bigger than what he could do alone.

Once outside, Arrow ran full-out. It was slightly downhill all the way to the church. Neither Roberta nor Jon knew where he and Saga were. Perhaps they hadn't discovered yet that they'd left the reverend's house...*with luck, they didn't.*

There were many cars still parked up and down the street from the church, as well as the four police vehicles parked directly in the loading zone in front. Arrow knew that the police suspected Jon of the murder of that tribeswoman and even his own son, Al. He heard them talking about it. Arrow didn't like talking to cops. But this was different than talking to the local sheriff about Burt. These cops were looking for evidence against Jon. And Arrow had it. If he showed the boots as proof that something bad had happened to Al, they would believe him. That kid never ever took those pink boots off. Never. The cops would believe him. *They have to.*

He slipped through the church's front door and down the stairs into the basement. There were more cops there than he realized. How many policemen rode in one car? Arrow stood just above the floor and tried to find Officer Merry. He was the one who found Saga that time. He knew about her and Arrow. It was easier to talk to people one knew.

He spotted Officer Merry next to the laundry room, taking notes on some tablet. Arrow wondered if they knew Hazel had all of this stuff carefully catalogued already? That girl was crazy about clothes and had a good head for computers. *She would lose her mind if these men ripped or damaged "her" merchandise.* Arrow smirked. Ada, Hazel, and Beth were three of a kind...well, no. Ada was in a class all by herself. Arrow practically growled as he thought of that woman. He would tell the police about her, too. The evidence was all over Saga's body. God, he hoped there was not more than he saw at the reverend's house. *There better not be...*

"Arrow?" one of the policeman called to him. "Arrow Turgis?"

Arrow spun around and faced a man with the badge name "Rogers." "That's me," he said. "I have the evidence you are looking for." And he pulled out the little pink boots from his jacket. "These were Al's. Jon Uolan's little boy?"

Officer Rogers didn't take the boots from Arrow; he just grabbed him by the elbow and took him to Officer Merry.

"Officer Merry?" Arrow staggered out. His throat felt dry. He was still holding the boots in his hand.

"Hello, Arrow. Nice to see you again." The man smiled. Arrow felt a slight ease in tension. "So tell me about these boots." And with his purple-latex gloved hand, he took them away from Arrow and deposited the pair into a plastic container labeled "evidence." Officer Rogers photographed them with his tablet and then wrote a label with a number and affixed it on the bag.

Relief flooded Arrow's senses like a cold Coke on a warm day—one responsibility released. And now another... For the next half hour or so, he talked of Jon and Al, then Ben and Mason, Burt and Ada, and about himself and Saga. He cried when he gave his suspicions about Mason's murder. And again when he described the scars, fresh and old, on Saga's legs. It was good to tell everything to someone. It felt like a heavy burden had been lifted off his shoulders. It got easier and easier as he talked. More police officers gathered around them, listening. There was total silence when he finished. They all looked at him. He hoped it was with sympathy.

"Need some water, son?" Officer Merry said and gave a bottle that someone else passed to Arrow. "Do you know where Mr. Uolan and Mrs. Hand are now?"

"Jon was back at Reverend Paul's house, just behind the church, across the little creek," Arrow said after he downed the whole bottle of water in one go.

Office Merry flicked his eyes, and several policemen left the circle of men surrounding Arrow. "What about Ada? Do you know where she is right now? And the reverend?"

Arrow shook his head. He had no idea. For all he knew, Jon had left the reverend's house too by now. But it was no longer his responsibility. With wobbly legs, he collapsed into one of the folding chairs.

There was a commotion up the back stairs. A door banged loudly.

"Help!" the reverend screamed. "Medical emergency! We need someone who knows CPR."

There was a rush for the door, and Arrow was left behind. It took a few moments for him to know what he wanted to do, and then he got up and rushed up the stairs, following all of the cops.

•••

Jon Uolan

Jon looked around, grabbed Roberta's bag, and rushed out of the reverend's house. He couldn't leave the bag behind. He couldn't take it with him. He ran down the street in the direction of Nora's house. He needed to use that computer again. And one of those chargers that Nora's late husband kept in the desk drawer might work for his phone.

The bag banged against his knees as he ran. It was stupid

to take the bag to Nora's house. He looked around. Aside from the reverend's house, the rest of the buildings on both sides of the street were empty. He was almost sure of that, despite the overabundance of seasonal decoration…or maybe because of it. A house just up ahead had a giant plastic snowman poking out of the evergreen bushes. He ran toward it. The snowman was big enough to hide the bag inside.

It was one of those models six feet tall, with three big white balls, a black hat, and an orange carrot nose, all molded out of one piece of plastic. Even with snow on the ground, this monstrosity would never look like it belonged. No one in their right mind would ever get one of these plastic things up north where he lived. The crooked smile was more scary than jolly, making the snowman more appropriate for Halloween than Christmas. But the bottom "snowball" was big enough for his purposes. Jon pushed the whole plastic snowman onto its side. There was a small plug at the bottom filled with water to give the snowman extra stability. He pried it out with his old hunting knife that he had found at the bottom of Roberta's bag. Unfortunately, the resulting opening was too small to fit the bag, so he used the knife to slit the plastic and enlarge the hole. He then carefully stuffed the bag into the snowman and pushed the plug back in. It no longer stood in place, but by pulling a few branches and weaving them together around the snowman's midriff, Jon was able to stabilize the giant plastic eyesore enough for it to stand on its own. It would have to do. Aside from those at the church, most of the decorations around Wilkins were hung, strung, and stuck with indifferent workmanship. With Aguguq's luck, no one would notice anything amiss before Jon had a chance to retrieve the bag.

Job done, Jon continued up to Nora's place. He couldn't think of any other place the kids would go to in the middle of a cold night. Jon thought of all the burns on Saga's legs, and his blood boiled. This town was evil. He couldn't understand why the gods wanted his people to move here.

Wilkins was small; just a few minutes was all it took to get to the B&B. The circular driveway was empty. Nora always parked there, so she wasn't home. There were no lights in any of the windows. Jon considered and then went around the back and used his key to get in. He didn't turn on any lights. He slid into the old office and pulled out the computer. He hoped his tribe had answers for him and he that had time to retrieve them.

The loading disk spun and spun. It was a very old computer. But eventually, Jon was able to log in to the mailbox set up by the tribe to read messages without sending them. There was nothing in the inbox but spam—the host company must have sold this email address to marketers. It made Jon angry. It wasn't their information to sell. But all it meant was that they would close this email account down and set up another one—SOP, standard operating procedure. He went into the draft folder. His email was there, and so was another one. He felt his heart beat faster. Finally, he was getting in contact with his people. He opened the draft and read: *Voted to move to Wilkins. Expect us soon.*

What? That was both a lot of information and not enough. Jon was amazed his tribe made a decision to relocate after many thousands of years of living on one particular patch of land. This was historic, for his people anyway. But what was "soon?" And did the people of Wilkins make a matching decision to welcome his tribe? He hoped so. Gods worked in mysterious ways. He liked it better when he could talk to Ay-Tal directly.

Now he needed to deal with police. He couldn't have his people arrive in the middle of the murder investigation. It was time to surrender to the authorities and tell them about Ada and Burt. The town of Wilkins needed to be cleansed of evil before anyone else could live here.

Jon turned everything off and trotted back to the church. The police was sure to still be there...he hoped.

• • •

Ay-Tal

Gray strands lifted the old plastic snowman and twisted inside. Moments later, the gun was wrapped in layers of squirming ropes, pulling it into the dirt below. After the short spurt of activity, the snowman was motionless again. The gun was carried mile after mile underground, scraping away any traces of residual DNA and chemical prints, until it was spat out above ground again next to the old garbage and debris along the railroad tracks, waiting to be discovered.

• • •

Paul Wolf

They all gathered in a circle around Ada Wilkins. The woman was cackling, rocking with hysterical laughter in a chair.

"Call an ambulance," Officer Merry ordered. "Now, tell me again, Reverend Wolf, what happened to Detective Hand?" He pointed to a pile of clothing on the floor of the reverend's office. A broken cup and saucer lay next the pile, surrounded by spilled liquid.

The reverend stood just behind Officer Merry, his eyes bulging out. He was sure Roberta was dead before he left the room. He had checked her pulse himself. "I..." he stammered, and, instead of continuing, he bent down to look at the shoes, stockings, a brown wool skirt, a simple white bra...

"Don't touch anything," Officer Merry ordered.

The reverend jerked back and looked up. Horror, fear, and disbelief were melded together in his face. He could feel it. "She was dead," he said.

"You said Ms. Hand was having heart spasms," Officer Merry said. "You said nothing about dead."

"I felt her pulse," he said. "There was nothing." He shook his head.

"Ms. Wilkins?" Officer Merry bent down to be eye-to-eye with the woman. "Do you know what happened? What happened to Ms. Hand?"

Ada looked around wildly, her eyes never focusing on anything.

"Ada?" The officer said her name quietly, almost soothingly. "Did you see what happened to Roberta?"

Ada alternated between giggling and sobbing, her breathing uneven, labored. "No one ever searches where the bodies are buried," she finally exhaled.

"Where should we search?" Officer Merry asked softly.

"Paul's house, of course," the woman said with a big smile.

The reverend backed away, his head hitting the wall of his office. Roberta was dead, he was sure of it. Sure. He looked at Ada; the woman was at her worst. He remembered how bad it was when Elsa died. This was worse. She was coming apart, and she was dragging him down with her.

"She has toxoplasmosis," he said to no one in particular. "It's all those cats. I told her to seek treatment, but she is so stubborn. Not that it would take, mind you. All those cats. Seven! Ada is a crazy cat woman. You've heard of crazy cat women, Officer? Well, it's all true." He felt like he was babbling incoherently but was unable to stop himself. "The disease is carried in the cat feces. The more cats, the more likely the person has the disease. The infection makes the cat owner get more and more cats. They can't stop themselves. Cat after cat. She got two just this year. I've told Burt, but he is probably infected, too. And the kids. They are all crazy. Makes mice into cat-loving zombies. Mice!" He practically screamed the word.

"What are you talking about, Reverend?" Officer Rogers asked.

"She probably killed the woman when I went to get help. Killed her and stripped her naked." Paul eyes blazed. He felt hot. *Where is the body? What did Ada do?* His hands shook. Far away, he heard the sirens of a coming ambulance.

He stood against the wall, as if roots had grown from his body into the foundation of his church. Officers with purple gloves and evidence collection tools came and started to take photos of Roberta's discarded pile. There were a pair of earrings and a necklace with little orange stones. He saw plain white underwear as the cops carefully lifted each piece of clothing and deposited them into separate evidence bags. The broken teacup and saucer were also collected. He had planned on pushing it out of the way before the ambulance came to take Roberta's body away. No one would have tested the tea residue, no one. *But now?* It was all going into a lab. They would know.

"Ada made the tea," he said. "She makes tea for everyone. Grows her own." His eyes followed the teacup into the plastic bag. A bit of amber liquid was visible. They would find out. Another officer collected Ada's cup. Paul glanced at the sideboard, where the electric kettle was sitting next to a collection of homemade teas. That woman would talk. She knew too much. He should have given them both the same tea. But it would have been too strange—two heart attacks at the same time. There would have been questions... "She was crazy," he said. "All these years, I've managed to keep her going. She was a productive citizen of Wilkins—"

"I am the mayor!" Ada screeched. "The mayor!"

The paramedics lifted Ada from the chair and placed her on the gurney, strapping her body in. She jerked left and right, up and down, but couldn't move her arms or legs. How long had it been? Paul was confused. All his sense of time was gone. *Where is Roberta's body? Where?*

● ● ●

Arrow Turgis

Arrow watched as Ada was wheeled into an ambulance. She looked insane, crying out that the gray worms ate Roberta's body. He was angry. Ada didn't deserve a hospital. He wanted her in prison: a dark, dank dungeon, hopefully held to the wall by heavy chains. She was evil. She was worse than evil, because she pretended to be good, hiding her vileness from the world by doing good. He hated her. More than hated her...

One of the police vehicles followed the ambulance out into the night. Two cop cars remained. Arrow turned back and went into the church.

There were still a few Wilkins folks loitering about, talking in small groups. Arrow had never seen the church open so late or so many still up and about at this time of the night. Or was it morning? People who lived around these parts didn't stay up late. Most were "morning people." But Ada's unexpected departure—well, unexpected to him; he had no idea what happened—was an obvious nexus of all kinds of speculations. As he walked past the groups of conversations, Arrow caught bits and pieces: "She would never have agreed to live with all those tribal people." "Ben, Mason, and now Burt. Poor woman's heart couldn't take it, I tell you." Arrow smirked at that one—Ada's heart was a lump of lakebed clay—cold, stinky, and slimy. "I heard the reverend tried to talk her into it, but she went crazy on him." "Killed Roberta just like that." The fingers snapped, and Arrow jerked his head toward the speaker. It was one of the men talking with the sheriff. That must have been a crazy rumor—Roberta couldn't be dead, could she? He rushed ahead. He needed to—

"Arrow Turgis." Officer Merry grabbed him by the arm. "I told you to wait below, son. What are you doing?"

"I was just... I was just... What happened to Ada?" He almost said "Aunt Ada" but managed to stop himself in time. It was a bad habit. She was no relative of his.

"Sounds like the stress got to her. But don't you worry about her. We have it under control. Now—"

"Someone just said Ada killed Roberta," Arrow interrupted the officer. "Is she going to pay for that? Is she going to pay for what she did to my sister? You can't let her get off easy. You can't..." He felt himself hyperventilating and tried to control his emotions and breathing. Cops never responded well to a freakout. He needed to appear mature and in control. If he didn't, they would take Saga away from him. "Sorry," he managed. "Just feeling stressed. Can we go get my sister now? She was at Mrs. Nelson's. I would feel better if I knew she was all right." He looked Officer Merry in the eye. The man seemed compassionate.

"We will send a car for her." He nodded and guided Arrow back down below into the church basement.

From the corner of his eyes, Arrow could swear he saw some of the walls crawl. He was so tired. He walked quietly.

Once the authorities got involved, everything took time. With luck, he and Saga would get justice. But if he could only ensure Saga's safety, he would be all right with that, no matter how much he hated Ada and Burt...and Jon and Roberta. "What happened to Roberta?" he asked again.

"We are looking into it, son," Officer Merry said and sat him back down on the folding chair. "Now tell me again what you were doing in Reverend Paul's home? You said Roberta and Jon were with you."

Arrow nodded.

"And then Ms. Hand left to go back to the church. Did you notice anything strange about her before she left?"

Arrow thought back. The thing was that the woman was perfectly nice, caring. She tended to Saga's wounds. She seemed genuinely moved by what she saw. "If it wasn't for Al's clothing and the gun in her bag, I would never have thought anything bad about her," he answered honestly.

"I see. The thing is, Arrow, the bag is no longer at the reverend's house. And neither is Jon."

"He must have taken it!"

"Perhaps," the officer said.

"You do believe me, right? The boots—they are evidence enough. Right?"

They both turned to look at the table, where the tiny pink rubber boots had been left in the collection bag. The boots were no longer there. Arrow jumped up. Officer Merry pressed him back down into the chair. And then several things happened simultaneously. Saga rushed down the stairs, calling for Arrow. Mrs. Nelson followed, walking slowly and accompanied by three strangers, two men and one woman. The strangers looked a lot like Jon—dark hair, ethnic Inuit features. The men both had gray eyes. Arrow was sure about the eyes. He stood up again, and Saga threw herself into his chest.

"It's okay, Arrow. It will all be all right now," she said into his jacket. "Jon's family is here to make everything okay."

Other policemen were descending into the basement. Officer Merry turned to face Jon's relatives. And then Jon appeared on the back stairs.

"Grab him!" Officer Rogers screamed. "You are under arrest—"

He didn't finish the sentence, for a small, golden-haired child ran naked, wearing only pink boots, from behind the stack of "sent mail" and jumped into Jon's arms.

"Daddy!"

Jon held the little boy, stroking his hair, and cooing softly into the unbrushed curls.

Everybody stopped and watched.

"So that's Al?" Officer Merry asked no one in particular.

"Jon's son," Saga said with a smile. "I knew he would come back! And those are his grandparents. See?"

"So Al is not dead?" Arrow felt silly asking. He was sure something bad happened to that little boy.

"Of course not," Saga said.

Arrow looked at his sister's expression and saw that she was lying. He just didn't know about what. Saga wiggled free from Arrow's embrace, went over to the kids' clothes table, and grabbed a pair of boy's sweatpants, a t-shirt, some socks, and a purple parka that sort of matched the one she was wearing herself. And then demonstrably, she walked over to Jon and Al and took the boy from his father's arms.

"You can't run around naked, Allie," she said. She looked around the room and harrumphed. "What? You've never seen a naked kid's bum before?" The way she said it made most people in the basement avert their eyes. Even Arrow felt the need to look away and give Al privacy while Saga dressed him.

But as he turned, he saw that Jon's parents, Al's grandparents, seemed shocked too. It was as if they have never seen that child before.

"So what is my son being arrested for?" the older woman with Mrs. Nelson asked.

Officer Rogers looked uncertainly at Officer Merry. Arrow tried to look at everyone at once—there was so much confusion on so many faces. Only Saga and Al seemed to be comfortable with what was going on.

Chapter Sixteen: Answered Prayers

Saga Turgis

"Thank you for coming back, Ay-Tal," Saga whispered into the boy's ear. He felt different than before. Younger, scrawnier. It felt as if there was not enough of him somehow, but so far no one else noticed. She helped the god dress and hide any differences underneath layers of clothing. "I think this should do it," she said and lifted the child back onto the floor. "Go make everything okay again."

Ay-Tal ran toward Amka and Tukkuttok, wrapping his arms around their legs, one each. "Grandma! Grandpa!"

Amka reached down and patted Ay-Tal's head uncertainly, while looking at Jon's face. Saga realized that she needed to step up and help. She went up to Jon's parents and lifted Ay-Tal to be eye level with his people. *Would they recognize their god now?* Amka smiled but shook her head slightly.

"Al told me all about Ms. Ay-Tal Blue," Saga said. "She sounds like a wonderful woman." And finally, that was enough. She heard Lenno Uolan exhale, his face breaking into a wide grin.

Amka leaned over and took Al from Saga, pressing him

close. She too was smiling now.

"Thank you, Saga," Tukkuttok said. And Saga felt warm and welcome all over.

"Mr. Uolan?" Officer Merry called, and all three men turned to face him—Jon, his dad, and his uncle. "I'm Officer Merry, and this is my partner, Officer Rogers." He stepped toward Tukkuttok and Lenno and shook their hands. Officer Rogers did the same. "We have some questions for you about Ms. Blue. The reverend told us that he spoke to Ms. Blue?"

"Reverend Wolf?" asked Amka over Ay-Tal's head. "We spoke with him. He explained his idea of having our tribe relocate to Wilkins. But I don't believe he ever spoke with Ms. Blue directly, did he, dear?" She turned to her husband, and Tukkuttok shook his head.

"As far as we know, the reverend didn't have such an opportunity," he confirmed.

"I see," Officer Merry said. "And did Detective Hand speak with Ms. Blue?"

"I wouldn't know," Jon's dad said. "Why don't you ask her?"

"Ms. Blue?"

"I meant your detective. Doesn't she work with you?"

"Unfortunately, it seems like Ms. Hand has gone missing."

"What?" Saga cried out. "But I liked Roberta. She was nice to us." She looked around the room, confusion and fear etched onto her face. Arrow walked over, took her hand, and squeezed it. Saga knew he didn't understand about Ay-Tal and Al. And she didn't understand Arrow's fears about Roberta and Jon. "What happened, Arrow? Did something bad happen again?"

"All I know is that Ada was taken away in an ambulance, and the reverend thought Roberta had been killed." Arrow talked quietly, but the whole room was hushed, and his voice carried. "By Ada," he added.

"Dead? Roberta is dead?" Jon cried out. He looked distressed. Freaked, even. Saga felt tears running down her own face. *How many had to die in this town before someone did something?* She watched as Jon turned to his mother with Ay-Tal still in her hands. "Is it true? Is Roberta dead?"

Saga saw Ay-Tal give just the slightest movement of his head; she noticed the telltale glistening of tears in the boy's eyes. And suddenly she understood—Roberta too was a god! Saga felt her world going dark. She sagged to the floor. A god was dead! Gods didn't die...but they died in Wilkins!

● ● ●

Saga woke up in a hospital room. Arrow was sitting next to her. He was asleep. Jon's mom was also in the room, sitting right by the bed.

"There you are, sweetheart," the woman said. "It's all fine now. You never have to worry again. I promise." The way she said "I promise" made Saga remember everyone else who had ever said that to her. There were a lot of people who had said that to her over the years, and what good had it been? "Yes," Amka said, as if reading Saga's thoughts. "But *I* mean it. You are part of my family now. You and Arrow."

"But..." Saga mouthed. She didn't want to wake her brother. He looked ashen with exhaustion. He could have used a bed to sleep on. Saga didn't even feel all that tired anymore. She looked around and saw that she was hooked up to a heart monitor and there was an IV drip attached to her arm. She always wanted to know what that would feel like. She decided it felt bad; there was a stream of cold swirling into her veins from the needle in her arm. *Bad.* It was a bad feeling.

"Ay-Tal is here to help us figure it out," Amka said.

Saga looked around for little Al. The sunny boy wasn't in the room, but, besides Arrow and Amka, there was a distinguished-looking woman sitting in a corner chair— strong chin, a slight widow's peak, dark, thick hair cut short with a few stray grays but not too many, full lips, and dark gray eyes. She had a long face and a slim figure, dressed in a gray skirt business suit. Saga glanced down; below the woman's knees were dark, leather elegant boots, good enough to jump trains yet stylish enough for any office.

"Ay-Tal?" Somehow, Saga recognized the god even inside the new body.

The woman's smile was warm and friendly. "I told you, Amka, that Saga would know me." Amka appeared to be surprised, and that made Saga proud. "You gave us quite a scare, Saga."

"I don't remember much," Saga said. She reached back to think. There was something about Roberta, the other god of small affairs. "Dead?" she suddenly exclaimed, remembering at the same time as she uttered the word. "Roberta can't be dead, can she? Gods can't die..."

Amka squeezed her hand; until then Saga hadn't even realized that Jon's mom had been holding it. "Unfortunately, child, gods die all the time. We are just lucky with ours."

"Ay-Tal?" Saga called to the woman in gray. "Don't die."

"I'm not planning to...not yet," Ay-Tal said. "There's too much to do. My whole tribe is driving down to Wilkins. They will be here in a few weeks. A lot to do."

"Your whole tribe?"

"Well, most of the tribe," Amka said. "Sometimes tribes lose coherence and dissolve around the edges. People move, resettle, get a different life. We've always lost people like that. Not everyone is content to live the same life generation after generation."

"But life in Wilkins will be different," Saga said.

"And that's also a problem."

"But you can't have it both ways," Saga argued.

"The reason some people leave is the same as the reason some people stay," Ay-Tal said. "So we will need to form a new tribe. A tribe that includes everyone who lives in Wilkins now and wants to stay."

"Some Wilkins folk will leave?" Saga asked. It seemed unthinkable—people in Wilkins seemed so set in their ways... "Oh!"

"You see? Same reasons," Ay-Tal said, nodding.

"You will make a new tribe out of us?" Saga asked the god.

"That's what I do," Ay-Tal said. "I bind people together and help them find a future where they all can be happy as a group. It doesn't work for everyone. There are those who will be pushed away, and those who will stay just on the edges, not really part of the tribe but not really outsiders either."

"Will Arrow stay?" Saga looked at her brother. He was snoring gently. She would hate to see him go, but she had already made up her mind to stay. She wanted to belong. She wanted that badly. Painfully. Stomach-churningly.

"I think we will find a way to make it worth his while," Ay-Tal said. "At least for another year. For Arrow and others like him."

"We are going to set up a college fund for all the young people of our new tribe. We are thinking of calling it the Mason Scholarship," Amka said. "But to qualify, they will have to spend a gap year between graduating high school and starting college in Wilkins, contributing to our community."

"How? How would they contribute?" It was a good name for a scholarship.

"There are a lot of things that need doing in Wilkins. For too many years, much of the town was left abandoned. We plan on making it a thriving community again."

"So, construction?" Saga asked.

"That too," Ay-Tal said.

Saga didn't understand but let it go. What it meant to her was that Arrow would stay with her for another full year after finishing this school year. It would make all of the turbulence of getting to learn how to live together with Jon's people easier. Well, easier for her. Arrow would have work to do.

There was a knock on the door to Saga's hospital room. Arrow was instantly up on his feet. Saga looked through the open door—Officer Merry and Officer Rogers were just outside.

"May we come in?" Officer Merry asked and then walked in without any further invitation. Officer Rogers followed. They tugged a big bouquet of colorful balloons into the room with them. Both were smiling at Saga, but she felt that their smiles didn't really touch their eyes. "Feeling better?"

"Much," Saga said and sat up a little more.

"Officers?" Amka said. "I was told that only family was allowed to see this child." She raised her eyebrows, and Saga saw the men shuffle a bit. She liked Jon's mom even more.

"Mrs. Uolan? A pleasure to meet you in a more..." He stumbled again—hospital rooms didn't seem to meet whatever criteria he meant to say. "A pleasure to meet you again," he finally finished.

Amka just stared at him, waiting for the men to answer her question. Arrow was about to argue, but Amka casually took his hand in hers and stopped him. It took an effort, Saga saw, but Arrow didn't say a word, he just glared at the cops. Arrow was always good at glaring, but Saga thought it wasn't helpful in most situations.

Officer Merry pulled up a chair and sat next to Saga.

"You look much better, Saga," he said again with the same stiff smile. "You gave us quite a scare back there."

"I'm sorry," Saga said. "I don't really—" She felt Amka squeeze her hand again and stopped.

"With you, Mrs. Wilkins, and Ms. Hand all taken ill at the same time, I feel like we should place the whole church under quarantine." It sounded like a threat.

Saga glanced at Ay-Tal. It didn't seem like the officers had noticed her in the room yet. And now she was hidden by the balloons. "I'm feeling fine now," Saga said again.

"Very good," Officer Rogers said. "I was hoping you were well enough to answer some questions."

"Officers," Amka said again. "This is a hospital room, and this is a sick child. A sick, abused child. One that you've failed to protect. One that you delivered back into the hands of her abusers, even after this child tried to explain to you—"

"Justice is never so simple, Mrs. Uolan," Officer Merry said. "There are many wrong turns. But we aim to get it right eventually. With both Mr. and Mrs. Wilkins too ill to answer our questions, we have to follow the leads we can. If Saga and Arrow," he glanced at Saga's bother, "are able and willing to help us—"

"I've already told you everything," Arrow said. Saga saw Amka give his hand another squeeze, and he didn't say any more.

"You've made very serious accusations against Burt and Ada Wilkins, as well as Jon Uolan and Ms. Hand."

"I—" Arrow started, but Amka gave him a stern glare.

"Obviously with Ms. Hand unavailable, we have more questions," Officer Rogers said. It actually sounded reasonable to Saga. "We still have a missing person case with Ms. Blue—"

"Ah, that," Ay-Tal finally spoke up. The officers turned at looked at Ay-Tal Blue.

Saga held her breath. *Cops versus God.* It was like a video game, like a story in a book. She didn't think these officers were particularly bad people, just obtuse when it came to believing children's complaints. But she had just learned that gods could die, so gods made mistakes too.

"For a room that allows only relatives, you have a full house, Saga," Officer Merry said.

"I'm an attorney representing Saga and Arrow Turgis," Ay-Tal said. "As well as the interests of Omuktal people and the people currently residing in the town of Wilkins."

"That's a lot of clients."

"But not at cross-purposes," Ay-Tal said. "I'm Ay-Tal Blue. Perhaps you've heard of me?"

●　●　●

Arrow Turgis

Since the decision to merge the townsfolk of Wilkins and members of Omuktal Tribe, there were several proposals on how to meld the two people spiritually. The town kept its old name—it was a practical solution that didn't require a lot of capital expenditure to amend the maps and other state and federal documents—but the people would identify themselves as Wilkins-Tal, using the old Yakut word for "chosen" to honor the newcomers and those who chose to stay and build something new. It felt right. Jon's father, as a tribal elder, suggested creating several totem poles celebrating the birth of a new people. The first totem pole would be made with a foundation carved from a local Wisconsin wood by the people of Wilkins. The top half would be worked by the tribe in a different wood: western red cedar, a traditional wood for carving totem poles up in Alaska. Once the tribe arrived into town, the totems would be joined into a single great one and placed next to the church as part of the merging ceremony.

"We want to work with the flow of the wood grain," Lenno Uolan explained to the woodworking class held at the Wilkins High School's shop classroom. He still had one arm in a sling, and his chest was wrapped tight to help his ribs heal. But his voice was strong, and he was obviously a talented teacher. Almost every student and even a few adults had signed up for a special course on totem pole-making from Jon's uncle. He was the master carver of the Omuktal Tribe.

Arrow was told that Ay-Tal's people traditionally carved their totem poles with a group of five elk on the bottom, followed by a whale, followed by a salmon. The different animals represented the deep past before the tribe crossed over into Americas, the crossing, and the present life dependent on the gifts from the sea, mostly salmon. Sometimes the carvers added a fantastical bird to represent an unknown future. Ay-Tal's Omuktal Tribe always presented a conundrum to modern scholars. Their art was very different from other native peoples in Alaska. Having a god living among the tribe's people meant some things hadn't changed for many thousands of years, for a god's memory was deeper than the tribe's. And when a god suggested artistic embellishments, the tribe listened.

The people of Wilkins decided on the American badger as their half of the totem pole. It was the Wisconsin state mammal, and it represented the same tenacity the people of Wilkins ascribed to themselves. After all, so many other small towns were left abandoned by modern life, but Wilkins was still here. And with the influx of new residents, it would be here for many more years.

Arrow listened from just behind Lenno. He liked the man. There was something simple about being able to focus on a task so completely that the world fell away. Totem pole carving was not like architecture, and yet there was a touch of architecture in there—it was more than just feeling the flow of the wood grain. The resulting structure had to balance. A well-made totem pole lasted generations. And when Arrow left Wilkins, his part of the pole would still be there, no matter how small his contribution.

"Arrow?"

He turned and saw Ay-Tal right behind him. She had the very unnerving talent of being almost everywhere at once. Arrow noticed that it freaked out the policemen too. He once saw Officer Merry jump when he didn't expect Ay-Tal to be there. Saga said that Ay-Tal had godly powers. He liked the woman, all right—she was working on making his and Saga's adoption into Uolan family final. How she managed to do in three days what usually took years, he had no idea. But when Ay-Tal wanted something, it got done. Those were godly powers, all right.

"I have a special project for you," she said now and pulled him aside. "I would like you to carve the tip of the totem pole."

"Really?"

"Sure. I think you have the talent to do it. I saw your carpentry work, and your art teacher showed me your drawings."

"She did?" It felt surprisingly good that someone noticed. Arrow had read that he had a better chance at being accepted into the architecture program if he could show some drafting skill. There were no drafting classes at Wilkins High School, but his art teacher had encouraged him to create very detailed pen drawings. He hoped it was good enough.

"I want you to carve a lark," Ay-Tal said. "I think it would be a fitting top for the pole and a nice memorial for Roberta."

"They never found her body, so how do you know..."

Arrow didn't like to say the word "dead."

"I know. You do too."

"The cops don't."

"They will come around eventually."

"They are digging out the reverend's backyard, looking for her body."

"They might find something, but not Roberta," Ay-Tal said.

Arrow could see that it made her particularly sad. He still didn't understand why. It wasn't like Ay-Tal ever met Roberta. Ay-Tal arrived from the north right after the detective went missing. Well, Saga kept saying crazy things, but she was very young and had been through a lot. Perhaps his sister needed a bit of fantasy to help her get over her trauma. He heard doctors talk about it. "Why a lark?" he asked.

"Some believe that larks are messengers of god," Ay-Tal said. Arrow made a face. He didn't mean to, but all this talk of tribal gods and such... "In the Lakota myth, these birds stand for Okaga, the god of the southern wind, bringing warmth and prosperity to its people. Some believe that larks are human spirits. Personally, I like the song that larks weave. And I know that Roberta loved them too."

"The last is the best reason," Arrow said.

"So you'll do it?"

"You mean do I want to have my carving crown the totem pole for the whole town? Yes."

Ay-Tal smiled, patted his head as if he was just a little kid, and left the room before anyone else had even noticed she was there. "Strange woman," Arrow mumbled.

• • •

Paul Wolf

"Tell me again what happened, Reverend." Officer Merry sat on the opposite side of the metal table from Paul Wolf.

Paul had refused an attorney—he felt that to get one was a sign of guilt. With Burt dying and Ada locked away in a psychiatric ward, there was no one to bear witness against him. They could dig his yard all they liked; they wouldn't ever find a thing. He had learned the hard way that fire was the surest way to destroy all traces of evidence. If only he knew what really happened to Roberta. *What could Ada have done to dispose of that body? Why would she strip that woman naked?* But however it turned out, Ada was more of a nut case than he even hoped for. Nothing she said would ever be admitted as evidence. "Deranged lunatic," he said just under his breath.

"What was that, Reverend?"

"I'm sorry, Officer Merry. I was just thinking of how much I underestimated Mrs. Wilkins's psychosis. I wish..."

"Yes?"

"I should have reached out to medical professionals," he said, shaking his head. "But my vows prohibited me from speaking out."

"Which vows would those be?"

"Confessional, of course. As you know, Officer, we can't just divulge what we hear from our flock."

"It was my impression that in cases of crimes or potential crimes, you have the responsibility to contact the authorities."

"If I even, for one second, believed that Ada was doing something... Well, but of course! But she said all sorts of things. Crazy things. It felt harmless to me, even if, in retrospect, it wasn't. It's always like that, isn't it? Hindsight and all." He produced a sad smile for the officer. People always believed men of god. His occupation—his life's calling—was as good as a shield. He nodded his head, expressing deep sadness and personal disappointment with the turn of events.

"So you still maintain that you have no idea what happened to Roberta Hand?"

"As I've told you, we went into my office. Ada was very upset about the vote. Roberta was kind enough to come in and help talk to Ada. She was supportive of the future that had the town of Wilkins merging with the Omuktal Tribe."

"Yes, it was an interesting idea."

Paul knew that this vote and the town's decision to invite the tribe to live in Wilkins were making national news. All of the coverage had been extremely positive. He was a hero for leading his congregation to such an honorable outcome. He had dozens of invitations to talk shows and news programs. More than he had the time for, really. He smiled again. *It is good to be appreciated.*

"The totem pole ceremony will be held on Sunday," he said, "after the service. I hope you and your partner will come." There were going to be people from all over the world in attendance and reporters covering that event. Global coverage. He leaned back, making the chair rock a bit. He was getting way too familiar with this chair and this interrogation room. *Yes, that's what it feels like—interrogation.* And yet they had nothing on him. It had been several weeks, and still nothing. And he was really too busy for all this. He was being extremely cooperative. "Well, if you don't mind, Officer Merry, I have so much to do. The tribe's people have been arriving, and with all the press it's just difficult to get all that needs doing done. So if you'll excuse me?" He stood up, and so did the officer. Paul tried to smile again and even extended his hand for a shake—it was good keep things civilized. He left feeling good about the interview.

● ● ●

The reverend pulled into his driveway. There was still police tape all around. They had totally dug up his back and front yards—something about a bag with a gun. He had no idea what they were talking about. *I never needed a gun.* Fortunately, he had seeds and tubers of his favorite plants safely put away for the winter. And Ada's garden had many duplicates. He had trained that woman well.

He parked the car and went to his front door; it was slightly open. He knew he left it locked—too many people buzzing about. Carefully, he pulled the door all the way open.

"Hello?" he called into a cold house. He always turned the heat off when he left—no point in wasting money or energy. His place was small, easy to heat. A few minutes of heater on full blast, and it was as toasty as he ever wanted it to get. "Hello?" he called again.

The living room and kitchen, clearly visible from the front door, were empty. Paul shrugged. Perhaps the stress of the police investigation and the whole do-good business was getting to him. The buses had started to arrive. The first few families had moved into their new homes. The whole town was buzzing with excitement. Never had WINGS's purpose been so clearly defined, so immediate, so visible. Wilkins would be known as the small town that saved the national disaster relief puzzle—*bring those suffering into your home!* It was his idea. His. He was the master manipulator. *So many strings to pull.* The business of doing good in the world was his family business. Every male for almost eight generations had worked to make the world a better place, to lead people to an emotional place where doing kindness was as natural as breathing.

He took off his parka—the winter chill was finally in the air to stay, as was proper for January in Wisconsin—and went to make himself some coffee. He never drank tea. Ever. Even from a supermarket. The water took forever to boil—"the watched pot never boils." He was about to pour the hot water over the grounds when something fell with a crash of breaking glass in his little hallway between the bedroom and bathroom.

"Hello?" He didn't call out this time, just whispered it, thought it really. He took the pot of boiling water in his right hand and tiptoed into the living room. It was still empty. He turned toward the hallway and nearly dropped the hot water onto himself. Mason, the boy he made dead, stood there looking over the photographs on the wall. One frame lay broken at his feet. Glass shards everywhere.

"Reverend Paul," the boy said. He still had the young boy voice—a slight squeak here and there. He was the same age he was when he died, not a day older.

Last time he had seen Mason's ghost, in the boathouse, it had been too dark to see the boy properly. Paul thought that someone was playing a trick on him, dressing in that old leather jacket that Hazel found in the Saint Paul donation crate. He had yelled then. And that kid ran away. Afterward, Paul wasn't even sure he really saw anyone. It was a strong possibility that his mind was playing tricks on him. There was too much going on, too much... But this time, there was a kid standing not even ten feet away from him.

"Mason?" Paul asked hesitantly. It wasn't him, of course. Mason Wilkins had been cremated. No one even knew where the ashes were any more. Saga, that stupid girl, stole them and then lost them. "Whoever you are, you have to stop now," Paul said in an authoritative voice. He was done with all of the stupid games these kids played. "You are trespassing, young man. The cops just happen to be outside—" The boy smiled, and the reverend couldn't finish. His heart did a jig in his chest. He almost dropped the hot water again, spilling a bit on his sock. "Damn!" That hurt. He straightened the pot in his hand again. "Don't make me use this," he threatened the boy.

"How have you been, Reverend Paul?" the kid asked. He sounded just like Mason. "Have you killed anyone else recently? Roberta, perhaps?"

How did the kid know about Roberta? The cops had kept the incident quiet for investigative purposes. The woman's body hadn't been found. Not yet. And Paul knew that he didn't have anything to do with it this time...well, other than the tea. But that was Ada's tea...an honest mistake on her part.

"Burt and Ben's parents," the boys said. "Ben. Elsa and her boy." Paul's eyes felt like they were ready to pop out of their sockets. "How many others?" The boy looked at him like he knew. "There were others, were there not? Even before you came to Wilkins. Yes. I bet there was at least one even back then. Some little old lady that needed someone to talk to? Or was it a single mom looking for help? A runaway? Someone with disabilities who couldn't protect himself, couldn't get away, wouldn't be believed if he did?"

Paul wanted to run but took a step forward and lifted the pot of boiling water. "I don't know what game you are playing, but I came home and found an intruder. This kid came after me. He broke a photograph and threatened me with a piece of sharp glass. I jumped away. Fortunately, I was boiling water..." As he said it, he threw the water right into kid's face. The water hit its target. The boy didn't even try to twist out of the way. He cried out, and Paul did too. And then the face stared to twist and melt. It wouldn't hold shape. The features expanded and collapsed, eyes twisted to the top of the head, ears migrated down to the shoulders. The leather jacket slipped. The t-shirt dropped to the ground. The twisting strands of gray flesh came together and fell apart, no longer holding the shape of a human body. There was no Mason, no body even. It looked like spaghetti with squid ink. Paul almost wanted to laugh. *I'm being terrorized by a spaghetti monster.* But instead of a laugh, a loud scream escaped his throat.

Paul took a step back toward the door. Then another. He found himself outside. The ground under his feet writhed and thrashed. He tried to move farther away from whatever became of Mason, but his legs wouldn't move. He looked down and saw that he was tied to the ground. The same strands of gray flesh were twisting up and around his legs, making their way up his torso.

"Help!" he screamed. "Hel..." Something slid into his throat. He found it difficult to breathe. Spots of color floated across his vision. Then darkness.

● ● ●

Officer Merry

"It was a heart attack," Officer Merry told Ay-Tal Blue again, holding the phone too tight against his ear. The woman made him nervous. They discovered Reverend Paul almost immediately—there were investigators on the premises. An ambulance was called, but the reverend was pronounced dead on the scene. Now the attorney, Ms. Blue, was calling, making inquiries. He had to explain yet again about Paul Wolf's untimely demise. The doctors said it was probably all the stress of the police investigation in and around his home and town.

"Officer Merry," she said.

"We know all about the town's emergency vote to ask us to leave, for the police to end the 'intrusive interference in your local affairs.' Really, I—"

"As far as I understand," she interrupted him, "the only outstanding issue is the missing gun."

"Well—"

"I've already given testimony on that point. The conductor shot at me. Jon Uolan tried to shield me with his body and then rushed me off the train, thinking that we were being attacked by a madman. You know how there were threats against my life after we won the Supreme Court case? There are people who are ignorant and easily misled to act in violent ways. Jon tried to protect me. He thought he was saving my life from some lunatic vigilante. Now, I understand that there seems to be a misunderstanding by the conductor. I'm not pressing charges. I could, but I'm not going to. I have more important things to attend to at this moment. But your work is disruptive to my work. To my people. To the town of Wilkins. To the children I'm trying to protect. I'm asking you to drop it. It would be so much easier for both of us, don't you agree?"

"But the gun—"

"Someday, it might turn up, Officer. Until that day, please allow this community to heal and to come together and grow. We seem to be attracting the attention of every news organization around the world as it is."

"And the case of Burt Wilkins?"

"He's dead now."

"And Ada?"

"From what I've heard from the doctors, Ada will probably spend the rest of her life under psychiatric care. It would be in the kids' best interest if you let that lie as well." The woman paused and let the telephone static sit between them for a long time, allowing him to make up his mind.

There was no upside. Not with all the media attention. Not without any bodies. Not with Reverend Paul Wolf and Burt Wilkins both dead. Not with Ada safely locked away.

"Maybe for now," he said, letting this strange woman win. "Thank you, Officer Merry."

He put down the phone and looked at his partner. The gun lay on the table inside the evidence bag. They could find nothing that tied Jon Uolan to the gun. The conductor had failed the lie detector test, not that that was admissible as evidence. But it was one more reason to step aside...*for now.*

"For now," Officer Rogers agreed.

• • •

Jon Uolan

Ay-Tal dug out Mason's old cowboy boots from the back of her car, threaded a cord through the pulls, tied the boots together, and went outside. Jon watched her throw the boots up over the power line. Once, twice, a third time... *Who knew that gods needed so many tries?* Finally, on the seventh throw, she got the cord tangled up with the wires, and the boots dangled high above the roadway.

"It's a new ritual I've heard about to celebrate Change," Ay-Tal said, getting back into the car.

"Sort of a farewell to the old and a clean start to the new? A death celebration?" Saga asked. It was just the three of them: Saga, Jon, and Ay-Tal. The god had decided never to use the body of that boy again. Thus the final goodbye.

"Sure, sure," Ay-Tal said. "And burn. And drown. And

throw from the highest peak. Scatter in the wind. Nail to the top of the bell tower and place under the corner stone. Set free on the ice flow. Tie to the back of wolf. Feed to the worshipers. Hide under the shifting sands. Sink in a bog. Conceal in a tar pit. Stuff in a maw of a tiger. Give to the monks as a holy relic—"

"Oh, stop it, Ay-Tal," Saga said with a nervous little laugh.

Jon understood that Ay-Tal was reciting death rituals that she had used in the past. In a way, a change was a death... followed by a rebirth. *Still, a bit gory that, especially with Saga around.* Jon had been a witness to a few godly changes now—one...no, two deaths, and two rebirths. He didn't really know if Al was gone for good, but the shoe tossing symbolized the final death of Mason, putting that boy to rest. He recalled other shoes dangling over the wires in Anchorage and D.C.—were they also memorials to some god changing her form?

"You can now pay for your shoes to be sent out into space. One of those space burials, you know?" Saga said. Jon thought that was a brave thing to say to a god. Even a god, who was very familiar and tangible like Ay-Tal, was still a god.

"Really?" Ay-Tal said. "Huh."

"And I've heard of people who turned their dead into lumps of diamonds," Saga said.

"I've heard of that service—make your loved ones last forever," Jon said. He remembered an ad for that on the Internet. He thought it silly at the time, but was it any more silly than placing a body out onto an ice floe?

"Humans have always been very creative when it came to memorials and death rituals," said Ay-Tal. "I remember mixing the ashes of a tribe's fallen hunters into the pigment used for cave paintings. The trek in the dark. The resonant cavity. The paint by torchlight. They were always mystical." It wasn't clear whom Ay-Tal meant by "they."

"You've witnessed prehistoric cave painting?" Jon asked. His god never ceased to amaze him.

"Not prehistoric to me," said Ay-Tal. "Who do you think taught the first groups of humans to seek shelter in caves?"

"How long?" Jon asked. "How long have you been around?"

"Long enough," said Ay-Tal.

"But why are you so free in telling me? Us? Isn't it a big secret or something?"

"It was never a secret," Ay-Tal said. "We have always been known to humans. We've been around since before humans left Africa. We took you, shaped you, showed you the world."

"How did people know you as a god?" Saga asked. "Didn't people use to worship bears and wolves and even made up creatures like Isis and Hathor?"

"Human explain their experiences using what's available at a particular place and time," Ay-Tal said. "Consider how humans experience sudden trauma."

"Like PTSD?" Jon asked. "I read that it was called 'soldier's heart' during the Civil War and then 'shell shock' during World War One. Some of our tribe members had 'post-Vietnam syndrome' after they returned from that war."

"Yes. Humans are very inventive. The name of the disease is always made to fit the times and the people," Ay-Tal said. "I remember when it was simply called 'severe nostalgia.' But yes, like that. And it is not just the names for the condition; the symptoms change too."

"But if the symptoms change, wouldn't it be a different disease?" Saga asked. *Good point,* thought Jon. He was continuously impressed by Saga's ability to calmly interact with Ay-Tal as if she was like any other adult in her life.

"All symptoms are taken from what's in fashion at that point in history, even as the underlying cause is very similar," Ay-Tal explained. "Sometimes, people lose their ability to talk or swallow, sometimes the symptoms of severe depression express as the inability to walk or the loss of consciousness. Some stop eating, as that became the way of expressing inner turmoil. It varies. And this is not limited to just cognitive malefactions. During and after World War Two, there was a worldwide phenomenon of seeing flying saucers. Something about how people at that time perceived technology, space exploration, and war, turned anxiety into sightings of green alien dudes in flying disks. But before that, humans saw sea monsters and dragons. Before that, gods and demigods of various kinds, witches, and wizards. There were all kinds of things that people believed ruled the natural world… Anxiety of the unknown always translates into a manifestation of fears steeped in the culture of its time. Humans see and experience what they expect to see and experience."

"So there were no green alien dudes before World War Two?" Saga asked.

"Nope. Not that I've heard."

"Hmm. So have you always assumed a human body for your godly purposes or—"

"Saga!" Jon tried to stop the girl. Sometimes Saga went too far.

"It's okay, Jon. Saga's question is a good one," Ay-Tal said. "We take on forms that work best for the people we serve."

"So not always human?" Saga asked, but Ay-Tal didn't answer. "Hmm. So why us and not some other animal?" She kept pushing the god for answers.

Jon cringed, but he also wanted to know the answers to these same questions. His ignorance had almost cost him and his tribe everything. He vowed to learn as much as he could. And he too often wondered about other species. Whales were intelligent and had deep emotional lives. They lived and loved and gave themselves to humans. *Or did people simply take?*

No, Jon was sure that his people never "simply took" anything. So why not whales?

Ay-Tal looked at him and Saga and smiled. "It was a choice," she finally said. "We could have gone with elephants, or whales, or even crows. But humans were chosen and we guided you, made you, really, into what you've become."

"So it wasn't evolution?"

"We were part of your evolution, your natural selection, if you will," Ay-Tal said. "We picked you, and the rest was history."

"Are you happy with your decision?" Jon asked. He thought back on all of human history, or at least those parts that he was aware of, and felt a bit unworthy of these gods' selection. *Could they have done better? Were humans grateful enough?*

"Happy enough," said Ay-Tal. "But there're always things to do. Big and small. Life to change for the better...or for worse. I think I will hang around with Wilkins-Tal for a bit longer."

"But now that the other gods have found you," said Jon, "will they let you? Will they let you stay with us?"

"They will keep an eye on me." Ay-Tal seemed uncomfortable with that, and Saga came over and hugged her. *The girl is offering support to a god!* Jon felt himself choke up a bit. He couldn't do that. Not even with Ay-Tal...well, he could if she was Al. It was confusing.

"I will have to pull my own share again," said Ay-Tal. "I won't be able to drop out and hide among my chosen people for generations. Time is moving swiftly now. I can't take a few thousands years off to rest again. There is too much work to do."

Acknowledgments

My friends and family have been full of encouragement, often reading each paragraph hot off the press, asking what happens next, and pushing me to go on. Their support means everything to me.

My husband, Christopher, and I co-write books together. On this one, he helped edit both the story and my grammar, improving the final book tremendously! Together, we also run Pipsqueak Productions: pipsqueak.com. In addition, I write a blog: interfaces.com. You can also find me on Twitter at @OlgaWerby

Allister Thompson was my editor on this book. In addition to fixing seemingly endless errors—spelling is not my strong suit—he looked for plot holes in my work. This book is much better because of his talent. You can find Allister (and hire him for all your editing needs) on Reedsy. com. He is a kind soul.

All errors between the covers and on them are entirely my own.

I would also like to thank Pixabay.com for creating an amazing site full of art available free under a Creative Commons license. The cover art for this book is partly created based on photographs and other media found there.

If you liked this story, please consider recommending

it to others. Reviews on Amazon and GoodReads are very much appreciated. Word-of-mouth endorsements and reader reviews are the holy grail for indy authors. Without these, our stories just gather e-dust. And I would like to write a few more tales of gods that walk among us and need encouragement!

Most of all, thank you for reading. Your imagination makes my stories come alive!

Other Books

If you enjoyed this book, I hope you'll consider reading some of our other novels. They're all available on Amazon or others places where books are sold.

"Many Worlds, One Life" series:
Suddenly, Paris (book 1)
Coding Peter (book 2)

"The Ornis Experiment" series:
Pigeon (book 1)
Birdie (book 2 is coming soon)

The FATOFF Conspiracy

Twin Time

Becoming Animals

"The Chronicles of DaDA Immortals" *series:*
Lizard Girl & Ghost

Harvest

To tempt you, I've included sample chapters from *Harvest*. Enjoy!

If you visit my site, Interfaces.com, please sign up for my newsletter. I write about once a month with offers of free books (from many indie authors) and with updates on my own work. In addition to my ramblings, you can get an ebook of my first novel, "Suddenly, Paris," for free! What a deal.

HARVEST
Olga Werby

ProLog

"The exton controls are not responding!" Marc shouted into his exoskeleton spacesuit helmet.

His exoskeleton was the heavy-duty dirt-and-boulder-mover type. *Move a ton with exton.* Right now, Marc was really just an intelligent bulldozer with life support. But the suit had disconnected from his D-tats, the personal computing device tattoos embedded in his lower arms and jaw, and his directional controls were busted. Now his exoskeleton acted with a mind of its own, moving him away from the construction site and out into the open Martian landscape. He needed to get back to the Malfy—an affectionate acronym for Martians Live Free, a city-sized habitat being built for the next wave of planetary immigrants.

"Marc?" his SB responded from the inside Malfy's operational center. "What's on the fritz this time?" Every contractor working outside was in constant communication with a personally assigned *safety buddy.* "I can't seem to toss the controls over to my side." In an emergency, Marc's SB could take over the controls of his exton and bring him in, even if he was unconscious.

"I've got nothing!" Marc was more irritated than scared. This was his second equipment failure in as many months, and their group of union builders had reported three more to the management since the start of the project about two hundred days ago. It was always the same MO: at the end of a shift, the movement controls failed to respond to their operators' commands, taking the builders out into the desert; and yet, after the rescue when the equipment was checked out, the engineers found nothing wrong with the extons. The first time it happened to Marc, he was even accused of faking the failure to get extra time off for hazardous conditions. As if construction work on Mars wasn't dangerous in and of itself. Fortunately, Marc's supervisor made everyone carry extra oxygen and a spare battery pack after the first few incidents. Just in case. Inconvenient for sure, but it was better than being stuck out of breath without a heater among the Martian dunes in minus 125 degrees Celsius.

"Send someone out to get me," Marc said. "It's an official request."

"Are you sure, Marc? You know if they don't find anything again—"

"I'm telling you, I've got nothing. Everything is dead on my side."

"Yeah, mine too," Marc's SB agreed. "I'll get Greg out there. But he won't be happy. He just got his exton off and you'll be cutting into his three days off period."

"Tell him that I'd go if it was him out here. And tell him to hurry up about it." The earliest he could expect Greg to arrive would be at least an hour, probably more—it took time get these darn things on.

● ● ●

Marc felt funky. His D-tats itched like crazy, probably from all of the energy pushed through them to try to reconnect with his exton. And now his comm was down, too.

As soon as he'd gotten over the rim of the crater, he'd lost touch with his SB.

It was lonely out here in the Martian landscape with no one to talk to and all the human structures obscured from view. Marc could only look ahead—his suit didn't allow him to turn his head—and before him stretched miles and miles of nothing but rust sand and red rocks underneath a yellow

sky. Someday this would be paradise, but Marc didn't expect to live that long. Still, it was decent pay, and the benefits were great. And, most importantly, all the construction workers were to be awarded a family subdivision inside the new MLF. Marc looked forward to moving his wife and a new kid he'd never seen out here from Luna Colony. Kids should run around on the surface of a real planet, his mother always said. In a few years, Marc would make his mother's dream a reality right here, on this dusty red rock. And when he did, he would be able to tell his kids that he built this place with his own hands. He would point to a boulder and say, "See that rock? Your daddy placed that rock." It was a satisfying thought…if only the equipment worked right.

He tried to will his suit to obey. Heat erupted around his jaw and down his neck. It took him by surprise—not an emotion he was used to. The off-world building crews went through years of training, and part of that training involved controlling one's thoughts. Spend too much attention on extraneous thoughts and emotions—like surprise and worry—and space got you. Cognition was a limited resource.

This fact about human nature was drilled into Marc, not just during training but from an early age. All Luna Colony children learned to focus and control their attention. Those who couldn't didn't make it to adulthood. It was different there now, in those modern Luna Live Free habitats—Elfys. But when Marc was young…

"Ahhh!" The scream seemed to rip itself out of Marc's throat without his conscious control. Pain twisted his arms inside his suit. He felt himself hyperventilating. Something was seriously wrong with *him*, not just with his exton. The horror of that realization hit him hard as the exoskeleton kept marching him inexorably farther from the base. He smelled cooked meat. It took all his willpower not to think where the

smell was coming from. The life support systems should have noted his elevated heart rate and responded.

Since his D-tats weren't working, Marc tried to blink commands directly into the suit. He drilled down several menus and selected a painkiller injection. He needed to get himself under control. Rescue was still at least thirty minutes away.

Sweat trickled into his eyes. It was difficult to see now. He felt cold and yet heat burned his arms, neck, and jaw. His teeth felt out of alignment. There was a constant buzzing in his left ear, different in tone and structure from the one in his right. But at least it was something he could focus on. He poured himself into the strange, asymmetric tinnitus. Bzzz, bzzz, swish, bzzz, bzzz, swish…

● ● ●

"I found him unresponsive."

Greg sat in front of a board of inquiry. Marc's death was the first among the Martian chapter of the Off-World Builders Union this year. Given that Mars was deemed a relatively low-risk environment, the death had attracted extra scrutiny from both the union leaders and the insurance representatives for the Martians Live Free project.

"Are you saying Builder Mark Kelly's communications were out? Or was he unconscious when you found him?"

"At first it wasn't clear, sir," Greg testified. "The exoskeleton continued to walk into the desert and wouldn't stop until I caught up with it and patched into it directly."

"So the comm was completely out?"

"Yes, sir. I wasn't able to control the exton from a distance, and Marc lost his communication a while before that." Greg wiped the sweat from his forehead. He hated answering stupid questions. Everyone already knew what had happened. Marc's D-tats had fried from some bad connection to his equipment. *Shit happens. Get over it. Move on.*

The interrogation went on for another hour, but at some point, even the insurance representative recognized that Greg had nothing more to add to the report he'd filed with the union. The conclusion was that this was a freak accident caused by improperly implanted personal computing device tattoos a decade earlier. The Luna Colony medical board was granted jurisdiction over the case.

Chapter One

"Sentient life's colonization of the Earth is fractal. Even within a single ecosystem, there are many species that possess intelligence and self-awareness. But only one species becomes dominant."

Professor Volhard took a theatrical pause here. Everyone in the audience knew where she was going with this, but it never hurt to add drama to a presentation.

"Obviously I am talking about humans. We are not the only intelligent, self-aware species on our planet—but we got lucky. We were blessed with favorable initial conditions, and our dominance was almost guaranteed. Lack of luck tends to permanently retard progress. Dinosaurs' loss is our win."

There were a few chuckles from the audience, but no big laughs. Varsaad Volhard sighed inwardly and moved on. She never knew how the lay audience would react, but this was all part of doing the book-selling lecture circuit.

Vars was tall and skinny with short, unruly, dark red hair and glasses to match. She looked a bit like a stick insect in her black pants and black sweater. For the tour, she was trying to dress more interestingly than normal—per instructions from her publisher—and so had added the bright orange scarf that her publisher sent in the mail. The instructions that came with the scarf told her to wear matching orange shoes, but

Vars didn't own any orange shoes, so matching black was as good as it got.

She hadn't failed to notice that the cover of her book—*Luck & Lock on Life & Love: The Human History of Conquest of Resources on Earth, Luna, and Beyond*—had the same color orange titles as the scarf. Her agent or someone in the office was obviously trying. Vars made a mental note to figure out who that was and thank them.

Vars talked for a while without paying attention to what she said—that was a gift that came with giving the same talk for the hundredth time. Fortunately, she was almost at the end of her book tour. Two more lectures and she would be done. She could go back to teaching and research—get her life back. This nomadic lifestyle wasn't for her. But before she got out of there tonight, Vars still had one more surprise argument for these people: a defense of space exploration.

She looked into the dark void in front of her. The stage

lights made the hundred people in the theater disappear from view—a plus for a shy researcher. And she was a true believer in the "what you can't see can't hurt you" principle. Not only had she opted out of vision-correction treatments, she regularly taught without her glasses, leaving all but the front row of her classroom a Monet-like blur. The trick worked well to relieve her agoraphobic anxiety.

"So, what are the prerequisites of space travel?" she asked.

There were a few shout-outs from up in the gallery—the cheap seats usually occupied by students. "Civilization." "Faster-than-light travel." "Aliens." They were on the right track, even if their sources were limited to science fiction movies. But Vars was an evolutionary socio-historian, and that meant she was trained to look both into the future *and* the past. She liked to think that her ideas about possible human future scenarios were well informed by historical precedents and intelligent extrapolations of cultural trends— meaning she wasn't just talking science fiction here.

"Let's start with something simple," she said. "Time." Time was never simple, but people always assumed it was. Everyone had experience with time, so everyone felt like they were experts on the subject. "Humans have a relatively long lifespan for a mammal. And we have the longest childhood of all animals." Well, that was true now. Neanderthal kids had enjoyed a longer childhood, but Vars didn't want to complicate things further. "Not only are we able to learn a lot before we plunge into adulthood," Vars continued, "we also have the time to use that knowledge. I'm sure we would all like to live even longer, but nature has ensured that we live long *enough* to transfer wisdom from one generation to the next, so our species can build on that, expanding our collective grasp of how the universe works. Each generation stands on the shoulders of all those that came before. Without a sufficiently long lifespan to learn and apply that collective mastery, space travel would just not be possible."

Vars tried to peer into the audience to check that they were still with her.

"So why not elephants or whales, you might ask. Both species live a long time and spend a significant proportion of that life as children." Vars didn't wait for answers. "Unfortunately, neither were lucky enough to evolve hands. Even the elephant's prehensile trunk can't compare with the nimbleness of human fingers. And whales have the additional disadvantage of living in an underwater environment. These are significant handicaps to developing space travel. So again, humans got lucky. We evolved to live on land, and we have the right appendages to be able to tinker with objects in our environment. To bend it to our will."

"Language!" someone screamed out of the dark.

Vars smiled. Language came up over and over again at each of her lectures. "Yes, language," she said into the darkened auditorium. "It's been said that language is the ultimate tool of mankind. Its greatest invention." There were sounds of agreement from the audience. "But are we the only species on Earth to possess language? Sure, human languages are incredibly sophisticated and versatile, far more so than those of any other species we have encountered to date. But until a few decades ago, we didn't even believe that there *were* nonhuman languages here on our planet. Now, of course, we know better. Dolphins, elephants, and even some birds have been observed using rudimentary languages unique to their species."

Vars stopped to listen to the audience. There were murmurings of assent, but also a few mutterings of rejection. The idea of animals inventing languages was very new still, but it was no longer controversial among her colleagues. Of course, politics was always way behind science. If humans were to widely acknowledge that dolphins communicated via language, then we might also have to recognize them as having some legal form of "personhood"—and that just wasn't tenable in the current political climate.

The dissent told Vars what proportion of the audience held human-centric views. It was about forty percent or so, judging by the noise. That was about average for this part of the country. In places like Berkeley, California, only one or two people in the audience dared to express such backward opinions loudly enough to be heard on stage. Most dissenters kept quiet, she knew. People were herd mammals, after all, and needed to be surrounded by others with similar views. That was how social echo chambers worked in the age of mass e-media.

"Language," she said, "particularly written language, is essential to passing information from one generation and one community to the next. Written language saved us from having to invent things over and over again—"

"Oral traditions!" someone yelled.

"Oral traditions are fantastic for capturing and communicating culture," Vars replied. "But they are lousy for transmitting technical information. There is no oral tradition of calculus." There was a murmuring of agreement. *Good.* "And before someone brings up apprenticeship, let me just say that I'm a believer in learning while being embedded in a community of practice. We see such educational approaches in species other than our own. Chimps routinely teach their offspring how to fish for termites with specially made twigs. Birds teach their chicks how to hunt and which foods are good and where they can be located. Cerrado, a species of monkey from South America, use giant hammer rocks to break tough palm nuts over carefully selected anvil boulders. It takes years for the youngsters to learn how to select just the right hammers and anvils and to perfect the technique for bashing open the nuts. So yes, apprenticeship works—but it has its limits. We are the only species on Earth to develop *other* intentional ways of passing on knowledge. Without written information, we wouldn't be in the process of colonizing Mars, or mining the asteroids, or having permanent bases on the moon."

Vars gave the audience a few seconds to absorb this. She wasn't done having fun with them yet. "But before written and oral language traditions, before the apprenticeship form of passing knowledge from generation to generation, there was another way. Nature's way. Evolution's way."

She stopped, giving her listeners a moment or two to guess the answer. Some nights, the audience got it almost immediately; other nights, there wasn't a clue in the house. Tonight, there was only silence.

"Evolution couldn't wait for humans to invent language. Survival depended on passing some information down the chain of generations." *Well? Still nothing?* "I'm talking about instincts, of course. Our drive to mate, to reproduce, to protect our children. Our will to survive against all odds. We've all experienced, or will experience, these instinctual needs. It's in our DNA, so to speak. But that's not the only hard-coded knowledge that we pass along to our offspring.

"I will focus on humans here, because that's what I wrote my book about. Which reminds me: I will be signing copies in the lobby right after the end of the lecture. I'm required to say this by my publisher." There were a few chuckles. *Good.* Vars hated dull groups. It was hard to speak without feedback. "Agoraphobia and claustrophobia, fear of dark places and of heights, ophidiophobia and arachnophobia, instinctual disgust of bodily fluids—blood, urine, pus, feces—all of these are innate for us humans. We are born to avoid tight places and grand expanses. We naturally avoid snakes and spiders even if we've never seen or heard of them before. But we have also learned to overcome these fears. We had to if we were going to go into space. Our spaceships are extremely cramped, and they float in vast expanses of space. Astronauts are forced to recycle their bodily fluids and to no longer be afraid of extreme heights and absolute darkness. Although I may never overcome my fear of snakes and spiders…" She shivered dramatically and earned a few more laughs. "And perhaps, one day, we will meet other explorers out there. And we might have more innate fears to shed."

Vars talked for another quarter hour about the importance of different sensory apparatuses and the need for access to easily extracted raw resources, but it was getting late, and she could feel that the energy had drained from her audience. She was tired, too. She needed to catch a redeye tonight and try to squeeze in a few more hours of sleep before another lecture tomorrow.

Before she was even aware of it, there was hearty applause, and then it was time for smiling, handshaking, and book signing. She'd come to learn that the only people who still bought paper books were the ones who attended these book tour lectures. She was grateful to all of them, and yet she couldn't wait to get out of there.

● ● ●

"Dr. Volhard?" The voice was a nice soft baritone. "May I have a moment of your time after you've finished autographing?"

Vars raised her head, a fake smile plastered on her face, and tried to identify the speaker. There were still half a dozen people waiting, each clutching a copy of her book. But none of those was the speaker. So she went back to signing, and soon enough, like magic, it was done. She rubbed her wrist, which had started to cramp up, and slid the contents of the table—brochures, pens, and leftover business cards—into her bag. She would deal with sorting it all out later.

"Coffee?" the baritone asked again. "I know you take it with sugar and milk. But I wasn't sure of the proportions."

Vars looked up again. A tall, slightly graying man in rimless glasses with a slight yellow tint was standing in front of her, holding a recyclable coffee cup. He was dressed in jeans, a dress shirt with no tie, and a wool jacket—easy elegance, her literary agent would call it. She tried to do something similar for these lectures—approachable, smart, and interesting were her original goals. But at this point in the lecture tour, all she could hope for was clean, awake, and present. Dressing in all black helped.

"I beg your pardon," she said. "Do you have a book for me

to sign?"

"That would have been lovely," the man said, "but I bought an e-version of your book."

"I can sign your data pad," Vars offered. She still didn't take the coffee from his extended hand. And she wasn't planning to.

"What a lovely idea." He smiled. "Do you mind if we talk a bit? I know you're tired—"

"And I have a plane to catch." Vars spoke more harshly than she'd meant to; the man did buy her book, after all.

She tried to go around him, but he wouldn't budge. She looked past him for a security guard at the door. Shouldn't someone be getting everyone out of here? Perhaps escorting her to a taxi? She was getting annoyed and a bit alarmed.

"My name is Ian Rust," the man said.

"Dr. Vars Volhard."

"Of course." He smiled again.

"I really do have to go, Mr. Rust," Vars insisted. She tried to push past the man, her suitcase ready to roll behind her.

"The thing is, Dr. Volhard, we really need your expertise as soon as possible," Rust said.

"Sir, I'm an evolutionary socio-historian. My direct expertise is rarely required on an *emergency* basis. Contact my university office, and I'm sure I would be able to fit you in during one of my ample office hours after I get back."

"Ah, but there are exceptions," he said. "We've read everything that you've published—"

"Everything?"

"Everything. And you have a unique set of expertise that my team at Earth Planetary Space Agency urgently requires." He pulled out his EPSA credentials. "Our car is waiting outside, Dr. Volhard. Won't you please follow me? Do you mind if I call you Vars?"

"Sure," Vars said automatically.

"Then please call me Ian." He handed the coffee to her.

EPSA was the umbrella agency that had taken over for NASA, ESA (European Space Agency), ASA (Australian Space Agency), and JAXA (Japan Aerospace Exploration Agency). So it wasn't entirely "planetary"—China and Russia still ran their own space exploration programs—but it *was* the largest and best-funded agency, and it was the one that was actively pushing the Mars colonization program and comprehensive exploration of the solar system.

Vars had always dreamed of working for EPSA, even as a girl. But somehow, somewhere along the way, her academic career had veered into anthropology, and then evolution, and then…well, here she was. The evo devo diva of anthropology.

And now she was riding down the dark, empty streets in the back seat of a black driverless car, with Dr. Ian Rust, head of the exobiology research team at EPSA, sitting by her side.

Chapter Two

Vars slept on the plane…or tried to. She was too confused, too keyed up to really sleep. That coffee might have been a mistake. Ian said that he couldn't tell her anything until they arrived at his EPSA office in Seattle, which was conveniently her own hometown where she lived with her dad. The man just smiled a lot and talked about how much he had enjoyed reading Vars's new book.

There was a strange edge to their interaction. If Vars hadn't believed Ian's credentials, she would have bailed on him a long time ago. Even so, she felt like she was being kidnapped. And, in a way, she was. She'd had to cancel the last two lectures of her book tour and apologize to her agent over and over again. Ian had promised that EPSA would send an official excuse letter, but Vars still felt like she let her agent and publisher down.

They landed at a general aviation airport, and another black car whisked them to EPSA's headquarters, just outside of Seattle's city limits. She was taken to a conference room on the top floor of the EPSA science building, which Ian called the "tree house." She immediately understood why—it was surrounded on all sides by a balcony planted with a row of trees and some shrubbery. It was quite nice, but Vars couldn't enjoy it; she was simultaneously exhausted and adrenalized.

It was just a matter of time before she crashed.

She must have looked it, too, because someone handed her a very big, very steamy cup of coffee. She sipped it gratefully, completely oblivious to how she came to be holding it. It was still very early in the morning, way before Vars even liked to get up, much less attend a meeting.

About a dozen EPSA people joined her and Ian around the conference table. Vars noticed that several paper copies of her book were laid out; some even looked read, with cracked spines and dog-eared pages.

"So," she said to Ian. "Is *now* a good time and place for you to tell me what this is all about?"

"Now is perfect," Ian said with a big smile. "We are very grateful to have you with us today, Dr. Volhard. This is my exobiology team." He pointed one by one to the people on one side of the table. "Dr. Alice Bear. Dr. Greg Tungsten. Dr. Bob Shapiro. Dr. Saydi Obara. Dr. Evelyn Shar. And Dr. Izzy Rubka."

Vars had heard of some of these people by reputation, of course, but never met any of them personally. EPSA people were a reclusive bunch, tending to mix with their own to the exclusion of others, even with the same research interests. It was one of the reasons Vars always wanted to join the organization—to get access to the best and the brightest minds and a chance to discuss the origins of life over coffee... But the introductions were happening so fast, there was no chance that she would remember how any of these names linked up with faces. Vars doubted she would even recognize these people walking down the street.

But Ian just continued. "And this group," he gestured to two men and a woman, "is on loan from JPL—Jet Propulsion Lab in Pasadena. Trish Cars, Dr. Ron Silverman, and Dr. Benjamin Kouta." Vars gave up on remembering who was who.

"And these two," Ian said, nodding to a pair of identical twins sitting next to him, "are Ibe and Ebi Zimov, our computer science wunderkinds from EISS, European Institute of Space Science."

Ian pronounced their names as *eye-bee* and *ee-bee*; it was the only introduction Vars was likely to remember fully, as the siblings were the most interesting looking pair in the room. They seemed young—Vars guessed not older than twenty—and she was honestly uncertain whether they were male or female or one of each. They were dressed the same— sweatshirts with the EISS logo embroidered on the left, black jeans, black canvas shoes—and both had their hair dyed jet black, shaved on the sides and long on top, falling over their eyes. Vars could see impressive sets of D-tats on the exposed parts of their necks and jaws and peeking out of the twins' sleeves. Other people around the room presumably had D-tats too, but nothing so obviously ostentatious as these two.

"And before you ask," Ian said, "yes, they are related to Dr. Sergey Aphanasievich Zimov."

That name sounded vaguely familiar, but Vars had no idea who Dr. Zimov was.

She also noted that the other two people present—two men in military uniforms—were not introduced.

"It's a pleasure to meet you all," she said. "Please call me Vars." She smiled at everyone, then turned to Ian. "But once again… Please, I'd very much like to know why I'm here."

"I was just getting to that."

She noticed that he looked tired, too. He hadn't slept much on the plane either. Then again, pretty much everyone in the room looked haggard. Deep circles under the eyes were the norm, not the exception.

Before Ian could continue, one of the women from the exobiology team spoke up. "In your book, Dr. Volhard, you mentioned an example of how robots developed by collectivist cultures would be less likely to kill. Would you mind elaborating on that?"

Vars didn't know what she expected—but it wasn't this. "You flew me out here before dawn to talk about *killer robots*?"

The discussion of robots in her book was just an illustrative example, and a frivolous one at that. It was just a funny way of explaining the differences in value systems between collectivist and individualist cultures. She'd almost cut it from the final draft, but David Gatewood, her editor, had insisted she keep it in.

"Of course not," Ian said. "Robots are just a small part of it. But if you don't mind answering Alice's question…" He gave Vars a pleading look.

"You're serious?" Vars still couldn't believe it. She'd worked four years on the book, and what had caught EPSA's interest was a stupid joke. *I guess David was right,* she thought. *People, even smart people, grab on to the most flamboyant metaphors.*

"Should I explain the differences between collectivist and individualist societies first?" Vars asked. She looked around the room; she didn't want to assume what these people knew, but at the same time, talking down to the top minds of the Earth Planetary Space Agency was completely unacceptable.

"If you don't mind," Ian said. He composed himself as if awaiting a lecture. In fact, every face in the room had that look of composed concentration that Vars was used to seeing in her grad students.

"Okay." There was nothing to do but move forward. She launched into her introductory lecture on socio-evolution. "While there are many ways of classifying the various human cultures that arose in the last fifty thousand years or so, one division that can be made is focused on the perception of the role of an individual within the group. In collectivist cultures, the group needs are judged *above* the needs of an individual; in the individualist cultures, it's the opposite, naturally."

"Naturally," echoed an older, tiny, dark-skinned woman with bottle-thick glasses and tightly cropped hair, the one who asked the original question. *Alice something.* Vars wasn't familiar with the woman's work. And she hadn't encountered too many people, other than herself…and well, Ian, who wore glasses. In his case, Vars was almost certain it was all about self-image. She wouldn't have been surprised if they were simple tinted glass. But Alice's glasses were thick corrective lenses and far from attractive. Most everyone had their vision corrected in this day and age. So either Alice had a strange affectation or an aversion to treatment. Or perhaps she had a defect that couldn't easily be fixed, which was rare.

"Logic clearly dictates that the needs of the many outweigh the needs of the few," said one of the youngish-looking men from the JPL team. Vars knew enough popular culture to know he was quoting a character from an old space-exploration series. *Star Trek?*

This is too basic, she thought, and she raised her discourse up a notch. "Let's just jump right into the robot anecdote. Robots designed by collectivist cultures would be less likely to kill. They would have a stronger focus on the *theory of mind*, understanding and taking perspectives of others—"

"Can you backtrack a bit?" Ian asked.

"Sure." Vars thought she now understood the Goldilocks zone she was to lecture to. "Consider guilt. Guilt is one of the strongest human psyche compulsions. We use guilt and embarrassment as tools for social compliance all the time. Guilt is motivational, so to speak. Our social media landscape is full of guilt traps. We finger people who don't pay taxes or contribute in a positive way to our society. We name people who don't recycle or who drop trash on the road or who still use personal transportation vehicles. We social-shame not only the anti-social behavior but even the way people dress and look."

A man in the back spoke up. "We are all familiar with cyber bullying, Dr. Volhard. EPSA is a large, multicultural organization, and we're all required to take classes and workshops in antisocial behavior and sensitivity training."

"I do too, as a university professor and researcher," Vars assured them. "But my point is that social shaming works."

"On robots?"

"I'm getting there," Vars said with a smile. "People from collectivist and individualist societies experience guilt differently. A person from a collectivist culture feels guilt as 'What will people think of me?' While someone from an individualist culture perceives it as 'How will I live with myself?' See the difference?"

"So outcomes vary?" Ian asked.

"Precisely! Consider a criminal," Vars said. "A person who commits a crime in an individualist culture can't escape guilt, for the feelings of guilt are experienced internally, whether anyone is aware of the crime or not."

"Are you implying that in collectivist cultures, a criminal won't experience guilt the same way?" Alice asked.

"That's precisely it, Alice." Vars made herself say the name of the woman to reinforce it in her memory—a simple mnemonic trick. "It's easier to commit a crime if you're convinced that no one will learn of it and you live in a world where it's only the opinion of your group that matters."

"So a murderer won't lose sleep over his deed if he was raised in a collectivist culture?"

"I'm saying that the guilt is assessed differently," Vars said. "And it's always about the extremes of the spectrum: the extreme form of collectivism, the extreme form of individualism. Of course, we live in a world that is both a little collectivist and a little individualist. I'm giving you the very antipodes to make my point clearer."

"Of course, Dr. Volhard," said Ian. "So the robots?"

"Yes, the robots. I'm getting to that, but first one more point." Vars took a big gulp of coffee. It was cold and bitter now, but she needed the caffeine.

She must have made a face, for Ian was instantly on his feet, getting her a refill in a fresh cup. She waited for him to sit back down.

"Thank you, Ian," she said, taking a sip. "Much better."

"My pleasure."

"And this is a perfect example of my next point: the theory of mind. Ian saw my expression when I took a sip from my cold cup and guessed that I was dissatisfied with my coffee."

"It was obvious," Ian said.

"To *you.*"

"I think it was obvious to everyone in the room," he said with a smile.

A few people chuckled.

"That bad? Well, good. Then everyone here has a good theory of mind. You were all able to interpret my feelings, thoughts, and experiences even though you had no direct access to my taste buds. The theory of mind is necessary for higher-order thinking skills. It's necessary for communication, for understanding multiple points of view. Not all animals on Earth have this ability, and even human children take several years to master this skill. Before the age of about four, kids are unable to switch perspectives and understand what motivates others. And even after that age, the theory of mind continues to develop into and throughout adulthood."

"The development of empathy," Alice said.

"That too. Empathy requires that we try to put ourselves in another's situation to understand how they might feel. This is different from sympathy, obviously, which doesn't require such cognitive acrobatics. So a child of five would flinch and hold their hand after observing someone get hit on the hand. It's almost like the pain of another is their pain."

"Are you saying that there's a difference in the development of the theory of mind between collectivist and individualist cultures?" Ian asked. He'd clearly read her book and was now helping his team to quickly get up to speed on the subject.

"Yes. In a collectivist culture, the theory of mind is paramount. The focus of collectivists is on others, so the success of the culture is dependent on nuanced social interactions that require complex cognitive activity and deep understanding of the feelings and motivations of others. In individualist societies, the focus is on the self, so the theory of mind is of less central importance."

"Thus robots designed by collectivist cultures would be less likely to kill," Ian said.

There were murmurs among the people around the table. Apparently not everyone was buying the conclusion about the robots.

"Didn't you just say that in a collectivist society it is easier to commit a crime?" Alice asked.

"Not easier, but with less guilt—and, even then, only so long as the crime isn't discovered by others in your group. In a collectivist society, as long as the crime remains hidden from the group, there are no ill consequences to the individual. But note that committing a murder requires a deep understanding of what others know, how they will react to the crime, and how they will feel about the perpetrator. One would need a deep understanding of the entire web of social interactions." Vars paused. "Again, I'm talking about extremes. But it stands to reason that robots created by collectivist societies would be designed with a focus on the theory of mind, with the ability to analyze problems from multiple perspectives. And such social cognitive flexibility puts more restraints on antisocial behavior than guilt alone."

"So the robots we design are more violent?" Alice asked.

The "we" came up a lot in Vars's classes. Everyone assumed that Western cultures were the most individualistic.

"Only if we design them so," Vars said. "But most of this is discussed in my book, and you clearly all have access to my work..." She trailed off meaningfully. All of this *was* in her book. It didn't make sense to her to be dragged urgently across the country for this predawn meeting. What did EPSA really want from her?

"Ibe," said Ian. "Could you run the short version of our presentation for Dr. Volhard, please?" He turned to Vars. "It's really the best introduction to our problem, and we can fill you in on details after."

The way he said "problem" made Vars uncomfortable.

Ibe and Ebi both got up and set up the presentation. One of them pulled up the oversized sleeve of his black sweatshirt and exposed an ostentatious set of D-tats on his right arm. That twin was a lefty, Vars noted, and a body-computing junky. She'd bet there was another, equally extravagant set of D-tats on the other arm.

She glanced around the room and noted a few other PCD

tattoos peeking from people's clothing. Vars heard that EPSA was heavily invested in cyberhumatics—the science of human implant technology and its connectivity with global networks and robotic extensions—so it wasn't surprising that D-tats were the norm among this group. But Vars had no implants, and it made her feel even more of an outsider.

Dark shades descended over the wraparound windows, cutting off the rays of the morning sun. The lights turned off, and the room was swallowed in a soft purple gloom. Vars yawned into the darkness—it would be so easy just to fall asleep in here, even with an almost full cup of coffee in hand. She heard others yawn as well. Yawning, she knew, was contagious among primates and other empathetic animals.

A 3D projection of the solar system lit up in the center of the conference table. The planets slowly rotated in their orbits. It was a very nice model, but of course it would be—this was EPSA.

"This is our solar system," Ebi said. Her voice pegged her as a girl.

Ibe spoke next. "This is Saturn. And this is Mimas." Based on the timbre of his voice, Vars judged him male. *So not identical twins.*

Using a combination of hand gestures and rapid tapping on his D-tats, Ibe zoomed in on Mimas, Saturn's closest moon. One side of the small whitish moon had a giant crater with a dimple in the center. "Mimas is primarily made of water-ice. As you can see, it's heavily cratered. The big one is named Herschel and is nearly a third of the moon's diameter."

"That's almost eighty miles wide and over six miles deep," Ebi added. "That pimple thing in the center is a mountain that's almost four miles high."

"That must have been some impact," said Vars. Based on the initial questioning, this was not how she'd thought the rest of the morning would go.

"It liquefied the little moon," Ibe said.

Most of the Saturn moons were well explored, and EPSA was actively working on establishing permanent science stations on some of them. But as far as Vars knew, none of the moons of either Jupiter or Saturn harbored anything more complex than simple bacterial life. Impressive, certainly, but old news now. And not something that an evolutionary socio-historian could help with. Vars's specialty was the development of self-aware cultures.

"A year ago, we detected a signal coming from Mimas," Ian said.

Ibe zoomed in on the giant crater and focused the image on the mountain. The rotation stopped, and the holographic image froze on a close-up. Vars could clearly see something protruding from the ice—a small, dark structure near the base of the central mountain.

Vars inhaled. She was no longer sleepy; all tiredness had been wiped clean. "What's that? One of ours?"

"No," said Ebi and Ibe in unison.

"And that's the main problem of the day," Ian said.

"You mean you don't know?" Vars asked. "It's been what? Twelve—"

"We have been able to divert one of our probes, and it arrived on site a few weeks ago," said of the men from the JPL team. *Ben?*

"So this picture..." Vars said.

"Yes, it's from that probe," said Ben. "We have detailed close-ups."

Ibe zoomed in even further, until the structure occupied most of the conference table.

"Wow," Vars whispered.

Chapter Three

The meeting lasted until late morning, until Vars just couldn't go on. Too tired, too much information, too much. Ian, seeing that Vars could no longer absorb anything new or contribute in any coherent way, insisted on taking her to an on-campus guest suite.

"My dad and I live just thirty minutes away," Vars protested, but Ian wouldn't hear of it. He and one of those guys in uniform—neither of whom had said a word the whole time—led her through the labyrinthine hallways. And without ever setting foot outside, Vars arrived at a small bedroom with a view of redwoods.

"I'll pick you up in a few hours and take you to lunch, okay?" said Ian. He smiled broadly and closed the door.

• • •

Vars's suitcase had made it to the EPSA guest room ahead of her and was waiting next to the bed, as was her backpack, which held her tablet and a few copies of her book. Even her raincoat was hanging on a hook by the door.

She took off her shoes and the fashionable orange scarf and thought about everything she'd heard. She still wasn't sure why EPSA wanted to talk with her, although she was thrilled to be included. This was the biggest thing ever. She was thankful for the alone time to process the information a bit. She needed to get a handle on what they were telling her. It was all so...so...incredible!

She pulled up her computing tablet and set it up on a desk by the window. Like her dad, Vars abhorred the PCD tattoos and had never even considered having one implanted. Well, nothing more than an ID microchip, which was required by law anyway. And the personal tablet, too, was an old-fashioned affectation. In her whole life, there had never been a circumstance or a place that didn't provide all of her computing or communication needs at any time she wanted it. Equipment was ubiquitous; in fact, for those who opted to get the new D-tats, it was never farther than their skin. But Vars's dad always used his own computing equipment, and she just picked up the habit.

She needed to get in touch with her dad. Even when work took them to different sides of the world, they talked every night, if only to exchange a few words. But last night, Vars had never gotten around to it, and she knew he would be worried about her. It was just the two of them—Vars's mother had died when Vars was just an infant, and they had no other family left, unless you counted some distant cousins on the other side of the world, in Norway or something. Her dad communicated with them only once or twice a year, and even then only out of a sense of obligation rather than familial closeness.

She considered *versing* with him but, at this time of day, her dad would be out in the field collecting samples. He did research on the effects of microplastics in the environment and tended to spend his mornings dredging through coastal tidal plains. It made more sense just to send him a note. She would tell him about her insane trip to EPSA later tonight when she got home. The idea of spending a night as a guest of EPSA seemed totally ridiculous—she lived just a short ride away.

She recorded a brief *vers*: *Dad, I'm back home in Seattle. Got invited to EPSA! Don't worry. All is good—talk tonight. Love you.*

She hit send. And nothing happened.

She tried again. Nothing. The blinking light on her tablet indicated no connection.

That made no sense. There was no longer a place on the Earth or the moon where communication devices didn't work. Even as far out as Mars, people complained when the services were down. Everyone was fully connected to the planetary network everywhere at all times. How else could anyone function?

Vars tried multiple times. She even restarted her PCD tablet—something she had never done before. But still nothing. Perhaps it was the room? *All those redwoods outside?*

She took the tablet out into the corridor. The man in uniform was standing just outside her door. He smiled. Vars smiled back, but her stomach did a double flip. She told herself that she hadn't been kidnapped, but clearly this man was guarding her in some way. *Holding me prisoner?*

"I'm not getting any connection in my room." She felt the need to explain and immediately got angry with herself. They couldn't keep her here against her will...could they?

"Dr. Volhard." Vars was sure the man was just about to salute her before relaxing his arm again. That was reflexive— years of training taking over. "Dr. Rust asked me to stay with you and help you navigate the facility when you were ready to resume work. Would you like me to escort you back to the tree house conference room?"

"No. I didn't get a chance to rest yet," Vars said uncertainly.

"Is there something I can get you? Coffee?"

"My connection doesn't seem to be working," Vars said again. She lifted her portable PCD to the man's face as evidence.

"Oh. Yes. Dr. Rust mentioned that the connection might not work here."

"Well, I need to get in touch with my father. Is there someplace I can go to do that?" Vars asked. "I didn't see any equipment back in the room." As soon as she said it, Vars realized it was true. There had been no public terminals there, which too was very unusual.

"I was only told to take you to the conference room if you were ready before Dr. Rust picked you up for lunch," the man said.

"I just need to send a message to my dad to tell him I'm okay," Vars tried again. "It's short. See?" She played the brief recording to the man and immediately hated herself for acting like a child who needed permission to talk to her own father.

"I'm sorry, Dr. Volhard. All I can do is take you back."

"Well, I don't like being out of reach like this," Vars snapped. Again she felt like a kid, whining about not getting what she wanted. Not that she had ever been that kind of kid.

Embarrassed, she stepped back into her room and closed the door. Perhaps she was just tired and misinterpreted what was going on.

She climbed into bed and placed her PCD tablet on the pillow. She watched the connection indicator show an error. She blinked. Blinked again.

The next time she opened her eyes was when a knock sounded on her door, four hours later.

• • •

"I should have introduced you earlier. This is Major Terry Liut," said Ian.

Vars smiled thinly at the man sitting across the table from her in the small EPSA cafeteria. She recognized the officer as the other uniformed man in the back of room during the morning conference. "Nice to meet you, Major Liut," she said.

Ian smiled. "Terry—we are very informal here—explained to me that you tried to contact your father?"

Tried and repeatedly failed. Even here, in the cafeteria, Vars had no connection on her tablet, and she had yet to see a single public terminal anywhere in the building. Perhaps that was because of EPSA's military component—the agency was a mixture of civilian workforce and the air force of its active member nations. Or perhaps all EPSA employees were required to get a PCD tattoo, so no terminals would be needed.

"Yes," she said. "I just want to let my dad know that I'm all right."

"And we're working on that," Major Liut said. "But you see, we ran into a little problem. We don't have Dr. Matteo Volhard's DNA profile."

Every human had their genetic code registered with authorities the moment they were born—or even sooner in cases of prophylactic genetic testing to identify possible medical problems. After the Keres Triplets asteroid fragments hit the Earth in 2057, wiping out half the human population and ninety percent of all other life on the planet, genetic testing had become a must. Even over a hundred years later, it was the only way to maintain a healthy gene pool.

"I assume it's just some error," Vars said. The Human Genome Heritage Project was regularly underfunded. Glitches were bound to happen.

"That's what we assumed at first. But it doesn't seem to be a glitch," the major said.

"So…what are you trying to say?" Vars asked. She was getting irritated.

"We ran your DNA sample this morning while you rested, to check it against your officially registered sample—"

"You did *what?*" Anger simply erupted out of her.

Ian raised his hands in a soothing gesture. "Vars, I know you feel like this is a big violation, but—"

"Violation?" Vars felt herself trembling with rage. *First kidnapping, then cutting off all my communication with the outside world and keeping me prisoner, and now this?* "So that's what the coffee was all about!" A dark realization hit her. "No wonder you kept giving me fresh cups. And, like a sucker, I just assumed you were being considerate and nice. All the while you were *stealing* my DNA from me."

"Vars—" Ian began.

"I think we should stick to formal address, Dr. Rust."

"If I may," Major Liut interjected. "Ian was very much against gathering your DNA sample without your explicit permission—"

"But he did it anyway," Vars spat. She needed to get out of here. As she scanned the room for exits, she saw that several other military personnel were stationed around the cafeteria, and all of them were now staring at her.

"He didn't have a choice," the major continued. "When your work was identified as necessary for this project, we had to look into your background. Your father's lack of genetic credentials was flagged."

"I assure you that was in error," Vars said.

"And *I* can assure you that EPSA doesn't make mistakes," said Liut. "At least not in this area. By law, we have to track all of our people's genetic material. We are charged with creating a genetically diverse population for off-Earth colonization. We take genetic diversity seriously."

"And I think you might have made a mistake this time," Vars said quietly.

"The only way a citizen of Earth, or of any off-world colony, would not be part of the Human Genome Heritage Project database is if he or she was born in one of the human seed vaults," the major said. "Are you aware of any information that might lead you to believe that your father might be a former Seed?"

Vars felt her head spin. There were several human seed vaults on Earth, one on the moon, and one planned on Mars. There was talk about establishing yet another one in the outer reaches of the solar system. The establishment of the Vaults was one of the governmental responses to the cataclysm that followed the Keres Triplets asteroid strike. As the nations of Earth recovered, they worked together to build the Vaults partly in order to ensure the genetic diversity of humanity. Individuals were selected by a secret set of criteria and spirited away into underground catacombs that were supposed to be impervious to all disasters. That was almost three-quarters of a century ago. And, in each year since, a genetic lottery had been held to deposit a few more babies into the Vaults.

The Seeds, as the humans who grew up in those communities were called, developed an almost monastic lifestyle. All were required to donate sperm and eggs to the outside world. The resulting embryos were highly prized by those interested in embryonic adoption. Seeds who reached the age of maturity at about thirty years old or so—Vars wasn't too familiar with their secretive ways—were allowed to make a choice to leave their society and join the general population or to stay and spend their entire lives below ground. Vars had heard horror stories of Seed children and adults being exploited for their unique genetics. She found the whole system detestable.

Now these men in front of her were hinting that her father was a Seed. That just couldn't be.

"My dad would have told me," she said. But even as she spoke, doubt wormed its way into her heart. No close family except for the "distant cousins" who lived in Norway, which just happened to be the location of one of the Vaults. *And Dad's extreme aversion to public communication terminals and D-tats...*

The major and Ian sat quietly, waiting. Furious as she was, Vars still appreciated the space to think. Would EPSA have a reason to lie to her? *They are the good guys, right?*

"I need to talk to my dad," she said finally.

"I figured as much," said Ian. "We've sent a representative to talk with him."

The major added, "And we would also like to run a blood test on you."

"You didn't get all you needed from my coffee cup?"

"We just want to be sure," Ian said. "I...we want you on our team, Dr. Volhard. You have a tremendous contribution to make to our understanding of how to even approach what we're dealing with. This genetic thing," he glanced over at the major, "will be straightened out, one way or another. If you could just overlook this very...this awkward start to our relationship, I'm sure you will find working at EPSA very rewarding."

"Are you offering me a job?" Vars asked.

"If we can straighten out this genetic mystery," said Major Liut.

Ian glanced sharply at the man and said, "Yes."

"I see," Vars said. A job at EPSA was what she had always wanted. *It's just...*

"And I would like you to start immediately," Ian added. "My department will smooth everything out with your university—"

Everything was happening too fast. Vars felt confused and conflicted. "I still have a few classes left to teach this semester," she said and realized that she was agreeing to the offer.

"That won't be a problem," Ian assured her. "We need you, Dr. Volhard."

"Where do I go to take the blood test?" Vars asked. She noted that as soon as she said it, not only did she feel better, but Ian seemed to relax. Even Major Liut's face was drained of some of its tension. *They really do want me.*

"If you'll follow me, please, Dr. Volhard," said Ian.

"We can go back to Vars."

"Perfect! Thank you, Vars."

● ● ●

The test didn't take long, or at least the top-level pass at the results didn't. The more detailed analysis would take a day or so. Vars felt herself holding her breath as they stood around the display in the medlab. It read:

The paternal haplogroup is E-M5021—a relatively common haplogroup, associated with Ashkenazi Jewish ancestry.

The maternal haplogroup is U5a1—a very old mitochondrial haplogroup that was part of the initial human expansion into Europe after the retreat of the ice sheets, 30,000 years ago.

Top-level analysis of potentially

problematic variants:

- *increased risk for age-related macular degeneration*

- *hereditary hemochromatosis variant detected*

- *lactose intolerance*

- *less likely to be a deep sleeper*

- *wet earwax variant*

- *variant for a high number of freckles*

- *dark red hair variant*

- *light skin pigmentation*

- *likely to taste a wide range of bitter compounds*

- *likely to consume more caffeine*

It continued on, but Vars stopped there. She'd never paid much attention to genetic testing—she always figured if there was something truly problematic, her dad and her pediatrician would have fixed it or kept track of it. At a minimum, she would have known about it. She did note that the list of traits didn't explain her slight epicanthic eyefold—but then who really cared?

"Your results are excellent," Ian said.

"And they match your genetic ID profile," added Major Liut.

"In fact," Ian said, "there's nothing there that would preclude you from going on an outer planetary mission—"

"Wait, what?" Vars was taken aback by the suggestion. Sure, she had always been interested in participating in some space program mission, *theoretically.* But to hear it said so casually...

"We've already obtained your health records, and you are

in fine physical shape for your age," Ian continued.

"You obtained my health records?" Vars felt violated all over again. How could her personal doctor hand over medical records without her explicit permission? There were laws against that.

"Your agreement to employment at EPSA—we have the recording of your assent for legal purposes—gave us permission to initiate a full background check on you and your father," the major said. "Medical records were obviously part of that."

Had she actually agreed to take this job? Vars wasn't sure she had, at least not without ambiguity. She never actually came out and said she would take the job offer...she didn't think. Then again, she knew she wouldn't turn down a chance to be part of Ian's team—and potentially go *into space* to investigate the strange alien artifact. Yes, of course she was taking the job. She just hated how all of this was being handled.

"And my father?" Vars wasn't sure what she had agreed to with regard to her dad.

"Once we explained the situation to him," said Major Liut, "Dr. Volhard volunteered to take the genetic test."

"When did you even have a chance to talk to him? No, hang on. You're saying he *volunteered*?" Her dad was a very private man; that would had been very unlike him to agree to genetic testing.

"Once we told him we realized who he was..." Ian said.

Who he was? "Do you mean to say that my father admitted to being an ex-Seed?"

Neither man answered the question. "We have his preliminary test here," the major said. "Would you like to see his results?"

Vars could only nod. This was all happening too fast.

The major typed a few commands on the D-tats embedded into his left arm, and the medlab display lit up with genetic information for Dr. Matteo Volhard.

The paternal haplogroup is E-M5021—a relatively common haplogroup, associated with Ashkenazi Jewish ancestry.

The maternal haplogroup is U5a1—a very old mitochondrial haplogroup that was part of the initial human expansion into Europe after the retreat of the ice sheets, 30,000 years ago.

Top-level analysis of potentially problematic variants:

- *increased risk for age-related macular degeneration*

- *hereditary hemochromatosis variant detected*

- *lactose intolerance*

- *less likely to be a deep sleeper*

- *wet earwax variant*

- *variant for a high number of freckles*

- *dark red hair variant*

- *light skin pigmentation*

- *likely to taste a wide range of bitter compounds*

- *likely to consume more caffeine*

"Something is wrong," Vars said. "This is identical to mine."

"At the top level, yes," the major said. "We will, of course, do a complete analysis of both of your DNA profiles. In the meantime, would you like to see how similar your genetic profiles really are?"

"Major, are you saying…?" Ian didn't finish. He looked as surprised as Vars felt.

"Dr. Varsaad Volhard and Dr. Matteo Volhard share over 80% of their genetic traits, according to preliminary DNA profiles," the major read out from his report. He looked Vars in the eyes. "Dr. Matteo Volhard is both Varsaad's father and sibling."

Vars felt her head spin. Her vision tunneled as she lost all of her peripheral sight to darkness. Someone kept repeating her name, but that was all she was able to process.

● ● ●

"Vars? Vars?" A woman's voice. "It will be okay. Here, drink this."

Vars felt cold water trickle past her lips. She took a real sip and swallowed. It felt good going down her throat. The cold spread into her chest.

She slowly opened her eyes. She was lying down on a hospital bed, still in the same medlab where she'd learned of the genetic results. The thick-spectacled woman from Ian's team, the exo-biologist, stood beside her. There was no one else in the room.

"Alice?" she said.

"I got here as quickly as I could." Alice had a look of real concern etched on her gentle face. Why had she come here? Why did she care how Vars felt?

"I'm okay," Vars said. "I'm just tired. No sleep. The stress of the book tour. The artifact you found. And now all this." She waved her hands feebly in the air. She wasn't sure how much Alice knew. "Did Ian tell you he offered me a job at

EPSA?"

"Yes. And that you've accepted."

Vars sat up, picked up the glass of ice water, and finished it. Dehydration was never a plus. "Do you know how complicated my genetic relation is to my father?"

Alice flicked her eyes up to the ceiling in a gesture that Vars somehow understood. *She's telling me that they're recording us.* Vars double-blinked to indicate that she'd received the warning.

"I know about you and Matteo," Alice said in answer to Vars's question. News certainly got around fast at EPSA.

"So...do we need to call someone in order to leave the medlab?" Vars asked. They clearly couldn't talk about

anything here—not privately, anyway. And she wanted to learn more about the Mimas artifact. She wanted to know why Ian thought she could help. And she wanted to know why Alice seemed so invested in her well-being. She needed to know if she could work here.

The complete book is available on Amazon. You can get a free ebook copy of my first novel, "Suddenly, Paris," by subscribing to my newsletter at Interfaces.com.